ISBN-9798763422573

For my maternal grandfather,

Thomas Downes,

who encouraged me to study science and engineering

CHAPTER 1

It started as a discussion. Soon it became an argument. A heated argument. Voices raised. They stood face to face, staring into each other's eyes. One nudged the other, and the nudges became pushes. Soon one had his hands around the other's neck, squeezing and pressing against the windpipe, restricting airflow, but a knee rammed into his groin. He staggered back, and as he looked up, an iron bar grazed his head. Blood poured from above his left eye, ran into his eye socket, and dripped from his chin. He dropped to his knees – his eyes questioning. The other's face twisted with rage. The metal bar hit again. This time there was a crack, and the left side of his skull turned red with bodily fluid. His eyes went vacant. He fell forward, cracking his head on the bare concrete floor. The iron bar bouncing on the hard floor echoed throughout the tiny room, then landed in front of a wooden stand, preventing the blood from flowing farther and forcing it to pool into a lake of crimson.

William McLellan was no more.

His attacker thought, What have I done? I need to get rid of the body. I need help.

The bloody rod was lifted, wrapped in a piece of a muslin that was found in the corner of the isolated room, and the floor was given a hasty wipe.

The stairs leading out of the room were narrow and shaky, and the body was too heavy for one person to drag up the steps.

Rain thrashed down from the heavens and hammered against the windowpanes. The storm sounds came in waves, driven by the gusts of the fierce winds. Claps of thunder punctuated the rhythm of the gusts, and lightning flashes added an eerie foreboding.

Once outside, the downpour diluted and washed away the blood from the back of the killer's left hand. Both hands shook, and despair took hold.

I know who can help me. I will find him.

CHAPTER 2

The red 1961 Triumph TR3 looked magnificent. Someone had polished its paintwork and chrome to within an inch of their lives. The proud owner, Jeff Mullin, showed Brad Willis into his garage. 'I've mounted its axles on house bricks to keep the wheels off the ground. If the rubber doesn't touch the ground, it will last longer and won't crack or perish.' The man spoke with a broad, mid-state accent. Probably Nebraskan or Kansan. 'You say that it was in an accident three and a half years ago?'

'Yes, that's correct.' Willis's voice was low, almost a whisper.

'That would be before my time. I bought it after I retired from the USAF just over three years ago. I served at Mildenhall.'

Brad Willis was only half listening. The orange glow from the low winter sun flooded into the garage and exaggerated the difference between the colour of the paint on the driver's side front wing and the bonnet. The difference was minute. Without the sun's help, Willis might never have noticed it. The wing was lighter than the bonnet, but only just. Willis moved his fingers along the gaps between the wings and the hood and found it was a little wider on the driver's side than on the passenger's, a sure sign of a past repair.

'Were you aware that it had been in an accident?'

'I guessed as much. Inside the hood, there is some stray paint from when it was sprayed.' He popped the hood up and pointed to a line of tiny red dots along its edge. 'Look here and here.'

Willis nodded. He was concentrating, trying to recall anything else he could drag from his memory. 'Was there an old-style metal Automobile Association badge on it when you bought it?'

'There was one on the fender, but the owner removed it before I took possession, so I replaced it with the one you can see. It's old but not as old as the original.' Willis ran his fingers along the bumper behind the badge. There was an extra hole where a broader badge once sat. This is the car, he thought.

'Do you have the seller's name and address?'

'I'm sure I had it at one time on the original logbook, but it's long gone now.'

Sophie, Willis's new wife, stood at the front door of the house chatting to Mary Mullin. Mrs Mullin shouted, 'Would you like a cup of tea?' Her accent, in contrast to Jeff's, was pure Essex.

Willis didn't fancy a cup of tea, but he had to make sure he got as much information from Jeff as possible. 'Yes, please, that would be lovely.' Willis waved his mobile phone, indicating that he'd like to take a photograph of the car. 'Would you mind?' Jeff nodded. When Willis noticed a tax disc on the windscreen, he waved his phone again, and Jeff nodded once more. He photographed the car and the disc and then checked both images to make sure they were in focus and clear. Tax discs were no longer used in the UK, but Willis imaged it, hoping it might reveal something about the previous owner.

Mrs Mullin stood patiently. She gave a broad smile and ushered them into the house. 'He spends too much time on that damn machine. He won't drive it in the winter in case it gets wet. What's the use of a car that you can only use when the sun's shining? I ask you.' She guided Sophie and Willis into the lounge. 'Now, how do you take your tea, my darlings? Sugar and milk?'

'Milk but no sugar,' said Sophie. 'The same for both of us, thanks.'

Mrs Mullin appeared with a bowl of chocolate hobnobs. 'These are my favourites.'

Willis estimated she was in her late fifties, but she looked a lot older. She tied her white hair up into a bun at the back of her head and wore little make-up. Her face was prematurely wrinkled, caused perhaps by her having spent time abroad with her husband in a very sunny climate.

Jeff was the exact opposite. He stood erect and fit. It was no doubt his military training that helped. A big tuft of bushy black hair surrounded his chin, but he would never have got away with hair like that in the US Air Force.

'Jeff, do you still have the service history for the car?' Willis was keen to keep things moving before they began socialising.

'I've got it here.' Jeff opened a drawer and pulled out a wad of paperwork. 'I used to keep it in the car but brought it indoors once I started to do the servicing myself. It's difficult to find a decent service garage for cars this age.' He handed Willis the book.

There was nothing of interest that Willis could spot. Another wave of his phone and another nod secured photos of the service record. As Willis handed the book back to Jeff, a piece of paper fell out from between its pages. 'That's just an old invoice for a repair,' Jeff said as he put out his hand to lift it.

'Would you mind if I look at it?' said Willis. Jeff stretched over and handed him the invoice. 'This could be very useful. It is dated before you bought the car, and it's even earlier than the accident. May I photograph this too?'

'No problem.'

'C'mon. Stop chatting and have a biscuit.' Mrs Mullin was pushing a tray straight at his face.

'Thank you very much. This is too kind. We didn't expect to impose on you so much.'

'No trouble, luv. We don't get that many visitors, so you are welcome.'

'Where did you buy the car, Jeff? Was it direct from the owner or through a dealer?'

'Neither. I bought it at a car auction. It was from Nelson's in Colchester, and you can have the sale number if that would be useful?'

'Yes, please.' Jeff handed Willis yet another piece of paper, which he duly photographed. Willis believed he had just about got every piece of information that Jeff had on the car, so they spent the rest of the afternoon in small talk, mainly between the women.

Finally, they had exhausted everything that they could talk about, so two cups of tea later, Willis and Sophie said their goodbyes. Mary and Jeff stood, waving like crazy as they drove out of their driveway and headed north on the A12.

'They are two very lonely people. I'm glad he didn't ask me about the accident,' said Willis. 'I would need to have lied because I wouldn't have wanted to put a stigma on his shiny Triumph by telling him it had killed my wife.'

'It wasn't the car that killed your wife. It was the driver.' Sophie placed her hand on his knee and threw a smile in his direction.

She is a dream person and more than I deserve, thought Willis. Here they were chasing after whoever killed Carole, his first wife. Any other woman might have resisted helping, but not Sophie. Nothing was too much trouble. She also understood how important it was to Willis to see this through. He had suffered from PTSD, Post Traumatic Stress Disorder, since the TR3 ploughed into his car, killing Carole outright. He had received treatment to help manage the condition. It had been ninety per cent successful. He had one short bout earlier in the year. Putting this investigation to bed might help push him the last ten per cent of the way to being completely cured.

He stole a glance in her direction. They hadn't yet been married for a full year, and their marriage seemed like only yesterday. Her mousy shoulder-length hair framed her face. Even looking from the side, he could see the green flecks in her hazel eyes and her lips turning up at the corners, giving her a continuous smile.

'Are we going to check out the car auctioneers today?'

Willis would have loved to, but he was emotionally exhausted. Seeing the car had taken a bigger toll than he expected. 'I don't think so. The sky is getting dark, and we're heading into a storm, so we had better head for home.'

Sure enough, the sky opened. Torrential rain poured down. The wipers on his windscreen struggled to cope. Rivers of rain streamed down the glass, making it difficult to see. The brake lights of the cars in front became distorted and out of focus. Long spikes of red stretched from the droplets that surrounded them, and the red lights were coming on more often. They came on every thirty seconds, then twenty, then every few seconds. Finally, they came on and stayed on. The traffic had ground to a halt. They were at a complete standstill. Minutes passed, then tens of minutes. Despite the heater being on full, and the fans blowing at maximum, the windows were steaming up.

Willis hit the navigation button on the dashboard, and the satnav burst into life. The map showed there were less than a hundred yards to the exit to Newmarket. He handed Sophie a tissue and asked her to wipe the wing mirror on her side to allow Willis to see back along the hard shoulder. He edged the car out onto the shoulder and slowly made his way towards the exit, followed by another four drivers that had the same idea. The line of cars slipped off the A14 onto the A142 and headed into Newmarket.

'We will have a cuppa,' he said, 'and yes, yet another cuppa, but I don't enjoy sitting in a stopped car for long.' He swung the car into a town centre car park, took an umbrella from the rear window sill and nodded to Sophie.

'You'll get us soaked.'

'Not if you hurry. There's a little café around the corner. We'll go in there. It's not far.' Because sensible people were staying put out of the rain, the café was almost empty.

While the rain ran down the outside of the windows, they ordered teas and some scones and sat back in comfort. They were warm and cosy.

'I'm sorry,' said Willis.

'Whatever for?'

'Seeing the Triumph has taken a bigger toll on me than I expected. I had to stop. I'm not feeling too well.'

'You should have said, darling. I would have driven.'

'It's not that. If you drove, it wouldn't have helped. I just needed to stop. I'm sorry.'

'There's no need to be sorry.'

'When I saw the car and the replacement wing, I couldn't help but see it ramming into Carole and me, and the memory of it reversing back and driving off without hesitation was so strong. I can see Carole's lifeless eyes. I'm so sorry. You don't deserve this.'

'I knew what I was getting myself into long ago. I am with you all the way, sweetheart.'

Willis's hands shook. He couldn't keep his eyes still. They darted all over the place. He was sweating.

'Is your PTSD coming on?'

'No. This is something else. I am thrown back to where I was all those years ago, and I'm not sure I'm ready to face this.'

'Then don't. Have a break. Take a few days off and go to Cambridge and do some astronomy. You are still an astronomer. Go back to work. Go into the Institute of Astronomy tomorrow and do something completely different. If you do, it will take your mind off it, and you can relax, then you can start afresh once you've had time to recover.'

Willis had brilliant blue eyes that Sophie loved, and his thick mop of brown hair made him look taller than his six foot two would have you imagine. He was muscular and broad, and these were all traits that Sophie had said she admired.

'Sometimes I wish Reilly hadn't given me the list of partial plate numbers that helped to trace the Triumph.'

'You would still be here and still looking, and you even hoped Reilly wouldn't send you on another assignment until this was over.'

Reilly worked for MI6 and used Willis as an unofficial investigator whenever something technical needed doing. As an astronomer, he could get access to places and institutions that would otherwise be impossible. He and Sophie had, only weeks ago, returned from an assignment in Antarctica. They had married at the south pole, and that was what they could *really* call a white wedding. Willis hadn't expected a list of car numbers from Reilly to be waiting for him on his return.

Until a year ago, Willis had little recollection of the accident other than being haunted by Carole's eyes staring at him after her death. He had undertaken treatment to help with his PTSD. It had included hypnotherapy. While under hypnosis, he recalled part of the number plate of the red Triumph that had hit them, and that's when all this sorry mess got out of hand.

After about thirty minutes, the rain stopped, and the sun's rays burst between the yellow and white gingham curtains that adorned the café's windows. They walked back to the car in silence.

The roads were still wet. Another forty-five minutes passed before they reached home.

Mrs Burns was waiting for them with two hot cups of tea and two Danish pastries. 'For such a supposedly clever man, you were crazy to go out in yon weather. Ye could huv had an accident driving in that. I think a' professors are mad.' Mrs Burns was Willis's Scottish housekeeper. She looked after him like a grandson. The bun in Mrs Burns's hair reminded him of his maternal grandmother. Mrs Burns's ample bosom was wrapped, as it always was, in a multi-coloured pinny. The gaudy garment enclosed her whole body, and she fastened it with a long strip of material made from the same cloth. Mrs Burns 'did' for Willis. She looked after the cottage when Willis was away. They kept her on when Sophie moved in because Mrs Burns needed the company. Her husband, John, was wheelchair bound, so she didn't have a social life other than meeting with Willis. She called Willis 'the professor', and he thought she did this only to annoy him. He hated being called that even though he was a professor of astronomy at the Institute of Astronomy, or IoA, at Cambridge University. In return, Willis would call her husband Rabbie instead of John and tease him about his poetry. Having Rabbie Burns living next door was an asset, he claimed. Both of them took it in good spirits, and Willis suspected John even enjoyed the teasing.

Ptolemy, Willis's cat, jumped up on Sophie's lap. He had all but ignored Willis ever since Sophie arrived. Ptolemy was named after the ancient astronomer who believed the universe rotated around him. The cat thought something similar, and he was probably right. Looking after Ptolemy was another thing that Mrs Burns 'did' for Willis. She fed him and housed him whenever Willis disappeared on his trips. He was more Mrs Burns's cat than Willis's, although she was now having strong competition from Sophie.

'I've put some money in the tea cabbie,' said Willis. The tea caddie was an old dented tin that Willis kept on top of his Welsh dresser, where he put money for Mrs Burns to buy food for Ptolemy. 'I've also transferred money into your Post Office account to replace the money you spent while we were away.' Mrs Burns always acted as though the money was unimportant. She closed the door and trundled back to her cottage by taking a shortcut across the back garden. 'Mrs Burns spent money from her pension to feed Ptolemy while I was away this year,' Willis told Sophie.

'She's a real asset,' said Sophie, 'and we are lucky to have her.'

'You're right, Sophie. I'll go to the Institute tomorrow and do some work. It will take my mind off things and help me relax. We can go sleuthing again the day after.'

CHAPTER 3

Willis arrived at the Institute of Astronomy early. He drove into the car park at 7:30. Parked right across from his car stood a red Mazda soft top. So much for trying to forget about the red car he had visited yesterday. He shook his head and headed for his office. Matt Quimby, an associate, met him in the corridor and asked how Antarctica had been.

'Bloody cold.'

'Congratulations. I heard that you've married.'

Willis confirmed he was and thanked him for his good wishes. He'd had to take the plunge, eventually. He told him Antarctica had been an interesting experience, and the extreme cold and isolation helped him to appreciate what he had here in England, but the food had been something else.

Matt asked if that meant he wouldn't recommend anyone to spend the winter there.

'The correct term is "winterover." Antarctica was a great experience, but six months of darkness was a long time, even for an astronomer.'

Quimby laughed. 'Still, you got almost unlimited time on the South Pole Telescope. I assume it was Sophie Fenwick you married?'

Willis said he had to fight for time on the telescope, just like everybody else, because it was a very busy instrument. Yes, he'd married Sophie, and the wedding was something else too. Willis stopped at the coffee machine and pressed the button for a black coffee.

They shuffled up to an oval table in the middle of the foyer. Matt asked if he had taken any photographs.

Willis told him he had taken plenty of the aurora australis. The southern lights were magnificent, but they'd taken very few of the wedding. There were some, but they were not for sharing. He followed his statement with a big grin.

Matt re-positioned a magazine so they could place their plastic cups on it without marking the table's polished surface. It was a copy of *Auto* magazine. On its front cover was a picture of a red Maserati. Willis smiled to himself. They're bloody everywhere, he thought. As soon as Matt lifted his cup, Willis lifted his and took the opportunity to lift the magazine and pretended to look at it with interest, then put it back on the table, face down. He leaned back in his chair and relaxed.

For the next fifteen minutes, they spoke about his work on the South Pole Telescope and his association with Sophie on the IceCube. The IceCube was a neutrino observatory, studying the smallest pieces of anything that could exist.

Afterwards, he went to his office and looked at the mass of unopened mail on his desk, and his email contained nothing to whet his interest. There were no offers of telescope time from the time allocation committees of any of the major world telescopes. He laid back in his chair in disgust. Following his visit to the South Pole Telescope, he had some scientific papers to write and publish, but he couldn't face starting them. After throwing his pen on the desk, he stood, locked the office door after him, and headed for his car.

When he arrived back at the cottage, it was only 9:30. Sophie was bored, too. She was sitting watching a TV programme about buying a house at auction and refurbishing it. Ptolemy was sitting happily on her lap. 'Let's visit Nelson's Auction House in Colchester,' he said. 'I can't stand the suspense any longer. I've tried telephoning them, but no one is answering, and the drive will do us both good.'

Sophie was on her feet and heading for her coat. She had got up so fast that poor Ptolemy was forced to jump from her lap onto the fireside carpet. Willis opened the door to the wood burner and threw in a couple of logs, saying it should keep it going until they got back, then closed its air vent to make it burn slower.

***

Nelson's Auction House was in a large industrial building. They made their way to a dingy room that doubled as an administration office. Willis produced the photo of the sales number on his phone to a short fat man in a brown stained overall coat who took a long breath and sighed. 'I'm not sure whether I can give you that information.'

'You probably want to keep your boss out of trouble. If you don't let me have it, the next call will be from the police.' Willis gave him the most serious look he could muster.

'I'll just pour myself a cuppa.' He walked through to the back shop and left the paperwork on the desk. Willis produced his trusty phone and photographed it, and then he took a paperclip out of an old Rizla cigarette paper tin on the desk and clipped a ten pound note to the paperwork.

'It came from an address in East Bergholt,' said Willis. 'Let's drive past it to see what it looks like.'

Sophie complained she was getting hungry and made a signal like she was putting a sandwich into her mouth.

'Let's look at this address first. Then I'll feed you.' He threw a kiss in her direction.

Number 13 The Mews was a large Victorian building with a dozen individual doorbells covering the front door. Willis pushed one, and nothing happened. He pushed the lowest button; it had the number '0' on it.

A deep voice answered. 'Yeah?'

Willis asked if he was speaking to the caretaker, but he knew no one else would have zero as a number.

'Yeah. Who's askin'?'

'Colchester Police. Please, will you come to the door?'

There was a long pause, followed by a click and a buzzing sound, and the door swung open two inches. 'What d'yer want?'

'Have you seen this man?' Willis held up his phone to let him read the name and address.

'Jim Pryce doesn't live here any longer.'

'Do you know where he's moved to?'

'I thought you lot would know that better than me. He's in jail. Has been for the last eight months or so.'

'Do you know which jail?'

'I don't rightly know, but I imagine it's one of the local ones. He owes two months' rent when he gets out. You make sure to tell him that if you see him.'

Willis turned around and walked to his car. 'C'mon. I'll buy you a sandwich or something.'

'… or something? Where's all the romance gone?'

'Okay, I'll get a pizza.' They both laughed. It helped break the tension. Pizza was the nickname they had for sex when they were at university.

She thanked him, but she'd just have a sandwich or a scone because they wouldn't want to get arrested for indecency in the heart of Essex. Sophie smiled at Willis the way that he loved, and it made him feel warm and fuzzy inside.

They found a small tea shop and sat at the window. Sophie said there was nothing like an afternoon cream tea to help you relax. The tea came in a pot made with proper tea. Even Mrs Burns didn't use real tea any more. 'I'll be mother,' said Sophie as she fitted the tea strainer over Willis's cup and poured. Willis watched the leaves swirl around and settle in a tiny circle at the bottom of the strainer. After he covered his scone with jam, he ladled on copious amounts of whipped cream. The next twenty minutes passed in relative silence. Both had jam and cream on their lips and faces and used tissues to wipe themselves clean.

'I will ask my uncle if he can find out which prison Jim Pryce is in.'

Willis looked puzzled and asked how he could help.

'He's a Detective Inspector. D I Jonathan Swallow is his name.' She waved her hands in the air, imitating the flight of a bird.

'You didn't tell me you have a relative who is a policeman.'

'I still have some secrets. Everyone must have some mystery to them.' Sophie removed her phone from her handbag and dialled. 'Hello Uncle, it's Sophie here. I'm fine, thank you. Mother is well too. I need a favour. I know, I know, I should call you more often, but I've been away for a year. I'm just back. It's a Mr James Pryce. He's in jail, probably somewhere in Essex or Suffolk. I need to know what jail he's in. Yes, I love you too. Does that mean you'll help? Pretty Please. Can you find out what he's in jail for? I know, I know, it's asking a lot, but it must have been in the public domain at the time he was charged, so it's not as though you'd be telling me anything confidential. It would just save me a lot of work if you could help. That's great. Thank you. You've got my number. I love you too.' She hung up. 'Let's go home and get some dinner. He'll likely call us later this evening.'

'That's magic,' said Willis, 'and I might even order two pizzas.' Sophie leaned forward and kissed his cheek.

At that moment, a black Jaguar car stopped at the lights outside. Sophie watched Willis's eyes. He was staring at the woman in the rear of the car. She was also looking at him. He dropped his teaspoon into his cup with a clatter. He was breathing in gulps and becoming breathless. Sophie stood up and put her hands around his neck to massage his shoulders. His muscles were rigid. Every part of him was tense.

'What's the matter?' she asked. Willis was silent. He didn't answer her. She looked at the woman in the Jaguar. She had short fair hair, and she was smiling. The woman was talking to someone on her mobile but, within a few minutes, the lights changed, and the car drove off. Willis's breathing remained irregular.

He slouched in his seat. 'Get the bill, Sophie, please. Let's go home. Would you mind driving?'

'Not at all, sweetheart. Will you be okay?' Willis nodded. She took the car keys and strode off to settle the bill.

They drove back to Madingley in silence. Sophie tried to start a conversation with Willis, but he wouldn't answer. He was in a different world. Completely unaware of what was going on around him.

Even when they arrived at the cottage, he remained silent as he went indoors and collapsed into the chair by the fire.

Sophie was worried. 'Should I call a doctor? You look as white as a sheet.'

Willis waved his hands in the air, dismissing the idea, and sat staring at the soft glow of the slowly burning logs on the wood burner.

Sophie felt his forehead. It was ice cold. She opened the vent to the fire, and a single flame appeared among the logs. 'I will make you a cup of sweet tea. I know you don't have sugar, but you look like you are suffering from shock.'

She returned a few minutes later with the mug of hot liquid. She put her hand behind Willis's head and the cup to his lips. At first, he resisted, but slowly he took a small sip and then another, then he took the cup from her hand and swallowed its contents in a single gulp.

'I saw her,' he whispered.

Sophie put her ear closer to his mouth. 'You saw her?'

'I saw her.' He waved his hand toward the Welsh dresser. The top of the dresser was bare except for a photograph of Carole. 'I saw her.'

Sophie stepped over to the dresser and returned with the photograph. 'You saw Carole?'

'Yes,' came the weak reply. 'I saw her. I saw Carole.'

True, the woman that Sophie had seen in the Jaguar had an uncanny resemblance to Willis's dead wife, but she said that she would never have made the connection without looking at the photograph. 'You know it can't be Carole. You know she is dead. Pull yourself together.' She was worried that she might not be appearing sympathetic enough, but he had to realise he was mistaken.

'I know,' he said. 'I'm sorry yet again. I seem to keep apologising. I think I'm cracking up.'

'There's no need to apologise, darling.' She sat on the arm of the chair and put her arm around his shoulders. 'You've had a lot of stress recently. Perhaps we ought to give up this investigation, at least for the time being.' Willis let his head fall onto her shoulder and sighed. He was still shaking.

Dinner continued in silence. Willis had lost his appetite and was picking at his food. They decided on an early night; they would go to bed and recover from the day's trauma. Sophie's mobile rang. It was her uncle, so she switched its loudspeaker on and laid it on the table.

'Right, I've got the information that you asked for. James Pryce is in Hollesley Bay Prison. It's in Suffolk, just to the east of Woodbridge. I think he might be in Hoxon Unit, but I can't be certain.'

'What's he in for?' asked Sophie.

'Car thefts mainly, but he's also been convicted for burglary. It's a category D prison, so it's not for too dangerous individuals. They put him away for three years, but he is due to be released soon.'

'How soon?' interjected Willis.

'In the next few months, I'd guess. He's qualified for ROTL, Release on Temporary Licence. That means he might even get visits outside the prison, but I can't be sure. To get that, he would need to be a trusted prisoner.'

'Wasn't Hollesley Bay where Jeffrey Archer the politician was sent?' asked Willis.

'You've got an excellent memory. After he left Lincoln jail, they sent him there. The locals call it Hollesley Bay

Colony, and it has quite a long history. Before it was a prison, they used to train people there who were planning to immigrate to avoid poverty, and it's also known as "Holliday Bay" because it has a very high escape rate. That's about all I can tell you, I'm afraid.'

'Okay, thanks. We'll arrange a visit,' said Sophie.

'You can't just turn up. You'll need to book a visit in advance.' He called out the gov.uk URL for Sophie to go online and book.

'That will take several days to arrange.' Willis snapped back.

'You could always try to call the Prison Governor? Tell you what, I'll call him tomorrow morning to see if I can get you in quickly. I'll tell him you're looking at an old cold case. How soon are you able to visit?'

'As soon as possible. Tomorrow if that is even possible.'

'Okay. I'll call or text Sophie as soon as I know.'

'Thanks, Uncle,' said Sophie. 'I'll promise to come and visit you soon.' She pressed the red button, and the phone disconnected.

'That sounds like a result,' said Willis. He was suddenly himself again, and Carole had been put to the back of his mind, at least temporarily.

Willis had a restless night. He tossed and turned. Sophie had to wake him several times when he started shouting in his sleep. About 2 a.m., she finally woke him and told him she was going to make a cup of hot chocolate for them both. 'You were shouting in your sleep. I haven't slept a wink since midnight.'

'I must have been reliving today. But it's getting interesting, so the sooner we sort this out, the sooner things will get back to normal.'

'Oh boy, I can't wait for that.' Sophie blew on her chocolate to cool it. 'Drink up and let's go back to bed.'

CHAPTER 4

Willis woke early the next morning. The first thing he did was to make a note to call the Institute to book two weeks' leave. He had already taken liberties in the last couple of days, but he didn't feel guilty about it, because Willis had put in more than his fair share of hours on research and writing scientific papers. While he was on leave, he was sure that he would do even more. He and Sophie had a leisurely breakfast and relaxed, waiting for Uncle Swallow's text. At 11 a.m. precisely, Sophie's phone pinged. 'It's from Uncle Jon Swallow, and we're on for 1 p.m. today. The Visitor Centre has been told to expect us.'

Willis estimated it was about an hour and a half's drive, so they'd better leave right away. He dialled Mrs Burns to let her know they would be gone for a few hours and to check that she would be alright to feed Ptolemy, but he needn't have bothered, because she always came over around 11 a.m. to check out everything was okay.

***

As they approached Woodbridge, Willis realised it would take longer than ninety minutes. He had forgotten that the prison was on the opposite side of the town towards the coast. He pointed at the satnav. The arrival time was 1.05 p.m. When Willis pressed harder on the pedal, Sophie swayed, and the car sped up an extra five mph.

As they drove past the entrance and headed for the car park, Willis admired the impressive building.

The Visitor Centre was well signposted. They went to reception and introduced themselves.

The uniformed officer said they were expected and asked them to follow her. They almost had to run to keep up. She took long strides and didn't look back to check if they were still there. She showed them into a small interview room and asked them to wait.

After ten minutes, Jim Pryce arrived accompanied by two warders. They were chatting, and everything looked relaxed. Once Pryce was in the room, one warden left, and the other stood by the door.

'You guys must be royalty,' said Pryce. 'I've never had visitors before without notice. You must have pulled some strings. And to get an interview in a room rather than the visitors' area? Now that is something.'

Pryce was a small thin man with mousy, untidy hair. His sharp features, along with his oversized moustache, reminded Willis of an oversized rat, and when he grinned, his yellowed teeth added to his sad appearance. He dropped himself into the chair at the other side of the table, and its legs squealed as they scraped on the floor tiles. Pryce slouched with his legs wide open, attempting to project a masculine image and threw his head to the side to toss a lock of hair back on top of his head. No sooner had he done it than it slipped back down onto his forehead. Willis took an instant dislike to him.

'What's this all about then? It must be important for the Governor to command my presence.'

Willis spun a piece of paper around on the desk. 'It's about this registration number. MN—'

'I know what the number is. What do you want to know? I might tell you if I feel like it.' Pryce grinned through his crooked teeth and put his hands on the table.

'You owned this car, I assume?' asked Willis.

Pryce tossed his head back and said that he didn't, that he'd only borrowed it for a job.

'What kind of job?'

'That would be telling, wouldn't it?'

'How long do you still have to serve?'

'About three months. If I behave, I could get out any day now.'

'Well, you had better start behaving, or you'll be here a lot longer than that. You drove this car at the beginning of April, three-plus years ago and were involved in an accident.'

'What if I was?'

'In that case, you are guilty of murder.'

'Bullshit. I never killed nobody. She's still alive. I saw her after it happened.'

Sophie heard Willis draw in a deep breath and hold his breath. There was a long gap before he spoke again. 'You saw her where? Where did you see her?' Willis was getting wound up. Sophie put her hand on his thigh and squeezed it. He calmed down.

'In town. In East Bergholt. She's been on the local telly nearly every week since I bumped her.'

'You bumped her?'

'Yes, that was all they paid me to do. To bump her car and frighten her.'

'Who paid you to do that?'

'That would be tellin' ye' wouldn't it?'

'I will recommend that they keep you in custody until after my investigation is complete.'

'You can't do that.'

'Watch me. You'll be held on suspicion of murder.'

'Murder? I didn't kill anybody.'

'You killed my wife. She was a passenger in the car you "bumped" three years ago, and I'm going to see you pay the full price.'

'Look, I hit Diana Bishop's car, and she's still alive. She's an MP. She's on telly all the time.'

'No. You hit Brad Willis's car with his wife Carole in the passenger seat. You killed my wife outright.'

'It was an accident. I only intended it as a bump. It was to give her a fright.'

Willis asked why he had to frighten her.

Pryce explained someone dropped a note and money through his letterbox, but he had no idea who it was. The idea was just to 'borrow' a car and frighten her. He didn't know who paid him or why they wanted her frightened.

'How come your name appears on the purchase receipt for the car if you stole it?'

Pryce explained that he'd waited for the damaged car to come for auction and had bought it. He grinned, pleased with himself for being cleverly devious.

Willis dropped a business card on the table and told Pryce if he remembered anything to call him. He said, in the meantime, he'd ask to have him detained pending further investigations. Willis would speak to the Prison Governor today. He stood and left.

As they headed back to the car, Sophie said she thought he'd kept his cool surprisingly well.

Willis told her he had surprised himself and asked her to contact her uncle and tell him what they'd discovered. She was to tell him Pryce had admitted hitting the car.

While Willis drove, Sophie called Uncle Swallow and relayed the message. He was worried that no one had witnessed the confession, and Pryce might withdraw it later. If he'd stolen the Triumph, the police would have fingerprints from the vehicle after they'd recovered it, but Jon said he would find out. If they matched Pryce's, then they'd have him. He'd alert the local police to have them investigate.

'That's that,' said Sophie. 'You're making progress at last.'

Willis asked if she'd look up Diana Bishop MP for him and to see if she could get an urgent appointment for them.

He assumed it would happen and drove towards East Bergholt.

Sophie was on the phone for ten minutes or more before she finally said, 'The soonest she can fit you in is Wednesday. That's when she holds her next surgery.'

Willis stopped the car in Woodbridge. He parked close to the station and headed for a little old-fashioned tea shop that he remembered from long ago. It was still there. He told Sophie they served lunches too. 'Order something for both of us while I make another call.'

The people at the table opposite tutted as Willis input the number, so he stuck his tongue out at them, and they turned and looked in the opposite direction.

'Hello, Mike? It's Brad Willis here. I'm in Suffolk. I need an urgent meeting with the local MP, Diana Bishop. Can you pull a few strings for me? It has to do with Carole's death. I'm making good progress.'

Willis nodded to himself and hung up. Mike Reilly was Willis's friend and contact in MI6. Willis had done Reilly many favours in the past, and it was Mike who had sent Willis the list of addresses of owners of Triumphs that contained the incomplete registration plate numbers and letters that Willis had supplied. Mike still owed him plenty, and Willis welcomed the chance to get Reilly to return some favours. He had solved problems in Antarctica earlier in the year and Kazakhstan the year before. Yes, he was surely due some favours in return.

Sophie returned with two lasagnes. 'They've got beef mince in them,' teased Willis. 'What about my vegetarian diet?'

'Sod your diet. You eat meat regularly. This is the best they have on the menu today, so it was this or a baked potato with beans.'

'Okay. Okay, I'll take what I'm given.' He smiled and patted her hand.

Sophie told him she was proud of him today. He'd never lost the plot once. Very nearly at one point, but he'd never lost it.

'That's not how I felt inside. I wanted to kill the bastard. I found who killed Carole, and there was nothing I could do about it.'

She said he should leave that to Uncle Swallow. He was a good DI and will follow through. She guaranteed it.

Willis remarked that the lasagne was rather good. He finished the plateful, wiped it dry with a slice of bread and asked what was for dessert.

Sophie suggested some lemon drizzle cake and custard because she knew he loved both. Not waiting for his answer, she stood and moved to the counter.

Willis's mobile pinged. The couple sitting across from him shuffled uncomfortably in their seats. 'Hello?'

'It's Diana Bishop here. You need to speak to me urgently?'

That was fast, thought Willis. 'Yes. I was rather hoping for a meeting.'

'You've got it. When the Prime Minister calls, I obey.'

'I'm sorry. But if it weren't urgent, I wouldn't trouble you.'

'I'm in East Bergholt. How soon can you get here?'

'In about half an hour. I'm having lunch in Woodbridge.'

'That's a late lunch.' Willis could sense a smile in her voice. It was uncanny. Certain ways that she used her vowels reminded him of Carole. She suggested he make it an hour. He should take his time, and she'd meet him in the pub in front of the church. He couldn't miss it.

Willis thanked her and hung up. The couple across the floor had been staring and listening throughout the conversation, so he cocked his head to one side and smiled. They looked away.

'There we go. Two lemon drizzle cakes with custard, enjoy.' Sophie placed them on the table facing Willis. 'I can't eat both of them. You had better have one,' she said, knowing full well that there was no way Willis would refuse a lemon drizzle cake.

'Very droll.'

'Eat it before I take it back.'

He told her they needed to be in East Bergholt in an hour. They had an appointment with Diana Bishop.

'That was quick.'

'Only the Prime Minister himself commanded her to come. Reilly has done us proud.'

Sophie advised they had better not be late.

The drive to East Bergholt took less than thirty minutes. They selected a table in a corner where it would be more private, and Willis approached the bar and ordered a couple of coffees.

Sophie said that Diana wouldn't be pleased with him, because he'd taken her away from something important.

'This is important too,' said Willis. 'Her life might be in danger.'

They sipped their coffees slowly, and there was half a cup of cold coffee remaining in each cup when Diana arrived. Fifteen minutes early.

She came and stood in front of Willis. His eyes glazed over. He didn't hear her say, 'I am Diana Bishop. You must be Brad Willis?' There was no one else in the lounge, so it was obvious he was. 'You had better close your mouth, Mr Willis.' Sophie turned and looked at Willis. His mouth was wide open, and he was staring at Diana Bishop, so Sophie dug him in the ribs. He jumped to attention.

'May I sit down, or do you wish I stand?'

'I'm sorry. I'm terribly sorry. You must think me very rude. Can I offer you a drink?'

'I'd love a black coffee, and I'd kill for a cheese roll if they have any left. I haven't had lunch yet.'

Willis went to the bar. He ordered three coffees and a cheese roll, but he couldn't keep his eyes off Diana. The resemblance was remarkable, and he could see why Pryce had mistaken Carole for Diana Bishop. They were identical.

Willis returned with the coffees. The waitress had said she would bring the roll to the table.

'So, what's this all about Mr Willis? You certainly know people in very high places. I was told to jump. Here I am, jumping.' She smiled at Willis.

He kept staring. Willis apologised for staring but said she reminded him so much of someone he knew. Diana had Carole's blonde hair; both wore it the same length, and she highlighted her eyes with the same green eye shadow Carole wore. He pulled out his wallet and handed the MP a photograph.

'Where did you get this? I'm sure we've never met before. When was it taken?'

'It was over five years ago. When she was still alive, she was my wife.' A tear dropped from Willis's left eye. Diana noticed it but chose to ignore it.

As she handed the photograph back to Willis, she asked what her name was.

'Carole. She was killed in a hit-and-run accident over three years ago.' He stuttered over the word accident because he now knew that it was anything but an accident.

'What I need to ask you is – have you received any threats in the last three years?'

'Why do you ask Mr Willis?'

'Call me Brad, please. Because I believe whoever killed Carol three years ago mistook her for you, and I think that your life was, or still is, in danger.'

Diana's face lost all its colour. She turned pale, and it was she who was now staring at Willis. 'I see where you are coming from, Mr Willis. Sorry…, Brad.' Her hand was shaking, and a small twitch appeared on the left side of her mouth, the same twitch that Carole had when she was nervous. 'Yes, I have received several threats. No, I have received *many* threats. It started four years ago, and I am still getting them.'

'Do you know why?'

Diana explained she was trying to get an old murder case reopened. Someone had a vested interest in her not succeeding. She had received multiple physical threats, and someone had run over one of her pets just after she had a note put through her letterbox. She'd had red paint daubed on her front door, and there had been many other things too.

Willis asked what the police had said, leaning forward, intent on her reply.

'Whose roll and cheese?' The waitress looked around until Diana claimed it.

'They have drawn a blank. I've complained to my colleague, the Home Secretary, to put pressure on them, but the police are stymied and have made no progress. I'm so sorry your wife was killed.'

'If it's any consolation, the plan wasn't to kill her. They just wanted her, you, frightened. The driver of the hit-and-run vehicle went too far, but he's in custody and will remain so for some time.'

'That's something, I suppose.' Diana tore a piece out of her roll and put it into her mouth. She even chewed the same way as Carole.

He had the urge to ask her if she was sure she wasn't Carole but controlled the impulse. He continued by saying that the driver was only a hired hand and not the real culprit. So, whoever was threatening her, was still at large.

'Is there anything that you can do to help, Mr Willis?' She was formal again. 'You are very resourceful. That is clear.'

'I don't know. It's not my line of work.'

'Of course, he'll look into it,' said Sophie. 'I won't get any peace at home until he sorts this out. Why don't you put a file together of everything that you have, or can think of, and let Brad have it? We will then decide whether we can take it further.'

Diana's eyes lit up, and she thanked them both very much. She would appreciate anything that they could do, and even if it only helped to move the police forward a little, it would be welcome.

Willis agreed they had a deal. Diana would send anything she could find to him. They exchanged cards, making sure that they included their mobile numbers.

Diana apologised for giving him the run around when he tried to contact her, but that was her secretary's job, and she was quite good at it too. She got so many weird requests, and they needed managing, but she would be at his beck and call anytime, day or night. If he needed anything, just call her mobile.

'That will be very helpful,' said Willis. 'Let me know as soon as any new threats arrive. It could be important to follow them up as soon as possible after getting them.'

'I asked my driver to come and pick me up at 4 p.m., so that will be him now.' The black Jaguar that Willis had seen in the tea room stood and waited until Diana was ready.

'Would you object if I took a photograph?' Willis waved his phone in front of Diana. She nodded and took a step back. Willis handed his mobile to Sophie and asked her to do the honours.

As her car drove away, Diana waved to them.

'Well, that's progress,' said Willis. Before going home, he wanted to stop off at the Boots store in Stowmarket to print off all the pictures he'd accumulated on his phone in the last few days.

Once the prints were produced, Sophie asked to see the picture of Carole that Willis carried in his wallet, and she compared it with the picture she had taken of Diana. Both agreed that the similarity was remarkable.

Willis admitted he'd struggled not to call her Carole, and he'd even considered asking her if she was sure that Diana Bishop was her real name.

'That would have gone down like a ton of bricks. I'm still surprised you didn't struggle with meeting her. I think if I had been in your position, I would have struggled a lot.'

'Oh, I struggled alright. I've just got better at not showing it, but I think that it's also helping my PTSD. If we solve this, I will be cured permanently.'

'Let's hope so,' said Sophie. 'Let's hope so.'

CHAPTER 5

'This coffee is too strong, Sophie.'

'I used the measuring spoon as you told me. It was alright last time.'

'You need to make sure it is a level spoonful. I watched you yesterday, and it was heaped.' Willis was very particular about his coffee. It had to be a particular Brazilian blend, and it had to be the right strength. Nothing else would do.

Sophie sighed to herself. It was a level spoonful. What Willis didn't realise was that his tastebuds reacted differently to coffee early in the day. She ignored his criticism and asked where he'd put the photograph of Diana Bishop.

'It's here,' said Willis. He stood and walked over to the Welsh dresser. He'd slotted the picture in front of the silver frame that held Carole's picture. 'It's remarkable. I could never imagine that two people could look so alike.'

'Should I be worried?' She made it sound like a tease, but she wasn't teasing.

'No, sweetheart. I've got over Carole. Really, I have. You have nothing to worry about from Diana. I only want to find out the backstory and what happened that caused Carole's death.'

Sophie wandered over to the dresser, stood on her toes and kissed his ear. That had been the right answer. She giggled as Willis turned around, took her in his arms and gave her a long passionate kiss on the lips.

'There, satisfied? I only have eyes for you. There goes another song title.'

'I think I'm satisfied. You can prove it to me later.' She had leaned over to return Willis's kiss when Mrs Burns appeared at the back door.

'Will you be going out agin today? You were hardly in yesterday at all.'

'We're not sure yet,' said Willis. 'It depends on a telephone call that we are expecting. If you want to start on the dusting, it's fine with us. We won't get in your way.'

'Are ye sure?'

Willis nodded and sipped his coffee. He lifted a copy of the Cambridge News to avoid her gaze. If she thought Willis was watching her, she wouldn't start working.

'What's this then?' Mrs Burns said as she started to polish the dresser. 'I see you have a new picture of Carole. Ah huvnae seen this one before.'

'Don't you remember that one being taken, Mrs Burns?' he teased.

'Ah certainly don't,' she scowled. 'Ah remember a' the photographs of Carole in the hoos.'

'I'm teasing you, Mrs Burns. That's not Carole. It was a lady we met who looks like her.'

'Now ah know you're teasing me. That's Carole, for sure. She's wearing her brooch.'

Willis jumped up and stood beside her. 'What the...?'

He raced upstairs. The noise of drawers opening and closing echoed throughout the small cottage. Then there was silence. Willis came down the stairs slowly, stopping on each step. He was holding a small brooch in his fingers. He swivelled the brooch on its pin and let the light reflect off the blue and green enamel of the butterfly's wings. Willis showed it to Sophie and told her Carole went nowhere without wearing this brooch. It was a gift from her parents when she was very young. He placed the brooch in the palm of Sophie's hand.

Sophie got up and moved toward the dresser. She lifted both pictures and returned to her seat. She held both photographs up close to her face, and Sophie looked between the pictures and at the brooch. 'It's not the same brooch,' she paused, 'Carole's brooch has blue forewings and green hindwings. Diana's brooch has the opposite. The forewings are green, and the hindwings are blue.'

Willis lifted the two photographs and compared them. 'Well, I'll be—' He slumped into a chair. 'Carole told me her parents gave her this brooch.' He grabbed his mobile, found Diana Bishop's card and dialled her number.

'Diana Bishop?'

'This is Brad Willis here. I have an urgent question for you. Where did you get the butterfly brooch you were wearing yesterday?'

'It's no use you trying to get one. It was handmade. I'm sorry. It's unique.'

'It's not that unique. I have one in my hand that's almost identical. Who made the brooch for you?'

'My father did. He made it when I was very young.'

Willis asked her if she could ask him if he'd made another, almost identical to your one.

'I would if I could, but my father is dead. He's been dead many years now.'

'Did he die in a car accident by any chance?'

'Yes, he did. But how did you know?'

'I need to come to see you. I need to see you today.'

'Alright. Alright. You can come to see me. How long will it take you? I have a meeting at 2 p.m.'

'I'll be there in an hour.' He asked her to text him her address along with her postcode.

'I certainly will. Why is this so urgent? What have you discovered?'

'It would be better if I told you in person. I'll see you in an hour.' He disconnected the call before Diana could ask him any more questions.

He turned to Sophie and repeated the story that Carole once told him. Carole had recalled her parents were in a car accident when she was young. Her father had died. This was just too much of a coincidence. He said he thought Diana must be related to Carole, but she'd never told him she had a sister or even a twin.

It took them over an hour to reach Diana's. Willis had been a little optimistic with his estimate. They drew up outside Diana's house just short of ninety minutes after his call.

It was a tall Victorian house made of red stone with black slates covering the tops of the bay windows. Stained glass patterns decorated the top panes of glass in each window, and each panel had rays of light radiating from a central sphere. They looked impressive. The driveway crackled as Willis drove over its loose gravel surface. By the time he and Sophie climbed out of the car, the thick, oak front door was already open.

'I've made you some tea and sandwiches. It will repay you for the coffee and cheese roll you bought me yesterday. Come in. There's quite an icy wind blowing.' She stood to one side as they entered a large hallway. 'The first door on the right. Go straight in,' She shut the door and kicked a soft cloth dragon she used as a draught excluder up to the bottom of the door. Sophie and Willis found themselves in a vast living room with a high ceiling and luxurious handmade settees. There were three settees in all, and they faced into an ornate, nineteenth-century Victorian St Anne's marble fireplace. A blazing fire was burning in the grate. It was most welcoming. 'Take a seat. Don't stand on ceremony. I'll be right back with some tea.'

Willis and Sophie sat together on one of the couches that faced sideways and assumed Diana would sit on the opposite couch. Willis reasoned that if Diana sat facing them, it would be easier to chat. When she returned with the tray, she didn't oblige but sat on the settee at right angles to them. At least Willis was on the side nearest to Diana. That would help a little.

Diana put the tray on the long glass table between them. She handed out plates and offered them the sandwiches. She poured out the tea from a real china teapot and into their cups via an old-fashioned tea strainer. Willis was impatient to get started, but he didn't want to start until the formalities were over.

'So, what is it you're so keen to tell me?'

Willis was chewing on a sandwich. He swallowed and said, 'Let's wait till we've finished the sandwiches if you don't mind? I think it'll be quite an eye-opener.'

Diana screwed her eyes up and turned her head to one side. She quizzically raised her eyebrows, then she nodded her head and took another bite from her ham and cheese sandwich. 'Okay.'

After they had eaten, she cleared the coffee table and appeared with a tray of After Eight mints. 'It's a bit early for After Eights,' said Willis.

'They're my favourite. Surely After Eights aren't too much of a distraction?' She grinned at Willis and offered him and Sophie the tray.

Willis took a mint but didn't unwrap it. He put his hand into his jacket pocket and placed the butterfly brooch into Diana's hand. She stared at it in disbelief, got up and headed out to the hall. When she returned, she was carrying her blue jacket. She held Willis's brooch against the one on her lapel. 'They're almost the same.'

'But not quite,' said Willis, 'the colours are reversed.'

Diana carefully unclipped the brooch from her lapel. She looked at the back of it. She did the same thing with the brooch Willis had handed to her. 'Look here,' she said, 'see this tiny mark on the back? It's a double heart.' She handed both to Willis. Indeed, both brooches had small double hearts stamped on their rears. 'That's my dad's trademark. Someone told me he used to make jewellery as a hobby. This is his signature. My dad made both these brooches.'

Diana sat in silence for a few seconds. 'This is an incredible coincidence. Can I ask where you got it?'

It was Willis's turn to be silent. He reached into his inside pocket and pulled out Carole's picture that he had removed from the dresser at Madingley and handed it to Diana, pointing at the brooch.

'You are going to tell me this is another picture of Carole, but I know it isn't. I don't remember this picture being taken.'

'I do,' said Willis, 'it's Carole.'

'Of course, it's me. Look at the brooch.'

After a suitable pause, Willis said, 'It *is* Carole,' and after yet another pause, 'and the butterfly brooch is almost like your one.'

Diana lifted the picture closer to her eyes. She walked over to a long dresser sitting against the far wall, opened a drawer and took out a magnifying glass. She stared at the brooch in the photograph for seconds before returning to the settee. 'Yes, I can see. It's almost the same.' She emphasised the 'almost'.

'Did you know you had a sister?'

'I never even suspected. After my parents died, I was put into foster homes. I was in a whole string of them. One was nearly as bad as the other. I tell a lie. There were a few good ones.'

He asked if she'd changed her name to Bishop.

'No, I've always been Bishop. For as long as I can remember, that is.'

'Carole's surname was Ford. Does that ring a bell?'

'No. Not at all.'

Willis said he had Carole's birth certificate, and it recorded her name at birth as Carole Ford.

'What was her date of birth?'

'It was the 26th of September, 1984.'

Diana's face went white. Willis thought she was about to pass out. He changed settees and put his arm around her shoulders. 'That's my date of birth,' her voice was weak and shallow. 'Carole was my twin sister.'

They sat without speaking for a few minutes while the revelation sank into Diana's brain. She lifted her mobile and dialled. She told Jennifer, her secretary, to cancel her two o'clock meeting and said she wasn't feeling too well and to hold all her calls for this afternoon.

Willis let Diana settle for a while, then asked, 'What does *your* birth certificate say?'

Diana disappeared to search for her birth certificate. She returned five minutes later. 'My certificate is a copy. A substitute. "Copy" is printed across its front. The original must have been lost when I was in one of the foster homes. The foster agency must have lost it. I do not know where Bishop came from, and it likely came from whomever I was living with at the time.'

Sophie said they ought to have another cup of tea and that she would make it if she showed her where the kitchen was.

'I'll come with you, Sophie.' Both the women disappeared, and Willis was left worrying whether he had done the right thing, telling Diana about Carole. Of course, he had. It was only right Diana should know she had a sister, a twin, even though it was too late ever to meet her.

After they finished tea, Diana reminisced about her past, how she had been swapped between families, and how it made her more determined to be a success and to have a role in life.

'There's something else you need to know,' said Willis.

Diana looked at him. Terror filled her eyes. 'What? There's more?'

Willis repeated that Carole had died in a hit-and-run accident a long time ago. The guilty driver was in jail. They'd traced him a few days ago. His name was Pryce, Jim Pryce. Willis looked at Diana for a sign of recognition, but none came. Some anonymous person had paid Pryce to 'give her a fright.' Willis used Pryce's words, not his. 'He overdid the scare, and the cars collided head-on.' He took a couple of deep breaths. They were as much for Willis's benefit as for Diana's. 'We can now confirm the intention was only to have Pryce frighten you.'

Diana sat in silence again but for longer this time. 'That makes sense, and it would be about the time I opened up an investigation into the cold-murder case that I told you about yesterday. It would have been an attempt to make me drop the investigation.' She shakily got to her feet and shuffled to the window. 'I had a twin sister, and I caused her death. How will I ever forgive myself? I should have let sleeping dogs lie.'

Willis said it wasn't her fault. It was whoever paid Pryce to drive into their car. The best thing to do was to continue with her investigation and make sure they caught whoever paid the killer. 'I, for one, wouldn't like Carole's, your sister's, death to be in vain. Let's join forces and find out who did this.'

'I have an unusual request. Would you mind if I asked you both to spend the night here?' She waited for Willis and Sophie to answer in the affirmative. 'I will order a takeaway, and we will open a bottle of wine.'

'We would be pleased to,' added Willis.

Diana said he could tell her what Carole was like because she wanted to know as much about her sister as possible. One never can tell. Something that he said might give her a hint as to her real background.

Willis glanced at Sophie. He was concerned that she might object to him recalling his past life with Carole, but Sophie smiled and gave the slightest of nods.

'That's an excellent idea,' said Sophie trying to brighten up the conversation. 'I can learn something about this misfit's past while we are at it.'

'I will try,' he said. 'But you both might need to wipe my eyes if I succumb and have a little cry now and then.' He wasn't joking.

CHAPTER 6

The takeaway was excellent. They enjoyed a not too hot curry and several glasses of wine. Willis was surprised when Diana produced the bottle of red wine, and he and Sophie exchanged glances when they read the label. It was Crozes-Hermitage. It was Willis's favourite and had been Carole's and his favourite tipple. When they mentioned it to Diana, it didn't surprise her. From their ongoing conversation, she had come to accept that there were things she had in common with her twin sister even though they had never met. The wine had removed some of Diana's melancholy after learning about her sister, but Willis and Sophie expected it would return the next day when things sank in, and she had overcome the initial shock. Despite the difficulties, the evening went well. They spoke about Diana's past life in foster homes and about as much of Carole's life as Willis had been privy to. Willis told her how he and Carole had met but left out the detail about being with Sophie first and then separating from her after university. Diana seemed as interested in Sophie's background as Carole's. They both thought that was a good thing because it helped keep the conversation balanced and not too morose.

After they had devoured the second bottle of Crozes-Hermitage, the alcohol started to take its toll. Diana produced an already opened third bottle without even indicating that was her plan. It was something else she had in common with Carole. Neither could refuse another drink once they had started.

Sometime around the middle of the evening, Willis got to his feet, swayed and looked up at an impressive oil painting of a middle-aged couple that hung above the fireplace. He asked who they were? Diana didn't know. A woman in one of her early foster homes had given it to her. She had told Diana that it looked like her. Diana had carried it with her from home to home, and she would take it out of its protective cardboard tube only when she needed cheering up. She didn't think they looked anything like her, but they had kind faces, and they were smiling. It made her smile when she looked at it.

One distinctive feature of Carole's was that she had 'missing' earlobes. At the base, her ears simply sloped backwards and disappeared, which was the reason she never wore earrings. There was insufficient flesh to support them. Willis noticed that not only was Diana not wearing earrings, but her ears sloped backwards the same as Carole's had done. What attracted his attention was the ears of the lady in the painting. Her ears did the same. It couldn't be a coincidence.

'If I am very careful, would you object if I lifted the picture down to have a look at it?'

'It's very heavy. You'll need to take extra care. The frame cost me a fortune.'

Willis signalled to Sophie to grab the other end, but the painting was a lot lighter than he expected. It glided down effortlessly, and they leaned it on the settee facing them.

'May I borrow that magnifying glass that you used?' Diana handed him the lens. They turned the frame onto its side, so he could see the signature, but it was almost illegible. As far as Willis could make out, it was Malcolm X. 'Assuming that it's not the American civil rights leader, he should be easy to trace,' he joked. 'It's a very well-executed painting. The brushwork is very fine, and the skin tones are excellent. Look at the lady's hair. You can make out individual strands and trace them back to their roots on her forehead.'

'Don't be so anatomical, Brad,' said Sophie. 'Enjoy the painting for what it is. It's a lovely painting. I'll give you a hand to put it back up.'

Before he lifted the frame, Willis tilted the picture towards the coffee table. 'There's something written on the back. I can't read it. It's down at the very bottom. Help me swing it around.' Once the picture was turned ninety degrees, Willis angled it to allow the light from the wall lights to reach it. 'My God. This is all too much.' Willis dropped onto the settee.

'What is it? What does it say?' Sophie insisted.

'It says, "Penny and Robert Ford – 1980".' Willis took a deep breath. 'Diana, I think these people are Carole's and your birth parents.'

That almost put paid to the evening. Diana insisted on keeping the painting off the wall, so she could look at it more closely. She kept staring at the faces of the smiling couple. 'I've read that inscription before, but I didn't know my family name was Ford. Now it looks like they are smiling at me. Trying to communicate.'

Willis could only try to imagine what Diana was going through. She had discovered a lost sister and looked into the eyes of her parents for the first time. How traumatic would that be?

Sophie swapped settees and sat beside Diana. 'This is so much for you to accept all at once.' She put her arms around Diana and hugged her tightly. They were both crying, Sophie more so than Diana. 'I think we ought to call it a night and go to bed early.'

'There's no way I can relax,' said Diana, 'you go if you want. I need to settle my thoughts. There's too much adrenalin flowing in my blood to sleep. I need another bottle of red.'

And so the night continued.

'Penny and Robert? I know their names now. I will start tracing them, discover where they lived, where they were married, where Carole and I were born.'

'It's a lot to take in,' said Sophie. 'You've got your whole life ahead of you to uncover these mysteries. Slow down. You've discovered so much, so fast. Give yourself time to absorb it. Then enjoy the discoveries.'

'You are both very kind. I've also made new friends. A new girlfriend and a brother-in-law. Or are you, my sister-in-law? I don't know.'

'I never thought of that,' said Willis. 'I suppose I'll need to add you to our Christmas list.' They all started laughing. It helped release the tension, but the wine was making its contribution too.

It was after 3 a.m. before they finally retired to bed. They were less inebriated than they deserved to be. The stress must have burnt the alcohol away. It was fun finding their rooms. Diana pointed. 'Here. No, here. Please take that one. I haven't looked out towels. I'll get them for you tomorrow morning.'

***

The next morning started late. There was no sign of Diana when Willis and Sophie woke after 10 a.m. The house was quiet. No one was moving. They lay in bed for half an hour after deciding it was bad manners to get up before their hostess. At 10:30, they dressed, and Sophie looked for Diana. She tried the door that she had seen Diana go into earlier that morning. It was empty. She found Diana lying sprawled, face down and fully clothed, across the duvet of a single bed in the smallest room on the landing. She woke her and led her to the room where she assumed she slept. Sophie stood outside the door until she heard the shower starting, then walked downstairs to join Willis.

'Let's put this picture back before she comes down,' suggested Sophie. Once it was in place, they collected the empty wine bottles and half-empty glasses of wine and took them into the kitchen. Sophie found a refuse bin under the sink and threw the wrappers from the After Eights into it. She stood the empty bottles in the corner, ready to be re-cycled. The wine glasses were rinsed, dried and placed end up on the draining board, and then they went into the living room and waited for Diana to come down.

'I'm so sorry,' said Diana when she appeared. 'I'm not a very good hostess. I left you to your own devices.'

'It was a great evening,' said Willis. 'We both enjoyed ourselves. It was exciting, but we enjoyed ourselves.'

'You can say that again.' Dark shadows made Diana's eyes look old. 'Thanks for putting the picture back up. We wouldn't have managed that last night. I had better call the office and tell my secretary to cancel today. Let's make some breakfast.' She headed for the kitchen.

Sophie followed. 'I'll help. Show me where you keep everything.'

Breakfast passed as though they had been friends for years. The conversation flowed freely, and there was no hint of stress from the previous night's experience. Willis wasn't sure if that was a good thing, but Diana was a strong character. She had shown some of that last night. He desperately wanted to talk to her about the threats she had received, but he and Sophie had discussed it before Diana came down from her room and decided, or rather Sophie had decided, that it would be better to leave that conversation for another time. Diana needed to recover from the shock she had experienced.

What is it they say about the best-laid plans of mice and men? After they had cleared away the breakfast dishes, Diana disappeared upstairs. She reappeared, carrying a large green cardboard filing box. A broad piece of plastic tape held its lid in place. 'These are the files I have accumulated from all the threats and oddball things that have happened to me. They are all photocopies. The police have the originals, and I have further copies in my surgery.'

Willis had almost forgotten that she was the Member of Parliament for Mid-Suffolk. She was showing her strength once more, but it would be difficult to discuss these events against the background of last night. 'Are you sure you want to do this now? You've had a lot thrown at you already. Wouldn't you rather leave this until another time?'

'Nope. This is important too.' She pulled the files out of the box. They were in neat folders and highly organised. 'I have them colour-coded, red, yellow and green. The red ones are serious threats, the yellow ones are less serious, and the green ones are of concern, but they contained no threats.'

'I'd like to format these in date order, too,' said Willis. 'When did they start?'

'About four years ago, as soon as I tried to reopen the case to clear Rob Moore's name. He claims he was framed, and I believe him. You would, too, if you met him. He's a lovely lad.'

Willis explained that most prisoners protested their innocence and were pretty good at convincing people too. Diana would have none of it. She suggested Willis visit him and then decide. He wasn't convinced, but that Diana was being threatened supported her theory that Rob might be innocent. The top file in the green folder held information on Rob Moore and described him as below-average intelligence and open to suggestion. It also said he was nineteen years old. There was a picture of him attached to the file with a paperclip. He looked younger than his age, but the photograph had been taken four years ago. He was young to be charged with manslaughter. It had been murder, but the judge reduced it following an appeal. Willis sank onto the settee, absorbed in his reading.

'Let's take the files home. You can read them at your leisure.' Sophie insisted.

'Go on. I will be okay,' said Diana. 'I've got used to the shocks from last night. I'll be fine. Go. I need some time on my own, anyway.'

***

They arrived back at Madingley in time for lunch. Sophie wasn't looking forward to cooking, so they visited the Three Horseshoes. It used to be the local pub but had upgraded to a restaurant. Like most pubs, it struggled to get clientele to visit, and the ban on smoking hadn't helped either. They sat at a twin seated table to the right-hand side of the glass extension that reminded Willis of a greenhouse. The restaurant had been one of the first to introduce dining pods. These were popular during the COVID pandemic. You sat in your safe bubble with friends and felt secure. Willis promised that if he ever got around to having a birthday party, he would hire 'a pod' and invite a few friends. Each pod would hold about a dozen diners. They could be as noisy as they liked in one of those, he claimed.

They ordered the vegetarian soup for Willis but settled on the Traditional Fish Pie for their main dish. He was a half-hearted vegetarian but ate meat and fish whenever it suited him. Willis used the excuse that he ate meat to keep his stomach enzymes in good condition, claiming that serious vegetarians lost the ability to digest some foods. He didn't like to think about the food he'd eaten during his visit to Antarctica. The cooks had served meat with every meal there. Despite the heavy food, he had lost seventeen pounds as a result of the cold temperatures.

George, the chef, came to their table to welcome them. It had been a while since Willis had visited. Had he upset him? Willis explained that he had been away for a year and had not long returned, but he promised George that he would see a lot more of them in the coming months. Before leaving, he recommended the fish pie, and George smiled when Willis told him they had ordered it already. He thanked them and moved on to the next table, where a couple was having difficulty deciding.

'I hope Diana will be okay by herself,' said Sophie. 'She has been through so much in the last twelve hours.'

'She'll be fine. Diana's a strong-willed lady. She's been living with threats, still getting on with her work as an MP and, at the same time, trying to re-open Rob Moore's case. We need another favour from your Uncle Swallow. If we can get hold of the case notes from the trial and any other police notes he can wangle, it would set us off running.'

'I'm not sure he will be comfortable getting you confidential police information, but he might be prepared to give us a verbal report on what they have if I asked him nicely.'

'I'm sure that will be enough. Diana will also get the court proceedings from Rob's solicitor because it's in his interest to give us as much detail as possible.'

The soup arrived. It was leek and potato. It was hot. They stopped chatting while they swirled the soup around their mouths to get it to cool. It was a thick soup, and getting it to cool took some effort. Eventually, Willis put his bowl to one side. 'We don't even know who it is that Rob is convicted of killing. I'm sure it will be in Diana's notes, but she didn't organise them in a way that makes them useful to our investigation. I'll see if I can pick up some A0 sheets of paper. They are almost four feet by three. We will summarise what we have on a few sheets, and maybe something will jump out and hit us in the face.'

'You are always optimistic. If the police found nothing, what makes you think you will?'

'One has got to try. One has got to try.' Willis had finished his soup, although it was still hot. It was just as well because the fish pie had arrived, and it was every bit as hot. Willis broke the surface of the pastry to let some of the heat escape and then sat back, contemplating.

'After we've finished here, let's head back to the cottage and get started on Diana's files.'

CHAPTER 7

The living room of their cottage was a mess; papers were strewn everywhere. They covered the carpet, the table, the chairs and the settee. A smaller pile lay balanced on the corner of the Welsh dresser. Mrs Burns had let herself in and then left in disgust. On the wall opposite the wood burner, Willis had 'Blue-Tacked' two sheets of A0 paper and had butted them together to make one long sheet. He'd hung them vertically, so he could add dates down the left-hand side and incidents on the right, but the sheets were still blank.

They began the arduous task of putting everything in date order. Sophie was sitting browsing the green file Diana had given them. According to Diana, it contained no threats but items that caused her concern. She pulled one out at random. 'This is a printout of an email. It simply reads "I am watching you". It could be of interest,' She threw it down on the carpet and removed another. 'This one reads "I hope you are enjoying your cheese roll", and it has yesterday's date, so they must have been watching her when she was with us at the pub.'

'Let me see that.' Willis leaned over and took the sheet. 'He's used the present tense, and that means he was in the pub or outside it, so he likely sent this from a phone.'

'Or a laptop with a data dongle.'

Willis told her to stop showing off. He went to the dresser and looked at the photograph Sophie had taken of Diana and him. He'd hoped to spot someone in the background, but it was a pity they'd taken only a close up of their heads and shoulders because it meant the background was blurred. Behind them, two men stood at the bar. One was looking at his phone, but it was too out of focus to be useful, so he put the picture back and returned to sorting the files.

'Didn't you tell me you'd used someone at Scotland Yard to trace emails for you when you were tracking the data tapes that were transmitted from CERN a couple of years ago?'

'You are a genius, Sophie.' Willis had contacted Bill Chalmers of the Porn Squad to trace where data was going from CERN, the European Organisation for Nuclear Research, near Geneva. Bill had used the squad's talents for tracing internet traffic and could tell Willis that the CERN messages were going to Kazakhstan. It helped them solve the investigation and led him to the culprits, but Bill couldn't tell him where the messages had come from, only where they'd gone. It was worth a try, though. If Diana's threat had come from a phone, it would be easier for him to trace.

Willis didn't have a direct line for Chalmers, so he sent him an email and requested a return call. He reminded Bill that Willis had contacted him, via the Home Secretary, a couple of years ago, for which he remained grateful, but he needed his urgent help again. Willis did not doubt that Reilly would help him contact the Home Secretary if needed, but he preferred to contact Bill to start with. Willis liked to cultivate his contacts. He remembered Chalmers as a short, thin man. He dressed untidily in a wrinkled shirt, so Willis assumed he was unmarried or not in a relationship. He had a distinctive stain on his tie, which he never seemed to change. He must have changed it by now, mused Willis. Chalmers looked more like a criminal than the men he was supposed to be catching.

Willis had settled down among the papers only minutes when his mobile rang. 'Hello, Bill. Thanks for calling back.' Willis pressed the loudspeaker button, so Sophie could listen in on the conversation. 'Yes, I need your internet skills again, and no, before you ask, it's not to protect some politician who's been breaking the law. It is a politician, but one that's been sent threatening emails – probably from a mobile phone.'

Chalmers told Willis that it was easier to trace calls and emails from phones and asked for the details of the MP and the source email address. He was pleased it was a Gmail address because they were easy to put a trace on, and many criminals used Gmail as their first choice. Willis explained the dot-gov email address belonged to Diana Bishop, the politician who was the victim, and it was the criminal who was using the Gmail address. Bill assured him that as long as one side used it, then it would be easy. He added that it could be done as long as they're not using a VPN. That would change everything. They used Virtual Private Networks to hide their identities, but there were ways around those too. The only thing Chalmers would need was permission to hack the dot-gov email system, and that would be a showstopper unless Willis could get the Home Secretary to call him and give her approval.

He was hoping he would get away without doing that, but Diana Bishop had a direct line to the Home Secretary, and he was sure she had her support because she was already aware of her problems.

Before Chalmers signed off, he checked he could call Willis on this number and agreed to wait for the Home Secretary to telephone. Only then would he get onto it.

'Yes. I'll be waiting too. Thank you.' They hung up. And I can also contact you on your number, thought Willis.

Willis called Diana and told her what he planned to do. She was very grateful and would contact the Home Secretary to get permission to have her dot-gov emails tracked, so she took Bill's contact details to pass on to the Home Secretary.

Sophie sounded encouraging and told him he'd started the ball rolling at least, but they'd need to be patient to see what Bill discovered.

Willis shook his head, said that Bill might discover nothing and suggested they get back to the paperwork. There must be something in here to give them a clue.

Sophie sighed, slipped off the settee onto the carpet and lifted another bundle and started reading.

After about two hours, Willis's temporary crime scene board was nearly full, so he added another sheet alongside the first two. 'I've added the time of day to each of the dated items. There seems to be a pattern. The emails usually come in around mid-morning or afternoon. Nothing ever arrived early in the day, around midday, or in the evening, and that might be trying to tell us something, but I don't know what it is.'

'I wonder why the threats have been going on for so long.' Sophie slid along the floor and parked her back against the settee. 'If Diana has got nowhere with her attempt to get the case reopened in three years, why would they keep trying?'

Willis believed it was because Diana continued to try. Her efforts have increased recently. It was only in the last month that she'd contacted Miriam Hodge, the Home Secretary, and that would have motivated anyone that wanted to stop her from stepping up her activities. Willis pointed to the list of times he had written on the sheets, and they looked suspiciously like pub times. He meant not times when a pub was open but when it was shut. If it were somebody that worked in a pub, they would be busy at lunchtime and in the evenings, so they might only send the messages between pub opening times.

'But pubs are open nearly all the time now. They rarely close.'

'What about a landlord?' Willis was staring into space. 'He would need to be there almost all the time, even if only to be seen. It's a thought, but let's file that in the back of our minds. Look at this email.' He laid it on the floor.

I'll come to get you if you do not give up. We will see whose going to survive this.

'And look at this one.' Willis dropped a second email beside it.

You're the one whose going to suffer. Stop now or else.

'What do you notice about these two emails? What do they have in common?'

'You mean other than they've used the wrong "whose" in both cases? It should be "who's" in both these messages.'

'Exactly. Let's do a quick recce through all the emails to see if we can find any other misspelt words.'

'The grammar is awful,' said Sophie. 'There are lots of double negatives, such as "you won't never succeed" and a few others.

'Here are another couple of wrong "whose" in two sentences.' said Willis. 'They won't prove anything. But we need to heed them because it means it wasn't a professional person who wrote these. We wouldn't have expected it to be, anyway.'

'Interesting. By looking at what the emails are saying, we've got no closer, but the style of writing is proving to be a strong clue.'

Willis said he needed a cup of coffee.

Sophie volunteered. She jumped to her feet and stretched her back. 'I'm getting stiff, and I need a rest anyway.'

Five minutes later, Sophie returned with the coffees. She pushed one in front of Willis. It was a little stronger than her one, and she put it down on a pile of paper sitting on the edge of the Welsh dresser. The papers wobbled. Willis watched it happen in slow motion, but there was nothing he could do about it. The papers and the cup fell onto the floor. The mass of paper covering the carpet protected it, but the cup bounced and emptied its thick brown contents over half a dozen sheets of paper. Sophie dashed into the kitchen and returned with a tea towel and tried to rescue the papers, but the towel absorbed the coffee, and the brown liquid saturated it within seconds. She rushed back and returned with another towel. Diana had used waterproof ink, so the printing hadn't run in the wet, but the papers were soggy and in danger of tearing. She lifted them as carefully as possible and hung them over the central heating boiler in the utility room.

'I'm going to tell Diana that you did it,' laughed Willis.

'Piss off. You can make the coffee next time.' Sophie put the last piece of paper over the boiler. 'Hey, look at this, Brad.'

It wasn't an email like the others; it was a letter. The coffee had sunk into the paper and exposed the watermark. 'It's a ship,' said Sophie, 'a tall-masted sailing ship.'

Willis got on his laptop and googled the names of pubs in Suffolk. There were hundreds. He refined his search by searching for 'pubs named after ships.' There were nine. Two he could dismiss as they were steamships. He checked the others' websites and noted their postcodes, then searched again. This time for pubs in Essex. He found fourteen on this list. Five were dismissed as unsuitable. He scribbled nine postcodes, turned to Sophie and said, 'How serendipitous. Guess what we'll be doing tomorrow?'

'Maybe you'll buy me a pub lunch in at least one of them?' She cocked her head snootily and walked into the living room. 'I bet you don't tell Diana I discovered the connection.'

'Humph,' Willis grunted. 'I still haven't had a coffee.'

'To hell with your coffee. I'm going to open a bottle of *vino*. I think we have something to celebrate at last. There's still a long way to go, but at least we've made a start.'

Willis said in that case, he was going to get a takeaway. He was going to order a pizza.

'You are such a naughty man. We've already eaten, and it's a bit late now for pizza. Let's just relax and have a few hours to ourselves.'

Willis told Alexa to play some romantic music, and his Amazon Echo burst into life. The dulcet tones of Alexa announced, 'Here is a playlist you might like, etc., etc.,' and soft music filled the room.

Willis and Sophie sipped their wine and enjoyed each other's company. Each relaxed. They had only taken ten minutes to tidy the reams of paper and put them in piles in the farthest corner of the room. They did it to avoid the scorn they knew would have come from Mrs Burns if they'd left them in situ. Alexa started to play the Carpenters' *It's only just begun*. It was one of their favourite songs. They had last heard it on their trip when they had danced together, shortly before they married. It would remain a special song. 'It's only just begun in this case as well,' said Sophie. 'Do you ever wonder how things will turn out when you start to investigate?'

'Not really. If I do that, I will get biased in my thinking and make the wrong decisions. No. I just go with the flow and wait for things to unfold as they happen. That way, my thoughts don't get cluttered with a lot of unrelated and erroneous ideas.'

'It must be good to be as disciplined as that, but my mind will often race ahead, and I'm wondering now who it is that the sender of the emails is trying to protect.'

'If we knew that, the case would be over and solved.'

'I know, but we could get a clue if we found out who the person was that Rob Moore allegedly killed, but we haven't done that yet.'

'I know,' said Willis. 'It'll be in Diana's files. We'll get there.' They'd only read about a quarter of them, and he thought they were doing fine so far with what they've discovered. As Sophie had said, they'd only just begun.

Willis put his arm around Sophie and hugged her. He was so glad that Sophie was helping him investigate Carole's death. It meant so much to him. Few wives would get involved in investigating an ex's demise. Sophie had stayed with him through all his treatment in St Petersburg, and she knew how important finding the car and the killer was to him. She had supported him all the way, and it couldn't be easy for her. He wasn't finding it easy, but he was driven to do it. Sophie had no such motivation, only her love for him.

He'd found Carole's killer but hadn't yet found who had paid him for her murder. That it wasn't his intention to kill her didn't reduce Willis's resolution in the least. He wanted to find whoever started the chain of events because he was sure he would never be free from his PTSD symptoms until he was found. Willis had never been as close to the solution as this, and he was determined to succeed. It was now or never.

Sophie bumped his arm. 'Come back to me. You are in your private world again. Just relax and enjoy the evening.'

'Sorry, I was miles away.' He kissed her. 'I'm going to order pizzas now. By the time they arrive, we will have started our second bottle of *vino*. You should be nice and malleable by then.'

'I'm nice and malleable now. What's keeping you?' She looked into his eyes. Willis could see the green flecks catching the light as her eyes dashed left and right, looking at each of his. Willis needed no more encouragement. He collected the bottle and glasses and took Sophie by the hand and led her upstairs. He was singing, 'It's pizza time again.' Sophie dug her elbow in his ribs and giggled.

The pizzas never got ordered, but they had pizza nevertheless.

CHAPTER 8

Willis had made a list of all the pubs he'd found whose names related to ships and put them in reverse order of distance from Madingley, with the farthest first. It would be a better use of time. They would drive out to the most distant one before any of them opened and then work their way home during opening hours. They might not get them all visited in a single day, but the logic still held. So, they would start in Essex and work their way northwards. There were sixteen pubs in all. Seven were in Suffolk and nine in Essex. This would take forever. 'Let's only do Suffolk to start with. It's more likely that the pub will be nearer home,' said Willis.

He hadn't considered how many pubs called *The Ship Inn,* or something similar, there were throughout the county. The first three they visited had that name and were easily eliminated. They didn't even need to go inside. All three had notices pinned to a board inside the door with food menus on. It was an easy task to lift the paper and check for watermarks. Two had watermarks but of the wrong kind. The third had a menu on headed paper without a watermark. Willis dismissed it as unlikely they would also have headed notepaper with a watermark. The menus looked professionally made and not produced on home printers. He was taking risks, but ones he was willing to take in the interest of time.

The next two pubs were more difficult. They had neither menus nor notices at the doors. They looked more like farmers' drinking establishments, and Willis eliminated them because they wouldn't have gone to the bother of having watermarked paper. It surprised him that any pub would have bothered with such elaborate embellishments.

The next pub looked more promising. It was the second last on the list in Suffolk. 'Sixth time lucky,' he joked. It was called *The Clipper Inn*. They passed by the *Lord Nelson* pub and headed south east along Duke Street. *The Clipper Inn* stood on the right-hand side. It was an impressive building and backed onto the river Orwell, and that wasn't too surprising for a pub named *The Clipper Inn*. There was a menu at the door, but it was on a card specially printed for the purpose. The logo on the menu and the pub sign looked very like the image on the watermark. It was a drawing of a ship with tall masts and a very slender hull. All the traits Willis expected to see in a clipper. As he walked in, Willis copied the landlord's name from above the door. Here, it was a landlady – a Helen Devlin.

Since this was probably the last pub they would visit that day, Willis ordered a half of Guinness, and Sophie asked for a Pinot Grigio. 'It's getting nippy outside,' said Willis as the waitress poured his pint.

'It's unusually cold for this time of year, and this chilled Guinness will make you feel even colder.'

'It's my favourite beer. Do you have a piece of paper that I can make some notes on?' The waitress ripped a sheet from a pad and handed it to Willis. He thanked her and took a seat at the table nearest the window.

'Damn. There's no watermark on it. That would have been too easy.' He strode over to the bar and showed the waitress a picture on his phone. 'Have you seen this watermark before? I collect unusual watermarks, especially from pubs and restaurants.' His phone showed the watermark clearly, but the printed message was too indistinct to make out.

'Yes, that's our watermark. Wherever did you get it?'

'It is part of my dad's collection,' lied Willis. 'I got the idea to take up the hobby from him, but this one is damaged. I spilled coffee on it, and he's not well pleased.'

'Hold on a minute.' She disappeared into a small room leading off from the bar and returned with several sheets of paper. 'Here you are. These should put you back in his good books. There are about a half dozen sheets there.' Willis thanked her profusely, ordered another round of drinks and gave her a generous tip. 'There's no need for that, but thanks,' she said, stuffing the five pound note into her apron pocket.

Willis brought the sheets back to the window. He held one up to the light. 'It looks as though we have found our pub.' On the paper was the identical outline of the ship they had seen through the coffee stain. 'This will give Bill Chalmers a head start.'

A tall woman with dyed red hair and a massive bosom joined the waitress at the bar. The waitress took off her apron and surreptitiously removed, from its pocket, the five pound note Willis had given her and then disappeared into the small room behind the bar. It was time for the afternoon shift to change. Willis glanced at his watch, 2:30 p.m. That is useful to know, he thought. He went up to the bar and ordered a packet of peanuts. 'This is a lovely pub. It's very comfortable. Have you worked here long?'

'I am the landlady,' she volunteered, 'and my man and I have been here nigh on four years now. We quite enjoy it. It suits our lifestyle.'

'Before you came here, did you run the *Last Anchor* up the road? Your husband's name isn't Bernie by any chance?'

'No. Alec and I came from London. We came for peace and quiet, and there are fewer problems in Suffolk pubs. Fewer disturbances and hassles.' Willis thanked her very much. As he returned to sit beside Sophie, he tore the packet of peanuts open.

'Alec Devlin is his name. That will help Bill even more. It should narrow down his options. All in all, it's been a very productive day, and I'm so glad we didn't start with Essex.'

'Me too,' said Sophie. She lifted her glass and clinked against Willis's Guinness.

'This Guinness is too cold for a day like this. Sup up your Pinot, and let's head home. Mrs Burns will have the wood burner going by now. It calls for another bottle of wine tonight.'

'If you keep up this rate of success, we'll both be alkies before we're finished.' She threw back her wine and followed Willis to the door.

***

As soon as Willis arrived at the cottage, he threw his jacket onto the peg in the hall and called Bill Chalmers. 'Have you made any progress tracing the email address?' he asked.

'I haven't heard from the Home Secretary yet. My hands are tied until she calls. I dare not hack a government email account without clearance. It's more than my job is worth.'

'Okay. I'll wait to hear from you. I have an idea where the emails originated from.'

'There's no advantage in telling me. If you give out clues, it won't affect the result one way or t'other. I'll trace it, or I won't, but I'll call you as soon as I hear anything.'

Willis thanked him and hung up. He laid Diana's papers back out onto the floor. 'Come and help,' he shouted to Sophie. 'We need to go through these and look for a mention of an Alec Devlin or a surname of Devlin. We also need to find the name of the victim. That's the next logical step.' They settled down on the carpet for a second time and methodically looked through the papers, reading every one for clues.

Willis was sure the link to *The Clipper Inn* wouldn't be strong enough for the police to take action. They needed to get a solid trace from Bill Chalmers, linking the pub and the sender of the emails.

The doorbell rang. A young man in a DHL shirt stood with an enormous cardboard box. 'A delivery for Mr Willis. I need a signature.' He thrust a keypad towards Willis, and he signed its tiny window. Willis held it up to check his scrawl. He was sure that only he would recognise the scrawl as his signature. It was illegible and extended beyond the limits of the tiny screen. Its curves turned into straight lines when they hit the screen's edges, but the young man seemed satisfied and dropped the box on the doorstep. Willis read the name of the sender. It was from Young's Solicitors and must be the transcript that Diana had requested from Rob Moore's trial.

As he struggled into the living room with the box, Sophie's eyes dropped. 'There's no room left on the carpet,' she said.

'This is important. Let's leave what we're doing and get stuck into this.' Willis dropped the box temporarily on the settee. Once again, they lifted the papers from the floor and arranged them in a neat pile in the corner. Ten minutes later, the carpet was covered with the newly acquired folders. 'They're in date order. That's something, at least, so we just need to read them.' If they only skimmed each sheet, Willis estimated that there would be over six hours of reading required, and by the time they had taken notes, it would be closer to eight. They couldn't split the task between them, because they would both need to read everything to get the gist of how the trial progressed.

The first folder revealed the name of the victim. The judge's opening remarks had made the revelation, and he was William McLellan, aged twenty-six, an unemployed labourer from Clacton-on-Sea. He had been married with three children. Willis dropped the folder and immediately called Bill Chalmers. 'Sorry to call you again. I need to find out if a William McLellan has any criminal convictions.' Chalmers took down the address and other details and promised to call back. Willis returned to wading through the transcript.

A witness had found McLellan dead due to blunt force trauma to his head and shoulders. The judge had described it as a particularly savage attack carried out in a fit of frenzy. The judge had continued by saying that whoever had committed this heinous crime had done so in anger and that it had been a spur-of-the-moment attack. Willis worried about the last statement from the judge. It was the jury's job to decide whether the crime was premeditated. Willis's sheets of A0 on the wall filled up fast because he stopped every couple of pages and made an addition to his list.

Several witnesses had been called to attest to Robert Moore's character. He had no previous, but the police had found a metal bar with the victim's blood on it in the boot of Robert's car wrapped in a blood-soaked rag. No fingerprints were found on the metal bar. Odd, thought Willis. If the killer had thrown it in the car, there would have been no reason to rush to wipe it. This suggested to Willis that someone had planted it there and pointed to Robert's innocence. His barrister had raised this issue at the trial, but he couldn't explain how the metal bar got into Robert's boot, and the wounds found on the deceased were consistent with the end of the metal bar. Robert couldn't account for his movements at the time of the victim's death. He was out walking on his own. There didn't seem to be any connection between Robert Moore and William McLellan. As far as the prosecution was concerned, they were unknown to each other, which made the killing especially heinous. No witnesses had been called for the prosecution, and the case rested on the bar being in Robert Moore's car. A DI Wilkin had made a statement that Robert Moore had admitted to the crime while in custody, but it had been a verbal confession, and he had withdrawn it once his solicitor arrived. The judge instructed the jury to disregard DI Wilkin's testimony. But the damage had already been done, thought Willis. The comment was lodged in the jurors' minds. If Robert Moore had a lower-than-average intelligence, he could have been coerced by the Detective Inspector to admit to the crime under duress, but that was a route that would prove unfruitful, thought Willis, so he would ignore that line of enquiry. An image of the metal bar was the only photographic evidence other than the hideous pictures of the deceased lying on a grassy verge. Willis could tell from the pictures that someone had attacked McLellan from behind and from the right. This suggested that the assailant had been right-handed. It was a long shot but noteworthy. But there were also wounds on the top of the victim's head, suggesting either the killer was much taller than the victim or he had continued to hit him once he had fallen to the ground. Willis studied the picture of the bar. It was unpainted and rusted, with four grooves running around its circumference. The two inner grooves were about eighteen inches apart. The rust had rubbed off the inside of the grooves. It was a clue what the bar had been used for, but Willis had no idea what that might be, and he could find no mention of these facts being raised at the trial.

It was after midnight. Both he and Sophie were staring at the four walls of the room, eyelids drooping and with dark shadows beneath their eyes.

'Let's go to bed,' said Willis.

'Oh, yes, please.' Sophie threw her arms around Willis's shoulders, and he almost carried her up the narrow stairs to the bedroom.

After thirty minutes, Sophie bounced around on the bed. 'I can't sleep,' she announced. 'I'm too tired. There's no way I'm going to get off.'

'Okay, I'll get up and make some drinking chocolate.' Willis had already been asleep. He staggered down the stairs. With his eyes closed, he missed the second bottom step, and he bashed into the wall. 'Bloody 'ell. I'll have a bruise tomorrow because of that.'

'I'll fetch the milk.' Sophie headed to the fridge. 'You said earlier that the killer was right-handed? I disagree.'

'How come?'

'If the bar in the car boot hadn't been moved before the police took the picture, then it would have suggested the culprit was left-handed. The picture shows one end of the bar unwrapped. The bloody side was on the right side. That suggests that a left-handed person placed it in the trunk.'

'Not necessarily. If they had wrapped and then lifted it, they could have rotated it.'

'It was a long bar,' insisted Sophie. 'It would have meant putting it down and walking around to the other side of it. Rotating it in your arms would feel unnatural.'

'What if he'd put it under his arm then swapped arms because it was heavy? He might have rotated it then.'

'It's not that heavy,' argued Sophie.

'I guess, in that case, we're looking for an ambidextrous man.'

'Hilarious. Who says it has to have been a man?'

'It was a particularly violent crime. It isn't the sort of thing a woman would do.'

'Okay, I'll concede that. It's an ambidextrous man we're looking for.'

'Sod off. Let's go back to bed.'

'It could have been two people,' Sophie shouted up the stairs after Willis. She dropped the two chocolate-stained mugs into the sink and ran some water over them.

'It's getting too complicated,' shouted Willis. His voice was muffled; the duvet was around his head.

CHAPTER 9

'We need to visit Rob Moore in prison,' said Willis. 'Diana will have visited him several times. I will ask her to arrange a visit for us.' He called Diana. She had a visit already organised to the prison with Rob's solicitor, Edward Young. She said that they should meet her outside the prison at 3 p.m. Diana would have their names added to the list of visitors. They wouldn't be visitors, but members of the legal team working on getting the case reopened because that's the only way she could get four people in to see Robert at the same time. He was in Hollesley Bay Prison, the same prison as Jim Pryce. Diana had convinced the prison authorities to transfer him to a category D prison. Because she was fighting his case, she argued it wouldn't be in his interests to escape. Being an MP carried some weight.

A warden ushered them into the same interview room where Willis and Sophie had met Jim Pryce. There was a wait of around fifteen minutes before they could bring Robert to see them. They used the time productively. Willis wanted to know what Robert had done on the day of the alleged killing. Where did he drive, and where did he park? Young said that Robert had stopped at the Neptune Marina to eat a sandwich, but he hadn't asked if he had left the car, and the solicitor told them he had also parked further along the river for a few minutes. Willis was still in the middle of questioning Young when Robert was shown into the room.

'Sit down, Rob,' said Diana. 'I've brought another two people today who are going to help us prove you are innocent. This is Brad and Sophie. Edward, you know well. Edward will help fill in any details they require, but I need you to answer all their questions honestly.' Robert nodded his head slowly, keeping his deep brown eyes fixed on the table in front of him. He looked even younger than his years suggested. Robert had jet-black hair, and it was cut short with a side parting. Willis couldn't see Robert's eyes, because his bushy eyebrows cast shadows from the overhead light.

'Will you look at me, Robert?' said Willis. Robert raised his head, looked at him and then lowered it back to its original position. Willis was sure he did it unintentionally. 'If I can't see your eyes, I can't have a conversation with you.' Robert gave a small nod of his head and raised his eyes to meet Willis's. 'How did you get your scar? The one on your cheek.'

Robert's eyes flashed sideways to look at Diana as though asking permission to answer. 'You can tell Brad anything you like. He's on our side.'

'My dad.'

'Your dad gave you the scar? How did that happen?'

'When I was little, I stole a pound from his wallet.' There was a gap. 'I wanted to buy my mother a birthday present.

He hit me with his hand. The sharp corner of his ring tore my cheek. When I told him why I had taken it, he said he was sorry and gave me five pounds to buy my mum a nice present.'

'Edward told me you parked at the marina the day that Mr McLellan was killed?'

'I didn't kill him. I didn't touch him.'

'I know,' said Willis. 'Tell me about the marina. What did you do there?'

'I ate my sandwich and watched the boats. I often look at the boats.'

'Did you leave the car while you were there?'

'Only to feed the gulls. I never eat my crusts. The gulls come and take them.'

'How long do you think it took you to feed the gulls, Robert?'

'My name is Rob. I like being called Rob. I remember walking up to where the big restaurant was, and I fed them there. It was only for ten minutes.'

'When did you learn to drive, Rob?'

'When I was seventeen. My dad taught me, and I passed a month after my birthday. I passed the first time,' he said proudly. 'The man told me I had driven perfect and didn't make any mistakes. He tested me twice, too, just to prove it. He asked lots of questions about the Code too. I got them all right. I surprised him when I knew all the stopping distances.'

'You're good at driving. Did you stop anywhere else than at the marina?'

'A big red yacht left and headed for the sea. I turned around and followed it along the side of the river for a bit.'

'Once it sailed away, did you stop and get out of your car?'

'Oh yes. There's a big stone wall along the road. I climbed on the wall, so I could see it going even farther.'

'How long did that take?'

'I sat for about fifteen minutes and ate my ice cream cone.'

'You didn't tell me you'd bought an ice cream cone?'

'I didn't buy it, silly. The man gave it to me. The man who liked looking at the boats too.'

'Did he tell you his name?'

'No. He was just a man.'

'What did he look like?'

'He was bigger than me, and he had a scar, like mine. Not as big, though.' Rob rubbed the side of his cheek, feeling for his scar. 'He had his hair done like a lady. It had a band around it, and it hung in a pigtail. It looked silly as his hair was all grey coloured.'

'Thank you, Rob. You've been very helpful. Did you go or stop anywhere else?'

'No, that's all I ever do. I drive there on Wednesdays after I pick up my dad's order from Stowmarket.'

'Is that every Wednesday, Rob?'

'Nearly every Wednesday. I wouldn't come if it was Christmas or New Year's.'

Rob's concentration was waning. Willis slid a piece of paper over the table and asked Rob to write his name on it. He was happy to oblige. Willis thanked him again and nodded to Diana and Edward Young to take over, but they hadn't any questions ready, because they were simply interested in getting Rob to feel comfortable in Sophie and Brad's presence. Diana explained they came to see him every two weeks to ask how he was doing and keep the familiarity going. Willis asked Rob whether he would mind if he came back to visit him. He said that would be great. They could talk about boats.

Once outside, Willis suggested they go to Woodbridge for coffee. The day had revealed a lot of new information. As Willis followed Diana and Edward's car, he complained to Sophie that no one had questioned Rob long enough, and they had assumed that because he was autistic, he couldn't answer questions reliably. They parked at the station and headed for High Street. Willis recommended the same little tea room he and Sophie had visited earlier in the week.

'You didn't tell me he was on the spectrum?' Willis was angry. 'Just because he's autistic doesn't mean he's unreliable. Why use the euphemism of below-average intelligence? He's a shit hot driver and has been since he was seventeen. He knows what he's doing.'

Diana grabbed Willis's hand. A shudder of déjà vu flowed over him. Carole used to grab his hand like that. She said they didn't know Willis well, either, so they weren't sure how he would react. Sorry, but they'd underrated him.

'Four coffees?' asked Willis. 'How do you take them? Don't tell me, Diana. You take it black with one sugar.'

'How did you…?'

'Just a wild guess.' Willis saw Sophie throwing daggers in his direction. 'And four Danish?'

When he returned, Diana announced that the day had been a success because they had the description of either the murderer or his accomplice, but she asked what was going on with the piece of paper and Rob's name.

Willis explained it was a private bet that he and Sophie had placed with each other. Sophie reckoned the murderer was left-handed, but he was not entirely sure. Rob was right-handed.

Diana asked why he thought the killer was left-handed? How could he deduce that?

Sophie jumped in, saying it came from the picture of the bloody bar lying in the car that Diana had sent with the transcript of the trial. The picture showed the bloody end of the rod positioned on the right, so they could deduce that the handle must be on the left. Therefore, the murderer was most likely left-handed.

She looked at Edward. He was a tall, erect man with dark hair and a neat moustache. He had intense blue eyes that competed with Willis's for brightness.

Edward argued that he could see the counterargument to that, and it would be useless in court.

Willis replied they weren't in court. They were looking for clues, and they should wait to see who was right.

'Stop bickering, you two.' Diana was using her politically won authority. 'We've booked a table for dinner. Why don't you come and join us? It's still a bit early, but by the time we drive there and have a drink, it will be time.'

Willis turned to Sophie. 'That would be an excellent idea.'

Diana suggested Edward would lead the way, and Sophie and Willis should follow him.

Willis tucked his car behind Edward's and asked Sophie if she thought they were an item.

Sophie thought it was possible. They had been working together for some time. It might have started when they put Rob in jail, but it also could be platonic because she had seen no sign that the relationship was anything other than business.

They headed down the A12 and cut off at Dedham. When they turned onto Gun Hill, Willis said he thought they were heading for Le Talbooth at Dedham. He believed it was an excellent restaurant, but he'd only been there once before. He should have guessed since Diana didn't live too far from there. The car park was almost empty when they arrived, but it was still early, as Diana had implied.

'Let's go into the lounge and order some drinks, then I'll upgrade our table to a four-seater,' said Edward. They collected their drinks while Edward was organising the table and wandered outside and along a broad grass verge that ran alongside the River Stour.

'Look at that lovely bridge,' said Sophie. 'Let's walk over it and look back at the view.' The walk took longer than expected. When Edward appeared, it took a little while for him to work out where they'd gone, and then he saw Diana waving from the bridge. They stood at the centre of the stone bridge and looked towards the restaurant. They could see tables and chairs sitting right up to the edge of the river bank, where a large white awning covered the outdoor tables.

'It's a pity it's wintertime and so cold. It's lovely to sit outside in the summer, and there's a small riverboat that moors here in the warmer weather and offers boat rides along the Stour. It's all very idyllic.'

Edward said he'd had a slight problem with the table, as all the tables for four had been taken. He'd had to move their reservation forward thirty minutes. He hoped that was okay, but everyone nodded in agreement.

'That means we won't have as much time to drink, so we'd better get more drinks ordered.'

'Hey, don't forget we have to drive home afterwards,' said Sophie. 'We can't afford to lose our licence,' she joked.

'You can both come home with me. You are part of the family now. We are related.' Diana tipped her glass to one side.

Sophie said that they'd see about that, tipping her glass in response.

Edward volunteered to fetch a menu.

As soon as he was out of earshot, Sophie looked at Edward and whispered to Diana, 'Are you and he…?'

'No. Not yet anyway. But it might be heading in that direction because Rob's case has been pushing us together. We get on very well together, and I think he feels the same way too.'

'We won't cramp your style by coming home with you. We'd hate to reduce your chances.'

'Don't you even think of it. We are not at that stage yet. If you stay, socialising might help. For somebody who can stand up in court and make his case, he is quite shy and needs lots of encouragement.'

'Okay. That's a deal,' said Sophie.

But she didn't need Sophie acting as a matchmaker either.

'Okay, I promise to behave,' said Sophie. Willis smiled; he had made no such promise.

Time flew by. The evening passed very well. So much so that they left their cars in the restaurant's car park and ordered a taxi to take them to Diana's. Sophie took Diana aside before they got into the cab and asked her if she'd told Edward about the discovery of her sister and parents. 'I haven't. Didn't you spot the look on his face when I mentioned we were related? I might need to explain that at some point.'

No sooner were they in Diana's than she produced a bottle of Crozes-Hermitage. 'You must buy this stuff in bulk,' said Willis.

'I have to. I drink it in bulk.' She giggled and poured four glasses of the delicious nectar.

The evening was still young. They had eaten early, and several drinking hours stretched out in front of them. At first, Willis drank slowly and cautiously, watching the clock, but later, all his inhibitions were thrown to the wind. Sophie was giggling in the corner with Diana. They were exchanging confidences, or so Willis assumed.

Willis asked Edward if they were a couple. He knew well the reply, but it was a way to open up the subject.

'No. Not really.'

Willis sensed a slight drop in his voice. 'You sound disappointed. Would you like to be?'

'Yes, but I'm not sure how she feels. Our relationship has been professional until now.'

'You'll never find out if you don't test the water.'

'I can't ask her outright.'

'Heavens forbid. You can never do that. Start simple by standing up close to her. If she doesn't move away, you can try something more daring. Sophie says Diana feels the same about you, and women know these sorts of things. Sophie is never wrong. Well, hardly ever.' He gave Edward a gentle nudge with his elbow.

'What is this thing about you two being related to Diana?'

'Hey, Sophie,' shouted Willis. 'When did you first taste this wine?'

'That would be telling.' She came over, nestled into Willis's chest and kissed his cheek.

Thank goodness, thought Willis. I've changed the subject. For now, anyway.

'We've always drunk this wine for as long as I recall, or rather, for as long as we've been able to afford it.' She looked up into Willis's bright blue eyes and mouthed a kiss in his direction. She's being bad, he thought. This is all a plan to make the evening more romantic for Diana's sake, so he mouthed a kiss back. He might as well play the game too. Willis placed his arm around Sophie and pulled her in close.

Diana said that the two of them looked rather friendly.

Sophie said that just because they were married didn't mean they couldn't have a nice hug now and then and tightened her arm around Willis to emphasise her comment.

Edward walked over to the coffee table on the pretence of picking up a handful of peanuts that Diana had set out. He lingered at her side and offered her a nut. She took one and popped it in her mouth. Diana stared into Edward's eyes, turning it into a sexy moment. Edward had relaxed. He was on a roll.

Sophie and Willis sat on one of the two facing settees, and Sophie deliberately sat very close to him. Edward sat on the settee opposite. Diana dropped beside him. She was even closer to Edward than Sophie was to Willis if that was humanly possible. Sophie lifted her glass and made a toast to good friends and good company. They returned the compliment, and everyone relaxed.

Two bottles of *vin rouge* later, everyone was feeling merry, and Edward had wangled his arm along the back of the settee and was almost hugging Diana. She, in turn, kept turning and smiling at him. Because of their closeness, when she turned, their faces nearly touched. 'Kiss her,' Willis whispered into Sophie's ear. She poked him with her forefinger and shook her head.

'Are you, or are you not, going to explain your comment about you three being related?' Edward asked Diana boldly. There was a lengthy silence.

Diana looked across at Willis. He raised his eyebrows and put out his hand, palm upwards. It was an 'over to you' gesture.

Diana leaned forward on the settee, so she could turn to face Edward less closely. 'Brad is my brother-in-law, or is it, my ex-brother-in-law?' Willis tilted his head to one side, intimating, whatever. She continued by telling Edward that over three years ago, as he already knew, she had started receiving threats from whoever killed William McLellan. One of the threats had been meant to frighten her. A paid thug, Jim Pryce, mistook Brad's wife, Carole, for her, drove a car at her and misjudged the distance, killing her in the accident. Diana stopped, took a deep breath, and then took a run at what she needed to say. 'Carole was my sister. A sister I didn't know I had. We were … we were twins.' She welled up, turned, looked at Edward, and then buried her face in his neck, sobbing. He instinctively wrapped his arms around her and pulled her close.

Edward looked across to Willis, his eyes vacant. Willis put his forefinger to his lips. Edward took the hint and said nothing.

Diana's muffled voice escaped from the confines of Edward's neck. 'I'm sorry,' she said. 'I've wasted your evening.'

Edward pulled her around so that they faced each other. 'You haven't wasted my evening. I've had a lovely cuddle.' They laughed. He kissed her face drying the tears from her cheeks with his lips.

Diana held his ears and kissed him full on the lips.

They huddled down together while Diana relayed the rest of the story to Edward. Willis didn't feel too comfortable hearing Carole's story from someone else's lips, but he was getting used to it, and it hurt less each time he heard it.

'Finally,' said Diana, 'the coup de gras.' She slurred her words and was swaying from side to side. 'Meet my mum and dad, Penny and Robert Ford. This is how they looked in

1980.' She swept her hand wildly at the photograph above the fireplace, staggered backwards, crashed onto the settee and fell into Edward's arms. He pulled her close and kissed the top of her head.

'It's been quite an evening,' said Edward. 'I'm sorry to hear about your wife, Brad, and it must be traumatic listening to this being repeated.'

Willis said listening did him good, and every time he went over it in his head, it affected him less.

'This might be a good time to head for bed,' said Sophie.

'I'd rather stay up for a little longer,' said Diana. 'Do you mind? I don't think I could sleep just yet, and I want the evening to last.' She looked at Edward and squeezed his hand.

Edward and Willis looked at each other, and Willis poured them another glass of wine. The freshly poured glasses sat on the coffee table between the settees, untouched. No one felt like drinking, but it didn't inhibit the conversation.

Diana showed Edward the brooch that had helped uncover the mystery. 'Did you notice that I have tiny earlobes and never wear earrings?'

'Yes, I noticed. I notice everything about you.' The combination of a surfeit of wine and the earlier events had loosened Edward's tongue. And more. He kissed her on the lips. They had broken the ice. Willis and Sophie were witnessing the start of a wonderful friendship. Edward asked if that would mean her real name was Diana Ford.

Diana said she supposed it did. But she'd been Diana Bishop all her life, and she wouldn't change now. Her mum, Penny, had small earlobes too. She turned to Willis. 'I thought I recognised you when we first met in the pub. Do you believe in unspoken communication between twins?'

Before Willis could answer, she said, 'God, it must have been difficult for you, seeing me for the first time? Now I realise why you were staring at me so intensely. Was it an even bigger shock meeting me? You knew I took my coffee black with one sugar.' The thoughts were spilling out of Diana at an increasing rate.

Sophie jumped in quickly to soften the intensity of the conversation, saying it was she who was more shocked, thinking they were bigamists. That would have been something. She smiled at Willis and kissed him.

The conversation was also making Edward more than a little uncomfortable. 'I fancy a coffee. Does anyone want to join me?'

'I'll come and help,' said Willis. He turned back towards the women. 'And two coffees for the ladies?' They were deep in conversation. Diana kept glancing up at Edward as she spoke. Willis could guess what the conversation was about. 'Okay. I'll take it as read. Coffees all around.' He followed Edward into the kitchen. Willis found the coffee, and Edward filled the filter machine.

'Thanks for your advice, Brad. It worked very well.'

'It certainly did,' said Willis. 'After we've had coffee, Sophie and I will head for bed. You make an excuse to stay behind with Diana a little longer.'

All four coffees duly arrived. Willis drank his in two gulps and showed Sophie the bottom of his empty cup. He wanted her to do likewise. She took the hint. 'We're off to bed now,' said Sophie.

'But we haven't finished our coffees yet,' said Diana.

'Take your time,' said Sophie. 'There's plenty of it.'

CHAPTER 10

'The house is very quiet.' Sophie turned over on the bed and shook Willis. 'I said, the house is very quiet.'

Willis answered that everyone was asleep.

'But it's gone nine o'clock.'

They dressed quickly and went downstairs. Fully clothed, on the settee with their arms around each other, lay Diana and Edward. As he headed for the kitchen and the coffee machine, Willis grinned, saying that he guessed Edward had broken the ice.

'Time to get up, love birds,' shouted Sophie. She gave Diana a shake. Both Diana and Edward sat up in surprise, partly because of how Sophie had woken them and partly because they were in each other's arms. Memories of the previous night returned, and Diana kissed Edward before rising from the settee. Sophie grinned at her and said it had gone 9 a.m. and thought Diana might have something she needed to do.

There was nothing that wouldn't wait till later. Diana stretched her arms above her head and leaned from side to side to stretch her body muscles. 'God, I'm stiff. It was a good night, though.'

Edward said it had been a very good night as he struggled with his collar and tie. He hadn't even slackened them.

Diana's eyes were drooping, and she said she couldn't remember what she had in the diary for today. Her morning had been written off, and she asked what was for breakfast.

Everyone staggered into the kitchen, and Willis had finished making coffee. As he readied the cups, the coffee machine was making its last gurgling noises. Diana searched in the cupboards and pulled out copious supplies of eggs, bacon and sausages. 'Where's the potato cakes?' asked Willis.

'What the…? How did you know I have potato cakes? Oh. I get it. It's Carole again?' She stretched up to the top shelf of the cupboard and produced a bag of potato cakes.

Mrs Burns often made potato cakes for Willis, but she called them tattie scones. Her recipe was different from Diana's. Mrs Burns's scones contained no eggs. But both were equally delicious. Willis smiled as he remembered Carole used to gorge herself on them.

Edward offered to drive them back to the restaurant to pick up their car as soon as breakfast was over.

Willis refused and said they would get a taxi.

Diana told him to stop being so chivalrous and to take Edward away from her because she needed to get some work done today. Diana pointed to Edward and then gave a dismissive wave but made sure he could see her smiling as she did.

Immediately after breakfast, Sophie and Willis left with Edward. Once they arrived at the restaurant, Willis advised

Edward to return to the house, if only for a few minutes, as it was important, he told him, to part on a romantic note, and it would set him up for the next time they met. Edward thanked Willis and drove off with some enthusiasm back to Diana's.

Sophie told Willis she'd need to watch him. Her husband was a real smoothie. She hadn't seen this side of his personality before.

He replied, saying it was a bit late for that. She'd married him. How did she think he'd managed that?

'I thought Linda and Gabi had talked you into it?' Drs Linda Foreman and Gabi Costa were a couple they'd met the previous year in Antarctica. Linda had teased Sophie and Willis that they should get married. In the end, it was a double wedding.

'They did encourage it, but the thought had been ripening for a long time.'

As soon as they were back and settled in the cottage, the floor became a mess once again. Papers and files covered the carpet. Mrs Burns arrived, took one look, turned around and headed back out. Not so Ptolemy, the cat. He was more than happy playing with the papers and skidding them across onto different piles, but Willis eventually picked up the courage to call Mrs Burns and ask her to take Ptolemy off his hands for a couple of hours. She gave her usual 'Humph,' called for the cat, and they marched off together.

Sophie said she was getting fed up looking through these papers, and every time they made a start, something happened to distract them.

Willis's mobile rang. 'Just like that,' she shouted.

'It's Bill Chalmers,' Willis said, raising himself onto the settee and grabbing a paper and pencil. He pressed the loudspeaker button, so Sophie could listen in. 'Yes. That sounds great.'

Sophie heard Bill say, 'You'll never guess where we traced the email address to.' She also heard the 'What?' uttered by Bill when Willis suggested it might be *The Clipper Inn* in Ipswich.

'Bloody hell. That's exactly how your boss, Mike Reilly, answered me two years ago before I could tell him the emails from Cambridge and CERN ended up in Kazakhstan. He knew already.' Bill checked whether Willis was sure he needed his help?

'Willis assured him he did. His suggestion had only been a hunch and would never stand up in a court of law.'

Bill added neither would the information he's given him, because he'd done it without a search warrant, and without a warrant, the evidence is inadmissible.

Willis asked him why he couldn't get a search warrant now. If they did, and it happened again, they'd have them.

To apply for a search warrant, you'd need due cause, explained Bill. Unless there was something Willis hadn't told him, there would be no sound reason for suggesting a warrant.

Willis would see what he could find out but asked if he could rely on him to keep the trace on the address.

'No comment.' Chalmers hung up.

He turned to Sophie and said that she had her wish. This was the distraction she'd wanted. They would need to go back to *The Clipper Inn* to see what they could uncover. Willis planned to telephone ahead to see if they could get a table for a late lunch. They'd be busy. He'd have to leave a recorded message, but if they left now, they'd be on time. Willis could check any reply, using the hands-free on his mobile as they drove. He handed Sophie his phone – he would be driving.

'We're going to wear out the surface of the A14 if we keep driving back and forth. The A14 surface is so poor quality that we don't need to contribute to its wear.'

As they passed Bury St Edmunds, Willis's phone bleeped. 'They say they have a table at 2:30, but that's the last serving they do. They want to know what you'd like to order?' Sophie waited for his reply.

'Shit. I never checked the menu.'

'They do cod and chips because I remember seeing it on the menu on our last visit, so we can't go wrong with that.'

'Okay, cod and chips, it is. That should please them as it's the easiest dish to make.'

Sophie pressed a few keys and hit the 'Send' button. She leaned back in her seat and enjoyed the rest of the ride.

When they reached the pub, the car park was nearly empty. Inside, only a few older men, who looked like farmhands, stood at the bar drinking ale. From its colour, Willis guessed it might be Adnams. They introduced themselves and took a table. Willis chose it near the bar from where he could monitor whatever was taking place. The same young waitress who'd served them the first time they'd visited came and placed serviettes and utensils on the table. She was most helpful and took an order for two white wines. Willis assumed she remembered the big tip she'd got on their last visit and was expecting another. When she returned with the drinks, she told them she finished at 2:30, and her boss would take over now all the lunches were finished.

By the time they finished their fish and chips, the young waitress had gone for the day, and Helen Devlin, the landlady, had taken over running the bar. 'Hello again.' She was being a good landlady and speaking to her customers. 'Not drinking Guinness today, I see.'

Willis said it was a tad too cold for chilled Guinness. 'Helen, isn't it?'

She thanked him for remembering and asked if there was anything she could get for him.

Willis believed they had everything they needed. But he asked if there had been a tall guy in here last week with grey hair and a ponytail and, if so, did he come in often?

Helen didn't recognise anyone like that. Was he sure it was here he'd seen him?

Willis was about to answer when Sophie cut in. 'That wasn't here, darling. That was in the Anchor up the road.'

'If it was the Anchor, it could be Billy. He about fits that description, but he's quite short, though.'

'Thanks, anyway. I am mistaken. How's business? It's quiet at the moment.'

'Afternoons are always quiet. That is why I choose this shift. It gives me a break before the evening rush starts.'

Willis thanked her and added, 'When does Alec start his shift?'

'He sometimes pops his head in for a pint in the evenings, after six, but he doesn't work shifts. He has a boat down in the marina, and the lazy sod's nearly always down there.'

Willis asked if it was a red yacht by any chance. 'A long sleek red yacht?'

'That's the one. Have you seen it?'

'I've often admired it,' lied Willis, 'and watched it glide in and out of the marina.'

Another customer attracted Helen's attention. She excused herself and headed across to his table.

'Maybe a visit to the marina is called for?' said Sophie.

'We're nearby and in the right place, so we might as well visit while we're here.' They finished their drinks quickly and left.

***

They parked in one of the restaurants in front of the marina and walked along the embankment. 'There are a lot of boats here,' said Sophie, 'so it'll take forever to find the right one.'

'I'm thick. I should have asked Helen for its name.'

'How about, *The Clipper*?'

'That would be handy.'

'It's moored over there. You're not very observant for an astronomer.' Sophie put her thumb to her nose, wiggled her fingers and stuck out her tongue.

'Put your tongue away. It's not ladylike.'

The Clipper was tied up in the second berth from the quayside. Willis ignored the sign that said 'No Public Access' and walked along to the yacht.

'Is anyone on board?'

'Just a minute.' A bald head popped up from below deck. 'Hi, what can I do for you?'

No ponytail here, Willis thought. He introduced himself and Sophie and explained that they had just been speaking to Helen. He'd told her he admired the yacht, and she invited him to stop by to see it.

The man replied that, by all means, they could come on board to have a look around.

'I am speaking to Alec?'

'Yes, I am he.' He said with perfect grammar. 'Come below.'

Willis imagined because it was a fast-sailing yacht, it would be tiny inside. It was huge. He estimated that it would have held at least a dozen people at a push. It certainly looked lived in. The main cabin was untidy, and there was a pile of plastic seats sitting in one corner.

'Forgive the mess,' said Alec. 'I had a bit of a party last week and haven't got around to unloading everything yet.'

'She's beautiful,' said Willis. 'How far do you take her out?'

'Just across the Channel. I've always wanted to go to the Med, but I haven't had the time. You know how it is, with the pub and other things? Would you like a cup of tea?'

'Coffee would be better if you've got any?' Alec took a can of instant from the shelf. Willis smiled and nodded. He was dying to ask him if he had a friend with grey hair and a ponytail but thought better of it. It would arouse his suspicions.

The three sat drinking coffee. They discussed how much time Alec had to mess around on the boat. He didn't take too much to do with the pub. Alec had got it up and running but left Helen to deal with it nowadays because she was much better at chatting to customers than he was.

The conversation dried up. Other than asking Alec leading questions about the investigation, Willis had nothing else he needed to chat about. Maybe he'd meet Alec in the pub and buy him a pint for his hospitality? Helen had told Willis that he sometimes popped in after six o'clock.

Alec said he'd look forward to that and helped Sophie to step over the gap between the boat and the jetty.

As they walked back towards the car, Sophie said, 'He didn't send the emails. His English grammar is too correct.'

'I know. We're back at stage one. We have no leads whatsoever.'

'He must go to Belgium often. Did you notice the heap of Belgian chocolate wrappers he had swept into a corner on the floor?'

'There were also Turkish cigarette butts in the ashtray. He's taking his time to clean up after his party.'

'That's men for you. There's no Helen on board to do the chores. Alec is very polite and courteous. He's been well brought up and has excellent manners. If he hadn't been bald, I might have fancied him.' Willis looked at her sideways and ignored the comment.

***

Once they were back at the cottage, Mrs Burns came in and started to complain. How was she to tidy up when they left papers all over the place? Willis explained she could clean everywhere except in the corners where they had piled the files, but she wasn't happy. Willis whispered to Sophie that Mrs Burns was in a complaining mood.

'I bet you'll be covering the carpet with the papers again today.' She stomped out and slammed the door.

Willis took a long slow breath. 'I suppose we will, at that.'

Sophie told him to cheer up. They would find a link soon.

It took half an hour to lay out all the papers in the positions where they liked them, and they knew it would take twice as long to put them away again. Sophie had put a yellow marker into the last file she'd looked at and had also put the files she'd read into a different pile from Willis's. This gave her a head start. She sat in her favourite position with her shoulders against the settee and with papers surrounding her legs. She worked from left to right. Those that she had read, she moved to her right-hand side, but the number of papers on her left side didn't look like it was getting any smaller.

Willis thought there must be a cleverer way to do this. They had looked at the accused, the pub that was the source of the threatening emails, and the man someone had hired to threaten Diana, but they hadn't looked at the victim yet. There must have been a reason he was killed. He had asked Chalmers to see if the guy had any previous. Bill hadn't got back to him yet.

Willis pressed a button on his mobile. He'd put Chalmers into the fast-dial memory. 'Hi Bill, did you ever find out if McLellan had any previous?'

Bill said McLellan had been arrested for aggravated assault and also for burglary. Also, he had allegedly attacked an East European. It was a witness who'd reported it, but the victim hadn't pressed charges, so he'd got off with that one. The burglary was at a pub in Ipswich. 'Shit, it's *The Clipper Inn*. I'm sorry. I wasn't aware of its significance when I found this.'

'What was stolen?'

'We gave the place the once over. The barmaid reported it when she came on duty, but the owners reported nothing missing, and they said that whoever did it left a right mess behind.'

'Was he charged on his own, or was he part of a gang?'

'There was one other. He was underage, so he got off with a warning and probation.'

Willis joked that Bill knew what his next question would be.

Bill chuckled and said he was Sam Cordell from Clacton, and McLellan had lived in Clacton-on-Sea too. They had been neighbours. Bill read out the address. Willis rushed to grab a pen and asked him to repeat it. He wrote it on one of the trial transcript pages. Sam was underage, or he was at the time of the offence, but his probation had expired, so Bill couldn't ask his probation officer to help.

Willis would just be straight with his parents and tell them he is investigating William McLellan's murder. He was sure they would help. Did Bill also have William McLellan's address handy? It would save him searching through a ton of paper at his end.

Bill read out the address, and Willis wrote it next to Sam's. But Bill warned that Willis mustn't give his parents the idea he was accusing him of the murder.

Willis thanked him for the advice and asked if there had been any other emails sent to Diana.

'A couple,' came the reply. But Bill still hadn't heard from the Home Secretary, so he couldn't act. Bill guessed they were worried about the privacy of the other MPs, so he didn't think he would ever get permission as it would lay the whole of the gov.uk mail system open to hacking. If they allowed it to be done once…

'I can imagine,' said Willis. 'I'll need to try something else.'

'One other thing. You didn't get the details of Sam Cordell from me; his files are sealed.'

'Okay,' he sighed. 'Chat again soon.'

'I guess we're going to sunny Clacton tomorrow,' said Sophie.

'I don't think it will be sunny at this time of year.'

Sophie stood and started sorting the paperwork back into its original piles. She warned Willis that he better not upset Mrs Burns any more than he's done already, so they made a single high pile rather than two smaller ones, hoping it would please Mrs Burns.

'We will visit Sam Cordell's address first,' said Willis. 'Although he is less likely to be at home than McLellan's parents, we can ask when they expect him back. We will then return to Sam's after he gets home.'

'Does it mean we can have a lie in?'

'If you like.'

'No paperwork tomorrow before we go out?'

'I had forgotten about it. We might have time for a quick look before we go. Anyway, we need a glass of wine this evening. We don't deserve it but, sod it, we'll have a glass, anyway. Which wine would you prefer? I'll look it out.'

'I think I'd like … anything but Crozes-Hermitage.'

CHAPTER 11

‘Come and look at this.’ Sophie was screaming at the top of her voice. ‘Look what Ptolemy’s done.’

Willis rushed in to find all the court papers scattered around the living room floor, with Ptolemy rolling on a nest of papers trying to make himself comfortable. The rustle of the paper and its texture were keeping him amused. Willis ran forward, waving his arms, and Ptolemy screeched and jumped onto the back of the settee. ‘Out,’ insisted Willis. ‘Out.’ Ptolemy slinked away more like a contrite dog than the arrogant cat he was. ‘Let’s just put these in one enormous pile. I think we’ve got almost everything we can get from them.’

‘I hadn’t finished the end of the trial,’ said Sophie.

‘Me neither, but it’s going to be the law of diminishing returns, and we will need to put in a lot more effort to get back very little.’

They collected the papers in a higgledy-piggledy manner and stuffed them into the original cardboard box in which they'd arrived. In this dishevelled order, it wasn't easy to get them all in, but they forced the issue and succeeded. 'We'll need to lock him out until we're finished,' said Willis.

'It's a bit late to think of that now.' Sophie gave the box a kick that rammed it hard into the corner of the room.

'Temper. Temper. Losing the rag won't help.'

'It makes me feel better.'

Willis let himself fall onto the settee with his head hanging between his long legs, but he immediately grabbed his knees and pushed himself up. 'Dammit, we can't just leave them like that. We'll need to sort them out.'

'We will but not today; *Mañana* will do.'

***

After lunch, they headed for Clacton-on-Sea. 'Don't drive so fast,' said Sophie. 'There are Average Speed Cameras on this part of the A12.' No sooner had she spoken than a black Porsche raced past in the overtaking lane, and when it got about one hundred yards in front, its brake lights came on hard. It screamed almost to a halt, with smoke rising into the air as its tyres burnt, causing all the following vehicles to brake. As they reduced their speed and slipped in behind the line of cars, Sophie said smugly, 'Told you.'

'It's Essex drivers. They are infamous for their crap driving.'

The rest of the drive was uneventful. They drove past Clacton Pier and almost out of the other side of town. They passed the well-manicured gardens that were tended by the Council to attract tourists to the resort. Some parts of the town were bright and jolly. Other bits were drab and ran down. After they passed the Martello tower, it became a particularly run-down area. Willis told Sophie these towers were built in the early nineteenth century after the start of the French Revolutionary Wars. This tower was robust with forty feet high walls that, according to Willis, were eight feet thick and sometimes even thicker on the side facing the sea, where cannon attacks used to be common. They passed a fish and chip shop on the left-hand side and then turned right into a small street that the satnav showed would lead to Sam Cordell's address.

Willis spoke to Sam's parents and explained why they would like to chat with him, but he did this in a very laid-back manner and assured them that Sam had nothing to worry about. They seemed to accept this but told him he'd need to return after four when Sam returned from college. Proudly, his mother told Willis he was studying electrical engineering. He agreed to return around a quarter past four and thanked them for their help.

'Exactly as I expected,' he said. 'I knew we'd need to come back later, but at least we know he will be in. We'll come back a little earlier than promised, in case he decides he doesn't want to see us. We will catch him if he tries to slip away.'

Sophie read out the postcode for William McLellan's parents' house, and Willis entered it into the satnav. As they drove in its direction, the quality of the houses increased. When they eventually reached the address, the houses were expensive, with extensive gardens and double garages. They parked alongside a black Porsche. Willis looked at Sophie. Surely not? All Porsches look alike, and he hadn't noted its number plate. They got out, but before going to the door, Willis stopped and put his hand on the bonnet of the Porsche. It was still warm. It could still be a coincidence, though.

In keeping with the rest of the house, the doorbell was ostentatious and rang with a harmony of bell sounds, much more complicated than Westminster Chimes. An elderly lady came to the door. Her dyed hair was bright red, and she wore a pair of colourful spectacles attached to a silver chain that hung around her neck. At a glance, she'd pass as Barry Humphries. She held her head back and looked down her nose through the half lenses at Willis, and he could feel her disdain burning into the back of his eyes.

'Yeeess?' she said, sounding like Mrs Bucket from the comedy TV series *Keeping up Appearances.*

Willis thought he'd play the same game. 'I am Professor Brad Willis from Cambridge University. I'm writing a history of crime in England and would like to include the murder of your son in my finished book. Would it be possible for me to impose on your time and ask you a few questions? I would, of course, give you full acknowledgement in the book.'

She looked Willis up and down and then said enthusiastically, 'Come in, come in, don't stand on ceremony. I am Mavis.' Willis introduced Sophie as his assistant and secretary, for which Sophie sent him a disdainful look.

'Would you like a cup of tea?' Her pronounced poshness was already slipping.

'Yes, please. That would be lovely,' answered Willis. She vanished into the kitchen and came back with a tray. It contained an expensive china teapot, a tea strainer, a selection of biscuits … and two cups. Sophie wasn't getting a cup of tea. Willis looked at Sophie and nearly choked, trying not to laugh, but he could see the frown on her face.

'I'll be mother,' she said, pouring milk into both cups. 'I do so like the milk to go in first, don't you? It makes the brew taste so much better.' She placed the tea strainer on Willis's cup and poured while holding the lid on with her forefinger. Her pinkie finger was poking up towards the ceiling.

'Yes, it does,' said Willis, humouring her.

'Now, what is it you need to know about our Bill?'

Willis was about to answer when a loud bang resounded from the hallway. 'What the fuckin' hell. Who left this here?'

Mavis jumped to her feet and opened the door. A laundry basket sat at the bottom of the stairs with its soiled contents spilled over the stairs and into the hall. 'You really need to be more careful. This is my other son Kenny. He's such a good boy.'

'And who are you?' Kenny barked. He had what some would call designer stubble. Willis chose to think of him as uncouth and unshaven. Otherwise, his clothes were immaculate, with designer labels prominent on his shirt and his corduroy trousers. A silver *TAG Heuer* peeked from beneath his shirt cuffs.

His mother cut in. 'This is Professor Willis from Cambridge, darling. He's come asking after our Bill.'

'That's a nice car outside,' said Willis. 'Does it belong to you?'

'It does. What of it?'

'I think you might have overtaken us earlier on the A12?'

'These idiots always go too slow on that road. It holds everybody up. It's a dual carriageway, for Christ's sake.'

'Language, Kenny. Watch your language.' Mavis shook her head.

'Where's dad?'

'He's out. I think he might be having a late lunch.'

'A bloody liquid lunch, you mean.'

Willis let the argument flow around him and listened with interest. Kenny couldn't possibly be earning enough, legitimately, to keep Mavis at this standard of living. Her husband, whatever his name was, was in the pub in the middle of the day, so he wouldn't be contributing much either, not honestly at any rate.

Kenny slammed the front door on his way out. The Porsche's throaty roar vibrated the glass in the windows and filled the room with noise. 'He takes care of his dad and me. Kenny's such a clever boy, and he runs his own business. It's an employment agency.'

'Where might that be?' asked Willis, not expecting a reply, but if he didn't try…

'My boy has a small office in Colchester, but he does most of his business online, so Kenny has almost no overheads, he tells me, because he usually works from home.'

'Gosh. He must have a powerful computer to allow him to do that?'

'He has. It has three screens attached to it. Would you like to see it?'

'I'd love to see it if you think he wouldn't mind?'

Willis nodded to Sophie and swung his head around as Mavis led him upstairs. Sophie took the hint and looked around the living room while they were upstairs. When she heard Willis and Mavis coming down the stairs, she moved back onto the settee but not before stealing a chocolate biscuit off the tray for badness.

After they sat down, Willis said, 'The sort of things I would be interested in hearing about William are things like, what school did he go to, and what did he work at, et cetera.'

'He started the employment agency that Kenny runs. They were both very clever even when they were younger. They didn't get high marks at school, but they learned a lot after they started work.'

'May I take your number, so I can call you as I work on my book?'

'Certainly, feel free to come back any time you like. I am always at home.'

Willis thanked her as he made his way to the door. Mavis was still waving when they turned out of the driveway and headed back towards Clacton town centre.

'I found nothing of interest in the room while you were upstairs,' said Sophie. 'I looked in a couple of drawers too. There was nothing out of the ordinary. Did you have any better luck?'

'Not really. I asked Mavis for Kenny's email address in case I needed to ask him or her any future questions. She didn't know it, but she let me look it up on his computer. It's a British Telecom internet address, so it isn't the one that Diana has been getting the threats from, but he might have several addresses, of course. I had to close a picture of a map to get to his email screen. I hope I put it back as I found it.'

As they drove towards Sam Cordell's house, they discussed the odd family that they had visited. Something crooked was going on. There was no way they could earn enough money, working part-time, as they did, to support a house of that size. The antique cabinet in the living room must have cost a fortune. They couldn't see how they got so much money by legitimate means. When they got home, Willis would do a Google search for employment agencies in Colchester but was sure he wouldn't find one associated with Kenny McLellan.

When they arrived at Sam's house, he was walking up the path towards the front door. While they parked the car, he looked around at them but didn't seem very interested. Sam would assume that the visitors were here to speak to his parents, so he opened the front door and walked in, leaving it ajar. They could hear him calling on his mother to tell her she had two visitors in the driveway before striding upstairs two at a time, leaving Willis and Sophie standing at the open door.

Mrs Cordell came to welcome them and invite them in. She told them to ignore Sam because he had no manners whatsoever. She offered them a cup of tea. Willis was about to refuse, but Sophie cut in and said she'd love a cup. 'I haven't had a cup all day,' she said for Willis's benefit. If looks could kill, Willis would have dagger wounds all over his body.

'Let's have a cuppa first, and then I'll fetch Sam. He'll be playing his computer game. That's the first thing he does when he gets home. He plays online with his friends. If we have a cuppa, he will have finished and be more willing to answer your questions. I have learned not to disturb him.' She disappeared for ten minutes and returned with a tray of tea and biscuits. There were three cups this time.

Sophie surreptitiously drew the biscuit she'd stolen from Mrs McLellan out of her pocket and took a bite out of it.

When Willis had introduced himself and Sophie earlier in the day, Mrs Cordell had introduced herself as Brenda. Willis asked her questions about Sam, such as how had his probation gone, how had he reacted to the discipline that it had forced on him, and how he was getting on now. All of Brenda's answers were positive. Sam had looked at things in a positive light. He had been glad to accept probation; he'd believed he would be sent to borstal.

'How long was he involved with William McLellan before you found out?'

'I'm not sure. You know how it is with kids. The parents are the last to know. We had no idea until the police turned up at the door.'

The door opened, and Sam came in. He threw himself on the settee with enough force to threaten its springs with damage. 'I told you to stop doing that,' said Mrs Cordell. 'These two people are here to chat with you about that crook William McLellan who got you into trouble.'

Sam's eyes widened. He fidgeted on the settee.

'Don't worry, Sam,' said Willis. 'We only want to ask you a few questions about McLellan. We're not interested in you at all.'

Sam visibly relaxed, and his body slouched into the copious cushions on the settee.

'Everything you tell us will be in confidence,' reassured Willis. 'We would like to know what McLellan had been up to, and if you were involved in any way, we don't want to know.'

Sam gave the smallest of nods.

'Where did you first meet McLellan?'

Sam met him while still at school. McLellan had seen him nicking a bar of chocolate and threatened to tell on him. He had then coerced Sam to help him break into houses. Because of his smaller size, he could get into places that McLellan couldn't.

Willis could hardly believe it. Sam was over six feet tall. Looking at the size of him now, he must have grown fast, and he said so in a way that sounded like a compliment to Sam.

Mrs Cordell volunteered that he had grown a lot in the last three to four years.

'I am interested in other people he might have been working with. Did you meet any of them?'

'Only Roger.'

'What was Roger's full name?'

'I only ever knew him as Roger. We would meet up before a job, and he would disappear again afterwards.'

Willis asked him what Roger looked like.

Sam said he was an older guy, quite tall with long grey hair.

Willis thought he would know the answer. 'How did he wear his hair?'

'In an ugly pigtail at the back of his head, and he tied it with a green ribbon.'

Willis was making progress at last. He pushed a little further and asked what else Sam remembered about Roger. 'Where did he live? What make of car did he drive?'

'He lived somewhere in Ipswich. Bill and I had to pick him up one time from *The Clipper Inn* when his car broke down.'

'… and what kind of car was that?'

'It was a red Mercedes. It was quite old and at least ten years old, I reckon. I can't remember the number. But I doubt if he'll still be driving it after all this time. It was quite a wreck.'

'Do you remember anything about picking him up from *The Clipper Inn*? Did you see him talking to anyone before he left?'

'Bill asked me to wait in the car. When Bill and Roger came out of the pub, they were talking to a bald-headed man. I couldn't see his face. The light above the door was shining down on his head, and it cast long shadows. Sorry.'

'You're doing well, young man. Don't be sorry. Is there anything else that comes to mind about either Roger or the bald-headed man?'

'That's all I can remember. It was a very short visit.'

Willis handed Sam his card and asked him to telephone his mobile if he remembered anything else. He thanked Sam and his mother.

He had one leg inside the car when Sam came running out. 'The bald man had a tattoo of an old-fashioned sailing ship on his arm. I suppose it was a clipper, like the *Clipper Inn*.'

'That's magic, Sam. You don't know how much of a help you've been. Thank you.'

***

They were on the A12 within twenty minutes and heading west towards Madingley in another twenty. They'd passed the Copdock Roundabout just as the queue of traffic started to build in time for the evening rush hour.

There were lots of bits of information they had collected, but nothing was pulling them together. They had found out Roger possibly knew Alec Devlin of *The Clipper Inn*, but Willis didn't remember seeing a tattoo on his arm, and he was sure he would have spotted it if Alec had one.

There was nothing else for it. He and Sophie would have to go to the cottage and open yet another bottle of wine. Willis convinced himself he could think a lot clearer with alcohol in his veins. He'd also call Sophie's uncle.

CHAPTER 12

'I could use my time better than travelling into Greenwich Village on a Sunday.' Willis was impatient, and he was letting it be known, but, at least, he would avoid the city's congestion charge.

'C'mon, you've met my parents only once since we married, and they haven't had time to get to know you. Anyway, Uncle Swallow will be there, and if you want to cultivate his help, you'd better meet him and get to know him too. He won't go on answering questions from an anonymous caller much longer.'

Willis gave a humph and pressed the car pedal down further. He complained there were lots of other things they needed to do, but okay, it was Sunday, and that severely limited what they could hope to achieve. They could have gone to *The Clipper Inn* to check if Alec Devlin had a tattoo or not. Then again, he would probably be on his boat, leaving his wife to do all the work in the pub.

Sophie said he should stop whingeing. He would get on very well with her parents, and she was sure that once he got to know Uncle Jonathan, he'd enjoy his company too. Willis couldn't know too many DIs in his line of work. The more policemen he knew, the better, and Bill Chalmers of the Yard would eventually get fed up with his requests, so it would be better if he spread them around a bit.

Willis knew Sophie was right, but this wasn't the ideal time to be cultivating contacts. He'd rather be out and about investigating than sipping tea with Sophie's parents. Nice as they were. He wouldn't even be able to have wine with dinner, because even on a Sunday afternoon, the drive back from London would need all his concentration. As if to underline the thought, a maroon car swerved in front of him on the M25 without notice. Bloody Sunday driver, thought Willis. He took a deep breath and resigned himself to the rest of the day being unproductive.

Willis passed the old observatory at Greenwich and turned right in the direction the bossy satnav voice told him, then drove into an avenue of trees that he thought would look lovely in the spring when they had regained their leaves.

Sophie pointed. 'Over there. Where the traffic cones are.' Her parents, Alan and Ruth, had put out a line of cones to reserve a parking place on the street for them. Two cars occupied the short driveway. The second car must belong to Uncle Swallow. Willis parked in front of the house, partly obstructing the drive.

'Here. You carry the wine and the chocolates,' said Sophie. 'And try to smile when the door opens. Try not to look like I've dragged you here against your will.' Willis just looked at her and tilted his head to the side. Isn't that exactly what was happening? He bit his tongue and smiled.

Once the introductions were over and the welcomes finished, they settled down in the huge comfortable lounge and had two dry sherries pushed into their hands. 'I'd better be careful with this,' said Willis, lifting his glass in an attempt to get a conversation started. 'With a policeman in the house, I better be on my best behaviour.'

Uncle Jon said, 'Watch me. You can keep drinking until I tell you to stop.' He smiled, took a sip out of his glass and placed it on the coffee table. Jonathan requested they get the business out of the way before they started to enjoy themselves. Willis had called him about William McLellan. He had been quite a lad. His rap sheet showed several charges for possession and one of grievous bodily harm, but there was one interesting thing, every time, he walked away free because he had a red-hot solicitor who got him off on every count.

Willis asked who might that be, leaning forward with interest.

'He was Arnold Swanson from Swanson Partners; they are a huge company.'

'He couldn't afford to pay for a top solicitor unless he was bent or someone else was bankrolling him. Where are they based? Colchester?'

'No way. He's a barrister and based at Lincoln's Inn, London, and you can't get much more prestigious than that.'

Willis said this was ridiculous. He couldn't be that well bankrolled. Somebody big must support him.

Jonathan said, 'Whoever it was would be big enough to have him killed if he didn't deliver on their demands.'

'There's no way we can find out who was paying the fees, I assume?'

'Right on the nail. That information is protected by privilege.'

'Oh well. Let's leave discussing this until another time,' said Willis, 'because we've come for Sunday lunch, and we had better be sociable.'

'… and I should think so too.' Sophie's dad had appeared at the door with a huge grin on his face and invited them through to have another sherry. Lunch would be ready in a tick, and they had so much to catch up on.

The family spent the next half hour discussing Willis and Sophie's stay in Antarctica. They handed pictures of their wedding around, and her parents made numerous comments about the coarse jumper of Sophie's that substituted for a dress during the ceremony. Sophie explained it was a wedding they would remember for the rest of their lives.

Sophie's mum made a choking sound. A tear escaped and got caught in one of her laughter lines just below her left eye. Sophie rushed over and grasped her hands. 'I know. I know, mum. I'm sorry that you and dad weren't there, but Brad and I have decided that we'll hold another wedding to renew our vows and to celebrate our marriage. Here. At home.'

Her mum gave a big broad smile and patted the back of Sophie's hand. 'That will be lovely, Polly.' She leaned forward and gave Sophie a peck on the cheek. 'Let's go through to have lunch before it gets overcooked.' Sophie walked to the dining room, holding her mum's hand.

Once seated, Willis turned to Sophie and whispered, 'Polly? Is that a new name I can call you now? You didn't tell me about that.'

'It's a nickname that mum gave me. I had a doll called Polly, and mum always calls me Polly when she is pleased with me, so I've obviously done the right thing.'

Willis didn't want to disagree, but it was a surprise to discover that he was to marry Sophie all over again. When he told her as much, Willis grinned mischievously.

'It will be safer. Anyway, we never did check that the celebrant who married us did all the paperwork properly.'

'There's still a chance that I might escape, then?' Willis winced as Sophie's elbow dug deep into his side.

***

The rest of the meal passed quickly while Sophie's mum and dad, Ruth and Alan, embarrassed Sophie with tales of her schooldays and childhood.

They had retired to the lounge and were sitting in front of a roaring open fire when Jon Swallow's mobile rang. 'Yes?' There was a long silence while Jon listened to the caller's information. 'Okay, yes. Fine.' Jon threw his mobile, and it landed on the cushion on his left. He turned to Willis and told him somebody had hacked the government's email account. They'd found a software worm on the system.

Willis found his mobile and called Bill Chalmers. 'I thought you couldn't look into Diana's email without government permission?'

'What are you talking about? I need clearance before I can go near the government website.'

'You mean you haven't hacked her email account?'

'That's a silly question, of course, I haven't. Has somebody else had a go?'

'It would appear so.' Willis's phone went dead; Chalmers had hung up. He looked at his handset as though it might shine some light on why Bill Chalmers had disconnected him. He turned to Jonathan and asked how he'd found out about the hack since he wasn't officially part of the case.

It had transpired the Home Secretary received information that someone had deleted two of Diana's emails. It came down the line of command and ended up in his office. The Home Secretary called MI5, and it came down from them.

Willis was about to ask how the chain of command ended up in Colchester when his mobile demanded attention. From the screen, he saw it was from Bill Chalmers. Willis thanked him for hanging up without warning.

Bill told him to never mind that. His group had received instructions to investigate in tandem with MI5. Diana Bishop had already approached Miriam Hodge, the Home Secretary, asking her to get permission to access the email system. They also notified the cyber group of the civil police in Colchester. This was serious, but the good news from Willis's point of view was that they now had a mandate to investigate. That meant Bill would have access to Diana's emails and could track the threatening emails she'd received. Bill said he needed to go. There was a lot to do.

'I will need to go too,' said Jonathan. 'I need to get back to Colchester. My team's already started, and I'll need to be present.' He dialled a number, told someone he was on his way, and then gave his apologies to Alan and Ruth before rushing out the door.

'I suppose you and Sophie will need to leave too?' said Mrs Fenwick.

Willis shook his head. 'There's little point in us rushing off. There isn't a contribution we can make, not this soon anyway, because it will take ages before they make any progress with discovering who sent the emails and from where.'

Mrs Fenwick nodded to her daughter, and she led Sophie to the kitchen, eager to discuss the upcoming wedding celebrations.

'Have another sherry then, Brad,' said Mr Fenwick. 'Tell me what an astronomer does.' Willis accepted the sherry gladly, and the two men huddled in a corner while Willis described the nuances of modern astronomy to his father-in-law.

***

Jon Swallow arrived at Colchester Police Station two hours later, slumped into his swivel chair and put both his elbows on the desk. 'What have we discovered so far?' He beckoned to his cyber specialist, Johnny White, to sit.

He was told they didn't rightly know yet. It was definitely a worm that a hacker had introduced, but they couldn't fathom how and when it was done. The government email system had pretty sophisticated security and was the gold medal standard experts used to judge security protection systems. The cyber specialist was puzzled. 'I can't imagine anyone being able to get a foreign algorithm installed. Unless—'

'Unless?'

'Unless it was an inside job. If someone in the email technical support section wanted to add something, they certainly could.'

'What if a user tried to load it? Someone with a dot-gov email address?'

'No way! There is protection against that. There has to be. Members of the public email their MPs all the time, and if there weren't protection, any incoming email with an attachment could instal a worm or virus.'

Jonathan asked if the cyber guy from MI5 had contacted them yet.

'I wrote his number on your pad, sir, and he would welcome a call as soon as poss.' Johnny White stood to leave.

'Hold on, Johnny, stay here while I call this guy. I might need your input.'

The phone rang for no more than two rings when an anonymous voice answered. 'Hello.'

'Hello, back. This is Jonathan Swallow of Colchester Pol—'

'Thank you for calling, DI Swallow. I've been waiting for a call. I'm Georgie Maclean, and I believe we'll be working thegither.'

Hearing his accent, Jonathan guessed Maclean was from the east coast of Scotland and volunteered that he, too, came from Montrose, but that was another story and a long time ago. He asked what they'd discovered so far.

Georgie Maclean explained the code that was found was sophisticated enough to target a single user, in this case, MP Diana Bishop. As far as he could tell, no other email accounts were affected, and he said that the probable reason was to reduce the risk of discovery because if they only targeted a single account, then the chances of discovering the worm would drop off considerably.

Jonathan put a proposal to Georgie. 'What if they didn't disable the worm but allowed it to remain on the system? Could they analyse it to see where it's sending its ill-gotten information?'

As far as he could tell, the worm had only been used to delete emails from Ms Bishop's system. That's how she'd noticed it. It might have already achieved its objective and never be needed again, but from Georgie's experience, the culprits would get greedy, and the temptation to see what else they could find out would be too strong.

Jonathan still wanted to know if they could get permission to leave it on and monitor its behaviour.

Georgie would ask his boss to clear it with the Home Secretary – Ms Bishop would also need to give her permission. But his bollocks would be on the line if the virus spread to any other email accounts or any important information got compromised.

'Submit the request in my name. That way, we'll both get our knackers cut off if it goes awry.' Swallow gave a throaty laugh before hanging up.

***

Brad Willis was in the middle of describing the 'light year' as a measure of astronomical distance to his new father-in-law when his mobile interrupted. It was Jonathan. He explained to Willis the plan that he and Georgie had concocted and planned to implement, providing they got permission from the Home Secretary, that was.

Willis would call Bill Chalmers and ask him to call Georgie's boss and put his tuppence into the ring. Myriam Hodges, the Home Secretary, was already aware, so any request of this nature wouldn't be unexpected. If Georgie were sure that it would only be used on one email account, Diana Bishop's, then Willis was sure she'd be minded to allow it.

After Jonathan had hung up, Willis explained to Sophie and his in-laws that they would need to head home. It was still early evening, but Willis didn't feel too guilty about leaving, because they had spent the entire afternoon at Mr and Mrs Fenwick's. He had also formed the start of a relationship with Mr Fenwick, who seemed genuinely interested in his work.

***

The drive back to Madingley was uneventful. Sophie bent Willis's ear with details of her mother's plans for their wedding party. His eyes rolled skywards, but he understood why her mother was enthusiastic about celebrating her daughter's marriage.

With a touch of melancholy, Willis mentioned that at least he didn't need to worry about getting his parents involved.

Sophie gave a small nod of her head and suggested he could always invite some other people to come along – maybe from his work?

He would think about it.

Willis's parents had died soon after he was born, and his grandparents had brought him up. After that, he was with his foster parents until he left to go to university. Maybe he could invite Mrs Sloan, his last foster mother, if she was still alive and if he could find her? That's what he would do. That could be a mini-project for him to work on later.

Sophie asked what his plans were when they got home. Her fingers played with the short hair on the back of his neck.

Willis told her she'd distract him while he was driving but turned and smiled at her. He reckoned he'd call Diana and ask her which emails were missing – if there was anything common between them.

***

When they arrived home, Willis made some coffee and then settled down to call Diana. Edward Young answered Diana's mobile. 'You're well in there now,' teased Willis. 'Answering Diana's mobile calls for her. Have you moved in?'

'Hilarious. What do you want, Brad? Diana's just gone to get some wine, and we're getting on just fine, thank you.'

Willis explained he needed to ask her some questions when she came back – and preferably before they finished their first bottle of wine but promised it wouldn't take long.

Diana took the mobile, put it on speaker and asked what she could do for him. Was he calling because he'd heard her email account had been got at? She addressed him as Dr Willis.

'I'm Dr Willis now. Am I? I suppose I should call you the honourable or the right honourable lady or something similar?'

'Okay, Brad. Knock it off. I want to have a drink with Edward. Tell me what you want to know.'

He needed to know about the two emails that were deleted – did they have anything in common, perhaps a similar subject, or had they come from, or been sent to, the same person?

She brought him up to date, saying three emails were missing now. All three were trivial mails, and there was no pattern to their content, their subject, or where they went to or came from. They were seemingly very ordinary emails. The only reason she'd noticed they were missing was because she'd searched for one to recover a phone number. It wasn't even an important number, and it was in the public domain. The number was that of the library at the House of Commons. She couldn't remember what they contained, but she was sure there was nothing of any great value in them.

Willis asked if she remembered any more detail to call him and let him know. She could expect a call asking for her permission to leave the hack in place to allow the specialists to watch the traffic on her account. They would likely sort out a temporary email address for her in case she needed to send anything confidential.

'I've had the call already and gladly gave my permission. We need to get to the bottom of this.'

Willis said if this worked, they should find out who was sending her the threatening emails too. Fingers crossed.

'Okay. Can I drink some wine now? It's still Sunday after all.'

'Sorry to have intruded. Enjoy your Crozes-Hermitage and have a glass for us.'

She said she would. Before Willis could answer, the line was dead.

'Leave the lovebirds alone,' said Sophie. 'We have enough love here of our own. Let's have an evening off from investigating and cuddle up in front of the wood burner.'

'That's a deal.' Willis put another log in the burner and turned the dimmer switch for the lights down to its lowest setting. He slouched onto the cushions on the settee next to Sophie and planted a soft kiss on her lips. Did the pizza shop do home deliveries on a Sunday? If they did, he would have one later.

CHAPTER 13

Rain was hammering on the thin roof of the car park. Its impact resounded throughout the multistorey building. The entire floor was empty apart from two anonymous black cars strategically parked about fifty yards apart. The door of the car nearest the entrance smashed closed, and its crash was followed by the sound of steel-tipped shoes hitting the hard concrete. A narrow rivulet of water poured from a blocked drain and crossed the walker's path, turning the near-white concrete a dark grey. As they stepped into the wet surface, the sound from the hard shoes softened.

A second man exited from his car and stood leaning on the low wall that surrounded the parking area. The wall looked down onto a narrow lane that ran alongside the building. The strength of the downpour forced a fine spray of water particles to hit his face and spectacles.

'Who are you? You're not the person I am supposed to meet.'

'Never mind who I am. I'm here to do the transfer. Have you got it?' The man with the steel heels spoke softly and precisely, his Oxford accent evident.

'Of course. It's in this bag. Do you have the money?'

'Of course. Are you sure it works?'

'I have tested it thoroughly. I deleted emails from the account to make sure that the program worked. It leaves no signature behind to reveal that anyone has visited the account.'

'Are the instructions fully documented?'

'Everything is as agreed. There is an instruction book in the case with the laptop. It describes every step in detail – even a fool could follow it.'

'Let me see it.' The taller of the two men walked closer and held out his hand, but as he did so, his coat swung open, and a gun holster flashed momentarily into view.

'You won't be needing that,' said the shorter man. He pulled up the collar of his polo-necked jumper and handed over the instruction manual.

The man in the long black coat spent the next few minutes in silence while his narrow eyes studied the manual.

'I need to see a demonstration.'

'That isn't part of the deal.'

'You can't expect me to hand over this much cash without first making sure that I'm getting what I'm paying for.'

'We will need Wi-Fi to give a demonstration.'

'There's a café across the road. We can go there. It shouldn't take long if everything is as exactly as you describe.'

The smaller man removed his spectacles, wiped the rain spray from the lenses and replaced them. He slowly looked up. 'Okay. There's nothing wrong with giving you a short demo. Then I'll be gone.'

***

The café was half full of people. Two men sat in opposite corners, engrossed in the screens of their laptops – another two would go unnoticed. They sat in silence until the coffees came, and the waitress disappeared. The taller man mentioned how unusual it was to have a waitress in such a small place. These were the first social words the man in the dark coat had uttered since they'd met. He took a sip of his coffee and nearly spat it out. After adding four sachets of sugar to the black liquid, he sipped it, nodded and spoke again. 'Okay. Let me see it. Show me it working.'

The smaller man nervously removed the laptop from its case, opened it and felt for the on-switch. After some minutes, the laptop played its usual jingle to reveal that it was now ready for action.

'Ronnie. My name's Ronnie,' said the smaller man as he reached into a pocket in the side of the laptop's case. 'This memory stick holds a small program. It's called a Virtual Private Network or VPN. It prevents anyone tracing where you are.'

'I know what a VPN is. Stop wasting time and get on with the demonstration.' He didn't acknowledge Ronnie by name.

Quickly Ronnie pushed the memory stick into a USB socket on the side of the computer. He opened his mouth to tell his pupil how to connect it and closed it again. From a poster on the nearside wall, he copied the network password into the laptop's window. After several seconds, the screen burst into life, and a window appeared. Ronnie explained. 'Here is where you enter the target email address. Here you put the domain name on its own. You'd use this if you decided, for some reason, to bring down the whole dot-gov network.'

The man's slit eyes opened wide, and he whistled. He glanced at Ronnie and then immediately back to the screen. Ronnie typed in an email address, and a list of emails appeared.

'Here it is. Which one would you like to delete? Press this button to delete an email.' Ronnie demonstrated. 'I recommend you choose one that contains nothing important, making it less likely to get spotted as missing.'

The man pointed to an email and told Ronnie to open it.

Ronnie obeyed. An email appeared describing a book that the recipient was reading. He then swivelled the screen around so that it faced his customer. 'All you need to do is hit *delete.*' A thick finger pressed the button, and the email disappeared. 'Now you need to delete it from the delete folder just like in any email system.' He added he could, of course, delete it straight from the list without ever opening it.

'But even that will leave a shadow of it on the system. A forensics expert would recover it.'

'No, he won't. This is where the program gets very clever. It locates its original position and overwrites it with garbage. There is no way any trace of the original email remains on the system. Oh! There's one other feature I haven't told you about.' He flipped back to the home screen to reveal a third input box. 'If you want to spy on a department, enter its name here.' He pointed to the third window. 'For example, you can access any of the Government departments. But they will contain a lot of crap to wade through – better to avoid that option if at all possible.'

He told him to type in "The Home Office." He turned his head to challenge Ronnie.

Ronnie obeyed, and pages of departmental emails filled the screen. The screen continued to scroll with email after email. 'This will continue for hours,' said Ronnie. 'You better have a large external disk ready to use this option, and it will keep running until your memory and disk are full. Press the F10 key to stop it.' The man leaned forward and pressed the F10 Key. 'Hold the same key and hit delete, and it will get rid of everything that it's downloaded. If you were to hit the Home Office, followed by a range of dates, it would only download emails between those dates. That is a lot easier on time and disk space, and it's the option I would usually use if I chose this feature.'

'That's a complicated program to run on a laptop?' The man turned to Ronnie expecting an explanation.

It came. 'All the clever stuff is on the dot-gov server. Ironically, their machine will do all the work for you.'

Ronnie's customer looked satisfied. He smiled, closed the laptop's lid, removed the VPN dongle and slid it into its case. 'I'm satisfied. Let's finish our coffees and go for your money.'

Ronnie nodded. 'How do I get in touch with you?'

'You don't. If we want you, we will be in touch; otherwise, this meeting never took place.'

***

The walk back to the car park took only minutes. This time with the tall man carrying the laptop in its case. He opened the car and threw the laptop on the back seat. He removed a second case. 'This is your cash. You have done well. Let's walk over to the light, so we can count it.'

'I trust you,' said Ronnie. 'I'd rather be on my way.'

'But I insist.' The man swung the case to his side and started walking towards Ronnie's vehicle. 'I don't want any comebacks after you've gone. I don't want you to claim that some of the money is missing.'

Ronnie hopped over the stream of rain that was still running across the car park floor. The man handed the case to him. He placed the briefcase on the top of the low wall and flipped the catches open.

It was empty – save for a couple of yesterday's newspapers.

His eyes opened wide, and he slowly turned his head over his right shoulder. The outline of a hand holding a pistol met his gaze.

'I don't see why I should give you the money. I have the program, and no one will ever know that I am keeping the cash for myself.'

Ronnie shook his head an almost imperceptible amount and opened his mouth. He twisted around, dropping the briefcase over the wall into the lane below. The newspapers fluttered slowly in the rain and landed in a puddle. The dull thud from the silenced gun hit his chest. His head smashed against the bonnet of his car, and his spectacles bounced off its surface, causing their legs to splay and twist at awkward angles. Ronnie slid down the black paintwork, leaving an almost invisible trail of shiny blood on its surface. He cast a look at the man holding the gun and, with his voice failing, said, 'It will go inactive after thirty days if you can't re-activate it with the correct password. My password.'

'Fuck.' The man's narrow eyes tightened, and he pointed the pistol at Ronnie's forehead. Another thud. A bright red spot appeared between his now vacant eyes.

CHAPTER 14

'This is crazy.' Willis swirled the remains of his coffee around the bottom of his teacup. 'It just makes little sense.'

Sophie had her mouth open and was about to thrust a piece of bacon into it from a strategically placed fork. She hesitated.

'We've got small-time criminals like William McLellan being murdered, and at the same time, we have the involvement of a high-level solicitor and a professional hack targeted at the House of Commons email system. I can't think what connection there might be between the two groups of people. They appear incompatible.'

'Are you expecting an answer? Can I eat my breakfast?' Sophie waved the fork precariously across the table – its small piece of bacon threatening to fall off.

'Sorry. I'm thinking out loud. But I am flummoxed. There has to be a connection somewhere, but I can't think what it is.'

Sophie said to relax that it would come to him. It always did. Just stop complaining and think the situation through; there was some sense in there somewhere.

'I know. I know.' Willis gave a long sigh and then drained what remained in his cup.

The common contact point for both groups of people was McLellan. He was involved with the lower chain but must have interacted somehow with the upper chain – enough that is for someone to finance a barrister to defend him in the past and then to get himself murdered. He must have been at the delivery end of whatever was happening while the money travelled to the end that reaped the major benefit.

'And enough for someone to threaten a Member of Parliament to keep an innocent man in prison for his murder,' said Sophie, speaking with her mouth full and slurring some of her words. 'That infers whoever killed McLellan was important to those higher up the chain. They had to protect him.'

'That was sound reasoning,' Willis said, but his thoughts were somewhere else. 'What have we planned for today?'

'It's Monday. We have put no plans together for the week yet. But I can see you're planning something. Come on, spit it out.'

Willis wanted to go back to visit Mrs Bucket, aka Mrs McLellan, hopefully without her younger son being present. If she'd let him, he'd like to get some more time on Kenny's computer. Willis was confident she did not know what was going on, so he would appeal to her ego and simply ask to look at it again.

'Hold on. Let me search for the employment company he's supposed to be heading up in Colchester.' Sophie walked to the lounge and hit a dozen keys on Willis's computer. 'This is the full list of employment companies that advertise in Colchester.'

'Open up each of them and check if they specialise in any particular type of employment.'

Sophie did as Willis suggested. Each of the companies showed the same variation in their lists of vacancies. However, when she reached the third company from the bottom, Zodiac Employment, she stopped.

Sophie pointed out one differed from the others and had more vacancies than they did, but the vacancies were for people with low-level skills. It also had a list of candidates that it could offer to employers with the same low skill levels. Why would they advertise vacancies and candidates at the same time instead of simply marrying them up?

Willis tapped the screen with his nail and suggested it was because they have a long list of illegal immigrants who'd come across the English Channel by boat – by a boat called *The Clipper*? Willis put his hands around his head and slumped down on the settee, deep in thought. 'Remember, we spotted a lot of Belgian chocolate wrappers on the floor of the craft. Maybe Alec Devlin hadn't held a party but had just unloaded a group of migrants. There were about twelve plastic chairs piled in a corner. If they were for his passengers, they certainly wouldn't have travelled in comfort.'

Sophie curled her fingers around his elbow. 'In the ashtray, there was a pile of Turkish cigarette butts, and that is even more suspicious. So where do we go first – to visit *The Clipper* or Mrs McLellan?'

Willis said their Monday was planned out. After lunch, they'd go visit Mrs McLellan, and then they'd visit *The Clipper*. With some luck, it would be dark or at least dusk by the time they got there, and Alec McLellan would be back at the pub enjoying his evening tipple, so they would have the boat to themselves.

'But he will have locked it. He's sure to have secured it if he had anything to hide.' Sophie's voice was almost a whisper.

'There are still things you have to learn about me, sweetheart. Wait and discover.'

***

After lunch, they departed promptly for Clacton-on-Sea. Willis called Mavis McLellan, introduced himself as Professor Willis, and she wholeheartedly invited him to come to the house for tea.

Willis stopped at the end of the road where the McLellan family lived to check that Kenny's black Porsche was not in the driveway. 'If you can, try to endear yourself to Mrs McLellan because I'll need you to distract her while I look at Kenny's computer.'

'That won't be easy. I didn't even get a cup of tea last time we met.'

The front door of *Dunroamin* opened before Willis reached it, and Mrs McLellan stood in the doorway with a radiant smile. 'Come on in, Professor.' As Willis entered, she cast a disdainful glance in Sophie's direction, but Sophie ignored it and followed obediently after Willis.

'Sit yourselves down. I'll make some tea.'

'Oh, Mrs McLellan, what a wonderful quilt cover. Did you make that yourself?'

'Oh, yes. I love to crochet. Each of the panels is hand made by yours truly.'

'How wonderful, but I've never mastered crochet. I think my fingers are too thick.'

'Nonsense. Let me just get the teas, and I will show you the secret.' Within minutes, Mrs Devlin returned carrying three teas, each in one of the finest china cups that Sophie had ever seen. Since her last visit, at least. She had started to bond with Mrs McLellan.

'What wonderful cups,' said Sophie, ignoring the fact that she'd seen them before. 'They are so delicate and fine and must have cost a fortune. How rude of me to mention money, Mrs McLellan,' she said. 'I'm so sorry.'

'Not at all. But call me Mavis. Let's have a cuppa, and then I'll show you the secret of fine crochet.'

Willis said he was hoping to look at Kenny's computer again to see the full size of the business that he was in charge of. Mrs McLellan gave a dismissive wave of her hand, indicating that Willis could do as he wished because she wanted to spend some time with his assistant. Willis lifted his cup and saucer, and as he headed upstairs, the last thing he heard was Sophie's voice saying, 'Please call me Sophie, Mavis, and I hope you don't mind me calling you Mavis? Thank you so much for being kind enough to show me your crocheting secrets.'

Willis swung the door to Kenny's bedroom open. He was relieved to find the computer switched on and running. There was no window on its screen demanding a password, so he got straight down to work. The screen displayed the same map that it had on his previous visit. This time he took more notice. It showed the estuary immediately outside the river Orwell. It contained navigational information, including sandbanks and showed the position of local buoys, but Willis didn't have time to study it. He leaned over and powered up Kenny's printer. After pressing the print icon at the top of the screen, he let the machine do its work. He searched for and opened the documents folder. A glance revealed a host of letters and documents – too many for Willis to read now, so he pushed a thumb drive into one of the computer's ports, and when it opened the File Manager program, he dragged the complete Document folder across to the drive. A progress bar appeared on the screen, but it was taking ages for the files to transfer over, and Willis estimated it was taking several seconds for each one per cent of the file. The window of the bedroom shook. Kenny had returned, and the vibrations from his Porsche shook the window panes in time with the unnecessary revving of the powerful car's engine. Willis was becoming nervous. He glanced at the progress bar. It was showing only seventy-five per cent. Surely, he would be caught red-handed? Suddenly, the bar rushed to one hundred per cent, and the small window closed. Willis pulled out the thumb drive without bothering to disconnect it from the system. He closed the window and reopened the screen showing the map. Willis ran downstairs two steps at a time and threw himself on the settee. He was trying to look relaxed when he realised he had forgotten his cup and saucer. They were still on the desk in Kenny's bedroom.

Kenny barged along the corridor and into the room where they sat. 'Any milk, mum?'

'What's left in the fridge is all we have left. I've just made some tea. If you want some, you'll need to go to the shop.'

'Fuck. This house is a mess. It's so screwed up.' He slammed the front door, and the windows shook for a second time.

Once Willis heard the car's engine fade, he turned to Mrs McLellan and said, 'I'm so sorry. I seem to have left my cup and saucer upstairs.'

'No trouble,' said Mrs McLellan. 'Kenny will bring it down when he returns.'

'I can't leave a mess in the boy's room – he keeps it so tidy.' Willis jumped to his feet and was upstairs and back down in seconds. He said he would put them in the kitchen. He rushed into the kitchen and placed the cup and saucer hurriedly on the draining board. As he turned, he glimpsed a three-ringed folder sitting on the worktop. It had a sticky label on its cover that read, *Sailing Schedule*. On impulse, Willis lifted the folder, tucked it under his jacket and walked back into the lounge with his left arm artificially straight, carrying the folder under his jacket.

Willis told Mrs McLellan he planned to publish an article about Kenny and his business in the Clacton and Frinton Gazette, but he'd like it to be a secret until it was published. Would she mind if he took a picture of her with his phone? He'd like to show her as the mother of one of the most successful businessmen in the town.

Mrs McLellan's eyes lit up. 'Then you'd better take it before Kenny returns,' she said enthusiastically. 'Would you like me against my best velvet curtains?'

'That will do nicely.' Willis snapped the shot with his free hand and dropped the phone into his only accessible pocket. 'We ought to go before Kenny returns because we don't want to spoil the surprise. Do we?'

'Okay, Professor, thank you for your interest in my boy.'

'And thank you for your lesson on crotchet.'

As they drove out of the avenue, Mavis McLellan was still smiling and waving energetically.

Once they were clear of the house, Willis tossed the folder onto Sophie's knee. She read the label and opened it on the first page. 'It's a schedule of planned sailing times between Ipswich and Ostend in Belgium. He's bound to notice this is missing.'

'I'm hoping that my thumb drive contains the same schedule. If it does, he might think his dizzy mother has thrown it out, and he will easily be able to print another copy for himself. If it isn't on the thumb drive, the boy will be in a shit load of trouble when his bosses find out. Now to visit *The Clipper*.'

***

The quay was quiet when they arrived. They parked in the same restaurant car park as last time and walked hand in hand until they reached the step-way leading to the boat. A wooden seat serendipitously stood immediately across from the gangway, so they sat for five minutes surveying the scene and checking who was moving about and to where. Once satisfied no unusual activity was taking place, Willis stood up while Sophie remained sitting, clutching her mobile to her chest, ready to call or text Willis if she spotted anything out of the ordinary. He removed a wallet from his inside pocket.

'Are those lock picks?' Sophie asked.

'See? I told you there were things about me you didn't know.'

'Being a house breaker wasn't one of the things I expected to discover. Are you sure you can do this?'

'It will be a piece of cake because this yacht is American and was imported many years ago. European locks have narrower openings and are more difficult to pick. I can use my thicker picks on this, which will make it a lot easier.' Willis took one last look around before hopping across the gangway and disappearing under the awning of the boat.

Sophie watched him struggle with the lock for several minutes. Finally, he disappeared inside. After another few minutes, Sophie joined him. 'I thought I would be less obvious in here than sitting outside on my own, but I was attracting some unwanted attention from male passers-by. The lock wasn't as easy as you thought?'

'Well, keep your eyes peeled on that window in case we get any visitors because there's no back door to a boat. The lock is European, and it's new. He's fitted it recently, so he has something he wants to keep under wraps – and he knows the difference between American and European locks.'

Willis headed for the cabin and opened a drawer. Nothing of interest caught his eye. He opened another. A bundle of loose leaves temporarily stapled on one corner lay in the bottom of the drawer. He lifted the bundle and called on Sophie. She looked at the sheets and agreed it was the same schedule they had lifted from Kenny McLellan's kitchen, so Willis put them back carefully in the same position from where he had taken them. Opening the third drawer revealed an old army pistol – probably WWII by the look of it. Willis put its muzzle to his nose and sniffed. There was no smell; it hadn't been fired, not recently, anyway. The fourth drawer was the most interesting. It contained a bundle of passports held together with a rubber band. He released the band and opened the first dozen or so documents to discover the pictures were of foreign individuals, but it was difficult to be sure because all the photos had different lighting, and their owners all looked like they had slightly dark skins. They certainly had dark eyes and jet-black hair, and there was a mixture of males, females and also a few children. Willis took several pictures with his iPhone and tucked the passports back into the drawer. This was a people-smuggling racket.

He said they'd seen everything that they could there, and they should go.

'Move it,' Sophie pulled on his arm. 'There are a couple of men crossing the road and headed in our direction.'

The men stopped and stood arguing. They were shouting and pushing each other around.

'Come on.' Willis headed across the gangway and straight for their car.

Relief flowed over them as they sank into the car seats. ‘That was a close call,’ said Willis. ‘Another few seconds, and we would have had a bit of explaining to do. Let’s get out of here. When they reach the boat and discover that their expensive European lock has been unlocked, they will be more than upset. Let’s head home. It’s been a productive day, and I can’t wait to discover what I’ll glean from the information on the thumb drive.’

CHAPTER 15

Willis and Sophie lay in bed longer the next morning. The previous day had used up much of their energy. Willis had almost been caught out twice, once at the McLellan's home and again at the boat. Even when they arose, they shuffled around the cottage in a half state of torpor. That was soon to change. When his mobile rang, Willis immediately recognised the voice of Uncle DI Swallow. 'The Met found the hacker of the email system.'

'Great,' said Willis, 'will they allow you to sit in on the interrogation?'

'That might be difficult – he's dead – murdered. He was shot twice, once in the chest and once between the eyes. They found Ronnie Merrick lying behind his car, jammed against the wall in a Westminster car park.'

Willis asked if the district was significant, as it was the same area as the House of Commons.

Jonathan didn't answer but gave a 'Humph' and continued saying that Ronnie had been a support engineer working on the government's email system. He would have had access to the system and would have found no difficulty adding a worm or something similar to the system. Merrick had impeccable references and had been an ideal employee for over eight years. While searching the scene, forensics had found an empty briefcase in the lane to the eastern side of the car park. Someone had emptied it before throwing it over, and it had likely contained the pay-off for the services Merrick supplied. Two soggy copies of a London newspaper lay in some pooled water in the lane, but they revealed nothing of interest. Interestingly, forensics recovered two sets of fingerprints from the catches on the case. One set was Ronnie Merrick's, and the other was still to be identified. In answer to his first question, a coat of arms of the House of Commons was found, in gold, on the briefcase's lid. Whoever killed Merrick was likely to be part of the group doing the hacking or one of their paid killers.

Willis said it looked like they had tied up a loose end and eliminated the source of a future leak.

Willis brought Swallow up to date on his visits to Kenny McLellan's house and Devlin's boat. Before Jonathan could intervene, Willis said he knew it wasn't admissible evidence, because he'd done it without a search warrant, but he wouldn't be asking him to investigate anything yet. There was more to be discovered there, and he'd keep him informed. Willis hadn't figured it out yet, but he reckoned the death of William McLellan was the key and the link between the people-smuggling business and a prominent member or members of the British House of Commons, and once he cracked McLellan's death, everything else would become clearer.

Jonathan's voice was edgy. He told Willis he was getting in way over his head. If he were in his position, he'd back off and let the police take over.

'No way. My ex-wife's sister's life is in danger because she is trying to have the investigation reopened to prove the innocence of a young lad who is incarcerated for a crime he didn't commit. I need to give that my priority.'

Jonathan suggested they could raid the McLellan's house and Devlin's boat on the strength of an anonymous call.

If Jonathan did that, he'd close all the avenues of investigation that might uncover who was hacking the system and who was threatening the local MP.

'But you've told me. I know about it, so I can't sit on this for long. If I do, I'll have the book thrown at me for sitting on evidence, and I'm too close to retirement to want to take that kind of risk.'

'I've got you. I understand. Give me some time, and I will promise you I will keep you up to date with everything that I do, and when you say it's time to act, we will act. Agreed?'

'Agreed.'

***

Willis leaned back on the settee and drew his fingers through his thick mop of dark brown hair. They had better get a lead on this soon. Sophie's uncle was getting nervous, not to mention the risks that Diana was taking every day she was at work.

'Can you smell burning?' Sophie stood and walked into the kitchen. 'It isn't here.'

'Maybe it's coming from the bedroom?'

Willis headed for the stairs but suddenly stopped. 'It's in the hallway. The carpet's alight.' Thick, noxious smoke was rising from the hall floor and attacking his nostrils. He ran into the kitchen and pulled a mini-fire extinguisher off the wall without releasing its catch, causing the bracket holding it to the wall to tear out its screws and shower a spray of plaster and *Rawlplugs* over the worktop. He raced back into the hall and released the extinguisher over the offending flames. Hissing and squelching noises followed, and as the flames subsided, even thicker black smoke than before replaced them. A deep layer of foam covered the entire floor of the small lobby. Sophie threw open the door to the cottage to allow the dense smoke to escape.

Willis turned the small foot rug over, ran his fingers across the binding on its rear and felt something oily. It was petrol, oil or something similar. Someone had poured accelerant through the letterbox and set it alight.

'They're trying to kill us.' Sophie's voice had risen an octave higher than usual.

'They're trying to frighten us. If they'd wanted to kill us, they would have done it during the night when we were in our beds.' Willis knew this was just a warning. They must have been followed yesterday while they were out and on the drive back to the Madingley. Some of the crooks knew where they lived.

'Whit's all this commotion goin' oan?' Mrs Burns appeared from the kitchen. 'Ah could see the smoke and smell the pong from way next door. Ye could have burnt the place doon. Ye'll need to mair careful. Give me that rug, and I'll get rid of it. It's way beyond any repair. You'll need to get another.' She lifted the blackened rug from the floor, marched through to the back garden and stuffed it into the waste bin. 'I've got stuff that I can spray in the hall to take that dreadful smell away. Don't you be doing any cooking in here till the smell is completely gone.' Satisfied that she'd said her piece, she marched out the back door and crossed the garden to go home.

'How stupid of us,' laughed Sophie. 'We will need to be mair careful,' she said, paraphrasing Mrs Burns's advice.

'Well, if nothing else, it helped to take the sting out of the situation.'

'Let's not get complacent. This is still serious. Why don't you fit one of those camera doorbells, then we'll see who visits and who comes to the door?'

Willis didn't imagine that they'd be back anytime soon. If they did, they would take a different approach. But he thought Sophie's idea was a good one, so he would fit a camera, and while he was at it, he would also fit proximity sensors to the front and rear of the cottage. Sophie's voice was audibly trembling. She wanted to know what would they do now. 'Somebody knows we are onto them. They'll be looking out for us.'

'We can hardly stop, can we? We've come this far. So – we've ruffled a few feathers – all that means is that we're getting close. Too close for someone's liking.'

Sophie said they should go through the boxes of papers some more.

Willis didn't fancy spending a full day going through papers again. He'd rather leave that until they had spare hours left at the end of a day, and as a full day stretched ahead of them, they needed to do something fruitful.

The idea to go to *The Clipper Inn* again for lunch came from Sophie because they could chat with Mrs Devlin again, and they might even see Alec there. It was a long shot, but it would be interesting to see how he greeted them. If he were aggressive, they'd know that someone had spotted them near the boat.

Willis thought it was a good idea but suggested they visit for an evening meal. There would be a better chance of meeting Alec when he came for a pint, and he wouldn't be able to get physical in a pub full of customers.

'But that means we'll have to wade through more of Diana's papers?' Sophie swallowed some of her words. That was what she didn't want to do.

'Oh well! Let's get to work.'

***

Sophie reminded Willis once it had gone 5 p.m. She looked at him, opened her eyes wide and held her hands with their palms up, inferring that they had done enough for the day.

'Okay, I agree,' said Willis. 'Let's get ready. It will be well after six by the time we get there, and if Alec is coming, he'll likely be there already or arrive shortly after us.'

They rode in silence for most of the journey while Willis rehearsed in this mind how he would react if Alec Devlin got nasty. He decided it wouldn't happen and settled down to drive at a moderate speed.

The bar was busier than they had ever seen it. The pub was full of bustling drinkers, but that shouldn't have been a surprise as it was a local drinking man's establishment. Willis forced his way to the front and caught the eye of the young waitress he'd met on their previous visit. She waved him to go back, and she came around to meet him. 'Come with me. There's a table left behind the pillar, and it's quite quiet. If you give me your order, I'll bring it over to you and save you from fighting the animals at the bar. Now. First. What would you like to drink?' Willis asked for a Guinness and Sophie a G&T. 'I'll be back for your food order.' She shouted the comment over her shoulder as she marched off. Willis was glad he'd given her a large tip when they'd last met, and he would be sure to do the same again this evening.

'It's very crowded,' said Sophie. 'I don't particularly enjoy places with too many people.'

'We have a comfortable seat here in the corner, and you won't need to struggle with the crowd again until we leave.'

'I hope we are serving you well?' Alec Devlin slid into the seat opposite Willis and touched Sophie's arm in a more than familiar manner. 'Where are your drinks? Haven't you been served?'

Willis explained that a very helpful waitress had offered to bring their drinks to the table. He added that she'd been most helpful.

'She's a fine lass but a tad standoffish.' He winked at him to infer Willis knew what he meant. The waitress came, dropped off their drinks and took their order for steak and ale pie. 'That's our favourite,' said Willis, 'but the portions are so large we have trouble eating dessert afterwards.'

Alec said he'd told Helen to reduce the portion size, so they could sell more desserts, but she wouldn't listen.

'It's busy tonight,' said Willis, for the sake of something to say.

'There's a model boat club here tonight.' He told Willis they met every other month and spent a couple of hours showing off their latest creations and getting quite inebriated while they were doing it, but it was very good for business. His regulars often objected, but he'd told them if they drank more, he would refuse the club entry. They thought he was kidding, but there weren't enough of them to make up for the increased number of pints the club bought.

'Two steak and ale pies?' The waitress appeared and lowered two steaming plates onto the table. 'Sorry for the delay, but we needed an extra shoulder to close the doors to the beer cellar. It jams, and with only one metal rod, it won't close properly. Enjoy your steak and ale pies.'

Alec said he'd disappear and leave them in peace to eat but warned them the pie was very hot.

'Well, that suggests it wasn't Mr Devlin who spotted us near his boat,' said Willis. 'Neither was it any of his friends, or they would have informed him.'

'… or he's waiting until the pub gets a little quieter to surprise you.' Sophie lifted her eyebrows in the form of a question.

'I doubt it,' said Willis. 'If he had been, he would have kept away from our table because he couldn't risk being seen chatting to us if he was planning something sinister.'

'Everything okay with your meal?' The waitress was hovering again.

Willis hadn't taken a mouthful yet. 'Yes, thanks. Once it cools, it will be fine.' She walked away, satisfied that she had done her duty.

The pie was delicious, and the portions were indeed huge, so they would be far too full to order a dessert. Willis had drunk most of his chilled Guinness to wash down the overly hot pie and was considering getting another when the waitress's voice shouted over the babble of the crowd. 'The same again, sir?' Willis held up his thumbs in agreement, and she vanished back to the bar.

'They can't tip the waitresses in this part of the country.' Sophie grinned and took the last swig from her G&T. 'I think we should make this our local because the service is so good.'

'I need to find the gents' toilet. This cold Guinness is going right through me.'

Sophie sat sipping her replacement drink until he returned. Willis appeared, carrying an enormous cardboard box. 'Guess what I've just bought? A model of a clipper – or should I say a kit for a model of a clipper.'

'What the…? You don't have any time to mess around building models. What do you think you are doing?'

'I didn't buy it for myself. I bought it for John, Mrs Burns's husband.'

This would keep John busy for hours, and it was something that he could do from his wheelchair. It had cost nearly a hundred pounds, and that was much more than Willis usually spent on the presents he bought for John, but this would take him ages to complete. Willis took a sip from his Guinness and felt very pleased with himself.

Alec Devlin came and joined them again. 'I see you've bought a kit of *The Clipper* – my *Clipper*. The model is based on my boat.'

'Really? I didn't know that when I bought it.' Willis said that would make it more personal when he saw it put together. He'd bought it for a friend, so he wouldn't be putting it together himself.

'Some friend you are. There will be hours of work needed to put that together. It's made of tiny pieces of wood, nearly every one of them different.'

Willis said his friend had all the time in the world. He had built models before, but this would be the most complicated one he'd attempted.

'Good luck to him. I'll need to speak to my other guests.' Alec rose and disappeared into the throng of bodies filling the pub.

'I think we ought to go now. I'm feeling quite tired anyway,' said Willis.

'The same occurred to me but didn't want to say so.' When she got to her feet, Sophie kissed him. As he passed the waitress, Willis pressed a five pound note into her palm. For his generosity, she rewarded him with a huge smile and a kiss on the cheek.

'You look as though you've got further with her than her boss did.'

'I didn't see you moving his hand from your arm earlier on.'

'Yeuch!' Sophie turned and kissed Willis once again.

***

When they were about a mile from the pub, Willis drove into a layby. 'Are your urges getting the better of you, Dr Willis?' Sophie said and licked her lips.

'Nothing like that. I just want to make sure that no one is following us.' He switched off the lights and the engine and waited for ten minutes before starting the car up again. Willis guessed he was just overly suspicious. He swung out of the layby and headed for the A14.

***

When they got to the cottage, Sophie said, 'I am ready to crash into bed and could sleep for a week. That's even despite the longer stay in bed we had this morning.' She opened the door. 'And no more fires; the hallway is still intact.' Sophie walked to the kitchen and offered to make a pot of tea since it was too late for coffee.

They returned and dropped onto the settee, each chewing on a ginger nut biscuit. 'What the…? Did you tidy up before we went out?'

'Of course not. I'm not that fanatical.'

'Where have all our papers gone? The charts have even been removed from the wall.'

'That's Mrs Burns for you. She insists on keeping everything clean.'

'Bullshit! I'll go next door, deliver the kit for John and give her a ticking off.'

Willis lifted the large cardboard box, put it under his arm and headed for the back door of the kitchen. Sophie put her feet up on a stool, took a bite from her ginger snap and waited for his return.

When Willis hadn't returned after fifteen minutes, Sophie decided to see what was keeping him. She found him kneeling on the floor in front of John Burns, describing the contents of the kit to him. 'What are you doing, Brad? I thought we were going to have an early night. I'm shattered.'

'… and ah'll no get any use of my kitchen table after he gets going on this thingie.' Mrs Burns didn't sound at all pleased.

'… and we're not too pleased that you cleared away all our papers and took our charts down from the wall.'

'Ah did no such thing, lassie. I wudnae touch yer private papers nor wud ah take yer chart doon from the wall!' Mrs Burns was angry at the accusation, and it made her accent even stronger.

Willis rose to his feet and ran back next door. He ran upstairs and checked the bedrooms. Whoever had been in the house while they were at *The Clipper Inn* had known what they were looking for. Only the paperwork they received from Diana was missing. Nothing else had been taken, at least nothing Willis could think of.

Mrs Burns and Sophie arrived from the kitchen. 'We're very sorry, Mrs Burns. We were too fast to accuse you. Please forgive us. Someone else was in the cottage while we were out and removed our papers.'

'Ah! That's alright, Professor, as ah'm not that easily offended, and it was a natural mistake to have made. But it's not only yer papers that are missing. Where's your favourite picture of Carole?'

Willis looked across to the dresser. A gap in the ornaments stared back at him from where Carole's photo had stood.

CHAPTER 16

Willis had a fitful night. He had only slept for short periods as his mind was focused on planning his actions for the next day. The idea of someone having entered his cottage was affecting him more than he would like to admit. He had not shared his concern with Sophie but knew she shared his worries. Her erratic breathing and restless movements told him she, too, was having a poor night. He gave priority to fitting outdoor sensors and cameras to the cottage. Because of the risks involved, he decided he needed two systems. First, he would fit a wireless system that would be in full view to act as a deterrent, but he would also fit a covert system high up and hidden under the eaves of the cottage's thatched roof. With little effort, the wireless system could be jammed using basic equipment easily available at any hobby electronic supply store. Whoever these people were, they would have access to the most technically advanced tools. Impatiently, Willis lay and waited for the seven o'clock alarm to sound. When it did, he was on his feet, showered, dressed and ready to start his tasks in fifteen minutes flat.

Sophie was up shortly behind him and suffered from a similar lack of sleep. On the kitchen worktop, were remnants of Willis's encounter with the fire extinguisher. Small pieces of plaster had lodged themselves behind the rim that surrounded the sink, reminding her of the dangerous position in which they now found themselves. While Willis busied himself measuring up cable lengths to enable him to fit his proposed security system, Sophie started to cook breakfast. It annoyed him he had to fit electronic devices to the outside of his historic and listed cottage. Cameras would distract from its Suffolk pink walls and look incongruous. As soon as this episode was over, he vowed to remove them. How soon would it be over? Would it ever be over? Willis pushed the negative thoughts from his mind and concentrated on the measuring task at hand.

When he had completed the measurements to his satisfaction, he devoured part of his breakfast quickly, much to Sophie's disdain. Vocally, she let it be known that she had taken time to prepare a full English breakfast, and Willis had only eaten half.

***

Within ninety minutes, Willis had returned with the necessary components for the system. He was wasting no time. From the garage, he took a short ladder that barely reached past the bottom of the thatch. He chose to fit the wireless system first because it was the easier of the two to fit, and if anyone was watching, they would see its installation and hopefully leave before he fitted the real thing. At one point, he spotted a black saloon car sitting at a distance along from the cottage, obstructing the church gates. Its driver was still in place. Willis got down off the ladder and walked towards it, but by the time he reached the garden gate, it had started and moved off. Perhaps it was only his imagination, as he was looking for danger everywhere. Because it was better to be more cautious than less, he forgave himself for worrying.

***

It was after dusk before he completed the work. Willis had managed to fit all the external components while it was still light and had completed the remaining wiring from inside. Working in the eaves under the thatch caused his eyes to run. Because the inner thatch was over decades, maybe even hundreds of years old, it shouldn't have caused any allergic reaction. Never mind, it was all finished now.

As he walked from the garden into the house with the noise of the alarm squealing at him, Willis asked what was for dinner. He pushed the reset button on its control panel, and all noise ceased.

'Hopefully, more than you ate at breakfast.' It still displeased Sophie that Willis had left so abruptly. 'And you left a bag of cable ties on my worktop in the kitchen.'

'I needed all the time there was available, and I finished just before it got dark.'

Sophie wanted the meal to pass uninterrupted, but her wish wasn't to be granted. The klaxon sounded off once again. 'What's all the din going on here?' It was Mrs Burns. 'Ah cannae get near yer hoos without all this racket going on.'

'I'm sorry, Mrs Burns. It's only temporary.' Willis rushed to reset the panel. 'It's for a project that I'm working on at the university, and I promise to take it back down as soon as I have a chance to test it properly, but it will mean that you won't be able to visit the cottage unless we are at home.'

'How will I get the cleaning done? I cannae keep working around your ankles when you're in. Can I?'

Willis explained it would hopefully only be for a couple of weeks, and he understood it was causing her problems, but it had to be done.

'Oh, Aye, we'll see how that works.' She marched back out the back door triggering the klaxon again.

'Clever thinking. It was good you found a reason to persuade Mrs Burns from coming to the house while we are out. It could be dangerous for her.'

Willis had spent all afternoon thinking of reasons to keep her away. They would also need to keep the cat indoors, and that might be more challenging. He'd set the sensitivity, so Ptolemy wouldn't trigger it, but if he got overly active, it could still go off.

'What a sorry state of affairs we find ourselves in. I can't believe that it all started with you searching for a red sports car.'

'It wasn't a search for a red sports car. It was a search for who killed Carole. That much we discovered, but we haven't found out who paid him to do it yet.'

Willis had put a second spoonful of food in his mouth when his mobile rang. He finished chewing and swallowed the food before saying, 'Hello, Jonathan. Have I got news for you!' Willis went silent. 'What? When? How? Hold on a minute, Jonathan.' He turned to Sophie. 'That's a coincidence. We were only just talking about him. Jim Pryce, the driver of the sports car, was found hanged this morning.' Willis returned to his conversation with Jonathan and pressed the loudspeaker button to allow Sophie to hear. 'I assume that it's foul play.'

'It happened in a room adjoining the laundry department in his prison. A bed sheet was cut into strips and then plaited to serve as a noose. It was a thick noose, and it would have taken Pryce a long time to die.' Jonathan couldn't imagine anyone choosing that way to go. Even Pryce must have realised that it wasn't a nice way to kill himself.

'What did the forensic guys say?'

They were still waiting on their report. Somehow the prison hadn't discovered the body until late today. He'd got through the check yesterday evening and this morning. No one had noticed he was missing.

'Sounds like there might be prison guards on their payroll.'

That's what Jonathan thought too. If there were, it would mean Pryce had been murdered. He'd know as soon as forensics came back, and they'd given the report the highest priority.

'By the way, I've checked out the contents of the thumb drive you gave me. When we meet, I'll tell you about it. It holds some supporting evidence, but it isn't giving any fresh clues to help the case.'

'Well, it was worth a try.' Jonathan Swallow hung up, and Willis turned to Sophie.

'What a fucking mess this is. Two killings so far. Two attacks on our house. The whole thing is getting out of hand. We're losing. They're dancing rings all around us. If we don't get a break soon—'

'Calm down. Eventually, they always make a mistake. We'll get a hook on this thing. Just have patience and keep at it – something always breaks – it will come soon.'

The klaxon was going again. Sophie walked to reset the panel while Willis rushed out the front door. A tall figure attempted to vault the fence, but his foot caught on the gate post, and he fell lengthways on the pavement. As he bent his knees to rise, Willis put his foot on the small of his back and pushed. A loud exhalation of breath and a scream of agony filled the night.

'What's going on here?'

'Stay away,' Mrs Burns. 'I've just caught an intruder.'

'Oh, my dear. Oh, my dear.' Mrs Burns ran back to her cottage and locked herself in.

'Right, you. On your feet.' Willis twisted his arm behind his back and led him into the house. Sophie handed him a couple of cable ties – large ones. He secured the man's wrists behind his back and attached another two cable ties to his ankles.

'I'm saying nothing. I'm not telling you a fucking thing.' The man was still breathless from the pressure of Willis's foot that had forced the air from his lungs.

Willis formed a fist and rammed it into his visitor's groin. He bent double and fell longwise on the settee. 'That's for violating my house and frightening my wife and neighbours.'

'I'll have you charged with assault.'

'Really?' Willis took a second swipe at the man's face, causing blood to spray from his nose and saturate the cushion. 'It's only your word against mine.'

Willis asked Sophie to call her uncle to say they had caught an intruder but not to rush.

Willis emptied the man's pockets in search of any information that could show who he was or who had employed him. The only thing he found was a handwritten note describing how to get to Willis's cottage. He pulled hard on the collar of the man's jacket, forcing his head between his knees and pushed his fingers into the rear left pocket of his trousers. 'What have we here? Well, it's only a set of car keys and a mobile phone. You won't need to tell us anything. These will be enough to identify you.'

Willis stood at the front window of the cottage and saw, alongside the church, a familiar black salon car with a passenger in it. Willis took out his mobile and dialled. 'Before you come to the cottage, Jonathan, stop and apprehend the man in the passenger seat of a black car parked in front of the church across the way. He is our intruder's accomplice.'

The unwelcome visitor staggered to his feet, the cable ties around his ankles causing him to wobble as he rose. 'I want to make a call.' Willis pushed him, and he crashed down heavily on the settee.

Willis tried to open his visitor's iPhone, but he required a password. 'Oh well, we'll find out who you are when the police arrive. One call to the DVLA, and they, the Vehicle Licencing Authority, will provide your name and address. It won't be long now.' Willis looked at his captive, and small beads of sweat had started to form on his temples. 'You could do yourself a favour. You'll be charged with arson, housebreaking and likely murder.' The tiny beads of sweat on the stranger's face had changed from tiny spheres to large droplets.

'Murder? I have killed no one. You can't pin a murder on me.'

'There's no one else to pin it on. You're the patsy, I'm afraid. Unless your friend in the car admits to killing Jim Pryce?'

'Who the fuck's Jim Pryce? I don't even know the name – never heard of the guy.'

'That's for the jury to decide. You're for the high jump, mate. You've been caught in my house … oh, it's not even worth explaining. Just wait till the copper from homicide arrives. It's not that often that Scotland Yard bobbies come out this far. You must be important.'

'I am innocent. When this murder happened, I am sure have an alibi. When did it happen?'

'So as you can get an alibi arranged? No way.'

'My name's Victor Shaw. I live in Clacton-on-Sea. I'm not important enough to need to kill anyone.'

'Prove it. Give me the password for your phone?'

The man froze and stared at Willis. He lowered his head and shook it. 'It's 920419, my birthday in reverse.'

Willis tapped the numbers into the iPhone, and the first thing that appeared was a video. A white triangle covered a shot of a desk computer. Willis pressed the triangle and watched while a recording of him entering Kenny McLellan's bedroom flashed before his eyes. Shit, he thought, I didn't think to check for cameras but now knew who had put the tail on him and likely stole the paperwork. Ten seconds later, Willis was reading McLellan's email instructing Shaw to recover the manifesto for the planned trips on Devlin's boat. Kenny didn't need to be a genius to connect the missing manifesto and Willis's uninvited visit to his house. They had enough to nail them now, but could Willis convince Jonathan Swallow not to go gung-ho and arrest Devlin and McLellan? First, they needed to find out who the big guys were.

The door to Willis's cottage burst open, and Jonathan Swallow marched in with another officer. 'We've arrested the guy in the car. He's talking his head off. There are some boxes of papers in the car that appear to belong to you. Your address is on one of the flaps.'

'… and was there a framed photograph with them by any chance?'

Jonathan turned to the uniform that accompanied him and said, 'Charlie, bring in the boxes from the car but leave the picture frame. We'll need that for fingerprints.'

Willis turned to Shaw. 'Why did you steal the photograph?'

'I wanted to let Kenny McLellan know you were friends with Diana Bishop. McLellan has been harassing her.'

'… and why was he harassing Diana Bishop?'

'I've no idea.'

Willis nodded at Jonathan, intimating that he should follow him into the kitchen. 'That's odd; why would Kenny McLellan want to prevent Diana from discovering who killed his brother? Either he killed him, or he's protecting whoever did. My money's on the latter. How come you got here so fast? You didn't drive from Colchester.'

'Just lucky because we were in Newmarket, so we were halfway there. But I think it's time to put Kenny under surveillance. We'll have a man shadow him when he leaves his house, and I'll ask MI5 to hack into his camera system at home. It's bound to be wireless, and they can do that easily.'

Willis asked about Devlin's boat.

By the end of the day, there would be a man watching it. Jonathan added it was just as well that he'd finished putting in his security system, but it was a pity he wouldn't need it now these guys were safely locked up and in custody.

'Typical,' said Willis, 'at least it did its task well.' But he wasn't so sure. It might still have a role to play.

While Swallow removed the cable ties from Shaw's ankles and replaced his wrist ties with handcuffs, Willis sat scrolling through Shaw's mobile. 'What is that?' Jonathan made a lunge for the phone.

Willis twisted to his left, causing Swallow's hand to fly into the air. 'You can have it in a minute after I've read some of these emails.'

'That is police evidence, so hand it over.'

Willis took several steps away from Jonathan and stood in the doorway to the kitchen, saying he had every intention to – in a minute or two. Swallow shook his head and joined Shaw on the settee.

'Here, you can have the phone. I have everything I need except its full list of contacts, if it has any. I'll like a printout of those once you get it back from forensics.' He dropped the phone on Swallow's lap.

The officer who accompanied Jonathan dragged Shaw to his feet and unceremoniously bundled him out to a waiting police car. Once he was out of earshot, Willis asked, 'Who was the other guy in the car?'

'He is just a sidekick, I think. He has a scruffy pigtail and is tattooed, but he isn't saying a word. I only said that to unnerve Shaw.'

'Does he have a green ribbon tying back his ponytail?' Willis asked more in hope than expectation.

'Yes, he has. Why do you ask that?'

Willis repeated the information that Sam Cordell had given him, then added that his name was Roger. He didn't know his surname, but he had a connection back to Devlin and his boat. If possible, Jonathan shouldn't give him the impression that he was in any way interested in him but should let him go with a caution or something, then put a tail on him. Whoever was assigned by Jonathan to follow him would find it easy because he always wore that green ribbon to tie up his ponytail. Roger was yet another person of interest in William McLellan's murder.

Jonathan shook his head in resignation and promised to do what he could.

***

After Jonathan had left, Willis turned to Sophie and said, 'It would appear that we are making some progress with the info from Shaw's phone and, with the tracking down of Roger, we now have something to investigate.'

'Was it worth it? We have a terrorised Mrs Burns and have desecrated this lovely sixteenth-century cottage with security systems.'

That wouldn't be a problem, intimated Willis, because he'd remove them when this was all over. But they had better invite Mrs Burns over for a cuppa to explain what had happened.

***

After Mrs Burns left, they slouched on the settee. 'I'm hungry,' said Sophie.

'I'm not surprised, because we haven't eaten yet.'

Sophie walked through to the kitchen, returned and slumped back down on the settee. 'Now the food's cold and soggy. It's ruined.'

'What time is it?' Willis looked at his watch and said, 'It's gone 9 p.m. Why don't we just order a pizza? There's still time to have one delivered?'

'That's a deal. While you make the call, I'll get the wine and glasses.'

'Maybe we can have some fun afterwards?' Sophie winked at Willis and poured a copious amount of wine into each glass.

Until the doorbell told them that pizza had arrived, they sat sipping red wine. It was fortunate that Willis had switched his security system off. They finished the first half of the pizza quickly, and the third quarter took longer, but the final quarter remained untouched and still in its cardboard box. Two bodies lay sprawled across the settee, fast asleep, and one of them was snoring. Sophie woke, dug her elbow into Willis, and he rose, zombielike, took her hand and led her upstairs. 'Tomorrow,' she said.

'Yes, tomorrow.' Within minutes, they were both fast asleep.

CHAPTER 17

Willis and Sophie slept deeply and soundly. It was past ten o'clock before the sound of Willis's mobile woke them. Still groggy, he put the instrument to his ear. 'Hi, Jonathan.' He asked what new information did he have for him on this fine morning? Had his prisoner escaped during the night?

Jonathan said he was nearly right. His prisoner hadn't escaped, but Devlin's yacht had slipped out of the marina during the hours of darkness. They'd taken the two watchdogs off duty after midnight, thinking that there would be no action after then. How wrong they had been.

Willis asked what would happen now.

The coastguards had been alerted and were looking out for them, and they'd commandeered a River Police speedboat to intercept it on its return. It wasn't certain that Devlin was on board, but the coastguard would stop it for an inspection and given the number of small boats bringing migrants across the channel, it would seem routine.

Willis believed they wouldn't normally come in at Ipswich, because the sea would be too wide there for quick crossings.

Jonathan said that was what they were supposed to think, adding if Devlin were crossing over to Belgium instead of France, there would be fewer government ships out patrolling that area of water. Even with radar, it would be difficult to spot them with the increased width of the sea at that point. He promised to give Willis a call as soon as he'd heard anything.

'Okay. I might as well go back to sleep.' He gave a lazy laugh and disconnected.

'It's after ten,' said Sophie, 'so we might as well get up. If we lie here, we won't sleep tonight, so we should get on our feet. I need a shower, anyway.'

It surprised Willis that Devlin left the house last night. With Victor Shaw and Roger, whatever his name is, in custody, he would have thought Devlin might have hesitated. Or maybe it was a desperate move to get an urgent trip in before Shaw or his mate gave away any secrets.

Willis redialled DI Swallow's number and said, 'Did you by any chance release Roger, what's his name, last night?'

Jonathan said, of course he had. Willis had suggested it was a good idea to let Roger – his surname was Lowden – off the hook and then follow him.

Lowden would probably have called Devlin and warned him that Shaw was in custody. Willis asked Jonathan if he was sure he was still under surveillance or whether he could have slipped away.

Jonathan thought it would be impossible to check without going to the house and knocking on his door, and that was out of the question.

But Willis suspected he might have slipped out and been on *The Clipper* somewhere on the North Sea. 'Okay, as before, call if anything changes, please.'

Sophie asked if he wanted some breakfast and threw her pillow in his direction. But he had better eat more than he did yesterday.

***

It was early afternoon before Jonathan called him back. The coastguard had intercepted the boat. The crew was in custody, but there were fourteen illegal immigrants on board. A man answering Roger Lowden's description had also been detained. Surprisingly, Alec Devlin was nowhere to be seen. It looked like Willis had been right. They had crossed over to Belgium taking a longer route, and they hadn't only gone to Ostend but docked at Zeebrugge as well. The coastguards had their logs.

Willis thought it odd there was nothing else on board other than the illegals. The immigrants were a good enough reason for the trip, but he'd been trying to explain why people higher up the food chain were involved. Fourteen immigrants wouldn't bring in enough money to interest them even if they were used later as modern-day slaves. That Willis had found fake passports aboard eliminated that idea because there would be no need to supply them with passports if they were to be locked up and working somewhere for a pittance.

The coastguards had impounded the boat because it had been used as a tool to execute their crime. Once forensics were finished with it, probably tomorrow, Jonathan would get Willis on board, and he could search it to his heart's content, but Jonathan was sure they'd found everything that was to be found.

Willis wasn't happy. It didn't stack up. This was only a small-time operation, bringing in a few tens of thousands, at least, or maybe a hundred thousand pounds at the most. That wouldn't be enough to motivate someone enough to hack a gov.uk website and threaten an MP – to protect the cover-up of a murder of an apparent small-time crook like William McLellan – unless, of course, McLellan wasn't small-time.

***

'Ah've come to clean up your kitchen.' Mrs Burns took over the room. 'Ah see you've had lunch, so I'll clean away the dishes and wash down the worktop.' Willis made a strategic move out of the kitchen; it was best not to get in Mrs Burns's way when she was working. She followed him into the lounge, waving her cleaning cloth in her hand. 'Anyway, you've got the use of your kitchen table. I cannae get near mine. John has that blasted boat spread all over it. And you should hear the language. He disnae normally swear, not much anyways, but he's fair going at it with that model you bought. John says he cannae get the bits to fit together properly. He thinks that whoever made the kit measured something up the wrong way, and the bits just won't fit together.'

'It's a very complicated model. He'll get the hang of it.' Willis told Mrs Burns the guy who sold it to him said it was the most complicated and intricate model he had ever made. But he had seen one assembled on a shelf in the pub where he'd bought it, so it would fit together.

'John's put together many, many kits, and he loves them. He's become pretty good at them. Sure, he put together yon model of Nelson's ship that sits on your dresser, and that was fairly complicated. I'm fearful that he'll lose the rag and smash the thing up.'

Willis agreed to come over later and give him some encouragement. That model had cost him a small fortune, and he didn't want John to damage it.

Mrs Burns shrugged and disappeared back into the kitchen.

***

As much as he tried, Willis couldn't get comfortable looking through Diana's legal papers with Sophie. Every few minutes, an image of John Burns smashing up a partly completed model of a clipper boat flashed into his mind. Eventually, he gave up and told Sophie that he was going next door to calm John.

He found John struggling with a small wooden shape, but to his relief, the ship was almost complete. 'Your good lady told me you were about to smash the model into tiny pieces, but here it is, and you've almost completed it.'

John said Willis should know what Annie was like. She always exaggerated everything. Sure, he had a couple of sticky moments, and he'd cursed a lot, but he'd eventually put it together. Almost together, that was. He couldn't get the insides of the boat to fit. They were too small. Neither the cabin nor the hold would fit snugly into the gaps designed for them. He had checked and double-checked the dimensions and the diagram, but he still couldn't get them to fit. They flopped around with about half an inch to spare around both components. He handed the pieces to Willis to try.

Willis lifted each small wooden cube and sat it into the hollow hull. No way could he get them to sit without physically gluing them to the base of the ship. Willis asked to look at the diagram. John handed Willis the main diagram and pointed to the offending area.

John said Willis would need to study the small diagram, too, because it showed how to put the cabin and the hold together, and it was very detailed and very clear, with little scope for error.

True enough, thought Willis, the instructions are explicit. He inspected the cabin and hold inserts and decided that John hadn't made a mistake. Both had been put together exactly as the instructions demanded.

'Give me a minute.' Willis walked back to his cottage and found the receipt that the model maker had given him. Once he was back with John, he dialled the number at the base of the receipt. 'Hello, you won't remember me, but I bought one of your clipper kits from you several days ago.'

'Ah, the man with the pretty girlfriend? I remember you well. What can I do for you?'

Willis explained the difficulty John was having with inserting the internal components into the model. 'It makes little sense. They don't fit.'

'Oh, I am so sorry.' He said there should have been four packing pieces supplied to bridge the gaps on each side. Hadn't he found them?

From an outstretched palm, John dropped four rectangular pieces of balsa onto the table and said, 'I thought they were real packing pieces because they were used to keep the layers of wood together before I separated them.'

Willis asked the designer if they were four brick-shaped pieces of wood about one by one by four inches.

'Yes, those are the ones. I'm sorry the instructions should have been clearer.' But he still didn't understand why they were needed because he had even gone back and measured the dimensions a second time to make sure. They were the right size, and the width and the size of the hull were correct, so he couldn't figure out where he'd made the error.

'Thanks for your help. No harm done. It's all sorted now.'

John thanked him for helping resolve the problem, and Willis headed swiftly home.

***

Within minutes, he was speaking to Jonathan for the third time that day. 'You *have* impounded Devlin's boat, yes?'

Jonathan said, of course. It had been done immediately. He'd told Willis he would impound it.

Willis explained that he'd spent the last hour trying to build a model of that boat.

'That's very interesting. I *don't* think,' said Jonathan interrupting Willis's flow.

'Shut up for a minute, Jon. The cabin and the hold won't fit in the model.'

'So…?'

'So … it means there are double walls in the boat with hidden spaces between the hull and the walls. Get forensics to remove the side panels, so we can see what Devlin is really shipping from Belgium.'

'I'll get it started immediately and call you back when I've got something.'

***

Two hours later, Jonathan was on the phone again. 'You'll never guess what I found in the cavity?'

'Do you think I'm fucking psychic or something? What did you find in the gap?'

Jonathan had found eight oil paintings – all old masters. Two were Van Goghs and another a Vermeer. All were on the hotlist as having been stolen from exhibitions or private houses in the last three years.

Willis hoped he hadn't irreparably damaged *The Clipper*?

'Why are you worried about me damaging *The Clipper*?'

'Because I want you to put the paintings back where you found them or at least paintings that look like them. We need to see who comes to collect them. Don't we, DI Swallow?'

'Bloody smart ass.' Jonathan hung up.

'This evening, I think we'll go out for dinner.' Willis was holding Sophie's hand.

'Are we celebrating?' Sophie grabbed his arm and hugged it.

'I think we can say that. But we'll be working too. Get ready. I fancy another steak and ale pie this evening.'

***

On duty in the pub was the young waitress that Willis had befriended. 'Where's the boss man tonight?'

'He's around the back, and he's been on the same call for nearly an hour.'

Willis leaned against the bar, slowly sipping on his cold Guinness. He sat on a high stool that was jammed in a corner opposite the door to the backroom. From here, he could make out half of the conversation that Devlin was having. 'Yes, I know. Don't keep repeating it. I am well aware. They don't matter, because they are collateral damage. Don't worry. The crew won't talk. Stay calm. I've reported the boat stolen. Whether they believe that is another thing. Stay calm. I tell you. Now go. I need to be seen in the bar.'

The door swung open.

Willis told Alec that since he enjoyed the steak and ale pie last time, he thought he'd try it again.

Alec apologised, saying that the steak and ale pie was off tonight, but they had some nice fresh fish caught that morning.

Not from your boat, Willis thought. 'It will need to be fish and chips in that case. We've had that before, and it is excellent too. By the way, that model I bought last time I was in—'

'Yes? What about it?'

'I found a mistake in it. Or my neighbour did.'

'A mistake?'

'Yes, the cabin and the hold don't fit into the hull properly. When they are put in place, there's a gap all the way around them. We had to use a few packing pieces to support it in situ.'

Never had Willis seen a man's complexion change colour so quickly. Devlin turned completely white, and he ran to the car park. Within a few seconds, he was back, and he barged into the back room. 'I need an address. I can't go anywhere without an address.' Once again, he ran back out into the car park.

Willis guessed that John's model clipper was about to become unique. As he returned to join Sophie at the table, he surmised Alec Devlin would either buy all the remaining kits or smash them to pieces. When the penny finally dropped, he would start panicking about who could work out that the panels in *The Clipper* were removable.

'What would you two like to eat this evening?' It was the young waitress doing her duty again.

'I am told the steak and ale pie is off today, so we will have fish and chips twice, please. Can we have cod? Take your time; we are in no hurry.'

Sophie leaned back in her chair. 'I guess we can relax for the evening. The pressure's off for a little while.'

The pressure was only off until, or if, Devlin realised Willis was one of the people who could discover his secret. Alec was panicking, and that was good.

'It's a pity this pub is implicated in whatever it is because it's rather pleasant. I enjoy eating here.' Sophie took a sip of her drink.

'Fish and chips, twice. Can I get you anything else, sauces, salt pepper…?' The waitress placed a hot plate carefully in front of Sophie and then Willis.

'That's fine, thanks. We have everything we need, thank you.'

They had finished their meal and were relaxing, sipping their drinks when Helen Devlin approached carrying a large brandy and dropped clumsily on one of the spare seats. 'Where has Alec gone now? That man is a liability. He's always dashing all over the place.'

'I think I heard him say he was going to meet Roger somebody.'

'Those two are inseparable. It's as though they are joined at the hip. I suppose I'll need to run the bar on my own until he deems to turn up again. Oh, well.' She lifted her not unsubstantial frame from the chair and headed back to the bar sipping her brandy.

When Willis turned to look at Sophie, her mouth was wide open. 'Close your mouth. It's unladylike. That's how to find things out – just bring them up in normal conversation. It's better than asking direct questions about Roger.' He reminded Sophie that Helen had denied knowing Roger earlier. That was interesting.

'I know we had a long lie in this morning, but I am tired.' Sophie's eyelids drooped.

'Me too. Let's head home. I wonder if I should tell John Burns that he helped solve a smuggling problem by not being able to finish his model?'

CHAPTER 18

'Stand still, will you? Are you people on drugs or something? Stop coughing.' As the officer guided a pair of the immigrants into a room in the detention centre, they tripped and fell against a door, smashing it against the wall. 'You're drunk. Get in there and sit down.' He was talking to the group without being sure whether they understood him. Not a word of English had been heard from them since they arrived. Not a word of any language had been said, not even between members of the group. He asked if any of the group could understand anything that he was saying. No reply. Nothing but vacant looks. Into the second room, he led two of the group's female members and pointed towards two chairs. At first, they didn't seem to recognise the signal that he was giving, then they staggered and crashed into a table that sat in the middle of the room. The officer grabbed one woman's arm, hoping to break her fall. It felt hot. 'Call a doctor. This woman needs treatment.' While this was going on, the other woman stood swaying and fell clumsily onto the chair. The guard briefly touched her forehead and pulled swiftly away. 'And so does this one.'

After leading the others into their allotted rooms, it became clear that some were suffering from fever, and others were disoriented and unbalanced. The coughing continued, and one of them became violently sick over the floor.

***

Willis's mobile gave its characteristic chirp. 'Hello, Jonathan.' There followed a long period of silence while Willis listened to what Jon said.

'When did this happen? You better seal off the boat until it can be thoroughly washed down. And all members of the forensic team will need to be isolated and checked. The immigrants have brought an infection with them from their travels.'

'We might need a tropical medicine expert,' said Jonathan, 'because some of them might have come from hot areas in East Asia.'

'How about you? Did you go on the boat?'

'No. Thank God. I touched the paintings, though, but they were protected behind the panels for most of the journey.'

'If I were you, I'd still get a check-up.'

Jonathan said that a doctor had already checked him out, but it was inconclusive because the doctor said he hadn't seen this mix of symptoms before. There were coughs, sickness, sore throats, and in the last hour, some were having difficulty breathing.

Willis wasn't happy and advised that the crew be kept separately. They would have been in contact long enough to be infected. Whatever the immigrants had, there would have been plenty of time for it to propagate, and the restrictive size of the cabin would have encouraged the contagion to spread.

Jonathan should tell his team not to go home before an expert saw them, just in case they infect their families. This group could have been together for two or three weeks before they arrived in the UK.

Everyone who had been on the marina was self-isolating in the cells at the police station until someone came to give them the once over. Jonathan promised to call Willis as soon as he knew what was happening.

Standing beside him all this time and listening in was Sophie, looking worried. 'I think they will be in isolation for more than a few hours, and I suspect they won't get released for a couple of days at least. It will take that long for any symptoms to manifest themselves.'

'… and the rest,' said Willis. 'Normally, it will take at least four days before any symptoms show.'

***

Two hours later, Willis received a call from Bill Chalmers with instructions to stay away from anyone associated with *The Clipper*. They had isolated the cause as a virus, but which virus was still to be identified. They had alerted the IFS, the Imported Fever Service, and they would advise whether laboratory testing was needed. The United Kingdom Health Security Agency, the UKHSA, in Harlow had been notified and was also investigating, but they suspected that this might be something serious. Just in case, they'd alerted PHE, Public Health England, at the Rare and Imported Pathogens Laboratory, the RIPL, in Porton Down.

'Near Salisbury? They are the big guns, and they were involved with the assumed Russian poisoning of Sergei and Yulia Skripal in March 2018. If they get involved, it will be very serious. Let's hope that it doesn't come to that. God, they run tests for viruses like Ebola, so fingers crossed we won't need them.'

***

The cyber specialists, Georgie Maclean and Johnny White, from MI5 and the Met, respectively, were working well together. They had copied a backup of the dot-gov system and were tearing it apart line by line, and it would be only a matter of time before they uncovered the worm. They were running a program to compare the latest version on the server with an old archived file that was over three months old, and if the plan worked, it would highlight where in the file the change had been made. The search results wouldn't be available instantly, because they would need to eliminate manually all updates loaded between when the archive was created and its current version. Hopefully, they would crack it within the next twenty-four hours.

That sounded like a promising result. But it would only allow them to delete the worm and wouldn't help them find out who was involved in the first case besides Ronnie Merrick.

'Maybe not,' said Chalmers. His boss had said that a 'leader' would have been required. That was a small bit of computer code needed to load the worm, and if they had failed to delete it after the worm was loaded, it might tell them where the worm came from and maybe who had loaded it.

'I can't wait for the next twenty-four hours to pass,' said Willis.

Chalmers told him the confinement period for an unknown virus could be anywhere between fourteen and forty-eight days, but if they identified it, it would be shorter because then they could test for its presence in the blood. He also warned Willis that Porton Down wanted the whole thing kept under wraps to avoid widespread panic. They would make a public announcement once they'd identified the cause.

'I'll look forward to your call tomorrow.'

Willis spent the next thirty minutes passing on Bill's advice to everyone he knew who had investigated the incident on *The Clipper*.

'That's snookered any hope we had of carrying out any investigations,' said Sophie. 'It will be too dangerous until we can find out what the infection is.'

Willis called Jonathan and established contact with the members of the team who were doing the surveillance of the McLellan household, including the MI5 team, whose plan was to hack into the camera system in Kenny McLellan's bedroom. The information came fast and furiously. From the MI5 team, he learned that Kenny had been aware *The Clipper* planned a trip out that night. They'd heard him speaking to Alec Devlin about the trip, but neither mentioned its reason or any details of its cargo. There was a call from a third party that they hadn't identified, because it was from a second mobile that they were unaware existed. The one side of the conversation that they'd heard discussed the delivery of goods to a pub in London. But they never mentioned it by name.

Willis discussed the outline of a plan that he had devised and asked if they could help him. It turned out that they could, so he thanked them very much and said he would call them later.

Willis held two crossed fingers in the air for Sophie to see because he needed some luck for his plan to work. He handed Sophie his phone and asked her to call Mrs McLellan after rehearsing the plan with her. They set off for Clacton-on-Sea amid trepidation about whether their plan had any chance of working.

***

'Kenny's car is still sitting on the drive. We'll need to wait until he leaves.'

'How can you be sure that he *will* leave?' said Sophie.

'He's young. He owns a Porsche. He likes the good life, so he'll go out. I give him half an hour.' Willis glanced at his watch. It read 7:30 p.m.

Courtesy of Mrs Burns, Sophie produced a Thermos flask full of hot steaming coffee. Between their hot breaths and the steaming coffee, the car windows misted up, so Willis opened a window, and a blast of frosty night air hit their faces. He shrugged his shoulders, intimating either we steam up or we get cold. The heat from the coffee was welcoming. At five minutes before 8 p.m., Kenny came out to his car, started the engine and vanished back inside. At exactly 8 p.m., he came out and drove away.

'See, what did I tell you?'

Sophie's answer came in the form of an elbow pushed into Willis's ribcage. She got out of the car, walked to the front door and rang the elaborate bell. Something similar to an embellishment of Westminster Chimes rang out. 'Ah, Sophie, my dear, I didn't expect you to come tonight when you asked to call.'

'I'm sorry if it's inconvenient, but I had to find out how to finish this crochet square that I'm working on. If I just take my hook out, the whole thing will unthread itself. I'm so desperate for your help.'

'Come indoors out of the cold, my dear. Just let me finish watching the end of my programme. I'm a big fan of this soap.'

'There's no hurry. I'll just hang my coat here in the hall while you finish watching.' Sophie placed her coat on the hook, and once she was sure that Mrs McLellan was comfortably seated in front of her telly, she quietly unlatched the front door and opened it a few inches. She then sat beside Mavis until after the theme music for the show had stopped, but not before she had also closed the door to the lounge.

Meanwhile, Willis texted his contact in MI5, and once he received an acknowledgement, he moved into the house and up the stairs. He looked into the left-hand drawer of Kenny's computer desk, where his contact told him he kept the burner phone. He switched it on – shit – it was demanding a password. Willis looked impatiently around, searching for a clue about what it might be. Nothing stood out. He had an idea. He typed in 920419 – the same number that Victor Shaw had used to unlock his phone. Willis realised that Shaw didn't look like he had been born in 1992 – more like 1962. The phone unlocked. Willis scrolled to the owner's profile page and soon found the number of the phone. He entered it beside Kenny's name in his own phone, replaced the phone in the drawer and moved swiftly downstairs and out of the front door, closing it behind him.

When Sophie's mobile pinged, it was the signal that Willis had made it safely in and out of the house.

'I feel such a dummy, Mavis. It was so obvious, so I must apologise for disturbing your viewing.' She rose and walked to the door with Mavis following behind. 'Please, come back again. You're always welcome.' Sophie disappeared out of the door and headed for their car, whose windows were, by this time, well steamed up.

'That's one lonely lady,' said Sophie as she got in and closed the door behind her.

'Yes, for all her wealth, she is very unhappy.' Willis doubted if she and Kenny had a genuine relationship. It's just as well that Kenny hadn't told her he'd discovered Willis in his bedroom. But he wouldn't discover him this time, because his MI5 colleagues had blocked the wireless signals from the cameras with white noise. When he looked at the recording, all Kenny would see would be a lot of white dots dancing on his screen.

Willis frantically keyed in data on his mobile, then he dialled a number and spoke. 'I've just texted you the number of Kenny's burner phone. How long will it take you to get it tapped? Great. I'll wait to see what we catch from this exercise.'

Because Willis had left the engine running, the windows had now complexly cleared of condensation. 'What now?' He turned and looked at Sophie.

'It's gone 8.15 p.m., and we haven't eaten yet.'

'We'll pass the *Clipper Inn* on the way home. We can always stop to see if they've any steak and ale pie tonight.'

***

It was 8.55 p.m. when they reached the pub. Willis's favourite waitress informed him he was just in time for dinner as the last orders were at 9 p.m. They ordered, and she disappeared to get their order completed before everything shut up for the night. From behind the bar, Alec Devlin appeared. 'I'll give you a full refund on the model of my *Clipper*,' he said, 'because I don't like the idea of people supplying faulty models of my lovely boat.'

'It's no trouble at all,' said Willis. 'I've thrown the inner bits away, and I've glued down the deck onto the hull. No one will ever see inside. Why would they want to look, anyway? It's a lovely model, and I'm well pleased with it.'

'That's an excellent idea. Close it up and hide it. I wish I had thought of that.'

'So, were you on *The Clipper* today?'

No, he hadn't been, because he had an accident and broke the rudder. It was in a dry dock being repaired and would likely be there for some time because they needed to bring the parts in from the States.

'That's a downer. I guess we'll see you around the pub more until it's finished?' Your lies are becoming more complicated, thought Willis because there were three stories now: the boat had been broken, it had been stolen, and the truth, it had been impounded by the authorities.

'That's what Helen wants, but I'll find some way of getting out. Here's your meal coming, but you cut it close tonight.'

'We were walking. Weren't we, darling?'

'And got lost.' Sophie snapped at him; she was learning to lie as well as he could.

'Enjoy your meal. I'm pleased that you are happy with the model.' Alec disappeared into the back room, and they could hear him opening boxes, presumably to change the model as per Willis's suggestion.

The meal was excellent as usual, and they finished their drinks in a near-empty pub. By the time they left, the temperature had dropped, and the sky was a myriad of stars. As they walked to the car, it was so cold that the stars stared down without twinkling. Willis couldn't resist giving Sophie yet another astronomy lesson as they crossed the car park.

'Let's get in the car and warm,' said Sophie. 'I don't know how you guys manage it.' Willis was about to explain it was all done indoors nowadays with computers when Sophie put her finger over her mouth, and he took the hint and shut up. He would have plenty of time to indoctrinate her. Eventually, he would convert her.

CHAPTER 19

The following morning the rain was lashing down from the heavens, and all the winter's downfall seemed to be trying to come on the same day. Huge droplets rattled the cottage windows and bounced off the panes. Even Mrs Burns hadn't dared to brave her daily crossing from her cottage to Willis's.

'I guess we're going to have a day at home,' said Sophie. 'There's little point in going out in this kind of weather, but it will mean staying at home and working through Diana's paperwork. There's probably very little we can extract from it now, but there's still twenty-five per cent of it we haven't looked at.'

Willis suggested the bad weather was probably a godsend. There was hardly anyone left to speak to who wasn't either in custody or quarantined. They were at a dead end. Devlin and McLellan were the only two still in circulation. Willis was hoping for a distraction, however short.

It came in the form of a call from Diana. She had heard that *The Clipper* had been impounded, and its crew and illegal cargo of immigrants were under police or other agencies' jurisdictions. She failed to mention the rest of the cargo, the paintings. Bill Chalmers had kept that under wraps, and it hadn't appeared in the general report. Willis brought Diana up to date on the immigrants and the virus but said nothing about the stolen canvases. He decided the fewer people who knew, the better because it was the kind of knowledge that could put them in danger. Diana hung up after Willis's briefing.

He turned to Sophie. 'The discovery of the stolen artwork is new information of which we were unaware when we were looking through the papers.'

Sophie couldn't see how it could have anything to do with the threats to Diana.

Not that Willis suspected a direct mention of the artwork, but there might be a reference to something else that made little sense without the knowledge it existed. He didn't know what he meant, but he'd recognise it when he saw it.

The suggestion came from Sophie that they blu-tac the spreadsheets back up on the wall. They contained nearly everything they considered important. Something might pop out and attract their attention, and it might also concentrate their thoughts.

Once the sheets were in place, some connections they had discovered made more sense. Knowing that it was Kenny McLellan who had harassed Diana allowed Willis to draw a line connecting the two names. He also drew a broken line between McLellan and Rob Moore. If he had been harassing Diana, it would be because he was interested in keeping the innocent Rob Moore in jail to prevent any further investigations into his brother's murder. Why he should want to prevent enquiries into his brother's death continued to puzzle Willis.

'Look at this, Brad.' While Willis had been studying the wall charts, Sophie had been skimming through some papers in the box that remained. 'It's a memo between Edward Young, Diana's solicitor, and someone called Archibald Pendleton-Smyth, a senior civil servant. He's copied him in with some of Diana's movements.'

Willis took the memo and read it. He pulled out the next bundle of memos from where Sophie had removed the first set. 'If you look at these sheets, it would suggest that there was some kind of plan in place to provide Diana with extra security. Pendleton-Smyth makes mention here of the allocation of someone being assigned to her for an extended period, several years ago.' He scribbled 'To be followed up' on the sheet and attached it to the chart with the other notes. 'Let's settle down and finish going through this last box of paperwork.' Within minutes the carpet was, once again, covered in papers. One advantage of the poor weather was that there was no fear of Mrs Burns arriving and telling them off for the mess they were making. Sophie found another note sent to the same man. It updated him on Diana's progress in trying to get Rob Moore's release investigated. Willis pinned it on the chart beside the other one. They spent another two hours reading the remaining contents of the box, but nothing caught their attention.

'Ye've messed up all the carpet again.' Mrs Burns was standing with her arms crossed like a school teacher witnessing a wrong-doing.

'I will clear everything away in five minutes, Mrs Burns. We've just finished.' Willis stood and carried the box into the far corner of the room. 'Does this mean that the rain has stopped?'

'It stopped ages ago. It was only a heavy downpour. Didn't ye hear yon thunder?'

'That's great news, Mrs Burns. You'll have the house to yourself because we are about to head out now the rain has stopped.'

'Are we?' asked Sophie.

Willis nodded as he lifted his mobile and dialled. 'Can we come and visit you, Edward? We will be in the area about mid-afternoon if you are available.'

Edward suggested they come that evening to join Diana and him for dinner.

'I'd rather not,' said Willis, 'because I need to discuss something with you on your own, and it would be better if Diana didn't hear. See you later.' Once he had noted the postcode Edward provided for his office, Willis hung up and headed for the kitchen. He pulled out a pan from the cupboard and prepared lunch.

***

By 3 p.m., they had arrived in Colchester. They drove along Lexden Road, turned left at Southway into Church Street, then after passing the converted church that had become the Colchester Arts Centre, they turned into North Hill, finally stopping where the satnav demanded.

'I can't see it,' said Willis. He walked up and down, but there was no solicitor's office in sight. 'I wonder?' He opened the door to a reception area of a *Regus* office. This company provided short-term, small, temporary rental offices for companies that were transient or in the process of being formed. Willis looked at the list of offices on the facing wall, and Edward Young, Solicitors, was listed the third from the bottom. They headed for the elevator and pressed the button for the third floor. When the doors opened, they walked into a spacious corridor with two glass-paned doors. The one on the left read, 'Edward Young Solicitor' in black letters. Willis pressed a button, a solenoid buzzed, and the door clicked open. Edward met them as soon as they entered.

'Sorry. I should have warned you I was in a temporary office.' He said it had become very much part of his everyday life that he'd forgotten to mention it, and other than Diana, no one else ever visited him there. His main office was in London, but he hadn't been there since he came to help Diana. He walked ahead. 'I have a coffee machine, but it doesn't make great coffee. I'd offer you a cup, but I remember you are very fussy about how you take your coffee.'

'A cup would be great, Edward,' said Sophie, 'but I am sure Brad will resist.' As the paper cup was placed in front of Sophie, Willis nodded and grimaced.

'Now, what's all the secrecy about?' Edward was supping his coffee with relish. 'What's so secret we can't discuss it in front of Diana?'

Willis leaned over and handed Edward the two memos they had recovered from the box Edward had sent to the cottage some days earlier.

Edward gave a long noisy sigh and dropped them onto his desk. 'I thought I'd removed all the indications of this from the boxes I sent. These ones must have slipped through.' Edward explained he hadn't wanted Diana to know he had put protection in place for her. She would have hated it. She would have complained that it would impede her day-to-day work as an MP. As it turned out, protection was in place for two and a half years without Diana even noticing. Edward had only cancelled it about six months ago but feared he might need to re-introduce it now the frequency of her threatening emails had increased.

'Who is this guy with the upper-class name?'

'Archibald Pendleton-Smyth is a very senior in the civil service. He knows which strings to pull to get things done. He's a friend of my family and gets involved when any head of state visits the UK, so it was logical to get him involved.' This was what Willis expected would be the case, and he agreed he wouldn't tell Diana what Edward had done or was about to do if he re-introduced personal protection for her. 'So, why don't you still come for dinner this evening. I'll call Diana and tell her I had to call you for some reason, and we'd met.'

'We'd love to,' said Sophie before Willis intervened. 'We women have a lot to catch up on, and there's no time like the present.'

***

By the time they reached Diana's, the smell of roast duck had filled the house. Sitting in the lounge waiting for them were three glasses, overfilled with Crozes-Hermitage. 'I'm drinking this like coffee,' Willis teased and took a sip from the nearest glass.

'It tastes a lot better than coffee—' Diana stopped herself. 'Sorry. I forgot you are a coffee aficionado. Perhaps you would prefer coffee, Brad?'

'Certainly not. This is far superior to coffee, but it's not possible to drink red wine as often as I choose to drink coffee.'

'Well recovered, Dr Willis,' said Diana as she came over and kissed him on the cheek. 'I have lots to tell you about my birth parents, but that can wait until after we've eaten.'

The meal was delicious. Willis and Carole's favourite meal had always been duck, but he decided it better not to mention the fact to Diana. Sophie's and his favourite meal was now pizza, and it wasn't the time to explain the history of how that came about either.

They settled down in the lounge with its two long, comfortable settees. 'Right,' said Diana, her voice full of enthusiasm. 'I have made some interesting discoveries.' She'd found an auction stamp on the back of the painting of Mr and Mrs Ford. She looked up at the painting and held out her mobile, so everyone could see a picture she'd taken of the stamp. So far, she'd found out where they lived, what her dad did as a profession, and why they sold the painting. It was a really, really sad story. She explained that her mother had been diagnosed with cancer that later turned out to be terminal. Her dad had sold off as many things from the house as possible to pay for treatment from the States that promised results. It hadn't worked. 'Shortly after my mother passed—' Diana stopped for a few seconds to recover her composure, '… when my mother passed, my dad's death followed not that long afterwards. I like to think it was from a broken heart, but he was driving and couldn't have been concentrating, so he still could have been thinking of mum. But dad crashed his car and was killed outright.' She still did not know how the painting got into the hands of a succession of her foster parents. That would be her next task, she added, wiping a tear that had dripped from her left eye.

'Where did your parents come from?' asked Sophie, trying to move the conversation to something more positive.

'They came from Oxfordshire, but they moved to Cambridge when they married. I can only assume his work took him there.'

'You've done very well,' said Willis. 'You'd make an excellent detective.'

'I didn't do it on my own. My secretary is into researching her family history as a hobby, and she took some time off to help me.'

Both Sophie and Willis agreed they couldn't wait to hear the next instalment.

Diana disappeared and returned with a wad of paper. 'Not everything is good news.' She handed the papers to Willis. Sheet after sheet contained threats against Diana. He read each one and then asked if she would make photocopies of each of them.

Once she was in her study, Willis turned to Edward and Sophie. 'These threats came from someone else. They're different from the earlier ones – unless; that is, the writer has taken a crash course on spelling and grammar.' He pointed out several examples of the word 'whose'. Each one was written correctly, unlike in the earlier emails, and the grammar was perfect.

Edward announced he was certainly going to re-start the protection for Diana. Things were getting serious.

'Agreed,' said Willis. 'We won't mention it to her.'

'We should be able to get a handle on who sent these. People have been working on the problem since we last met.'

At that point, Diana returned and handed Willis the copies she had made. 'Let's change the subject and enjoy the rest of the evening.' Edward held his thumbs up high, and everyone followed suit.

After giving Sophie a quick nod to follow behind her, Diana stood and wandered into the kitchen.

'You're going to tell me how you and Edward are getting on? I hope.' Sophie smiled and stood close to Diana. 'No one will overhear from in here.'

Diana explained things weren't all good. 'Oh yes, we are getting on pretty well, but Edward always pulls back every time an opportunity arises to become intimate. I suspect that Edward might not be committed to our relationship.'

Sophie put her arm around Diana and said she needed to remember that Edward had been very shy not so many days ago. It had taken ages for him to even put his arm around her on the settee, let alone pick up the courage to kiss her.

'I know,' said Diana. 'We snog on the settee every evening, and his shyness seems to have disappeared, but there hasn't even been a hint of wanting to try anything more physical than snogging.'

'Give him time,' said Sophie, 'it will come. Now, come back into the lounge and have a drink.'

***

The evening proceeded entertainingly. Sophie kept her eyes on Diana and Edward and sent her a wink every time that Edward snuggled up amorously beside her. Finally, they settled down and relaxed, but not before Willis had updated Diana on the latest news about *The Clipper* and the immigrants' infections. Once again, he left out any mention of the paintings – Edward hadn't heard about them, and he thought it better that it remained so.

About 11.15 p.m., Sophie stretched her legs and suggested to Willis that it was time for them to go. She collected her coat, said they would see themselves out, and left Edward and Diana sitting snuggled up on the settee.

Once they were underway, Willis turned to Sophie. 'I'd better follow up those emails first thing tomorrow. They are much more aggressive than the previous ones, and they are longer. They go into detail about what will happen to Diana if she doesn't desist from her investigations. There is also a good chance that the team working on the dot-gov email system might have turned something up by now. I also plan to go into my office in Cambridge tomorrow as there's something I need to get advice on.'

CHAPTER 20

Driving into Cambridge can be difficult during the morning rush hour, but Willis used a back double he'd discovered that bypassed most of the heaviest traffic. He drove past his usual office at the Institute of Astronomy and parked in a space he found close to a large red brick building several hundred yards farther along the road. He took the lift to the top floor and visited a little-known department on the south side of the building.

Theresa Quigg was a tall woman of ample proportion that Willis had met many years ago on an assignment to South America. She specialised in profiling terrorists and criminals. On his last visit, she had successfully identified the writer of a blackmail letter with such uncanny accuracy that Willis had identified its sender immediately. Willis held no such high hopes for this visit, but he would welcome any help that Theresa's skills could provide.

'Dr Willis,' were the only words she uttered as he approached her desk.

Once again, Willis required help – any help he could find. He dropped a tin of *Quality Street* chocolates noisily on her desk. 'Pretty please, Theresa – HELP!'

'You remembered to bring the correct currency this time. You know I can always be bribed.' She tore the strip of Sellotape from around the tin's lid and prised it open.

'Leave the bribe alone. You haven't provided information yet.' Willis made a joking gesture of pulling the tin out of her reach.

'There's a charge for my quotes, too,' she said, pulling the box back to the centre of her desk. 'I prefer the green triangular ones. I'll eat those first while I listen to your wild story. It is wild, isn't it? It usually is.' She pushed the chocolates back in Willis's direction and nodded her head, signalling that it was okay for him to take one.

He stretched over and selected a chocolate, taking care to avoid the green ones. 'This time, the story is unimportant. What I need is a rough outline of the type of character who might have written some threatening emails – his background – his education.' From his case, he removed a manilla folder and slid it across the table.

'Why are you so sure that it's a man who wrote them?'

'I'm not, but I'm hoping you can confirm either way for me.'

Theresa pulled out a pad from a drawer in her desk and started asking a series of questions, such as the gender of the person receiving the threats, their age, the part of the country from where Willis expected the emails might have come, and the age of the recipient. Willis supplied as many answers as he could to Theresa's questions but warned that some of his answers might be approximate. The only answer he knew with certainty was Diana's age since she shared her birth date with Carole. The closest he could give as to where he thought the emails had originated was East Anglia or London.

He apologised if his answers weren't helpful, but they were the only data he had to go on at the moment.

'There's enough here for me to make a start. I can tell you right off from the phrasing and wording that they were almost certainly composed by a man.'

Willis recorded the distinction she was inferring between being composed and being sent. He made a mental note and enquired what other information she could garner from a quick read.

Theresa continued to describe the sender by saying that he was highly educated, a confident individual with a university education and from London or the west home counties.

Certain words that he used excluded him from coming from Essex or East Anglia, and he was over fifty years old.

Willis challenged her on how she could tell his age.

Certain phrases came in and out of fashion. There were a few revealing 'tells' that placed him in that generation. Also, despite the emails being threatening, he showed some deference to the fact he was writing to a woman. His wording came across as threatening, but the use of aggressive words was restricted. Yes – she was sure he was definitely over fifty – no doubt at all. But that was all she could give him today. She'd need more time to study the individual word usage and frequency. To do that, she'd scan every email into her computer and run a comprehensive analysis. If he got out of her hair, she could let him have the final results early tomorrow morning. Willis was about to say that tomorrow would be great when she added, 'But, it will cost you more than a tin of chocs. I'll expect you to take me for a slap-up lunch in Cambridge.' Willis held out his hand, and they shook on the agreement.

Instead of driving back to his cottage, Willis headed to his office at the Institute, where he got on the phone with Georgie Maclean, the MI5 cyber specialist. There was a decision he'd had to make whether to call Maclean or Johnny White, Jonathan Swallow's expert. It was always better to cultivate new contacts, he thought, hence the reason for calling Georgie. After all, he would already have the perfect 'in' if he ever needed Johnny's help. He could get it via Sophie's Uncle Jonathan. If nothing else, Willis's actions were always tactical.

From the very beginning, Georgie was hedging his bets. He was evasive when Willis questioned him on his findings. Willis would get nowhere speaking to Georgie. This was an obvious cover-up, so he called Bill Chalmers, who had a direct line with Georgie's boss in MI5, to request his intervention. It was imperative Willis discover the source of the emails. Bill agreed to call his contact to see what he could do but warned that 'MI5 is MI5', and they held power all of their own. Willis thanked him, and Bill promised to call him back when he had any news. Being the impatient person Willis was, he immediately called his second contact, Johnny White.

Johnny was much more co-operative. He wasn't surprised that MI5 didn't want to release the information. They would need to keep what they'd found under wraps for the time being, at least. He didn't know where they had traced the emails to. Even he had been pushed out of the loop when they'd got close, but he could tell Willis it was someone very high in Westminster. Which department it was, he had no idea, but it believed it needed to protect the sender.

Willis wasn't surprised. If something like this were to hit social media, it would go viral and embarrass the Government. He thanked Johnny for the information and asked if he found out anything else, would he call to tell him? Johnny agreed but added that he thought the people in charge had permanently disenfranchised him from the investigation. If another line of enquiry opened or anything changed, he'd let Willis know.

***

'If you think I have any answers already, get lost.' Theresa Quigg was not pleased Willis called her so soon after leaving her office.

'Keep your hat on,' snapped Willis equally aggressively. 'I have some more information that might save you a load of work. The person who sent the emails is—'

'STOP!' She said she didn't want to hear it. Any additional information he gave her would influence her decisions and result in him getting an inaccurate assessment of the sender. All the information she required was running on her system. To get a reliable result, she used standard inputs and nothing else because the result must be reproducible every time she ran it. If there were any inaccuracies, she could correct them later, and additional inputs would screw the algorithm up to the point that it became useless. She told him to get off the line and book a table for them for lunch tomorrow.

The last thing Willis heard was a chuckle from Theresa as she disconnected his call. That was him put in his place.

***

By the time Willis arrived back at his cottage, he was twitching and irascible. He was making progress in small steps – tiny steps and much smaller than he would have preferred. Next on his list to call was DI Jonathan Swallow, which was more to update Jonathan rather than in any hope of gleaning new information. 'I'm fine,' said Jonathan in answer to Willis's question as to how he was doing. 'But…' there was a long pause, 'others are not so lucky.'

'Are the others seriously ill?'

'The immigrants are in quarantine. People from Porton Down are all over the place. They are still investigating but are highly suspicious that the virus is a strain of the Nipah virus. The main reservoir of the virus are bats found in tropical regions in the Far East. It's carried, not unlike Ebola, from central Africa and, from what I'm hearing, is every bit as deadly.'

'I have heard of that virus – it is particularly nasty. Transmission is unpredictable.'

Person to person transmission could take place, but it was inconsistent between outbreaks. Close and direct, unprotected contact between people with the virus was a major transmission risk. In Kerala, in 2018, they recorded it as the most dominant method of transmission. The time that this group had spent in the confines of *The Clipper,* plus whatever time they'd travelled cramped together before that, would almost certainly have ensured they all caught it. The worse news was that the incubation period was typically within four to fourteen days, but, on one occasion, forty-five days had been reported. That meant Jonathan was likely to be in isolation for at least that long. What Willis didn't tell him was that, for those who showed the major symptoms, the mortality rate was between forty per cent and seventy-five per cent. There was no known cure. The result, in serious cases, was meningitis and encephalitis, both inflammations of the brain and usually resulted in death. Willis was confident that Jonathan and the forensic team would be safe. Their contact time had been minimal; however, he wasn't so sure about Roger Lowden's prognosis. Willis told Jonathan to keep away from anyone with flu-like symptoms, stomach problems or fever.

'No chance of that, Brad. Everyone here is in solitary confinement. I'll be as bored as hell, but I'm happier to be safe than sorry.'

'Does your team still have eyes on Devlin's boat in case anyone tries to recover the paintings?'

'Of course, it does. My phone's working fine, so I'm still able to manage things from here, but I fear if what you tell me is accurate, the powers-that-be will prevent anyone from boarding the boat, anyway.'

'… but the potential boarders won't know about the embargo and will try to board behind the backs of any security attachment. The security patrol won't be expecting anyone to have an interest in the boat now that it's been impounded. With many millions of pounds of art treasure hidden on board, it will be irresistible for them not to try to get it back. So, you had better have a second group watching the boat.'

After making a promise that he would keep Jonathan in the picture, Willis hung up and immediately called Bill Chalmers for the second time that day. He was in the throes of giving Chalmers a rollicking for not telling him about the seriousness of the situation with the virus when Chalmers interrupted him. 'I wasn't told. This is the first I've heard of any virus.'

After Willis told Chalmers which virus they suspected, its symptoms and the end prognosis, Bill gave a long slow whistle. Silence reigned for several seconds before he spoke. 'This is too important for even the Metropolitan Police to be told. As it's a matter of national security, it will be on a need-to-know basis only, and you had better not spread what you know around, or the men in dark suits will come and take you into custody.'

Willis hadn't thought of that. He might be on sticky ground, having told Jonathan, especially if he repeated it. He made a mental note to call him and tell him to stay schtum.

***

From the corner of his eye, Willis saw sunlight coming from the front door of the cottage. 'It's only me,' shouted Sophie, 'I've been shopping. You might come and give me a lift in with the bags.' He jumped to his feet, grabbed the last two remaining bags from the car and carried them into the kitchen. 'You were out for so long I did something productive while I was waiting for you. Shopping was the obvious choice.'

'What did you buy besides food?'

'Some pantie hose and a new pair of shoes.'

'Any more shoes, and you'll need to change your name to Imelda Marcos.' Sophie's upstairs wardrobe was full of shoes. Every time she opened the door to get something out, she was met with a shower of miscellaneous shoes spilling out onto the floor. 'Don't you think you have enough?'

'A woman can never have enough shoes – anyway – these are the first pair I've bought since we married – assuming we are married, that is.'

'Okay.' Willis conceded. He'd give her that. He guessed he must have as many textbooks as she had pairs of shoes. But, *they* stacked a lot neater in rows on a shelf, not scattered all over the inside base of a wardrobe.

'Make a coffee and relax. I've bought you some lemon drizzle cake to help you relax.'

While he considered what and how he should tell Sophie about the danger her uncle might be in, Willis put on the coffee percolator and scratched his head, trying to improve his concentration.

Once they were seated, Willis still hadn't worked out the best way to impart the worrying news to Sophie, so he took a bite from his lemon drizzle cake as a proxy for breaking the news to her. Eventually, he finished, having taken the smallest possible bites from the cake and sipping his coffee as slowly as he could. The unavoidable moment of truth was upon him. Before he could speak, Sophie said, 'You look worried. Have you had a bad day?' That was the 'in' that Willis needed.

'I've had some bad news. Come and sit over here, so I can tell you.'

Sophie's face turned sallow, and she dropped onto the settee beside him. Willis related to her what he had discovered during the day. He described the illness that was partly diagnosed, saying that he suspected all the immigrants had contracted it. After that, he told her about the name of the suspected virus and its incubation period – all of this was to postpone, as long as possible, his final sentence. 'Uncle Jonathan was briefly in contact with the migrants before they took them into custody, and there is a possibility that he might have been infected. They have, therefore, put him into quarantine. He is in isolation and might well be for up to forty-five days until they can be sure that he isn't carrying the virus.' Willis felt Sophie's fingers tighten around his arm. He quickly added that, from current best evidence, the virus wouldn't have been transmitted if he had been in contact with infected people for only a short period. Uncle Jonathan would have been in contact for a very short time if indeed he had been in contact at all. Everything they were doing was precautionary only. The entire team, including the forensics guys, had been quarantined.

Her fingers slowly relaxed, allowing the blood to flow once more into his arm. 'I understand. I also agree it isn't too serious yet. We'll stay in contact with Uncle Jonathan daily until we are sure that he is clear. I'm certain that he is.'

Willis realised how much he loved Sophie. Her strength was incomparable with that of any other woman he had ever known.

'Is there any more lemon drizzle cake?'

CHAPTER 21

As the sun set and the sky transformed from dusk into true darkness, two short oriental men stepped out of their stretched limo. They had set the satnav to deliver them to their target postcode in SW1P. One wore a black suit and the other, a white one. They walked the short distance to Thames House, which had the innocuous address of 11 Millbank, London. While they waited, they stood on the opposite side of the road and surveyed its architecture. Three dark double doors stood centre stage and contrasted against the white brick of the building, while four globe lights illuminated the seven steps that led up to the main entrance.

'Not long now, Mr Yin.'

'Only minutes to go, Mr Yang. I am ready. I have it safely in my hand.'

'Good. It's dark, so it's your turn, Mr Yin.'

'It will be my pleasure, Mr Yang.'

The man in the black suit glanced at his watch. 'Any minute now. I have timed him, and he operates like clockwork.'

'It must be boring to be so predictable,' said the white suit.

'That's one thing no one can accuse us of being.'

'Certainly not, Mr Yin.'

The left-hand door opened, and a wheelchair exited, carrying a ruddy haired individual. Its owner steered the chair down the left ramp, specially constructed to allow the stairs to be avoided, and released his grip on the drive wheel, allowing the chair to free-wheel down the slope.

The black suit took a step forward and stopped beside a lamp post.

When the wheelchair reached the bottom of the slope, it turned left, and its owner's hands once again drove the vehicle ahead.

A black outline followed his progress along the pavement, keeping its distance while the other member of the team made his way back to the limousine. When the black suit reached the pedestrian crossing, he paused and slipped his right hand from his pocket. The orange beacon of the crossing illuminated the red label on a glass syringe, making it contrast against his black sleeve.

The wheelchair swivelled and faced the crossing, and its driver looked right and left, waiting for the oncoming traffic to stop and grant him access. After three vehicles had passed, a small blue Volkswagen stopped to let him cross. His red hair nodded in gratitude to the accommodating driver, and he heaved on both wheels to drive him across swiftly. As he mounted the ramp on the far side, he turned sharply left and headed down the hill. He had only just released his hands from the wheel to allow the chair to coast down the slope when a hand reached over his shoulder. Pain shot down his neck and arm. He turned and stared into an oriental face as his eyes glazed over, and his head fell limply onto his left shoulder. The dark figure took a step back as the wheelchair accelerated down the hill and careered into a knot of workers coming from the opposite direction. A group standing by a bus stop scattered, amid screams and shouts, as the chair continued down the hill. The chair gave a wild swerve to the left, bouncing off a bus shelter, then a bigger one to the right before crashing into a metal railing and toppling its occupant onto the concrete walkway.

The man in black ignored the crowd that collected around the prostrated body lying at their feet. He turned, smiled and walked slowly to join his associate in the limo.

'That was easy, Mr Yin.'

'It always is when it's well planned, Mr Yang. Our employer should be well pleased with our result.'

'Indeed, I expect he'll have more work for us before long.'

A white sleeve pushed the automatic gearstick into drive, and the long car moved smoothly away with the dignity of a hearse, revealing the double yellow lines it had been covering. No one in the city would notice it was displaying a set of bogus registration plates.

The sound of two men chuckling faded as the vehicle sped along Millbank.

'He pays us well, and he's paid us even more generously to have his target terminated outside the offices of MI5.'

CHAPTER 22

Even before his morning alarm sounded, Theresa Quigg was on the phone. 'I thought I'd get to you before the rest of your day takes charge, and you get distracted.'

'I would have preferred to have slept a little longer,' said Willis, his voice still coarse from being awakened too early. He asked what she had for him on this sunny day.

'Nothing that I can give you in writing. We'll need to meet, face to face, because what I will tell you is for your ears only and is very sensitive and dangerous.' Theresa said there would be an abbreviated email on its way to him after they'd met, and it would summarise all her findings, but she wanted to speak to him about a few extra things she'd discovered that she had no intention of putting in an email. If he had ordered a table for lunch at the usual place, she'd meet him there at noon – it was better not to leave it any longer. His mobile went silent as she abruptly hung up.

'Who was that, sweetheart?' asked Sophie as she turned around and put her nose next to Willis's on the pillow.

'It was an old and very useful friend from my undergraduate days.' Willis told Sophie he was due to meet Theresa for lunch but was afraid that he'd have to go alone.

'So, this is one of your ex-girlfriends, I assume? How tall is she?'

He said she was a very intelligent lady but not one that he'd choose to meet socially. The alarm on his phone sounded, and Willis reached out and switched it off. He'd need to call the restaurant to bring the time forward to noon, but it wouldn't be open this early. 'What shall we do for the next hour?'

Sophie switched off her bedside light and nuzzled up close. The warmth of their bodies intermingled for the next forty-five minutes.

***

Well before the due time, Willis was impatiently sitting at their table in the restaurant. He repeatably looked at his watch, hoping Theresa would appear earlier than expected, but it was ten past noon before he saw Theresa's outline enter the swing doors. The waiter pointed in the general direction where Willis was sitting, and she headed over. Theresa was usually a cheerful person, but her smile was missing as a waiter tucked the chair under her knees.

'Which wine would you like?'

She shook her head. The wine could wait until after they'd chatted.

Another waiter came over and hovered, expecting to collect an order. Willis asked if he could give them fifteen minutes. He gave a curt nod and vanished. 'This is very intriguing. Whatever you've discovered sounds important.'

Theresa frowned. She suspected that he and Ms Bishop might be in danger. She'd be as precise as possible, considering the science and art of the analysis she'd completed. And she suggested he didn't take notes but confine everything she'd tell him to memory. He'd get an email containing the mundane stuff, but it would be better if she gave him the serious stuff verbally. That way, there would be no record of their communication.

Willis raised his eyebrows in anticipation and gave a minuscule nod in agreement.

'Okay. Prepare yourself for some surprises.' Theresa leaned forward until her head was nearly at the centre of the round table. 'I have already given you a rough outline of the person I suspect wrote the emails, but there's more, much more.' Theresa explained that the writer of the emails had been educated at Oxford, was or had been involved with government at a fairly high level, and had a direct link with the Cabinet Office. The technical vocabulary that the writer used was compatible with having spent time with Cabinet ministers and probably even the Prime Minister. Theresa digressed to say she was concerned that Willis might be getting himself in too deeply because the person she was describing would be a powerful man who would have powerful allies. She took a deep breath before her next revelation. 'He is likely unmarried, and I am about ninety per cent certain that he is gay.' She wasn't certain, he had to understand, but she suspected it was highly likely. Some phrases that he used while writing to a female, Ms Bishop, suggest that was the case. 'If I were you, I would use this last fact as additional information and not as a prima facie fact. On some occasions, I have been known to be wrong. There was one example in 1995—'

'Okay, I've got the point. This is dynamite. I must say that I'm not surprised. There is other information taking me in that direction – not about the fact that he might be gay – but about his affiliation to government.'

She repeated that he was getting into a very dangerous position. Any threat to this person would cause a reaction so powerful that Willis would be swallowed up in what followed. She should tell him to keep his head down but knew better than advise that. 'Be VERY careful, Brad.'

Willis spotted the waiter hovering again. 'Is it time to order, or are there more surprises to come?'

'Don't you think that's enough for one day? If you carry on, your life will be in danger. I'm serious, Brad. You're in deep this time.'

'White or red?'

'White. It's too early in the day for me to drink red.'

Willis signalled to the waiter for the wine list and menu. After they'd ordered, they reminisced about their wilder days on campus. She asked what happened to the nice girl he was seeing back then? What was her name? Sophia? They had been very close.

'Sophie – Sophie was her name. I married her. We live locally in Madingley.'

'Well, I'll be... I always suspected that you were right for each other. Kids?'

Willis said they had only been married about a year, so no kids, but that was a long story and best kept for another occasion. He added; however, they were planning a second wedding celebration soon, and Theresa would certainly be top of his list to receive an invitation. It was the first time he'd seen Theresa smile since she arrived.

***

Once lunch was over, Willis rushed back to Madingley to read his email from Theresa, in case there was something in it she had overlooked during their two conversations. He skimmed the email. Theresa had been thorough. Willis could hear the conversation repeating in his head, with her highlighting the more mundane facts. He had safely tucked away the verbal report she'd given before lunch in a separate part of his memory. Willis shared his new information with Sophie and stressed the dangers that Theresa thought they were in. All he got in return was a shrug of her shoulders and a 'what's new' comment. He got more reaction when he informed her he had invited Theresa to their wedding celebration. 'Good. I'll see what she looks like.' She pulled him close and pecked his cheek. 'That's all you're getting. I am exhausted after our physical efforts this morning.'

Willis dropped onto the settee and called Bill Chalmers. 'I have some news for you. I got some information back from my profiler.' He relayed everything that Theresa had told him during lunch.

'We're getting into some deep water. I have some information to tell you, and then it'll be obvious why I make that claim. On his way home after work yesterday, Georgie Maclean was murdered.'

He told Willis someone had given him a lethal injection as he left the MI5 building to go home. He had died in minutes, in full view of the public, but no one had reported seeing a fucking thing. What was almost more worrying than his murder was how his killer had found out he was working on the dot-gov system. This information had been shared only on a need-to-know basis. This supported Willis's profiler's opinion that someone very high up was involved.

Willis felt physically sick. For someone to be murdered outside of the MI5 building is so audacious that it beggars belief. What arrogance. He walked over to his drinks cabinet and poured himself a large brandy. 'This means we close ranks and tell no one what we're up to. Even using our mobiles could be dangerous. Haven't I read somewhere that WhatsApp is encrypted? Using that might help, but even a government might crack WhatsApp if it targeted it. We will need to keep communications to a minimum – talk only when we have to – and that will restrict us immensely.'

'Agreed,' said Bill, 'but if we go off the books, it will hamper how well we can operate. Access to support will become difficult, but we have done something like this before.'

Later that afternoon, Bill was due to meet with his boss, and he would have a chat with her to hear what she would say. Only if she thought it safe would they bring the Commissioner of the Met into the loop.

'Won't she get into deep crap if she doesn't inform the Commissioner?'

'You bet she will, but that might be necessary, given the circumstances. As long as she records her actions and puts the records in a secure place where she can recover them afterwards, she should be covered.'

'Okay, next time I call, it will be on WhatsApp.' Willis hung up and dropped his mobile on the coffee table. The next thing was to decide whether to call Jonathan. He was certain that Jonathan Swallow was one of the good guys but worried that he might expose him to danger, given that he was in quarantine and possibly vulnerable. Fuck it. He'd call him.

'I'd better keep my mobile fully charged,' said Jonathan. 'You're calling me a lot. Luckily, I've borrowed an iPhone charger from the staff.'

Only a few minutes passed before Willis had relayed his findings and reported on his conversation with Chalmers.

Jonathan sounded seriously worried. Long pauses interrupted his conversation as he responded to Willis and agreed that going off the books was the only way to proceed. He was worried that his conversations might not remain confidential once he had spoken to his team; therefore, he would ensure he made only the lowest level of information available to them. Clearly, it worried him to hold things back from his men, but if he told one member, the entire team would know, and control would be lost.

'I have something to tell you,' he paused again, his voice unsteady, 'the medical investigation team moved Roger Lowden just after lunch because he's developed some of the advanced symptoms of the virus.'

'If you are worried, don't be. Lowden spent hours on board *The Clipper* close to the infected immigrants. He was bound to get it. But I am surprised that his infection has developed this soon. You had little or no contact, so the chances of you contacting anything are infinitesimal. So, don't worry. Your confinement is only precautionary.'

'I hope so.' But Jonathan didn't sound convinced. 'I had my laptop delivered today, so I will do some searches to see what I uncover. While I am in here, it is unlikely that anyone will hack my personal account.'

Although not one hundred per cent convinced, Willis agreed it would be safe. If he cut off every means of communication, no progress would ever get made. Some risk-taking was necessary. As soon as he'd hung up, Sophie came and sat with him in silence, each staring into the other's eyes, sharing their worry but saying nothing.

***

It was clear that the group of Willis, Chalmers and now, Swallow would have to be very careful. Every conversation they had would need to be as secure as possible, and even if the Commissioner got involved, there would be no guarantee that they would make any progress. It surprised and disappointed him to know that senior members of government departments had so much apparent power and could get away with so much. His mobile rang and interrupted his thoughts.

'Hello, Diana, give me some good news, please.'

'I have some great news for you. I have been given a role in the Government. It's a non-ministerial role, but it's a rung up the ladder. It's only a junior position but a start. My contribution has been recognised.'

Willis's heart sank in his chest. This could be a ploy to bring Diana under control – to observe her. 'Which department will you be responsible for?'

'Her Majesty's Revenue and Customs.' Pride emanated as she spoke each word.

Willis's heart sank even lower. Was he being overly suspicious, or was Diana's appointment engineered, so that somebody could see and control her actions, maybe to keep her so busy that she couldn't continue to follow up on Rob Moore's case? If any department could keep track of smuggling, Revenue and Customs would be it. In the short term, Diana wouldn't be in any danger. That was Willis's assessment, and he hoped, to God, he was right. If he weren't, the consequences would be unthinkable. This was a big step for Diana, so he had better not stand in her way. 'Congratulations! Well done! You deserve it. You must tell me how you get on. When do you start?'

'I have started. I am due to go into the office tomorrow to pick up a portfolio of urgent tasks. At long last, I have something to get my teeth into.'

Willis wished her good luck and advised her she had better have an early night. Tomorrow she would need to be bright and bushy-tailed for her first day. He hoped her memory was good; she'd need to remember a lot of new names.

She told him that was one thing she was good at. Diana met so many people during the weekly surgeries in her constituency that she got great practice. She would chat later but thanked him for his good wishes, after which she hung up.

Willis was about to ask her the name of her new boss and kicked himself for failing to do so. He would ask the next time they spoke. By then, Diana would have learned a lot more about her new role and department.

'That's great news for Diana,' said Sophie, having heard every word of the conversation.

'Yes. It is,' Willis said slowly and deliberately, clipping each word as he spoke.

'You don't sound very confident.'

'It's nothing. It's only me. I suspect everything that moves, but I am sure everything will be fine. She's a very capable lady, and nobody's fool.'

Sophie reminded Willis what he'd heard about Roger Lowden's deterioration in health. In reality, she was searching for reassurance that her uncle was still safe. He squeezed her arm, 'I haven't had so much confidence in something for such a very long time.'

She revealed the surprise that she'd baked homemade pizza for dinner. Willis rolled his eyes. 'You're crap at making pizzas from scratch. Every time you try, something goes wrong. Either you burn the pastry around the crust, or the whole thing is soggy.' He wasn't disappointed. With great care, he removed a piece of pizza from somewhere near the centre, avoiding the soggy bits and cut it into segments. 'I'll still be hungry after this, so we had better get the cheeseboard out to fill the gap. Anyway, I prefer pizzas brought in. It reminds me of our university days.'

Sophie snuggled up close to him and kissed him on his cheek but not before biting his ear until he screamed.

CHAPTER 23

The building looked sad. Its dark orange walls needed a thorough clean. The doors had, at one time, been white. Now they were a deep yellow due to lack of care. It was a building no one expected to use, so they had allowed its maintenance to lapse, and it had very much fallen into disrepair. As the officer showed Willis into the observation room, its door squeaked, and he had to put his weight against it to get it to open. Inside, it reminded Willis of a police interrogation room – on the observer's side, that was – except that there was no one-way mirror. Instead, an eight-foot by a three-foot, double glazed sheet of glass separated him and the patient. On the wall, immediately to the right of the window, hung an old plastic telephone. It could have been there for anything between thirty and forty years. The officer lifted it, stepped to the centre of the window and pressed an intercom switch. 'There's someone here to see you, Mr Lowden.'

'Unless it's a doctor, I don't want to see anyone. Now fuck off.'

Willis took the handset from the officer and nodded to him it was okay to depart. 'I'm an expert on your condition,' Willis lied. 'I'm here to give you an update. But first, I have a few questions for you.'

'I've already told the officer. Go fuck yourself.'

'No one has told you the outcome then? That's serious. I'd assumed that someone would have broken the news to you by now.'

'What do you mean, *broken* the news to me? What does that mean?'

'It means, Roger, do you mind if I call you Roger, that you have caught NiV, a very serious virus. Its full name is Nipal virus, and there's no known vaccine or treatment to cure it.'

'What does that mean? I'm going to fuckin' die?'

'Well, Roger—'

Lowden interrupted Willis by saying, 'I'm going to fucking die, am I?'

'It's very difficult to diagnose, Roger. It depends how long you've had exposure to the virus and which strain it is.' Willis was flying by the seat of his pants. 'I assume that the giddiness has started, and you have hot fevers and possibly a severe pain in your head?'

'Dizziness – yes. Fever – yes. But I have no pain in my head.'

'That's encouraging. It means that the meningitis stage hasn't started yet.'

'What meningitis stage? People die from meningitis. Don't they?'

'Indeed. It's very serious. That's why we need to discover the source of the virus. All the passengers on board *The*

Clipper are much too far gone to help us. They cannot speak even their own language. You are the only person, still conscious; that is, who can tell us where you picked them up from.'

'Okay. Okay. I'll tell you. They came on board at Zeebrugge after being transported from Bulgaria in a truck, but they came from somewhere a lot farther east than that. I have no bloody idea where they came from.' Lowden dropped the handset, put his head into his hands and wept.

'We need to find out.' Willis shouted into the mouthpiece, but Lowden didn't hear him above the sound of his sobs. Lowden's sobbing subdued, and he lifted the receiver to his ear. 'We need to find out,' Willis repeated, 'and before the meningitis sets in. Then it will be too late to do anything. Someone must know where these people came from. C'mon, Lowden, give me a name. You're running out of time.'

Lowden started sobbing again, making his words almost indecipherable. 'Speak to a guy called Kenny, Kenny McLellan. He might know where they came from because I, as hell, don't.'

Thank you, thought Willis – progress at last. 'Where else did you stop *en route*?'

'What's that got to do with anything?' He spat the words out.

'Because we need to know who else, the fuck, might have given you the virus,' Willis said, every bit as defiantly.

'We stopped at Ostend to pick up some things.'

'Good. We're finally getting there. Who was it you met in Ostend?'

'It was a guy that Kenny told us to meet. I don't know his name, but he came to the boat and handed over the goods. And before you ask, I don't know what he delivered.'

You fucking liar, Willis thought. 'Describe him. Was he tall? Short?'

'He was tall. He wore a long black coat and looked odd – he had narrow slits for eyes – and he carried a gun. We were not supposed to see it, but it was visible under his coat.'

Willis said it wasn't much to go on. If they didn't find this guy, he could die. Willis waited for his reaction.

Lowden said that was all he knew, honest. Willis should speak to Kenny. 'Please, speak to Kenny.' He could tell him who it was. 'He organised everything that happened. Someone a lot higher than him was pulling the strings, but Kenny was in contact with him.'

'What about the owner of *The Clipper*? Where does he fit in?'

'The posh bloke? He just hires out the boat.'

He added that he'd known what they were doing with it and had turned a blind eye. But he was as guilty of smuggling those people as the rest of them.

'You normally wear a green ribbon in your Ponytail, so why are you wearing a red one today?'

He explained that green meant it was safe – it was their code. Red let everyone involved know that they were carrying cargo, and they had to be doubly careful. Lowden paused. 'How the fuck do you know I usually wear a green ribbon?'

Willis decided he would find nothing more from speaking to Lowden, so he stood and headed for the door.

As he walked away, he could hear Lowden calling after him, pleading with him to speak to Kenny. The desperation in his voice was palpable. The sound faded as the officer who brought Willis led him back along the corridor to the exit. But this had worked so well with Lowden that he would try the same approach with Kenny McLellan.

***

Willis told Jonathan he would like him to arrest Kenny McLellan, bring him in on a charge of smuggling immigrants, put him into isolation and arrange for Willis to have a one-to-one conversation with him.

'Arrest him, Brad? There's hardly enough evidence to arrest him. The first thing he'll do is to demand to see his expensive lawyer.' Jonathan Swallow was far from happy at the suggestion. 'He'd be a free man again before you could blink an eye. The best I can do is to bring him in for interrogation, but that won't put him under much pressure, and he'll just clamp up and say nothing.'

'How about Victor Shaw? Have you still got him in custody?'

'I have charged him with breaking and entering, and of course, he is in custody.'

'And no powerful lawyer has come to his aid?' Jonathan's silence confirmed his statement. 'Then I want to speak to Shaw. Can you arrange that?'

Jonathan promised to call him back in a few minutes. Willis started the two-hour drive to Colchester and connected his mobile to the Bluetooth system in the car to await Jonathan's call. He was on the A12 and turning into Colchester when the call came. Jonathan read out a postal code for Willis to input into his satnav and told him that was where Shaw was being held. He was to ask for Sergeant Rose, who would take him to Shaw. Rose was one of his proteges, and Jonathan told Willis he would be co-operative as long as he didn't overstep the mark. The Sergeant knew how serious this situation was.

***

Sergeant Rose was every bit as Willis expected, for he was a smart young man, aware of the rule book but not fearful of using common sense. He was everything that Willis needed. Now, all Willis had to do was to find out how far from the rule book Rose was willing to stray. 'This way, Dr Willis.' Rose marched ahead of him and said he had instructions to only listen in and not get involved – unless he had to, that was.

Willis thanked the sergeant and hoped he had broad shoulders. Rose gave a non-committal shrug with his neck and smiled.

Victor Shaw jumped to his feet as the door to his cell door opened. His eyes darted back and forth between Willis and Rose, questioning why they were there.

Willis sat on the cell bench from where Shaw had risen. He asked him to sit and said there was a lot that he, Shaw, needed to tell him. Shaw was in deep shit. They had put together everything that he and McLellan had been up to. All they needed now was his confirmation, and if he helped, they would put in a good word on his behalf.

'I don't kn-ow what you mean. Who are you anyway?'

'I will be the man who can probably get you get off a murder charge, but only if you co-operate.'

'Mur-der? I told you before. I have fuck all to do with any murder.'

Willis said they would see. But he'd leave that for the time being because there were other things he needed to check first. If he answered correctly, it would tell Willis whether he was to be charged with murder as well as breaking and entering. Roger Lowden had spilled all the beans, and Willis just needed to put a few extra details on the bones of Lowden's story.

'Roger won't have told you a bloody thing. He's not a snitch.'

'Roger has caught a deadly virus off the people he imported illegally on Devlin's boat. Roger will probably die. He's talking, hoping to get better medical attention.' He had also told them about the visit to Ostend and about the man they'd met there with narrow eyes. While he was at it, he also told them why they'd met the man.

'You're bluffing. He never told you all that.'

'How did I find out then – about the people smuggling and the artwork hidden in the boat's panels? If you have any sense,' Willis said, 'you'll try to use your little knowledge to negotiate a deal.'

Shaw leaned back against the cold brick wall of his cell, his eyes moving erratically in their sockets and his brain trying to weigh up the situation he found himself in. 'Okay, but I'll need a deal. I'll only talk if I can get a deal.'

Willis told him he couldn't promise anything, but they had put nearly all the pieces together, and time was running out. 'It is a matter of who gives me the information first, and the longer you leave it, the less information you will have to negotiate with.' They'd arrested Kenny McLellan. Willis had started lying, so he might as well continue – in for a penny – in for a pound. 'If Kenny talks before you—'

'Okay, what do you want to know?'

'To start with, who organises the migrants to be smuggled?'

It was a small-time crook, according to Shaw. He was a crook that Kenny knew. But they only smuggled them as a cover. Sure, they made money on them, but they were only there in case the boat got challenged by the coastguards. If it were stopped, they would charge the crew with smuggling but wouldn't look any further. They recruited a load of patsies, like Roger Lowden, to sail her. That meant they wouldn't suspect anything else was going on, and the paintings would be safe. They also wouldn't look for anyone else to charge. This had been the first time the coastguard had stopped the boat. The guy in charge was very careful because he was in a prominent position and, with his reputation, couldn't risk being caught.

'I'll come back to the government guy in a minute.'

At the mention of the government guy, Shaw's eyes twitched, and he looked away. Willis was pleased that he had dropped that snippet in.

'Where do the paintings get picked up from?' Willis knew it was Ostend but needed to know who in Ostend was involved.

Shaw poured out information as fast as he could think. He didn't know the tall guy in Ostend or his name, but it was the same man who always came with the stolen art. He was a friend of the government official who was in overall charge or, at least, an associate of his. Shaw suspected they worked together. And no, he didn't know who Mr Big was, where he worked or what his name was. He'd heard the man in Ostend tell someone that he had travelled from Vienna, but that was all he knew, and he assumed the paintings came from there. Oh, and the boss man had a very posh accent. He thought he must have been a university guy or someone similar. He also heard him speaking German or what sounded like German to him.

Willis asked him to tell him about Kenny. How did Kenny communicate with the guy in government?

Shaw explained they had been issued with mobiles that they could use only for that purpose. All the phones had the same password, just like his, 920419. The contact numbers had been preloaded, and they were only allowed to call those. Kenny had contact with the boss man. The boss man, in turn, had contact with Kenny and Devlin and so on. It worked because only those who needed to got involved. It was all quite secure.

'So, Devlin is in the know too?'

'Of course, he is. He had his boat modified, so they could hide the stuff behind the panels.' Shaw suspected the entire plan had been devised by Alec. He also knew Devlin was friends with the top guy. 'I guessed that much because they both spoke the same, posh like … like they'd been to a private school.' He'd overheard Devlin on the phone once, and he'd joked about calling him 'Sir' and then burst out laughing. Devlin had also ribbed him about how much money he threw around. If he were short of ideas on how to spend it, he could invest it in the pub.

'Where does Devlin keep his burner phone?' was the next question from Willis.

'It's always on his person, usually in his shirt pocket. He guards it like gold.'

The story was making sense. Willis was pleased with what he had gained so far but was running out of minor facts to bait him with, so he would give up and call it a day. If Shaw remembered anything else, he should tell Sergeant Rose, and the sergeant would get in touch with him. But Willis might have more questions, and if he did, he would be back.

As soon as he'd thanked Sergeant Rose for not contradicting him, he used the station phone to call Jonathan. He told him to have his guys bring in Devlin under some pretence. He should lift him from the pub in the evening and make sure his phone was in his shirt pocket before taking him. Willis would give him the password for the mobile, which was a burner. When he had taken him to the station and removed all his possessions, he must find out the number of the phone. As soon as that was done, Jonathan should release him, and Willis would have a tap put on the mobile. 'We're getting close, Jonathan. If we solve this, it will help your career no end.'

'I've told you already that it's too late to do me any good. I'm too close to retirement. But I'll have my team do that this evening.'

Feeling satisfied that he had completed a good day's work, Willis drove back to Madingley. He'd tell Sophie of his success and deviousness, and then they would relax. But first, he would call Bill Chalmers to have him request a warrant to tap Alec Devlin's mobile. That it was only a burner might speed the process significantly.

Shortly before 5 p.m., a voice that Willis recognised called. The Met had been listening in on McLellan's second phone. He had called a number in Whitehall. They had the number but now needed to wait for the phone company to tell them who owned it. If it were another burner, and since Bill Chalmers was certain that it was, they wouldn't be able to give them the owner's name. However, they were ready for the next call. They would triangulate it to find out where it was. Although its position wouldn't be spot on, they should get a rough idea of where the caller was, but it might take several calls before they can know, for sure, where the owner was based. They could combine many approximate locations via a process they'd developed, and then they could average several inaccurate locations to get a more realistic position for the user. Out of interest, the rough position placed the caller in the Department of Revenue and Customs.

'Why does that surprise me?' Willis thanked Bill Chalmers and poured himself a large glass of red wine.

CHAPTER 24

As soon as breakfast was over, Willis and Sophie called Diana and invited themselves over for lunch. Willis made the excuse that he had to share some information with her, which was, in fact, the truth, but it didn't seem so, because he'd got used to telling lies so often. Presumably, to discuss women's matters, Sophie snatched Willis's mobile and disappeared into the kitchen. Willis slumped on the settee, unsure of what to do next. In his mind, he had the start of a plan. He would warn Diana she needed to be careful in her new role and suggest it might be possible she's been given the position because someone higher in the department wanted to watch her. No. That wouldn't work; it might undermine Diana's confidence. After wrestling with the small number of options open to him, he decided he would simply give her the facts and let her draw her own conclusions.

When they arrived at Diana's, Sophie insisted on spending some time with her while she prepared the food, and Willis assumed it was a continuation of their earlier chat. Sophie was, no doubt, giving her advice on men – and Edward Young in particular. Partly because of procrastination and partly because the opportunity didn't present itself, Willis left his discussion with Diana until after they had eaten.

'You're very quiet, Brad. You have hardly said a word since you arrived.' Diana handed him the coffee packet to let him see it was Brazilian coffee and his favourite blend.

'I thought some important matters were being discussed, and I'd better not interrupt. Thank you for getting this coffee. You are very observant.'

'You both didn't invite yourselves over, so Sophie could give me advice on my love life, so what's the reason you're here, Brad?'

'As I said earlier, you are very observant. What I have to tell you must remain within these walls, and not even Edward must know about it. The Government has classified it as top secret.'

Diana nodded and sat back in her chair, waiting for what he had to say.

Starting from when the illegal immigrants were discovered, Willis ran over the background and filled her in on what he had discovered about the linkages between the boat owner Alec Devlin, Roger Lowden and Kenny McLellan. Against his better judgement, he told her how he had lied to Lowden and to Shaw to help extract the facts from them. He told her about the involvement of Sophie's uncle, the London Met and MI5, using the name of the last department to re-emphasise the importance of secrecy. Willis took a deep breath as he prepared to tell her the tough part. When they'd tapped McLellan's mobile, they discovered he had been calling someone related to the Government. To be more precise, he had been calling someone in HM Revenue & Customs. Willis stopped speaking, and the silence reigned for over a minute.

Diana's face dropped, and when she finally spoke, it was as a question. 'You think that someone has placed me into the Department for a secondary reason?'

'It's certainly a possibility, but it's no way a slam dunk. However, it would be a big coincidence if you were chosen for that department completely indep—'

'… completely independently? You're telling me that someone in Revenue and Customs has put me there to monitor me?'

Willis said he was fearful it might be the reason she had been selected

'Well…,' Diana paused for a second, '… two can play at that game. If someone wants to keep an eye on me, then I'll have to keep an eye on them. All I have to do is discover who the hell it is.'

Willis asked who had offered her the position.

She explained the offer had come from the Prime Minister, but he hadn't made the decision. One of the other ministers might have advised him, probably from the Home Office. Someone would have advised Myriam Hodge from lower in the organisation. It could have been a civil servant and someone quite junior. That's how these things happened. There is a surprising amount of informality. 'Final approval will have come from much higher up. However, I will make enquiries but will need to be careful in case I reveal my hand.'

'It would be a natural thing to ask about. You could be asking out of gratitude?'

'Okay. I will. I am due in the Department tomorrow, so I will ask.'

Willis asked how much she knew about the responsibilities of the Department.

She understood a lot. But as far as the day-to-day workings were concerned, she was at a complete loss. That's why they'd given her an induction manual. Diana walked over to the drinks cupboard where she had left her briefcase and brought it over to where Willis sat. She pulled out a folder and handed it to Willis. 'There's nothing confidential in it, so there will be no problem if you want to read it.'

Willis skimmed the pages. There were thirty, and it took him some time. 'Are there any links between the Department and the coastguards? I can't see any mention of it here.'

She said there would be links because the Department handled Customs and its revenue. So, there would be contact with the coastguards, but she believed that direct interaction would be a very rare occurrence. The coastguards were an autonomous department. Any actual link would be between the Department and the Clandestine Channel Threat Commander. This was a position that interfaced with the Home Secretary and the Minister for Immigration Compliance. The Commander's role was to help to make the Channel route unviable for illegal small boat crossings. Willis would find the definitions of each of these roles in the manual.

Even the Ministry of Defence got involved from time to time. It had recently received a formal request from the Home Office to assist the UK Border Force in the Dover Straits, where migrants have been attempting to enter the UK. There would be plenty of opportunities there for interaction, but she couldn't see how anyone could influence the operations of so many people.

They wouldn't necessarily have to influence them, thought Willis. If they could find out what the other departments were up to, it would make their smuggling activities a lot safer, allowing them to avoid patrol boats and cross the Channel in relative safety.

Sophie cut in. She couldn't understand what their motive could be. If it were only the money, it would ruin the career of anyone who got caught doing this.

Money was the only tangible thing that these smuggled people and items could be converted into. But Willis thought they were asking the wrong questions. They should ask why did someone need such a great deal of money, and he wasn't convinced it was only for greed.

Diana said her eyes and ears would be open every minute of the day while she was in the office, and if anyone took an unhealthy interest in what she was doing, she would notice.

'Great! Anything you find out will help our case. I believe we might be close to proving Rob Moore's innocence and getting his case reopened.'

'That's terrific news, Brad, and while we are discussing good news, I must tell you I, or my secretary and I have tracked down information about my dad.' They had discovered he worked as an accountant in a small company in west London. They gave her his last known address, and she asked to visit the house. The current owners had found a cardboard box of miscellaneous objects, and her dad's name was on some of them. This box had been sitting in their loft for decades, and they had planned to throw it away but never got around to it. The papers contained lots of information, especially about her dad's time in the war. It made for interesting reading. As well as the papers, the cardboard box contained another wooden box, but she was fearful of damaging it. It was locked.

Willis asked to see it. Diana looked on in amazement as he took his wallet of lock picks from his inside pocket, smiled in acknowledgement and got to work on the lock. 'This is one of his party tricks,' volunteered Sophie. 'I've only recently discovered that he'd received his training from criminals.'

As the box lid opened, Willis said, 'The good guys trained me.' He handed the box back to Diana for inspection.

Inside, she found a cloth rag wrapped around a heavy object. When she unwrapped it, she stared in disbelief. 'It must be my dad's ex-army pistol, and it's still loaded.' She rotated the weapon around to look at the cylinder.

'It's safe,' said Willis, 'because the safety catch is on, but I'd disarm it if I were you and not leave it lying around with bullets in it. I know it's been unused for many decades, but the bullets might still be viable.'

Diana re-wrapped the gun in its original oily rag and laid it on the side of the table. Underneath, she found several envelopes addressed to her mother, Penny Ford, that her father Robert must have sent to her while he was abroad. She held the envelopes up to the light to inspect the army stamps on their corners, then she slipped the envelopes back into the box and placed the revolver with its rag on top. 'For later,' she said, her voice breaking as she spoke, causing her words to come in a whisper.

'I think it's time to go, Brad,' insisted Sophie as she pulled on his sleeve. 'Diana will want to be alone with her treasure chest.' Diana sat staring at the box in front of her and experiencing a host of different emotions.

***

In a little over an hour, they arrived back at Madingley. Willis headed straight into the kitchen and set up the coffee percolator. He was uncertain whether Diana would share what he had told her with Edward, but it wouldn't matter, because he was on their side and might even give Diana useful suggestions and advice. He picked a Tunnock's caramel wafer biscuit from the tin, took a bite, and pondered what to do next. Everything would depend on what Bill Chalmers and his team found when McLellan next used his phone and whether they could work out an accurate position for the person he spoke to. Whoever it was, they needed a great deal of money. It was common for people in high places to become targets for blackmailers. Perhaps someone could have discovered something of consequence or had some proof that incriminated the person being blackmailed. How might it be possible to find out what that could be? Without knowing who was being blackmailed, there was no way they could discover this. Willis's best bet was first to concentrate on finding out who was calling the shots in this affair. Only then would he have any hope of discovering his motive. He called Chalmers and said, 'Any news on the trace yet on McLellan's contact?'

Chalmers said they were much closer. There had been three calls so far to the number, but the conversations were short, with the only information exchanged being times but not places. Whoever was running this was ultra-careful. The better news was that they'd triangulated two calls. Because one had come from somewhere other than the office, it needed to be discarded. But the other two were helping them to home in on an accurate position. In another twenty-four hours, they should be able to tie it down to an individual office. Chalmers admitted it was slow, but it was the best they could do.

'That third call – do you have an approximate position where the caller was?'

Chalmers could give him the GPS co-ordinates, but it was nowhere of interest. Perhaps he had received the call while walking along the Thames Embankment.

'Let me have the co-ordinates. I have nothing planned for this evening. Sophie and I can drive into London and go for a walk along the river to discover where the co-ordinates lead us. It's a long shot, but you never know.' Bill read out the numbers, and Willis entered them into a tracking app on his phone, then re-checked their accuracy with him before hanging up.

'Fancy a visit to my club this evening, sweetheart?'

'What's the big occasion? I should have known – it's work?'

'It is. But there's no reason we can't have a little R and R at the same time. Beforehand we'll need to do some surveillance along the Thames Embankment because I need to see what is of interest near to the GPS co-ordinates Chalmers gave me.'

***

Two hours later, they stepped off the train from Cambridge and asked the taxi driver to take them to the Thames Embankment.

'What Embankment are you wanting off at, mate? There's Chelsea and Victoria on the North Bank and the Albert Embankment on the south side. They are long roads and depending on what one you want will depend on what route I take. If you know what I mean?'

'I'm not sure. But I have the co-ordinates on my phone.'

'Okay, gimme them, mate. My phone will take us there.'

Willis read out the co-ordinates twice to ensure that the driver had entered them correctly and then leaned back on his seat to enjoy the ride.

'Ye don't know where ye're goin'? Is it a surprise for the missus or something, is it?'

'Something like that.'

'Well, I never, mate. I've never delivered somebody when they don't know where they're going.'

'Say no more, or you'll spoil the surprise.' Willis hated taxi drivers who chatted the whole time pretending to be friendly, hoping to get a bigger tip.

'As you like, mate. As you like.'

The ploy worked, and the rest of the journey continued in silence.

Several minutes later, the cab drew to a sudden stop. 'It's here, mate. Some surprise. There's nought here to see. That'll be fifteen quid.'

When they stepped out of the taxi, Sophie took Willis's hand. 'He's right. There's sod all to see here.'

In front of them stood three modern high-rise buildings. The building closest to them was eight storeys high. Willis said, 'We need to remember that the GPS position only approximates where the call was made from. It could be this building, right in front of us, or the one on either side.' Willis used his phone to photograph the names on each of the three towers. 'Let's grab another taxi and head for my club.'

***

As they entered The Athenaeum, a waiter welcomed Willis by name and led him to a table next to two tall windows decorated in burgundy and gold velvet curtains. It was Willis's favourite table, and from here, he enjoyed a view of the entire Coffee Room and, had it been daylight, a view of the Coffee Room Terrace. After ordering two glasses of the Club's excellent wine, Willis turned to Sophie and said, 'It wasn't entirely a waste of time. Maybe our high-ranking friend has a mistress or someone that he brings to an apartment on the Embankment. It would be worthwhile asking Chalmers to find out if anyone owned an apartment in the London SE1 postal code.'

'Stop theorising,' said Sophie. 'You'll only build prejudices into your investigation that will create bias in your thinking later on. Let's relax and enjoy what's left of the evening.'

CHAPTER 25

Two men, one wearing a black suit and the other a white, stopped and looked up at the eight-storey tower block.

'To the top, Mr Yang. All the way to the penthouse suite.' It annoyed Yang that they needed to go there to get instructions. Their employer could just have texted them on their phone because it was anonymous enough. Going up on that lift gave Yang the creeps. It accelerated so fast it left his stomach on the ground floor.

'Stop complaining, Mr Yang. You say the same thing every time we visit here. You said that the last time too. Coming here causes us such minor inconvenience, and we get paid well for the tasks we are given, just like last time and the time before that, so this will be no different.'

They walked past the private receptionist, who was busy with his computer screen. He didn't look up. His job was to challenge anyone who entered the building, but even if he had seen them, he would have let them enter. They had been there many times before, and because their appearances were easy to remember, he could easily recognise them. As the glass lift door closed with a swish, Mr Yang put his hand on Yin's coat sleeve and squeezed his arm. It was quickly removed with a look of contempt and placed on the handrail that surrounded its interior. 'Stop grinding your teeth, Mr Yang. We will be there in no time.' When the lift reached the top, its sudden deceleration caused both of Yang's hands to grab the rail. Once the doors opened, they stepped out together, but Yang rushed with much more enthusiasm than Yin to get out the open doors. Once out, he released a long hiss of air from between his clenched teeth.

There was only one door on the landing, and Yin's fat forefinger pressed the black button on its jamb. It flashed bright red, and a crackling noise almost completely obscured the voice. 'Yes?'

'We're here as requested, sir.' Yin assumed that his accent sufficed to tell the occupant who was calling. It wasn't. From above their heads, two white lights switched on, illuminating the hallway, causing them both to look up at the CCTV camera that was mounted above the door. The light extinguished, and a buzz indicated the door was open. They were free to enter.

The door opened directly into a large spacious lounge filled with multiple leather settees and chairs. Drinks cabinets lined opposite walls. As usual, no one was in the room. A man's voice echoed from a speaker on the ceiling above them. 'Gentlemen, you executed your last task satisfactorily. I am very pleased. Therefore, I would like you to complete yet another two tasks for me. Is that acceptable?' They answered in unison, confirming that it was. 'On the table, you will find an envelope. Inside, you will find both your payment for your last assignment and my instructions for your next tasks. Please take a seat, read them, and tell me you fully understand what I am asking you to do.'

Both men dropped onto the nearest settee. Yin read the first sheet before passing it to his partner. There were three sheets in all. After they'd read the third page, Yin stood and answered. 'It seems very clear, sir. You have given us the two targets' names and the two addresses where we are likely to find them.'

But if he didn't object, they'd prefer to complete their assignment indoors this time, suggested Yin. There would be less chance of leaving evidence.

'Whatever. I want the tasks done in two days. Check the dates I've given you, and do them on the stated days. I will need to be about my business when the deeds are done.'

The man closest to the table said he fully understood. They would complete it exactly as he wished, on the correct dates and at appropriate times.

'That is all. What are you waiting for? Go!'

'Yes, sir,' said Yang. They headed for the door and waited for its buzz to allow them to exit.

Yang showed no hesitation in getting on the elevator and sending it speeding to the ground floor. This place made him twitch, and the sooner he got out of the building, the better. As they passed the receptionist, he looked up with a puzzled look on his face but immediately looked down, attempting to ignore their exit.

'I'm always glad to get out of there,' said Yang. 'That guy isn't to be trusted. He always hides away, and we are taking all the risks without knowing who is giving the instructions.'

Yin explained it was better that way. It was safer for everyone. He paid them well enough for the simple tasks he asked of them, and Yin was happy to keep taking his money.

If it hadn't been for their Russian friends who'd introduced them, they would never have found this customer.

'Someday, we might not come out of there alive, and no one will know we've ever been there.' Yang was sweating profusely. 'Perhaps we should leave a record of our visits and our instructions with someone, just in case?'

'That's an interesting thought.' They headed east from the front of the building towards the underground car park where they'd left their black limousine.

Yang mentioned that one of their targets might be more challenging than any other they had done. They'd never had to deal with anyone of this status before. There might be security to deal with. That would make the job a lot more complicated, and it would mean they would need to be careful. They would be extra careful with this one, and they would plan it out to the nth degree. 'It will be done when it's dark, Mr Yin. That is your speciality, and it will also be safer since we can spot any security lurking around at night.'

'I agree. By then, other tasks will have been completed, and it will have been a while since I took the lead, so I'll be due to take my turn.'

'According to our instructions, we have two days to wait before we can do it. Our employer will need to get his alibi lined up, so we have plenty of time to consider how to go about it.'

'You know, Mr Yang, maybe we should consider retiring at the end of this year. We have worked hard and have enough money.'

'Maybe, Mr Yin, but I enjoy my work so much.'

CHAPTER 26

No lights shone in the compound where they'd stored *The Clipper* – the electricity supply had been cut, plunging the area into inky blackness. The intense darkness made the flames from the craft illuminate the faces of the firemen, causing them to appear and disappear with every flicker. The firefighters' heads and hands contrasted against their black uniforms and made their hands and heads seem disjointed, even suspended in mid-air, as they played the hoses against the doomed yacht. By the time the emergency services arrived, a ladder, used by the intruder to gain access, had been removed from the side of its raised hull and laid on the ground. Three hoses sprayed water simultaneously into the cabin. It was such a limited space that the fire had spread quickly, but this also meant that the water could reach the seat of the fire equally fast. Within minutes, billows of black throat-catching smoke replaced the flames that had danced around the deck. The hoses continued spraying for several minutes more to ensure that any fuel in its tanks would cool, avoiding an explosion. After the smoke had completely disappeared, two men wearing full facemasks climbed on board and searched the cabin. 'As expected,' shouted one man after lifting his mask, 'there's no one on board. Whoever did this set the fire left immediately and didn't even bother to take the can containing the accelerant with him.'

The other man instructed him to come down. They could inspect it when it got light – they would leave it to cool.

***

Standing about fifty yards away, half-hidden behind a wooden hut, stood a man in a black coat. He raised binoculars to his narrow eyes and peered at the remains of the boat. Fuck, he thought, I wanted the fucking thing to burn better than that. Never mind, it's enough to do the job. With that, he bundled eight rolls of canvas under his arm and headed for his car.

***

By 7 a.m., Willis's mobile was playing several chords from *Bohemian Rhapsody*. It was his new ringtone. He jumped out of bed and had the phone at his ear in one robotic action. He listened for several minutes as Jonathan informed him of the night's excitement. Willis would grab some breakfast and be right there. Jonathan read out the postcode of the compound while Willis hastily scribbled it on a pad at the side of his bed.

'You haven't noticed I am calling on my landline from home. They've released me from quarantine. The other members of the team that visited the boat have also been sent home. Poor Roger Lowden is suffering badly, but the doctors say he is responding to anti-viral treatments, and they are optimistic. The news about the immigrants is mixed. Three of them have died, but it looks like the others are recovering.

They gave me the all-clear, so I'll meet you beside what's left of the Devlin boat.'

'That's great news. Tell me about it when we meet.' So much for using WhatsApp, thought Willis. He dropped his mobile onto his bedside cabinet and turned to Sophie. 'Good news. Your uncle's out of quarantine and will meet us at the customs compound in a couple of hours. The bad news is that someone has got to *The Clipper* and set it alight, so taking it out of the water and putting it up on those "stilt things" they used to stand it on wasn't such a brilliant idea. C'mon, get up. We need to eat something, then get going.'

Sophie complained that ten to fifteen minutes wouldn't make much difference, and Uncle Jon would wait. 'Did you tell him I'm glad they let him out?' She rolled over and buried her head in the pillow.

***

The satnav took them into the middle of the open countryside and then led them up a muddy path to an area surrounded by an eight-foot-high metal fence. The track followed around to the right and past a small guard's hut standing inside the open gate. Willis could see three cars parked about twenty yards farther on, so he drove behind the rear car and parked. He suggested they'd better get their wellies out and put them on because the mud would get worse the closer they got to the knot of men in the distance. From the group, a hand raised and waved to Willis – he nodded to Jonathan and headed towards him. As he trudged through the wet mud, sucking sounds emanated from his soles and threatened to tug the boots off his feet.

When he reached Jonathan, he asked, 'How bad does it look?'

Jonathan raised his eyebrows. It was pretty bad.

Despite the heat, the smell of the accelerant remained. Whoever had done this had poured enough of the stuff to burn a battleship. But Jonathan answered the question Willis was dying to ask – yes, the wall panels had been removed, and the paintings were taken before the fire was started.

'I don't know whether to be sad or happy. I'm sad that your guards didn't catch the arsonist but happy that the paintings aren't destroyed.'

'The guards will be in my office this afternoon. It wasn't exactly a demanding job to do – all they had to do was to keep their eyes on one item.'

'There's little point in letting Devlin remain free,' said Willis. 'We'd better have him in him and charge him with smuggling.'

Jonathan walked over and spoke with one of his sergeants, then returned to Willis.

By the time they got back, Devlin would be in Colchester Station waiting for them. Jonathan spat out a collection of smoke, dust and saliva and marched off towards his police car.

***

Before they interviewed Devlin, Sophie disappeared to a nearby café while Jonathan and Willis met in a side room to discuss strategy. 'I realise this is an unusual request, but I'd like to question him first,' said Willis, 'I've already tried a tactic with Lowden and Shaw that worked well. If you're comfortable, I will try the same with Devlin?'

'Somehow, I imagine I will live to regret this later, but okay. Go ahead. There's little to lose at this stage.'

Willis walked into the interview room where Alec Devlin was waiting. He had a solicitor with him. 'I see you're ready to be charged?'

'What the—'

'Yes, that's correct. I'm the guy who's been watching you and eating your greasy fish and chips.' Willis thought the fish and chips were delicious, but it was better to start as negatively as possible. He would tell a lot of lies in the next hour, so he might as well start with the fish and chips. 'Where were you on the night that William McLellan was murdered?' Willis slipped a sheet of paper across the desk and pointed out the heading that gave the date of the incident.

'I wasn't—'

Devlin's solicitor leaned forward and whispered something in his ear.

'No comment.'

'Very well. You'll certainly be charged with people trafficking and with the importation of stolen artwork. We have the guy in custody who torched your boat last night, and we've recovered the paintings.' Two more lies. Devlin's hands were shaking, and he looked at his solicitor for advice. Yet another whisper.

'No comment.'

'I thought the Vermeer was especially nice. I would have liked to have owned that one but not so much the Van Gogh. Both are worth a few pennies, I would imagine – certainly enough to kill for. So, I don't think we'll have difficulty convincing a jury of your guilt.'

Devlin's eyes were darting from side to side, settling anywhere but never meeting Willis's gaze.

A 'no comment' followed another whisper.

'… and there's Georgie Maclean, of course. He was murdered too.'

'I don't know any Georgie Maclean.'

'That's odd. His notes mention you. There are lots in there about emails to an MP and hacking of email accounts, and Government accounts at that.'

Devlin's solicitor leaned forward to whisper yet again, but he pulled back and gave a dismissive wave of his arm. As he did, his sleeve slid up to his elbow, revealing a tattoo of a clipper on his forearm. Willis looked at Jonathan to confirm he had seen it. 'Yes. Okay. I loaned out my boat for illegal use, but I'm no murderer, and I have sent no emails to any MPs.' He stopped and looked at his solicitor, who was shaking his head. 'If you want someone for that, it is Kenny McLellan who sent the emails. I suspect Kenny killed his brother in a rage and framed somebody else for it. I know an MP was trying to reopen the case to exonerate someone called Moore, and Kenny didn't like that idea.'

But, Willis explained, he had copies of threatening letters sent from his pub. Someone had been silly enough to use the pub's stationery containing a watermark.

'It certainly wasn't me. Watermarks are common. There must be more than one of them the same.'

Devlin's commitment to the statement was clear. Willis believed him and left the subject for now. 'Once they had landed, where were the immigrants going?' Willis turned and smiled at Jonathan, who was sitting with his head buried in his hands.

Devlin explained they filled vacancies in Kenny's employment agency. It was a win-win situation. Their only risk was that the boat would be stopped and searched. If it had, he would have got an email as it was happening, and he would have immediately reported the boat stolen. The plan was that the crew would get charged and jailed, but no one had told them that, of course, and they would have been well financially rewarded for whatever time they spent inside.

Willis pushed a blank sheet of A4 paper and a pen in Alec Devlin's direction. He instructed him to write everything he'd told them, and if he did, Willis was confident that they would drop the murder charge. He also asked him to fill in a full resumé of all the jobs he'd held and the schools; etc., he'd attended. They might use that as a character reference.

Willis stood, and as he walked to the door, he said, 'You've done the right thing, Alec. Don't let your lawyer convince you otherwise.'

'What the fuck—' Jonathan spat the words out.

'I got results.'

'But you'll likely cost me my pension. His lawyer will claim you've got the confession from him by lies and coercion. The case could fall apart in court. And what's this crap about asking him to fill out a resumé?'

'None of my lies affected his confession. They did, however, affect the information he gave us that implicated Kenny McLellan. So, settle down and relax. I asked for his background because maybe he is associated with the top guy. They possibly attended the same school together.'

When they reached the front desk at the station, Sophie was already sitting reading a novel. She was frowning. She'd waited a while. 'You told me you'd only be half an hour. Instead, you took well over an hour. That's going to cost you.'

Willis kissed her on the cheek and apologised. 'I didn't think it would take that long either. I'll make it up to you later.'

'You had better. I've drunk so much coffee my eyes are ready to pop out.'

***

They drove to Diana's. Willis had called while on the way to let her know they were coming and teased her by telling her they had some good news to impart. Diana was sitting with coffee already made and with Jaffa cakes laid out on the tray.

'Right, you two teasers, what's this excellent news that you have to impart?'

Willis set about telling her about the fire on Devlin's boat and imparted to her details of the subsequent interview with Alec Devlin. Devlin said he believed that William McLellan's brother Kenny killed him in a wild rage. It would have given him a motive for keeping Rob Moore locked up for the murder. But they shouldn't tell Rob yet. They still needed to prove it. It was only Devlin's opinion that Kenny did it, and he might well renege on his story later, but it was an important pointer in their investigation. They had, at last, something to prove.

'That's great news.' Diana held up her coffee cup in a mock toast.

'We also suspect that Kenny McLellan also sent some of the threatening emails.'

'Only *some* of them?'

Willis said there was evidence that at least two people sent the letters and emails. In some, the grammar and spelling were poor, and in others, the writer had used excellent English. Two people, at least, must have sent them, or one brilliant person masking his or her identity. He doubted it was the latter. The differences were too consistent.

'Terrific. I will get Edward to get the case reopened tomorrow.'

'I'd rather you didn't do that,' said Willis. 'It is far from certain that we have the right man. If you start the ball rolling, it will also let the cat out of the bag and alert the culprit that we have discovered something.'

Diana said she'd better not tell Edward, because he would be keen to get the process started. Ever since they'd begun, he'd been looking for a reason.

Willis thought that was a good idea. They would tell him as soon as they were sure of their facts.

Diana walked to the window. 'How long will the police security men be outside my house? I feel I'm the one in prison and being watched everywhere I go.'

'Not long now, Diana,' said Sophie. 'Brad and my uncle are making excellent progress and expect to discover the truth soon. Be patient.'

'Have you made any other discoveries about your parents?' asked Willis.

'I can't discover new things every day. I've got a job to do too. And before you ask, I have discovered nothing about who is interested in keeping tabs on me in the Department. Whoever it is, is taking great care not to reveal himself or herself. It's not keeping me from doing my job, but I am being as observant as I can. Oh! I meant to mention Edward is coming over later today. Would you both like to stay for dinner?'

Willis and Sophie exchanged glances before Sophie answered. 'We need to get back. We're falling behind at home, and there is a lot of domestic stuff we need to do. Anyway, it's about time we invited you to join us. We can't keep imposing on you every time we meet.' Diana held both of her thumbs up and nodded as they moved to the door.

'… and don't forget, no mention to Edward until we are sure.'

***

'That's the first time we've left Diana's house sober,' said Sophie. 'I thought we'd better give them some time together.' Sophie told Willis that Edward appeared to have lost some of his newly found confidence and was backing away from Diana. They would need some quality time on their own to remedy it.

As they turned into the main street leading to their cottage, Willis asked if they ought to stop to get a takeaway. Sophie said she had a meal partly prepared and ready to go into the oven. When they approached the cottage, two men in black coats raced out of the front door and vaulted over the front garden fence. Without thinking, Willis swerved the car to chase them. They ran ahead, but Willis was closing fast. The setting sun was shining in his eyes. He gave a blast on his horn, and the runner closest to him turned to look over his shoulder and, as he did, tripped and fell. Willis had no time to brake – there was a dull, sickening thud, and the car gave a heave and came to a halt. He watched as the dark outline of the intruder rolled over the windscreen, mounted the roof and landed on the road, blocking the driver's door. Willis saw the second intruder vanish into the distance, his coat flailing in the air as he ran. The door wouldn't open. The man had landed propped against it. Fearing that he might hurt him more by opening the door, Willis signalled to Sophie to get out and climbed over the passenger seat to get onto the road.

Willis felt for the man's pulse. He was alive. There was no blood, but his breathing was erratic and shallow. Willis thought it best not to move him in case there was some internal injury. Willis called for both an ambulance and the police. He took his jacket and covered the figure, hoping to retain some of the man's warmth.

The ambulance arrived first.

When the police arrived, Willis explained what had happened. After handing him a breathalyser, the officer in charge insisted that Willis accompany him to the station. Willis told Sophie to telephone her uncle to rescue him. When Sophie approached the cottage, the blue light from the alarm was flashing. Somehow, they had disabled the alarm.

***

It was only the second time in his life that Willis had been in a cell. Several years earlier, the South American police had temporarily incarcerated him for shooting a rebel while rescuing one of his companions, and he hadn't liked the experience one bit. This time, the officer deemed he had acted recklessly and had contributed to the man's injuries. When he arrived, it took Jonathan over an hour to convince him that Willis had acted naturally, though the situation forced him to divulge a little about the case they were working on. Nevertheless, the officer insisted on keeping Willis in overnight until he got advice from his superior. Jonathan had to give in to the officer's decision and told Willis he would check that his cottage was secure.

After her uncle had left, Sophie returned to visit Willis. She teased him through the bars, saying he was lucky they hadn't stayed at Diana's and swallowed more of her Crozes-Hermitage before leaving. If he had failed the breath test, he would have been in even deeper trouble. She would order a pizza for him.

It would be yet another pizza story that they could boast about to their friends.

CHAPTER 27

It was after 11 a.m. before the call from Bill Chalmers convinced the senior officer to release Willis. Once he was out, Sophie drove him to the cottage because he wanted to see for himself what the intruders were after. Nothing was out of place, and nothing was missing. Only the indentations in the settee cushions revealed they had even been there. This worried Willis. It meant that they had waited some time for their return with evil intent. He turned the cushions over and squeezed each one to form its original shape and to drive the negative thoughts from his mind.

Just in time for lunch, Jonathan arrived to give him an update. 'Your intruder is in Cambridge Hospital, unconscious. According to the doctor, he will probably stay in a drug-induced coma for some time while they check for brain damage. Other than he has East Asian features, we know nothing about him. He carried no identification. But the doctors are worried about his condition.'

'Don't expect any sympathy from me,' said Willis. 'They sat on my settee waiting for us to get home. There can be only two reasons they might want to do that, either to chat to us or to kill us, and I doubt very much it was the first one. I don't understand why they ran away as we approached. If they'd waited for us, why would they have run off?'

Jonathan joked, 'Maybe they are allergic to cats, and Ptolemy came in and chased them?'

Willis ignored his comment and asked if the East Asian was carrying anything lethal that he could use.

'Nothing that we've found, but we haven't searched all his clothes yet, so he might have been carrying something. I will check. It is a pity you've chosen to live in such a quiet little village with no security cameras anywhere. I thought you told me you'd installed an alarm? Why didn't it go off?'

But he had set the alarm on that occasion. Sophie had found its blue light flashing when she got to the door. They had disabled its klaxon, allowing them to enter and wait in silence. However, Willis explained that he rarely set it now, because he had an elderly housekeeper who visited and needed access. Since he didn't want to burden her with the alarm code, he'd usually leave the system dormant. After all, he thought the risk of more unwelcome visitors was negligible. He was wrong.

Accepting that no information would be got from his hospitalised and unconscious assassin, Willis asked Jonathan if they could go to speak to Alec Devlin once more.

Sophie was adamant she wasn't coming. She had better things to do than sit in a café or police station while they interrogated the same man again.

***

'I can't speak to you without my solicitor,' said Devlin.

'I don't see why not,' said Willis. 'You didn't take his advice the last time, and that was a good decision. You have the Inspector here on your side, trying to get you handled leniently. Now shall we continue, or do you want to wait until your lawyer arrives?'

Devlin looked down at the table and nodded.

Willis asked him to answer for the benefit of the recording machine.

'Yes.' The word was barely audible, but Willis saw the LEDs on the machine flicker, confirming that it had recorded the weak reply.

'Two East Asian men—' Willis stopped and watched for Devlin's reaction. Nothing came. 'Two East Asian men broke into my house last evening, and I believe they intended to kill me.' Still no reaction. 'What can you tell me about the men? Before you answer, think carefully.'

'I know nothing of these two men. They might have been part of the group that Kenny McLennan smuggled in, but why they'd even know about you, let alone want to visit you, I have no idea.'

Another setback. Willis believed Devlin knew nothing of the men. 'How does the guy at the top of all this get his dirty work done?'

'I told you. Kenny McLennan is capable of killing, and I think he killed his brother, but other than him, I have no suggestion that I can give you. Honestly.'

Again, Willis believed what Alec Devlin was telling him. The man was almost a wreck and would try anything to lessen his personal problems.

'If you think of anything you've missed, will you contact me? If you tell the Sergeant, he will arrange a call.'

Once they were out of earshot, Willis suggested to Jonathan that they pull out the personal resumé that Devlin had completed on their last visit.

Devlin had done a thorough job. Every single job he had, even those from his schooldays, he had meticulously described – right down to the paper round that he did while still at school. Devlin's parents had brought him up well and had encouraged him to earn his own pocket money by taking part-time jobs. The items Willis was interested in were those where his career might have crossed with someone in a government department. He suggested making a photocopy of the last page to see what Bill Chalmers could match up with government employees. Willis took a picture of the page with his phone and sent it as an image to Bill with a note, asking if he could check Devlin's jobs against others in the civil service or elsewhere. He wanted to know whether Devlin had worked with anyone in the past. Anyone who could be involved in the case. Devlin's list of jobs wasn't long, for he had led an idle life before becoming involved in running a pub. Chalmers replied by text almost immediately.

No. What you are asking is against regulations. But I will see what is available in the public domain. I will have my team check out Wikipedia and other public sites. I'll let you know. Don't hold your breath for a quick reply.

Willis showed the reply to Jonathan. He could have told him that if he'd asked. There were controls designed to protect an employee's personal information.

After placing his mobile on the table, Willis took a long slow intake of breath through his nose. 'I guess I knew that already, but a man's got to try. Bill might still find something out on the internet. Let's wait and see.'

'What are your plans for the rest of today?'

'Sophie promised Diana and her solicitor friend they could come to dinner. She's hosted us several times, but we've never reciprocated. I think I'll suggest to Sophie that we invite them this evening. After spending a night in the cells, I'd like a relaxing evening free from stress and worry, and a nice glass of *vino* would be welcome too.'

When Willis arrived back at the cottage, the first thing he did was to put the suggestion to Sophie. She was up for it but thought that since most of the afternoon had passed, Diana wouldn't have enough time to organise Edward. As it turned out, it wasn't a problem. When Sophie called, Edward was already with Diana, so it made it simple to arrange. They agreed on the time – 7 p.m. Sophie set about sorting out the evening's menu.

'Should I prepare the guest bedroom while you do that? It is a wonderful opportunity to push Diana and Edward closer together.'

Sophie gave him a peck on the cheek. 'See? I knew you could be romantic.' She giggled and wriggled as Willis tickled her under her ribs.

'See? I remember where you are ticklish.'

As a result, preparing dinner was delayed by over an hour.

***

'What a picturesque cottage.' Diana walked around the lounge, inspecting the walls and windows. 'It must be listed.'

'It is,' said Sophie.

'And it's a pain to get anything done,' said Willis, 'because there are so many regulations to follow to make sure it keeps its original features when any changes are made. Sit down and have a drink.'

'Not before I show Diana around upstairs,' said Sophie, winking in Willis's direction. He turned to Edward and offered him a drink. As Willis watched Diana's heels vanish up the narrow staircase, he realised that the women's conversation needed to take priority.

'Any chance of a brandy? I've had my hands full this week with Diana.'

Willis asked why.

'She's been very impatient trying to move our relationship forward, but I'm not ready for that yet.'

'Well, neither of you are getting any younger. Don't leave things so long that you regret it.'

'It's nothing to do with age.' Edward said he wasn't ready for that step yet. It had only been two years since he'd lost his wife, and he was still unable to forget her.

Willis said it wasn't about forgetting. His wife Carole had been gone for almost four years, and he still thought about her every day. He walked over to the cabinet, lifted Carole's picture and handed it to Edward. 'They even look the same, so I can empathise with every thought you have, but Sophie and I have discussed it and agreed that there will always be a place in my life for Carole. She generously agreed, even though she had never met my wife. Do the same with Diana. I think you'll get the same reaction.'

Edward took a swig from his brandy and leaned back in his seat, shaking his head, unconvinced. As he did, Diana and Sophie appeared near the bottom of the stairs. Diana's heel snagged in the stair carpet, and she flew into the room with her arms high in the air. Edward jumped on his feet, took two steps across the room and caught her in his arms. They stopped, smiled at each other and mouthed a kiss.

'Sophie has prepared the guest bedroom; in case we decide to stay. We can have a proper drink if we do.'

Edward stood, put his glass on the coffee table, and asked Willis where the toilet was. He disappeared in silence. 'See what I mean, Sophie? The man's impossible.'

'Give him time,' said Willis. As soon as the opportunity arose, he would share Edward's conversation with Sophie.

The evening passed quickly. But Willis found the opportunity to tell Sophie about his conversation, and she, in turn, shared it with Diana, making her feel a lot happier about Edward's reluctance to get more involved. Diana said she would talk to Edward about his hesitancy and concerns, but it wouldn't be tonight. She'd wait until the time was better suited.

The meal went well, and both congratulated Sophie on her cooking. 'That's why I married her.' Willis cowered down and wrapped both arms around his head as though protecting himself from a blow that he knew would never materialise.

'And so, you ought. You'll pay for that later.'

Willis straightened up with a huge grin on his face. 'Dessert, anyone?'

***

It was after 11.30 p.m. before Diana and Edward rose to leave. As Edward collected his coat from the stand in the hall, he heard Diana tell Sophie that she hoped they would stay over on their next visit. Sophie wished so too and planted a kiss on both her cheeks.

Standing by the front garden gate, they waved at Edward's car until it vanished at the end of the street. 'That's an odd affair,' said Sophie, 'but I do hope they work things out.'

'They will. I worked my way through the same flood of emotions that Edward is struggling with, but I got there in the end.' He turned, smiled and kissed Sophie fully on the lips.

'I'd like to think I helped you a little through that phase?'

'You did, sweetheart. You did.' Willis thought about the word sweetheart. It brought back the memory of a discussion he had with his grandfather before he died. His memory of his grandfather's words was crystal clear. *You should find a nice girl and make her your sweetheart – then make sure she remains your sweetheart for the rest of your life.*

He thought of Sophie. He had succeeded in taking his grandfather's advice. So far.

CHAPTER 28

A low scratching noise interrupted Diana Bishop's sleep. I must do something about that damn mouse in the loft, she thought. She closed her eyes and fell asleep again. Minutes later, her eyes opened again. The scratching was now a scraping sound and much louder and impossible to be made by her small, annoying mouse. She lay beneath the duvet, wondering what was causing it and resisted the temptation to get out of bed into the coolness of her bedroom. Two sharp snaps followed each other in quick succession. Her feet were on the floor, and she struggled to walk, groping her way towards the dim light escaping through the thick bedroom curtains. Other than the faint outline of the window, the room was in absolute darkness. Her hand parted the double curtains. She looked up and down the street. Nothing. She leaned forward to see the access to the front door. Still nothing. She shrugged her shoulders and returned to bed, letting the warmth of her duvet restore a comfortable temperature to her chilled legs. Her eyes closed, and she dropped off.

Then a crash.

She sat up erect. She looked at her LED alarm clock. The time, 2:05 a.m., shone out in red numerals. She sat shaking, twitching, and a hot flush enveloped her senses as sweat exuded from her open pores. She concentrated, listening for more sounds. There was a momentary silence before a low metal clang carried up the stairs. She froze. Someone, somebody, was in the house. A pale glow escaped under her bedroom door from a safety light illuminating the outside landing. She stared, terrified that the glow would darken to tell her the intruder was outside the door. Instead, there came a gentle squeak of wood twisting. The warped third-bottom step always groaned when someone stood on it. He was coming up the stairs. Fuck. The threats were coming to fruition. He was going to kill her.

Then the dreaded event happened.

A shadow interrupted the glow from under the door. It halted at the mid-point behind the door splitting the glow into two distinct parts. Her heart was racing. Diana's breathing became erratic. Her eyes opened in a stare. The whole of her body was trembling.

Then the thing happened she had feared most. The door swung open. Silhouetted between the door jambs stood the dark outline of a figure, its long coat moving as the man slowly opened its flaps.

'Ms Bishop? Ms Diana Bishop?'

Diana nodded, but there was no way the intruder would see her response in this dim light. Three loud shots filled the room. The mauve wallpaper became temporarily visible from the flashes coming from the gun's muzzle. Diana Bishop's eyes closed, and she fell back on the bed.

CHAPTER 29

When she opened her eyes, the sun was already streaming in through the disturbed curtain she had opened earlier. The bed was wet with sweat. 'Thank Christ,' she whispered, 'what a fucking dream.' As she sat up, the damp sheet peeled from her back and tugged her back onto the bed. The glow from the LED clock told her it was 8:08 a.m. She had overslept.

Then she noticed it.

The bedroom door was open, and sunlight from the stairwell window illuminated the doorway. She placed her palms on the surface of the bed and slowly raised her body. She continued pushing until the view of the bedroom floor was no longer blocked by the corner of the bed. Bit by bit, the outline of the prostrate figure came into view, its arms outstretched in front as though attempting to break its fall.

Diana shook. Her whole body vibrated, and her hands covered her face. She opened her mouth to scream. But no sound came. She thumped the mattress with her right hand,

and something heavy bounced into the air, tumbled and fell on the bedroom carpet with a loud thump. She looked over the edge of the bed, and there, lying on the carpet, was her father's ex-military pistol.

Now Diana screamed. She screamed so loud that her throat blocked in protest. Tears poured from her eyes, and she collapsed in the bed in a hysterical fit. Minutes passed before she settled, but the sobbing continued.

***

Bohemian Rhapsody's ringtone caught Willis's attention, and he lifted his mobile. 'Hello, Diana. What can I do for you this sunny morning?'

'I've killed him. I've shot him.'

'Hold on, Diana. For heaven's sake, slow down. Who is it you have killed?'

'A man came into my bedroom last night – I shot him. He's lying on the floor, and the carpet's covered in blood. Help me, please.'

'Stay where you are. Do nothing. I'll get someone to come to see you.'

Willis was immediately on the phone with Jonathan. 'It will take us too long to get to her, so can you have Sergeant Rose from Colchester get there pretty damn quick to settle her down? I am leaving now.'

***

Willis was on the A14 heading for Diana's, speeding and cursing the average speed cameras as he did. He increased his speed to seventy-five mph, then risked approaching eighty. If I get stopped on his road, he thought, it'll delay my arrival. Once he was sure that he was free from the cameras, he put his foot down. Cars in the overtaking lane obligingly moved over to let him pass.

Then it happened. Willis spotted a blue flashing light gaining fast. He eased off the pedal and slid into the inside lane. The lights cut in behind him. I'm for the high jump now, he thought. His dashboard light flashed, and Jonathan Swallow's name appeared on display. 'It's me who's behind you. Cut in behind me and follow.' Jonathan's car cut out into the overtaking lane, and, with his lights still flashing, he blasted his siren to clear the road ahead. Willis tucked in behind him at a safe distance and put on his hazard indicators to prevent anyone from cutting between them. When you are in a rush, time always seems to pass quickly. Soon, they approached the Copdock Roundabout. Although both its sets of traffic lights were showing red, the two cars cut in front of obedient drivers who had watched them approach and had slowed or stopped. Soon they were on the A12 and nearing East Bergholt.

When they arrived in front of Diana's house, they were met with a chain of parked cars outside. Not only had Sergeant Rose parked out front, but the forensics van was there too. They had beat them to the scene, which wasn't surprising. Waving his card, Jonathan took the stairs two at a time, and Willis followed. Once in her room, they saw Diana still sitting on the bed with her knees under her chin and swaying back and forth. Sergeant Rose sat at her right side with his arm around her shoulders. When he saw DI Swallow, he rose to let him take over.

'Tell me what happened. Take your time. There's no hurry. Sergeant, fetch her a cup of hot sweet tea, please.'

'She's suffering from shock,' said Willis, and as he did, the wail of an ambulance stopped in the street outside. 'Let's get you to the hospital. You're in shock. Sophie will come to see you. She's on her way as we speak.' Two paramedics manhandled Diana with difficulty past the corpse spreadeagled on the carpet. Diana's eyes fixated on the black bundle as they attempted to guide her past and through the narrow gap remaining between the door jamb and the sprawled legs of the body. They led her downstairs and into the waiting ambulance.

Once he was alongside, Jonathan looked questioningly at his forensics guy. He responded immediately. 'Three bullets in his chest. He was facing the woman when she shot him. The gun is an ex-army pistol, and we're having it checked. But it is very old, and it's a miracle that its ancient ammunition worked considering its age.'

'Her father saved her life.'

'What are you saying, Brad?'

'Nothing. I was only thinking out loud. She showed this gun to us a couple of nights ago. Diana had discovered a lot about her dead father, and her discovery included a box of letters,' Willis paused, 'and her father's ex-WW2 pistol. If she hadn't, she wouldn't be alive now.'

'We've taken pictures, Inspector,' said a voice coming from another white forensics suit leaning over the body. 'We are ready to roll him over. Have you seen everything you need to?' Jonathan nodded, and the deed was done.

'Christ. It's the guy from the hospital,' snapped Jonathan. 'How the fuck did he get out?'

'He didn't.' Willis was looking closely at the corpse's face. 'It's the one that got away. It's the second man that broke into Heritage Cottage and who was waiting inside to kill me. I wonder why he moved his attention away from me towards Diana.'

With a flick of his wrist, Jonathan flung open the blood-stained flap of the body's overcoat, pushed his gloved hand into its inside pocket and pulled out a sheet of A4 paper. He read it and gave a long, slow whistle. 'Read this, Brad.'

Willis read aloud, ‘Prof Brad Willis 4 p.m.’ He read the next line. ‘Diana Bishop MP 2 a.m.’ He took a few breaths before continuing. ‘At the top of the sheet are two dates. One matches the date they broke into my cottage. The other is today’s date. Both times have been added in biro. These are the instructions for our murders. The two assassins had flexibility with the times they killed us but not the dates.’

‘That’s handy. We’re looking for somebody with a cast-iron alibi on both these days, and that’s very helpful, I have to say.’ Jonathan folded the paper and dropped it into a waiting evidence bag. He bent down on one knee and studied the label inside the coat. ‘His tailor is based in Munich, but look at this. It looks like there’s a word written in ink on the label. It says “YIN.” I wonder what that tells us.’

Jonathan headed downstairs and stood in front of his sergeant. ‘Thank you, Inspector Swallow.’ Sergeant Rose was replying to a compliment that Jonathan had given him because he had tackled the difficult task of calming Diana.

‘The front door hasn’t been forced, so how did you get in, Sergeant?’

‘Someone removed the whole of the kitchen window, Sir. It was a very professional job.’

‘Why am I not surprised, Sergeant? Why am I not, in the least, surprised?’

‘I think I’ve seen everything here that I need to,’ said Willis, ‘so I ought to go visit Diana, and I imagine Sophie will be there by the time I get there.’

‘I’ll come with you, just in case Diana is up to talking, but I promise not to push her if she isn’t.’

***

By the time they arrived at Colchester Hospital, Diana was sitting up in bed and giggling with Sophie. She’d made a miraculous recovery. As Willis and Jonathan approached her bed, she said, 'Take this woman away from me. She is incorrigible.'

'Don't I know it.' Willis kissed Diana on the cheek. 'Inspector Swallow here has something to tell you.'

'I have?'

'Tell her about the note.'

'Ah, yes, it seems,' said Jonathan, 'that you are a bit of a hero. The man you killed was about to kill you. I found a piece of paper detailing his instructions with the dates and times of two murders.'

'… and mine was the other name on the list.'

'In that case, I'm very glad to be of service,' she said and threw an air kiss at Willis. 'But you'll also need to thank my dead father. He's the one who saved me by giving me a weapon in time to save my life.'

'Then worked his magic on the ammunition to keep it viable over the years,' Willis said.

'Have you called Edward yet?' asked Sophie. 'He will certainly want to hear all the details.'

'I've already called him, so he knows, but he needed to fly to Paris today. His company is bidding for a big legal contract. He'll come to see me when he's back early this evening.'

'I'm sorry, folks. There are only two people allowed to visit at once.' A nurse stood at the foot of the bed. 'One of you will have to come back later.'

Jonathan immediately stood, threw a kiss in Diana's direction and left.

'I suspect they'll let you out later,' said the nurse. As she walked off, she turned. 'You don't seem to be showing any signs of stress.'

'If they release you, you'll need to come home with us.' Sophie squeezed her hand. 'Your house will be a crime scene for the foreseeable future.'

Diana agreed she would but only for one night because she had a flat in London she used when attending Parliament as an MP. She would stay there for the next few weeks. Diana's chest rose and fell. 'Well, the bastards won't stop me from doing my job. No way!' She said that the residence she used in London housed several MPs because of its proximity to the House of Commons.

'It's a pity that Jonathan has already left,' said Willis. 'He will need to be told to move your security to your London flat. Thinking about it, why didn't your security man intercept the intruder?'

Willis called Jonathan, who was still driving and asked the question. He hadn't passed East Bergholt yet, so he would divert to Diana's house to check.

Diana said she would speak to the Home Secretary. Once she hears what has happened, she will surely assign security from MI5 to guard the London premises.

From behind Willis's head, a voice said, 'Ms Bishop? If you sign this, you will be free to go. I have given you the all-clear.' The doctor pushed a clipboard holding a form in front of Diana.

'Well, that's that. Will you drive me to your lovely cottage?'

After twenty minutes, Willis's mobile was again playing the ringtone by Queen.

'Yes? Okay, thanks.'

He put his phone slowly down on the seat. 'They found your security man lying behind your rubbish bins. He's been garrotted.'

CHAPTER 30

'I've come from the hospital, and our unconscious friend is still just that, unconscious.' Jonathan Swallow had called Willis as soon as he'd left the patient's bedside and arrived back at the station. He told Willis that the doctors feared he might never regain consciousness. After a couple of days, they'd removed the drugs they had used to induce the coma, but he remained completely unresponsive with very weak brain activity.

Willis didn't intend to sound unconcerned, but he wasn't. After all, the bastard had intended to kill Sophie and him. It was a pity; however, they might not extract any information from him regarding who paid them to complete their assignment. He told Jonathan as much.

Jonathan had gone through his belongings, and he'd found something interesting. He was wearing a white shirt and a black tie. His counterpart, the man that Diana shot, wore the opposite, a black shirt and white tie. They also wore opposite coloured suits – black and white. Jonathan said they needed those, so they could be told apart. He gave a short laugh, pleased with his humour.

Willis suggested he look inside the coat and tell him what it said on the label.

There was some heavy breathing and the thump of footsteps as Jonathan made his way to the evidence lockers. 'Just a minute, and I'll pull the coat out. Right, what are you looking for? The label is identical to the other one and from the same Munich tailors.'

'Isn't there a name in ink written on the label – perhaps "Yang" is somewhere on it?'

'Yes, I've found it. It's faded a lot but is at the bottom of the label where it said "Yin" on the other coat. I'll be—'

'Yin and Yang. In ancient Chinese philosophy, yin and yang were two Chinese words meaning dark and light, negative and positive – two opposites. Hence two different coloured shirts. Two different coloured suits. Two complementary colours. Each was the opposite of the other. I might be going too far, but it might also make sense why Yang was at my cottage waiting while the sun was up, but when it set—'

'... and Yin attempted his part of the assignment, to kill Diana at night – in the dark. But it all seems too far-fetched.'

Willis asked if he had found a syringe in his belongings.

'Yes, we did, but we haven't analysed it yet.'

Willis said he'd find it was some form of quick-acting poison, and it would match that used to kill Georgie Maclean. If Willis were right, since Georgie was murdered after the sun set, Yin would probably be the killer. They had divided their tasks up based on each of their personal or superstitious preferences. Either in the light or the dark.

'What a load of—'

'I agree, but it doesn't help us find out who hired them. Any luck with tracing the phone number that McLellan's been calling?'

Jonathan said that the information was being improved as they spoke. They now had half a dozen calls traced, and they had more or less pinpointed the location of the office, but the reason they hadn't acted on it was that another location had shown up. It was on the Albert Embankment and was the same location that Willis had asked for previously when they could only provide an approximate location.

'Okay, who occupies the office where the phone is?' Willis was impatient.

'It's a civil servant in Diana's department, but he isn't as senior as we thought. He's certainly not senior enough to pull all the strings that have been pulled recently. That would need someone higher up, but there's a possibility that whoever made the calls used someone else's office.'

'I'm coming to Colchester. It's difficult having his conversation on the phone. I'll meet you in a couple of hours.' Willis gave his apologies to Sophie and told her he was going to visit her Uncle Jon.

***

'Here's coffee,' said Jonathan, returning to his desk once Willis was seated. He knew it wasn't real coffee as it came from a machine, but he'd have to put up with it unless he fancied grabbing their electric kettle and making some, and, even then, it would only be instant. Willis grunted and took the tiniest sip that his lips could manage.

Willis thought it was time to bring McLellan in. If they did so, they would have enough to arrest him.

Jonathan agreed but pointed out that it would put a stop to any further investigations using the phone. Willis made the counterargument that more calls wouldn't help, and they couldn't barge into a government department without due cause. They would have to find a reason and from whom better to get it than McLellan.

DI Swallow agreed to set it up. They would visit McLellan's house after 7 p.m. when they knew he would be home. They would invite him to come in to start with, but if he didn't co-operate, they would bring him in. Doing that might mean there would also be the chance they could delay the arrival of his highly paid lawyer a little longer while they questioned him.

'And while I put the fear of death up him.'

'Behave, Brad. Only if it is necessary.' Jonathan was beginning to appreciate Willis's techniques.

***

At 7:30 p.m. exactly, after having watched Kenny arrive thirty minutes earlier, Jonathan and Willis knocked on the front door. Another two officers waited in a second vehicle in case needed. No one answered. A loud thump and crash echoed from behind the house. Kenny McLellan had jumped from his bedroom window. Willis made a move to chase him, but Jonathan grabbed his arm and nodded his head to the left. A uniformed policeman appeared through the side garden gate, holding Kenny by the collar of his shirt. 'We're nothing if not professional.' Jonathan grinned at Willis. 'Now, my man, where were you off to? Did you think we were burglars?'

'I thought, I thought… I don't know what I thought.'

'Okay, you're free to go back in if you want, but we'd like to ask you some questions about your brother's death. You'd like to help us. Wouldn't you?'

'Of course, I would. But best not to do it here. My mum gets all upset every time we talk about Bill's murder.'

Jonathan offered to drive him to Colchester, where they could talk in private. This was all happening remarkably easily. As Kenny slipped into the back of Jonathan's car, Jonathan asked what age Bill was when he died? Kenny answered he was twenty-three, but he was very grown-up for his age. Willis noticed the respect that Kenny was showing for his elder brother and doubted whether Kenny could have murdered him … unless Kenny was playing them … unless it had happened in the heat of the moment.

Kenny continued to talk freely about William, adding yet more compliments and saying that he had taught Kenny everything he knew. He added that he, Kenny, had been a fast learner, but his mum never treated him as well as she did Bill. Kenny said that his mum thought the sun shone out of Bill's asshole. He was quick to add that he was every bit as good as his brother.

The car pulled up outside the station, and Kenny continued talking about his brother as they walked in.

After leading Willis and Kenny into an interview room, Jonathan disappeared to get coffee and biscuits.

'You're that professor guy who visited mum? What was that all about?'

'I work at Cambridge University.' That wasn't a lie. 'I am studying crimes and novel methods of solving them. Like your brother's murder, for example.' That was only a partial lie. 'So anything you can tell us that might help would be terrific.' That was the truth.

Jonathan placed three cups of coffee and a packet of Jaffa cakes in the middle of the table. Willis cast a look at Jonathan that he understood. 'Sorry. That's the only coffee we have.' Kenny started to devour the Jaffa cakes as though the World Health Organization had announced a world famine.

Willis asked him to tell them again what happened the day that his brother was killed.

It had been late evening, and he had gone out to meet some friends. Kenny stopped to swallow, and Willis took the opportunity to push the Jaffa cakes farther in his direction. William had told his brother he would be out for about thirty minutes, and that was the last he ever saw of him. Kenny stopped chewing, a sign that telling his story was affecting him. Bill had told him he was going to the pub called *The Clipper Inn* but never reached it. The next thing was cops knocking on his door, saying that Bill was dead.

'You don't have any idea who the person was he was going to meet, or why?' asked Jonathan.

'Only that it was with something to do with his business. That's all I know. That's all I told the cops at the time. I know nothing else.'

Willis believed him. What he said, he'd said with feeling and with more conviction than a trained actor.

'Tell me about the smuggling.' Willis tried to stress him.

'What smuggling?'

'C'mon, Kenny, we know all about the smuggling. You use the immigrants to feed into your employment agency. You advertise vacancies, and then you fill them with illegal immigrants.' Kenny's face turned the same colour as the sheet of paper lying in front of him, and he took a deep gulp. His Adam's apple danced frenetically. 'I've no idea what you mean?'

'Of course you do, Kenny. We know all about it. Alec Devlin spilled everything. It'll now be a matter of how much of it we decide to charge you with.'

'But Alec Devlin doesn't kn—'

'You're right. Alec Devlin doesn't know everything, but he knows enough to get you into a lot of deep crap.'

Something was odd. Why hadn't Kenny asked for his high-powered solicitor?

'Was the use of the immigrants part of the plan, or was that something you did on your own?' Kenny's face flushed, and he shrugged his shoulders. Willis took a chance. It was now or never. 'You are getting in very deep here, and I think you ought to call your solicitor. I'll fetch a phone.'

'No. Don't. I'll tell you everything.' He took a nervous slug of his coffee. He was supposed to hand over the immigrants to the guy who was paying them. Kenny didn't know his name. He'd arranged all meetings by phone, and they'd turned up and made the exchange. Money for people. He could never be sure how many there would be. Neither could they. Some would cancel at the last minute. This meant he could cream off several on every trip and use them in his agency. As a result, he could make double the money they paid him.

'It means you can't call your solicitor, because he would find out about the theft and tell whoever is paying him about your side-line.' Kenny was nodding faster now. 'If he'd found out, he would have you killed just like your brother?' Kenny was physically shaking now. 'Or perhaps you killed your brother because you wanted to take over his business?'

'Don't say that. Don't ever say that. I would never kill my brother. He meant everything to me.' His head hit the table with a thud, and he sobbed uncontrollably.

'Alright,' said Willis. 'But, you know who *did* kill him, don't you? He was killed for the same reason you'll be killed when this comes out.'

'But Bill wasn't doing the same as me. It was my idea only. I started it after Bill was murdered, so that wasn't the reason for his murder.'

'Tell us who murdered him. Who killed your brother?'

'I don't know. I have no idea, but if I did, I would kill the *bastard*.'

Willis said they were going to leave him on his own for a while to think about what he'd said and to consider any other things he hadn't yet told them. Willis stood and beckoned Jonathan to follow.

Once certain he couldn't be overheard, Willis said, 'He's shit scared. They will eliminate him if they ever find out. Even if they won't, he thinks they will, and that is every bit as good.'

'So, where do we go from here?' Jonathan didn't sound as confident of success as Willis.

First, they would tell him to call his mother to tell her he would be staying away on business overnight. If he continued to help them, they would offer him protection. Then they would take time to put their plan together slowly and carefully. The next thing they needed to do was to interrogate him about the phone calls he makes to the person who is running this. Once that was done, everything should fall into place.

CHAPTER 31

'Let's leave Kenny sweating for a while longer. I'd like to visit *The Clipper Inn*. Come on. I'll buy you lunch.' Willis stood and waved to Jonathan to follow.

'You would make someone a fine commanding officer, Brad. Does Sophie do everything you tell her as well?' Sarcasm dripped from every word.

'She only does the things that she wants to, but I think you'll want to join me for lunch today, so shut up and get in the car.' Willis gave a wide grin displaying two rows of dazzling white teeth. 'It's only a minor thing I remembered, but it's small things that make all the difference. Don't you agree? Details are important.' Willis didn't expect an answer, and none came. 'You'll like the food at this pub. It is excellent.'

***

When they turned up at *The Clipper Inn*, it was still too early for lunch. 'We don't start cooking until noon.' Willis's favourite waitress had run to his side, apologising profusely.

Willis said it didn't matter. They'd have a couple of beers while they waited.

'A Guinness as usual, sir?' she said, smiling at Willis. '… and your friend?' She looked at Jonathan.

'I'll have an Adnams.'

'You know something,' he paused, 'but I don't even know your name,' said Willis pouring out his charm.

'It's Marie, sir.'

'You know something, Marie? I've never seen inside a pub's cellar. Any chance…'

'Of course, sir. The pub's quiet. Follow me.'

Willis turned to Jonathan, intimating he should come too. Jonathan cast his eyes upwards but did as he was told.

Marie guided them down a very narrow and steep set of shaky stairs into the pub's basement. She pointed out wet patches on the cellar floor where water had accumulated and told them to avoid stepping in them. 'It is a *very* old building,' said Marie, who had stopped, facing a pair of sturdy, thick wooden doors. She explained they were the original doors from when the pub first opened over two hundred years ago. If she let them in, they would need to help close them again because they would stick, and it would need at least two people to close them. Willis nodded. She pushed against the single metal strut that held them, with her back propped against the wall for support. 'It's very stiff,' she said. Willis pointed to the rod to show it to Jonathan. His eyes nearly popped from their sockets. 'There should be two of those,' said Marie, noting Willis's interest, 'but one's gone missing, and it needs a second one to stop the doors from bulging outwards.'

Willis remembered their meals had been delayed one time when Marie needed to lend a hand to close them. He recalled her telling him about the doors. 'How long has it been missing for?'

'For years and even before I started working here two years ago. We keep saying that it needs replacing, but she gets angry when we mention it, so we stopped.'

'By "she" you mean Helen Devlin, the landlady?' Marie said it was, and Helen didn't use very complimentary terms when she was angry either.

Marie pushed on the rod again, but this time much harder. It sprung out of place, and one of the enormous doors sprung open and hit Marie squarely in the face. She wiped her face with her sleeve and ignored it, so no doubt it was a regular occurrence. Marie set about explaining how they set the kegs up, what their cooling jackets did and how the cooling system kept the cellar cool until the beer was pumped upstairs. While she spoke, Willis nodded every so often, but his thoughts weren't on her words but on a group of dark patches protruding from below one of the stands supporting the kegs. Jonathan had already seen them and was impatient to leave the cellar.

Willis picked up on Jonathan's impatience and suggested to Marie that they should go upstairs before the landlady arrived, in case she got into trouble for showing them around. Marie looked relaxed and told them that the landlady wouldn't arrive until after they stopped serving lunches. She would sit upstairs in her flat watching daytime telly until the meals had finished, but she agreed she had better get back upstairs before other customers arrived. All three of them pushed against the oak doors to bring them close enough together for the rod to fit into place. On the third heave, the wood groaned, and the sound of metal falling into place confirmed that the rod was finally secure. Willis took one last look at the seated rod and noted two circular scrapes caused by forcing it into the latches.

'Thank you for showing us around, Marie,' said Willis while he pushed a folded ten pound note into her hand. It wasn't until they arrived upstairs that the sweet taste of fresh air hit their lungs, replacing the dank, fusty, stale air from the cellar.

'Now, gents, what would you like for lunch?' Marie held her pad ready. 'Everything's on today both, your favourite, the steak and ale pie and cod and chips.'

Jonathan's phone rang. 'Okay. I'll be right there.' He turned to Marie. 'I'm sorry, but I will need to go – work calls.'

'I'll need to go too,' said Willis. 'Thank you for your help. But we'll be back soon.' Of the last statement, Willis was very confident.

Once they were back in the car, other than Jonathan's admission he'd used a trivial telephone call to leave the pub, they sat in silence for several minutes.

Willis said he remembered Marie telling him, on a previous occasion, that a pole or rod was missing from the cellar door, but it didn't register as significant. 'I think we've found out who killed William McLellan. It has to be Alec or Helen Devlin, and from our conversation with Alec, I don't think he did it.'

'Hold on. We'll need to get the blood on the floor analysed to check that it belongs to William, but, with alcohol swilling around the cellar, it could easily have been compromised – not to mention how long it's lain there.'

'But Helen doesn't have to know that.' Willis winked.

'Let's get back to the station.' Jonathan was jubilant.

'Still happy to do what I tell you?' The rest of the journey took place in complete silence.

***

'I need a search and an arrest warrant,' Jonathan shouted as he strode towards his office. 'And I need Helen Devlin's bank records checked.' There was shuffling, and pads were lifted to take down the details.

'We need to be careful,' said Willis. 'There's plenty of evidence that the murder was committed in the pub's cellar, but there's nothing that proves it was Helen Devlin who did the deed. We don't even have a motive.'

'It was her or Alec, and if she tries to land it on her husband, he will tell us everything he knows.'

'But I don't think Alec knows anything about the murder. He's convinced me he doesn't. Let's speak to Kenny McLellan again. He's only next door.'

Kenny jumped to his feet when his cell's door opened but sat down again, ready for questioning even before Willis and the DI could take their seats. Jonathan aimed straight for the jugular. 'Tell me what role Helen Devlin played in your little scheme.' Kenny shook his head. 'Now. I'm only going to give you one chance to come straight with me. Tell me.'

Kenny didn't hesitate. He said she organised everything to do with the immigrants. Helen sourced them and organised Alec's trips to bring them in. She'd put pressure on William to feed some of them through his company, but William was having none of it. Kenny tried to convince him it would earn him extra cash, but he was stubborn. So, when William was killed, he jumped at the opportunity. Life was too short to miss opportunities like that. It became a right little earner.

'Did Helen know you were in favour of trafficking the immigrants?'

'Of course, she did. She even asked me to have a word with Bill to convince him.'

'How long did that conversation take place before William's body was found?'

'Only a matter of days. Are you saying that Helen killed my brother?' Willis leaned back in his seat and raised his eyebrows. 'You are. The *bitch*. I'll kill her myself. Right. Get your notebooks out, and I will tell you everything I know about Helen Devlin's involvement from start to finish.' Kenny didn't stop talking. He spoke for an hour, giving times and approximate dates and promised that his computer could provide the dates accurately. When he had finished, Willis simply said, 'Now tell us about the paintings.'

'I ca—I can't tell you about the paintings – they'll kill me. They have assassins who sort people out who don't do what they're told.'

'They did have assassins, but one is dead, and the other might as well be. There are no assassins, so talk.'

'There's the guy who delivered the painting to the boat in Belgium, a tall guy with narrow eyes. Is he dead?'

'He's in custody.' Willis lied yet again.

Stress visibly fell from Kenny McLennan's shoulders, and he relaxed. He said the paintings were sourced from somewhere in Europe. He was told there was a gang not only stealing to order but also acting as fences to sell on works of art, stolen earlier, whose 'owners' had failed to convert into cash.

'… and?'

'And then the paintings are sent to London. A black cab used to come and collect them. Where they ended up, we have no idea. The cab came without us having to order it. I guess now that Helen Devlin would have telephoned someone to say that they'd arrived. Other than that, I do not know.'

'Stop lying, Kenny,' said Willis. 'We know the full story, and we only need your input as confirmation.' Jonathan turned and cast an unbelieving glance at Willis. 'We know who it is you call in London, and we even have his mobile number. Will I read it out to you?'

Kenny slouched even further down in his seat. 'Okay. So, you know everything. In that case, you can tell me his name for as sure as hell I don't know it. He's just an anonymous voice on the phone to me.'

'That can wait for later.' It was the first ploy Willis had used that turned up barren, so he would need to backtrack. 'I think that the person you spoke to was merely a stand-in to take his calls. Describe his voice to us. What kind of accent did he have?'

Kenny said that was an easy one. It was just like speaking to Alec Devlin – the same accent and almost the same voice. On one occasion, he thought he was speaking to Alec, and the guy got all shirty when he called him by the wrong name.

'So why were you calling him other than to tell him the paintings had arrived?'

'That was all. No, that's not true. I also told him when the immigrants arrived and if there were any problems, but there never were. The people smuggling was only a cover for the paintings coming in. He was terrified that if the boat got raided and the paintings were taken, he would need to answer to a big boss somewhere.'

Willis and Jonathan rose, saying that they would return soon with more questions.

Back in the incident room, Jonathan was surrounded by people providing information. One group pushed two warrants in front of him. Another reported that Helen

Devlin's bank account was extremely healthy and much too healthy to be supported from income from the pub alone. What's more, yet another group reported that not only had she put the pub up for sale, but she'd put it on the market for a ridiculously low price, far below its actual worth. There was no doubt remaining. She was in this up to her armpits, and she was planning a quick getaway as soon as she could sell the pub. Maybe she would disappear before she completed the sale and have the cash forwarded to her by her conveyancing solicitor.

They would need to act, and they would need to act quickly.

***

Parked along the road leading into the marina stood four vehicles. In the front three police vehicles, there was one with Jonathan and Willis, while the other two were full of supporting police officers. Behind those, a white van held forensic personnel. The plan was that Jonathan, followed by Willis and two female officers, would enter the pub and arrest Helen Devlin. Two male officers would wait in the third car and enter, but only if called for.

Once the pub was ready to close for the afternoon and the last customers had left, one of the women officers approached the bar with Jonathan while the other waited outside. Helen Devlin was polishing a wine glass as they entered. She held it up against a light above the bar to check her handiwork. When she spotted the woman officer's uniform, the glass crashed onto the tiled floor, and Helen Devlin made a rush for the rear door. Jonathan stopped and leaned casually on the corner of the bar. Within seconds, a sheepish Mrs Devlin returned to the bar cuffed to the second female officer who'd been waiting in the car park to stop her escape.

Jonathan told her she was under arrest and read the screaming landlady her rights. 'I've done nothing,' she kept shouting as Jonathan instructed the officers to take her to the station.

From behind the bar, Marie appeared. 'You? You are a policeman?'

After explaining that he was only helping the police, Willis told her she would need to go home, and the pub might be closed for some time. She opened the cash till and removed two twenty pound notes, and put them in her pocket, explaining that it was her wages for the day. She drew Willis a look of contempt as she marched past him, heading for the door, but as she did, she was stopped by an officer who asked for her contact details because they would need to speak to her later. As she exited, two white-suited forensic officers carrying equipment entered and asked Jonathan what he wanted them to test. He directed them down to the cellar. Thirty seconds later, the crash of an oak door, then the rattle of a metal rod hitting the stone floor, was followed by a string of expletives. 'Oops! I should have warned them about the door.'

Willis ran down the stairs to apologise and tell them that the rod was evidence and that they should bag it with anything else they found. The senior of the two, whose forehead was red with contact with the door, looked at the condition of the bloodstain below the kegs and said he doubted whether they could use it, but he would do the best he could.

Jonathan left two officers alongside the forensic team with instructions to declare the place a crime scene and to board the doors and windows securely when they left.

'Let's have a word with our friendly landlady. Yours truly would like a chat.' Jonathan waved to Willis. 'I'm glad that I have you to tell me what to do.'

CHAPTER 32

'Your lawyer has arrived.' Sergeant Rose opened the door, and a short man with a comb-over hairstyle entered and sat opposite Helen. 'Let us know when you've prepared, and we'll come in and ask our questions.' The man placed his briefcase on the table and nodded to the Sergeant, who exited and closed the door firmly behind him.

'Her lawyer is here, at last, sir,' said Sergeant Nigel Rose, poking his head around the door of Jonathan's office.

'Thanks, Sergeant.'

Jonathan waited for the door to close, then leaned towards Willis. He said he was worried that she'd get the same high-powered solicitor to arrive to represent her as Kenny McLennan did when he had been arrested on previous occasions. It was just as well for them that Kenny thought he had something to hide from his high up friends, for if he hadn't, the station would team with over-paid solicitors.

'Don't let looks deceive you.' Willis stood up and walked to the window. He didn't think that there would be much for them to do for the next couple of hours. 'Why don't we call Diana to tell her what we have will all but clear Rob Moore's name for the murder?'

Diana was elated when she heard. Tomorrow she would arrange a visit to Rob's prison to tell him the hopeful news. And yes, she would bring her security escort with her for protection during the trip. She thanked Willis and Jonathan for all the work they had done, bringing the culprit to justice.

Willis warned she had only been charged, and there remained a long way to go yet before they could confidently say that justice had been done.

'I know. I know, but the wheels are in motion, and that is good enough for me at this stage. She thanked Willis again and said goodbye.'

According to Jonathan, there was an excellent Italian coffee place a hundred yards along the street. They might as well sit there while they waited, and they could plan how they would handle this interview.

***

Willis gave a 'so-so' wave of his head when he tasted the coffee.

'As good as that?' Jonathan grinned. 'That's high praise indeed – I'll need to come here more often. This interview – we need a plan.'

Willis's plan was simple. Jonathan should let him take the lead exactly as he did with Kenny McLennan and would only stop him if he stepped over the line. It had worked with Kenny, and there was no reason it shouldn't work with Helen Devlin. If Willis said anything out of order, it would isolate Jonathan from at least some of the blame.

'Agreed.' Jonathan was holding his spoon and playing with the froth floating on his coffee. 'But if I say your name at any time, you stop. Agreed?'

'Agreed.'

Jonathan iterated it wasn't exactly a shut and closed case. If her lawyer has any sense at all, he will challenge them to prove it was she who had killed McLennan and not somebody else from the pub.

'We will need to get the evidence one way or the other,' Willis said.

Jonathan's mobile pinged. He read the text. 'They're ready for us. Let's see what we can achieve.'

***

'I am DI Swallow, and this is Brad Willis, a police consultant.' Sergeant Rose took up his position beside the door. Jonathan made all the usual comments for the recording machine stating the names of those present but stopped and looked at Helen Devlin's solicitor.

'You have no evidence to hold my client. We will reserve our situation until you produce such evidence.' The lawyer sounded defiant, but that was what they paid him to do.

'Please may I have your name for the record?'

'I am John Philips of William Glover solicitors.' He placed a business card on the middle of the table.

'Well, we will need to produce some evidence for you.'

Jonathan said traces of blood had been found on the cellar floor. In the fullness of time, they would be shown to have come from William McLennan, with whose murder his client was being charged.

'In the fullness of time?' echoed John Philips, making it sound like a challenge.

'When they visited her cellar, Forensics found one of a pair of metal rods identical to that used to bludgeon Mr

McLellan to death.' Willis looked in Helen Devlin's direction. 'The cellar doors are missing such a rod.'

'No comment.'

'Very well. Let's change the subject. Threatening letters were sent to a Member of Parliament on headed paper belonging to Helen Devlin.'

Devlin's eyes darted to her solicitor and then back to Willis. 'No comment.'

'The killer of William McLennan is left-handed. You are left-handed, Mrs Devlin.'

'That proves noth—' She swallowed hard, 'No comment.'

'You admit to being left-handed?'

'No comment.'

Sophie's words haunted Willis. *If the bar in the car boot hadn't been moved before the police took the picture, then it would have suggested the culprit was left-handed. The picture shows one end of the bar unwrapped. The bloody side was on the right side. That suggests that a left-handed person placed it in the trunk.*

Sophie had been right, and he had been wrong.

Willis revealed they had checked Helen Devlin's private bank account. It currently contains over four hundred and fifty thousand pounds. That was a lot for the owner of a pub that isn't full every night. There was also the fact that Mrs Devlin put her premises on the market at an unusually low price, and from that, they could deduce she planned to leave the country as soon as possible.

'I am selling the pub because Alec has been arrested, and I can't run the place without him.'

'You haven't needed him in the past. You complained he was always on his boat and never helped you. Look, Helen, the amount of evidence against you is huge, and it will grow once the DNA results are back from the blood in the cellar and from the blood-stained bar that you used to murder the young man. Not to mention we have your fingerprints to check against those found on the bar.' Willis tapped his fingers impatiently on the table. He was lying again.

Helen Devlin was swaying in her chair, clasping and unclasping her hands and looking at her solicitor. He nodded in her direction, prompting her to answer as they'd rehearsed. 'If we can cut a deal, I will tell you everything.' Her solicitor grabbed her arm.

'I'm not at all sure we will be able to strike a deal unless…' Willis stopped to allow the tension to increase, '… unless you can prove that someone else coerced you into killing the boy, or that it was self-defence.'

She glanced at her solicitor.

'We need a break. I need to confer with my client.'

'This meeting is paused at the request of the accused's solicitor at 21:30.' DI Swallow pressed a switch, and the machine's red recording light extinguished.

'Coffee?'

'No comment.' Willis grinned.

'You might want some later. This could be a long night.'

No sooner had Jonathan received his coffee and taken the first sip when Sergeant Rose returned. 'She's ready for you, sir.'

'He was an idiot and completely useless. I've sent him away.' Jonathan looked at the empty chair where John Philips had sat. Stretching over, he put his finger on the record button to press it. 'Not yet,' said Helen.

Slowly, Jonathan pulled his hand back but said, 'I need to record that your solicitor has left at your request.'

'Later. After we've talked.'

'I can't promise you anything,' said Jonathan, 'but if your information is useful, I will make sure your input is taken into account.'

'Not good enough.'

Willis stood. 'You'd better call your man back then.' He walked to the door.

'Okay. Okay. You're a hard man to negotiate with.'

Jonathan said it was less a matter of negotiation and more about what he could achieve. But he had to be honest with her if she'd killed the boy…?

'I might have my charge reduced to manslaughter.'

'That's not how it works. It will be for the court to decide, but I promise I will put everything that you tell us in front of them for consideration.'

Jonathan asked Sergeant Rose to fetch Helen a cup of tea and some biscuits. Willis reluctantly conceded that a cup of station coffee was necessary.

Helen started by telling how she'd organised her husband to bring in the immigrants. She was the brains behind the whole thing. Her contact in Europe, whom she'd met in the pub and struck up a conversation with, suggested the idea while Alec was boasting about his boat to some customers. The smuggling had gone on for at least four years; it was a good earner and helped support the pub. When Willis reminded her of her bank balance, she added that the paintings helped too, but she would come back to those. She had attempted to convince William McLennan to skim off a few people from every trip and to feed them through his agency. That's when things started to go wrong. She and Bill had a stand-up argument. They went down to the cellar, so no one could hear. Helen made the mistake of pushing Bill during their shouting match. He'd fallen over and then charged at her with his fists flying. She grabbed the bar from the door for protection and lashed out. The next thing she knew, Bill was on the floor, unconscious and bleeding. He'd stopped breathing. She'd tried to resuscitate him but failed. She'd driven to the Marina to get Alec to help dispose of the body, but instead, she'd spotted an unlocked car and hid the evidence. The rest they knew. She'd dumped the body and discarded the rod in the parked car. She had tried to prevent Diana Bishop from re-opening the case for obvious reasons.

'Tell us about the paintings.' Things were going better than he expected. Willis was pleased but impatient.

The paintings had been where most of the money had been made. Bill and now Kenny would call a mobile number to have them collected from his house, but it was all done secretly. She told them what they'd already learned from Kenny about the black cab collecting the paintings, but she said that it also dropped off a bag of cash. She would take most of that, meaning Kenny was merely a go-between in the transaction, even though it had been both Helen and William who had first contacted the buyer and got things running. Helen argued that she and Alec had taken all the risks to bring them into the country. She dug into her bag and produced a mobile phone that she would use should anything go wrong with the delivery or with Kenny's part of the transaction.

Willis lifted the mobile, switched it on and input the password. The same contact number appeared he had seen on Kenny's phone.

'How did you know the password?'

'Carry on,' said Willis, 'don't let me interrupt you.'

'You know more than you're letting on. Don't you?'

'We know a lot. We'll check everything you tell us against what we already know. Carry on. I don't want to be here all night.'

Helen Devlin was on the back foot and looking nervous again. She told them the rest. All the exchanges between them and the buyer were supposed to be done anonymously, but on one occasion, she drove and waited outside Kenny's house when she knew a pickup was to be made. When the black cab arrived, she followed it into London and along the bank of the Thames. It stopped outside a high block of flats on the Albert Embankment, where the driver handed the package to reception. He then picked up two additional bags and delivered a sealed bag containing cash to Kenny McLennan, who passed it on to her. She did not know who received the second bag.

Probably a pay-off for the driver, thought Willis, but why would he need it in a bag? They wouldn't have paid him so much that it needed a bag.

Helen was speaking again. She had no idea who it was she was calling when she pressed the call key on the mobile, but it sounded much like Alec. One time, she even accused Alec of trying to trick her, but he denied everything, and besides, he wasn't devious enough to go to such lengths. If she hadn't taken the lead, nothing would have happened. And he certainly couldn't have afforded an apartment on the Albert Embankment, so she knew it wasn't Alec she had called.

***

It was after 2 a.m. before Helen Devlin stopped talking. Jonathan told her she would have to put everything that she'd said down on paper and sign it. In the end, there were twelve pages of writing, and Jonathan insisted on typing them out before he left for home. All the station staff were long gone except for a duty officer, a couple of uniforms, and of course, the ever-reliable Sergeant Nigel Rose.

Both men's eyes were drooping when Jonathan arrived with the paperwork shortly after 3:30 a.m. and handed both the printed copy and the handwritten copy to Helen to read. 'I have corrected some spelling mistakes you made, so please carefully check that you agree with everything before you sign it.'

Jonathan put his hand around Willis's shoulders, led him into a corner of the room and whispered. 'In several sentences, she has explained whose fault she thought caused a particular incident to occur. In each case, she wrote "whose" instead of "who's", so this matches some letters that Diana received. I'll keep her handwritten statement as additional evidence. That part of her story is true. We incorrectly accused Kenny McLellan of writing them.'

'I think almost all her story is true,' said Willis. 'There were only a few revelations that we were unaware of. The other parts we already knew but needed confirmation.'

Jonathan folded the sheets, gave Helen her copy and put the rest in his pocket before telling her she would remain in custody.

The door of the room burst open.

'I am Arnold Swanson from Swanson Partners. There's no need for Ms Devlin to stay here any longer. Please release her immediately. You had insufficient evidence to bring her in, let alone to charge her.'

Jonathan stepped forward and stood between Swanson and Devlin. 'I'm afraid you're too late, Mr Swanson of Arnold Swanson, Solicitors. She's been charged. She's staying right here, and she's signed a full confession.'

'My client signed it under duress, and she sighed it without legal representation.'

'On the contrary, sir. She had access to her solicitor. She voluntarily waived her right and sent him packing.

Everything that she told us is admissible in court.' Jonathan took a step closer to Swanson.

'We will represent her now.'

'If she so wishes, that will be the case. It's now after four in the morning. I, for one, have had a long day, and if you wish to represent a potential client, please return tomorrow morning. Mrs Devlin will still be here.'

'You will be sorry, Detective Inspector. Your career is about to come to a swift end.'

'And, so I think, will be the career of whoever is paying you, along with your company's reputation for secretly aiding and abetting a known art thief.'

'A *what*? Don't talk ridiculous, man.'

'An art thief.' Jonathan repeated the words slowly and patted the pocket of his jacket.

'We will see about that tomorrow.' He marched out and slammed the door.

'That's sorted him out,' said Jonathan.

'I think we have another problem.' Willis stared at Jonathan. 'How did they find out that Helen Devlin was in custody?'

CHAPTER 33

'You had better come to the station.' Jonathan spoke quickly.

'It's only 9 a.m., and I didn't get to bed until gone 5. What is so urgent at this time of the morning?'

'Arnold Swanson is back and demanding to speak to *his* client. Helen Devlin isn't awake yet. She went to bed at the same time as we did. Therefore, I have told him he'll have to wait until she rises.'

'Good thinking. I was so tired that I stayed in a *Premier Inn* last night, so I'm only twenty minutes away. I'll be on my way as soon as I get dressed.'

Exactly twenty-three minutes later, Willis was standing next to DI Swallow's desk. 'I have an idea. Let me take the lead again when the interview starts. I want to find out how important money is to these people.'

***

Shortly after 10 a.m., they met in the interview room. After the formalities were over, Arnold Swanson kicked off by saying for the recording machine, 'I'd like it put on record that you have accused my employer of being an art thief. Will you please confirm that for the record?'

Jonathan was about to speak when Willis put his hand on his arm. 'I can confirm that. For the same reason, will you confirm whether you meet your employer at Whitehall or his Albert Embankment address?' Swanson's Adam's apple did a jump up and down. He wriggled in his seat and swung his head towards and away from his assistant several times.

'I need a few minutes to discuss with our client.'

'But she hasn't agreed to be your client yet?' Willis threw the gibe over his shoulder as he and Jonathan stood and left.

'What was all that about? That was confidential police information.' Jonathan's words were a half-octave higher than normal.

'Don't worry. It won't go anywhere. I doubt if it'll even get as far as whoever hired them. Money is important, but in the legal profession, reputation is even more important. I would be surprised if Arnold Swanson wants to represent Helen Devlin, now that he thinks we know who his employer is, and now he believes our statement that his employer is an art thief also to be true.'

'But we don't know.' Jonathan threw his arms in the air. 'This better work if it doesn't…'

Sergeant Rose appeared at Jonathan's desk. 'Mr Swanson would like to see you now if you don't mind?'

'Asking for permission? He's on the back foot.' Willis slapped his hands. 'I'd love to play poker with that man.'

When they entered the room, Arnold Swanson remained standing. 'We have taken instructions. We will no longer represent Ms Devlin. Thank you for your time, and I apologise for forcing you into the office so early.' He lifted his briefcase, and he and his assistant left.

Helen Devlin asked what had just happened. Jonathan took great pleasure in telling her that Messrs Swanson had realised that her contact in London would be arrested soon, and they needed to wash their hands of any involvement with him. Willis told her that if it was any consolation, they wouldn't have helped her case. She'd managed that herself by the information she'd already given the police.

Jonathan mouthed, 'Sleep?' to Willis.

'There's no way I can sleep now. I need to go to visit Diana. There's something I need to check, and it would be better if you came too.'

***

As they expected, Diana was at home when they arrived, and she told them that the Home Secretary had insisted she take a few days off to recover from her earlier trauma. Although she would be at home, there was no way she'd be idle, as there was so much to do as MP for her constituency that the time would be well spent. She brought tea, and her hands shook when she filled the cups. Diana was clearly still traumatised. She took her left hand and placed it on her right wrist to steady the shaking. Willis lifted the milk jug and filled each cup without asking.

Willis waited until she was seated and finished the first cup of tea. 'Did you see Edward last evening?' She nodded, and as she did, Willis imagined the light caught a tear in her eye. 'Did you mention to him about Helen Devlin's arrest?' She nodded again, but this time the nod was much smaller. 'There is something I need to tell you.'

'You need to tell me that Edward isn't who he seemed to be?'

'How did you know?' Willis screwed his eyes up.

'Because he texted me today to say that he needed to go to Paris permanently, and he didn't know when he'd see me again, if ever. He didn't call me. He sent me a fucking text message to break it off with me.'

'I'm so sorry, Diana.' Willis slid over and took her hand. 'I started to suspect when he avoided getting more involved in your relationship. It's no wonder that every effort by you to solve Rob Moore's case foundered. Every step you took, he reported back and was used to make your actions counterproductive.'

Diana asked why they would want to keep Rob in jail? What would they have to gain?

'It kept the police's attention away from Helen Devlin. She confessed yesterday to killing William McLennan. If she had been arrested, it would have messed up their plans and stopped her from fulfilling her part in a smuggling scheme.' Willis kept the details to a minimum and didn't burden Diana by telling her about the stolen paintings just yet. 'I believe Edward worked for a company called Arnold Swanson instead of the company he told you he did.'

'Surely, what he was doing was illegal? You can charge him?'

'I am sure we will find something to catch him on,' said Jonathan. 'The hardest part will be to trace where he is, and I'll bet he's certainly not in Paris.'

Willis pulled a piece of paper from his jacket. 'I can tell you the registration number of his car, and even if it turns out to be a rental, there will be an audit trail back to trace him.'

'I've lost my short-term boyfriend,' said Diana, 'but I'm learning a lot about my past family and my newly found family.' She smiled and poked Willis in the ribs. Willis's ribs were sore with all the poking they'd received recently.

***

Before they returned to the station, they stopped off at Colchester General Hospital, where Jonathan asked to speak to the consultant caring for the only remaining live assassin, Mr Yang – or should that be, half-alive assassin? Willis couldn't imagine a high civil servant, if that's what he was, hiring two such men to kill on his behalf. If only they could talk to Yang, their problems would be all but over. But, as he suspected, it wasn't to be. The consultant told them not only was the patient still unconscious but that his brain activity was reduced. Therefore, in his opinion, it was likely that he would never regain consciousness and soon would need to be taken off life support.

'Where's the car they drove?' asked Willis. 'It must be somewhere near Diana's House. Yin will have left it there. It's likely parked somewhere blocking someone's driveway.'

***

And so, it was. The stretched black limo sat two streets away from Diana's house and had been left unlocked with keys in its ignition, ready for a prompt getaway. There was no need to check the records to discover who owned it, for in the unlocked glove compartment were Yin's driving licence, insurance documents and house keys. Jonathan noted the address in East London before calling for the vehicle recovery service to come and remove it to their compound. While he was waiting for them to arrive, he searched the boot, where he found an assortment of chemicals and syringes. 'These two killers were nasty bastards. There are devices here to kill that boggle the mind and enough of them to kill scores of people.' He lifted a pistol by putting the stem of his ballpoint pen through the trigger guard and turned it around to check the ammunition. Holding the gun close to his nose, he took a single sniff and confirmed it had never been fired, not recently anyway. After he'd logged and packaged everything, Jonathan placed the plastic envelopes and paperwork onto the back seat of his car. 'How anyone could have such a perverted mind baffles me. Those two must have been sick. They needed help.'

'I know what kind of help I would have given them. The same kind that Diana dished out, except it would have been a lot slower and more painful.' Willis looked at the syringes. 'One of these was in Yang's pocket when they searched his coat, so that must have been his plan for Sophie and me. Possibly he intended to inject us while we slept.'

Jonathan agreed the syringes were the same as those used in Georgie Maclean's demise. But they needed to drop this evidence off at the station and go on to East London to see what these keys revealed when they opened the door of number 11 Greyshade Gardens.

'Greyshade?' said Willis. 'Typical. Even the name is halfway between dark and light, Yin and Yang. I suppose they were so fanatical that they needed something compatible with both of their obsessions?'

'We will soon know, my dear Brad. We will soon know.'

***

As they entered the street, they slowed, assessing the houses. There was a set of four houses in each row. Three rows on each side filled the terrace. When they reached the first semi-detached house in the third row on the left, they saw it. The large square black sign with a white border and white numerals stood out. Even without reading its number, they would have surmised that this was the correct house. Black and white curtains added to the building's starkness, with the upstairs windows displaying black curtains and downstairs, white. After they parked in front of its driveway, Willis sat for a few seconds trying to imagine what would drive a person to take on such a strong lifestyle.

After turning the key in the lock and pushing the door ajar, Jonathan waited for the sound of an alarm. Silence. As he suspected, the black box hanging on the outside wall was a dummy and merely to deter intruders. Everything in the house was black and white, so much so that it was uncomfortable on their eyes. Willis pushed the door closed behind him. 'Christ. How can anyone live in conditions like this?' Jonathan didn't answer. He pushed forward into the lounge. Above the fireplace hung the familiar circular black and white swirls of the Yin and Yang logo. Upstairs was similar. Nothing but blinding contrast.

Willis pulled open a drawer in one of the bedside cabinets. 'Colour at last.' Notebooks and a host of ballpoint pens lay jammed inside. Similarly, the second drawer was stuffed with a host of miscellaneous objects, making it difficult to open and close. 'I have drawers like this at home.' Willis chuckled. He took a deep intake of air when he opened the bottom drawer. 'Come and see this, Jonathan.' About twenty syringes lay higgledy-piggledy covering its base. 'I wonder how many poor souls these two bastards executed during their careers?'

'And that wasn't their only method of execution.' Besides the gun they'd found in their car, a black Glock 19, 9 mm pistol lay hidden in a cardboard box at the bottom of the wardrobe, surrounded by small bottles of oil, nitro solvent, brushes and rags needed to clean and maintain it. Another box held a Glock 43X, 9 mm with its silver slide and associated maintenance tools. 'It's easy to see who owned which gun. Yang preferred the silver-topped 43X despite its maximum capacity being only 10 +1 rounds compared with the Glock 19's standard capacity of 15.'

'I'll have forensics come and give the place a thorough going over,' said Jonathan.

'Come and see this.' Willis was holding up a sheet of paper in his gloved hands. 'It's the order to kill Sophie and me. Written in the corner is a phone number. It's the same one we've been tracking, and would you believe it has Devlin written beside it?'

'I don't believe it. I was sure that Devlin was telling the truth, and he had nothing to do with the killings. Also, it means that Helen Devlin hasn't been completely truthful either.'

They both spent the next hour searching for other evidence. Eventually, they gave up and headed back to the station. 'If we get back in time, we will speak to Helen Devlin before they transfer her to a holding cell in prison.'

When they reached the station, they found two officers waiting for the necessary paperwork to allow them to collect Helen Devlin, so Jonathan and Willis rushed through to where Helen was being held and questioned her. 'You haven't been completely honest with us,' said Jonathan. 'Your husband is involved more than you told us. He ordered Willis's murder and that of his wife. Speak up, or you'll lose any benefit you might have gained.'

Helen Devlin burst out laughing. 'That wimp? He wouldn't have the balls to order someone's death. I don't know where you got that idea from, but I can assure you that it's bollocks. I have lived with the man for most of my life, and I can assure you he did no such thing. He's not man enough.'

They walked out of the room and out of earshot. Jonathan turned and glanced at Willis. 'Have we been mistaken? Did the order come from Devlin, or was it an order to kill Devlin?'

'I have to agree with Helen. There's no way that Devlin seems able to order someone's death.' Willis frowned and drew his hand through his thick mop of hair. 'That's a loose end, and I don't like fucking loose ends. We need to visit Alec Devlin tonight.'

***

When they arrived at the prison, the Governor was very co-operative. He walked them through to the interview room. Alec Devlin was led in. His eyes inspected his toes, and his shoulders hunched as he walked. 'We need to have another chat, Mr Devlin,' said Jonathan. 'You haven't been entirely honest with us. Have you?' He pointed to a chair, and Devlin sat down, his head still facing down.

'I have told you everything I know. I don't know what you mean.'

'In that case, won't you tell us who it was you put the contract on?'

Devlin said he couldn't, because he had done no such thing. He could never order anyone to be killed. The rest of the interview was unfruitful, with Devlin denying all knowledge of any order to kill. All the while, he wriggled in his seat like an innocent schoolboy accused of some ill-doing. In the end, they gave up and had Devlin taken away. After asking the Governor to stay behind, and in case they had it completely wrong, they told him about their fears that someone unknown might have issued a contract on Alec Devlin. The Governor agreed to put a guard on Devlin during exercises and to restrict him from mixing with other prisoners. Because he was awaiting trial, he would have a cell to himself, and that would also help.

On the way back to the station, Willis asked Jonathan if he believed Devlin.

Jonathan's answer was confident. 'Definitely.'

'Me too. Then the only explanation remaining is that the contract has been taken out on Devlin.'

CHAPTER 34

Radiating from three tall narrow windows, feeble rays of moted dustlight illuminated a worn, dark orange carpet and gave the impression of warmth. But it was cold. The heating hadn't been switched on in this room for months, if not years. Winter sun from the leftmost window bounced off the long tabletop and threatened to blind the man sitting opposite. He rose and pulled on the curtain, making the room even murkier.

'We must hasten the shipment,' said the man standing with his back to the light. 'So far, everything that could go wrong has. Alec and Helen are in jail, and young Kenny McLennan is also in trouble. How could Helen have been so stupid to not only have killed William McLennan but also to have admitted it? I can't understand her thinking.'

The man on his left appeared to be more senior than the others. 'What's done is done. Once the crates are loaded and their contents distributed, we will stay low for a while.

Alec's boat is destroyed, and we will struggle to find another gullible victim to act at our beck and call.'

'But, Robert, we still haven't collected all the cash from the previous shipment.' The man directly opposite him had interrupted, and his voice trembled as he forced the words out.

The man answering to the name Robert smashed his palm on the table. 'It will be here. I followed it up yesterday, and they will transfer the money by tomorrow evening. We can't expect our customers to part with such large sums until they've had time to authenticate the goods. How many units are ready for shipping?'

The fourth man, who had been silent up to now, sat bolt upright in his chair. He said all twelve were ready. He addressed Roberts as 'sir' and treated him with great respect. It had taken longer to add the eight paintings from the last shipment. He added that some of the separating tissue between the canvases had been disturbed. He assumed that someone had inspected them and therefore knew of their existence.

Robert said that was impossible. If someone had known they were behind the panel in *The Clipper*, there was no way they would have arrived there safely. 'They were still there before you set it alight?'

'Of course, they were,' he said, squeezing his already narrow eyes together. 'I'm just saying—'

'Don't just say. Just do as you're told. Our house of cards is falling apart, and if we don't get the packages off our hands soon, they will be dangerous evidence of what we've been up to here.'

'The trucks are due to arrive in the next few days, and as soon as they're loaded, the canvases will be gone for good.' The man with narrow eyes tried to regain his composure.

At that moment, the door burst open, and a scruffy, overweight man wearing an open-necked shirt with exposed trouser braces barged in. 'Yin and Yang are both dead. If they have left any evidence, we are for the high jump.'

'They came with your recommendation, Draghi. If there is any comeback, I will hold you personally responsible.'

Their references had been excellent, Draghi said defensively, his Essex accent dominating. 'I used them before, and they performed good. I asked around like I always do. Know what I mean? They didn't fail nothing.'

'What are you planning to do about it?' Robert waited for Draghi's answer, but he only looked on with his mouth open. 'Okay. I'll make a suggestion. I want you to destroy their house. We must burn the building and everything remaining in it. We don't have time to search it, so this will be the quickest solution.'

'But—'

'But nothing. Go NOW!'

'The coppers is there already.' The braces man was now shouting. 'Guys with white outfits is all over the fucking place. It's too late to burn it.'

'For fuck's sake.' Robert's expletive was in sharp contrast to his natural Oxford accent, but listening to Draghi's imprecise grammar, giving him bad news, caused it to slip. 'Helen Devlin is the weak link in the chain. If she talks, we are in trouble. I want her silenced. For good. Do you think you can do that small task?'

'Yes, Guv.' Draghi snapped his braces elastic against his chest and marched to the door.

'Use the instructions I've given you. And don't mess it up. Do it yourself. Don't delegate.'

'You two,' he said, pointing to the men opposite him, 'I want you to split the packages between you and take them home. Take any empty crates and boxes with you too. Don't show your faces here again until you get a call from me. I need this house to be so squeaky clean that, if it comes to a search, there will be no evidence and no sign that anything has ever gone on here. Got it?' Two heads bobbed up and down out of time.

Robert turned to the man sitting beside him and told him they would need to keep away from this place until they returned to supervise the transfer. When the trucks arrived, they would return.

They walked out from the long table, and the room was once again empty.

The draught from the closing door disturbed the dust motes and made them dance wildly in the artificial breeze. The same breeze lifted a sheet of paper, swept it across the room and tucked it neatly under the hems of the dusty green curtains that covered the middle window, but the men were long gone by then, and no one remained to notice.

CHAPTER 35

As Willis pulled up his usual chair to face him in his office, Jonathan said, grinning, 'You're making a habit of coming here, but I better give you an update.' He had received feedback from the tracking they'd carried out on the phone at Whitehall, and, from the information they'd captured, it turned out the phone was in the personal office of the Deputy Chief Executive and Second Permanent Secretary of Her Majesty's Revenue and Customs. His name was Archibald Pendleton-Smyth. His was the second-largest department in the civil service, and only the Department of Defence was larger. Pendleton-Smyth was responsible for around fifty thousand colleagues in all.

'That was the person who Edward Young contacted about getting protection for Diana. Isn't he a bit senior to sort something like that out?'

'Possibly. But he'll have someone lower down who would take care of it.'

'If Edward wasn't who he'd said he was, why would he worry about Diana's safety? Maybe the memo wasn't about her safety but about knowing where Diana was and what she was up to?'

Jonathan said that they would know soon. The Met was to visit him today. Two very senior plain-clothed detectives have asked him for a quick interview with the idea of keeping things at a low level until they could find out what was going on. This Pendleton-Smyth guy was so senior they would need to tread safely. This was how police careers could come to a premature end. As a result, they might never hear what the outcome of the interview was. Even Bill Chalmers might not remain in the loop, although he had been responsible for triggering the investigation. On the other hand, if it uncovered a definite, provable misdemeanour, they would hear very soon.

An officer rushed into the office, interrupting the proceedings and dropped a report in front of Jonathan. 'Sir, there's been an incident at the prison.' He turned around and left as quickly as he arrived.

As Jonathan read the report, his face visibly changed colour. 'Helen Devlin is dead. The prison is investigating the cause. There is no sign of injury on her body.' He rose and grabbed his jacket. 'Are you coming?' Willis sprang to his feet and followed him.

***

When they arrived, the pathologist had already stretched Helen out on the table in the medical unit. The doctor looked up as they entered. 'Her skin is discoloured. There are no bruises on her neck or anywhere else. I suspect the cause of death is poisoning, but we won't be certain until we have a full post-mortem and get the toxicology results back. I am ninety-five per cent certain that poison is the cause.'

'At what time did she die?' asked Willis.

'Shortly after breakfast. Someone could have slipped something in her food.'

Behind them, the door opened, and the Prison Governor entered. He said, 'I don't think it was the food that was got at. She'd partly eaten a box of chocolates a visitor brought for her yesterday evening.'

Jonathan said, 'I need to see her cell. Is it still as it was when she died?'

'It's taped off as a crime scene,' said the Governor, turning to lead the way. The prison had several single cells or rooms that were kept specifically for prisoners who were awaiting further investigations or trials. Helen Devlin's cell was one of those. When they entered, a box of Milk Tray was spread across the floor, its contents spilling out, covering almost every corner of the small room. 'One might assume that she took unwell while eating the chocolates and had dropped the box and its contents,' said the Governor, pointing to the box's flattened lid. 'We found her lying on top of it, and that's the condition we found it in.'

Sticking out from beneath the bunk, with only a corner showing, was a sheet of paper torn from a three-ringed notepad. It caught Jonathan's eye. After removing a handkerchief from his jacket pocket, he lifted it and read it aloud. 'Happy Wedding Anniversary, darling. I'm sorry we can't be together today.' Jonathan folded the paper, using the handkerchief, and laid it on the table. 'Alec Devlin sent this. I do not know how he managed it because he is still under lock and key but manage it, he did.'

They marched into Alec's cell, which was only about fifty feet away. 'It looks like you're guilty of murder too.'

'Really? Who was it I am supposed to have murdered?'

'Your wife.'

The blood drained from Alec's face. The change in skin pallor surprised Willis as there was no way he thought any feeling remained between Alec and his wife. Devlin put his head in his hands and wept. After raising his head, he said, 'I've been locked up here for days. How could I possibly have killed her?' It was only then that Willis remembered they had concealed Helen's arrest from him.

'Because she is in a cell only feet away from here,' Jonathan shouted, 'so you could have used anyone to send her chocolates.' When Alec asked why on earth would he send his wife chocolates, Jonathan said it was to celebrate his wedding anniversary.

Alec stretched out, lifted Willis's wrist and looked at the date on his watch. After a pause, he said, 'It is indeed our anniversary, but we never celebrate it. We never send each other presents. Why would I start now? I didn't even remember that it was our anniversary, and nobody else knew when we got married because we never talked about it. I didn't even know she was in prison.'

Jonathan insisted that was why it had to be him. Helen would have remembered the date. Otherwise, she would have been suspicious about receiving such an odd gift.

'Show me the note.' Alec held out his hand.

'I put it into evidence,' said Jonathan, 'but it read *Happy Anniversary, darling, I'm sorry we can't be together today,* followed by several kisses.'

'Nonsense. I never called her darling – ever. I have a special name for her, but we haven't used it in years. And kisses? You must be joking?'

They left Alec weeping into his hands and retreated into the corridor. 'I believe him,' said Willis, 'and I don't know why, but I believe him. Why would someone poison his wife and attach a note that identified him as the sender? If Devlin didn't know we arrested his wife, how would he know where to send the chocolates?'

'It's a prison,' said Jonathan. 'Every prison has a grapevine. It wouldn't have taken long for him to have found out.' Willis argued the other prisoners wouldn't have accepted Alec yet, so he wouldn't be part of any grapevine. Jonathan dismissed his argument, saying that it could still have happened. They agreed to disagree.

Jonathan's mobile pinged. 'I am needed back at the station. Bill Chalmers needs to speak to us.'

***

Once they were back, Jonathan closed the door to his office and switched on the loudspeaker on his mobile. Bill Chalmers's voice was low and almost inaudible. 'The officers spoke to the Second Secretary. He knows nothing of a burner phone. He gave them permission, in fact, he almost insisted, that they search his office. His assistant was out for the day, and they searched his office too, but there was nothing to report. There was no sign of a burner phone and no sign that anything else was out of the ordinary.'

'Science is science,' said Willis. 'The techies detected the phone in his office, so it was there. They couldn't have done a thorough enough search.'

They heard Bill take a long, slow intake of air at the other end of the call. 'These guys are professionals. If there were anything there, they would have found it. Trust me.'

Willis asked if they could put a tail on him to see what he did outside the office. Willis sounded desperate.

'Right? Are you asking me to request a tail be put on the Deputy Chief Executive of the second-largest ministerial department in Whitehall? I want to survive long enough to retire. No way. You must come up with another plan.' After tens of seconds of silence, they said their goodbyes and hung up.

Because they would need some time together to come up with a better plan, Willis asked why Jonathan didn't come to Sophie's and his tonight to have some dinner. This whole thing was getting out of hand, and someone else might be killed. 'Talking of being killed, did you put a guard on Alec Devlin just in case he is telling the truth?' Jonathan shrugged his shoulders in disbelief but called the prison and ordered a twenty-four by seven guard put on the prisoner.

***

'Hi, Uncle Jon.' Sophie put her arms around him and, standing on tiptoe, kissed him on the cheek. 'We're having roast duck tonight. I hope that's alright?'

'It'll be better than what I would cook at home. Ever since your Aunt Jane passed, I have been living very simply and eating very basic meals, so anything will be an improvement.'

'Anything? Okay. I won't expect a compliment tonight.' She giggled and threw him another kiss.

'I said anything would be an improvement, but that doesn't mean I don't appreciate good cooking when I taste it.'

The duck breast *à l'orange* was perfect, and Jonathan wasn't hesitant in saying so. His compliments came fast and furiously until Sophie, embarrassed by too many, asked him to desist. 'You've only got ice cream for dessert,' she said. But seeing Jonathan's mouth open yet again, she interrupted. 'I know, I know, it's your favourite. I remember Aunt Jane told me but just keep quiet and eat it. Pleeeease?'

Willis leaned over and tugged on his sleeve. 'I wish I could get off so easily. If I don't compliment her, I get frowned at.'

The men sat in the lounge drinking cans of Stella Artois while the Manchester United game played in the background with the sound turned up just sufficiently to let them hear the cheers announce when goals were scored. The conversation kept returning to Helen Devlin's murder and who else could have known the date of their anniversary. They might have told a member of staff in the pub, but none of them would have the wherewithal to have someone killed while in prison. Jonathan decided to investigate whether any relative or employee of Alec and Helen would know the date they were married.

Willis asked why was it that when you turn the sound down on a television set, it lures you into giving it your undivided attention.

As a cheer from the set struggled to reach their ears, Willis's mobile rang. 'Hello, Bill. Are you working overtime tonight? What? I can hardly hear you. There's a lot of traffic noise.' The noise dropped. Bill must have cut into a doorway or something similar.

Bill was tailing Mr Posh-Civil Servant. He'd met a friend after he'd left the office. From what Bill observed, he would hazard a good guess that he was gay. When they'd met, he'd showed a little too much affection.

'That's a strike against him, Bill,' said Willis. 'My profiler, who rarely gets things wrong, said whoever wrote the threatening emails to Diana showed signs of being gay. So, he could be our man. But I thought you'd said you wouldn't order surveillance on Pendleton-Smyth, because it was too risky?'

'I didn't order it. I'm doing it myself. But it means that anything I discover can't be used in court. If I get caught, they'll throw the book at me.'

Willis said he should worry about the consequences later. It was more important to discover what was going on first. Bill asked him to hold for a few seconds because his target had waved down a taxi, and Bill was struggling to find a second cab to follow him. Once he had found one and was safely inside, he continued to report that the pair had spent over two hours in *The Belle Pub*. He paused, waiting for Willis's reaction. When it didn't come, he said, '*The Belle Pub*?' Still no reaction. 'It's one of the most well-known gay bars in London. I've been sitting there drinking a half-pint of shandy and attracting a lot of attention – and I don't mean I was in danger of blowing my cover either.' Willis gave a silent smile. 'I can tell when you're grinning, Brad Willis. It isn't amusing.'

'Sorry, Bill, but I find it immensely amusing. I bet you are still wearing your work clothes too, and those will make you stand out like a comedian at a funeral. Where are they going now?'

After reading out a street name, Bill said they were heading west along the Strand and then turning up Regent Street. He asked Willis to hold again, then added that he suspected they were going to the casino. Five minutes later, the confirmation came. Bill said he was about to hang up as he planned to follow him into the *London Vegas Casino*, and he'd call him later if it wasn't too late when he got out.

Jonathan, who had only heard one side of the conversation, was leaning forward with his eyes wide open, begging for an explanation.

Willis repeated everything that Bill had told him, including the bit about the gay bar, and added that as Bill wasn't the tidiest of dressers, it was surprising that he got any attention at all.

In all the excitement, they had missed the end of the Man U game. Jonathan switched over to The Sports Channel and listened for the result. It took ten minutes of replays and near-misses before he discovered that the match had ended in a draw, and everything now depended on the away game scheduled for next week. With a shrug of discontent, he pressed the red button on the remote, and the screen went blank. 'What do we do now? Shall we wait up for Bill to call us or go to bed?'

'Bed. Casinos get very active after midnight. If we wait for Bill to telephone, we will be up all night.'

Jonathan didn't need any further persuasion; he was on his feet and heading for the stairs.

'What the hell is that?' Sophie sat bolt upright in bed and dug her elbow into Willis's side. He groaned and turned over. 'Answer your bloody mobile, will you? It's on your side of the bed.'

Willis glanced at the time on the red LEDs of his bedside light. 'It's 4:35 a.m. Who the fuck could this be?' Then he remembered. 'Bill. Couldn't this have waited until the morning?'

Bill was talking fast and furiously and spilling his story out as fast as his mouth could cope. Archibald Pendleton-Smyth was a gambler. He was a big-time gambler and a big-time loser. He'd made a tour of all the casino tables, one after the other, and when he'd failed to win on one, he'd move to another, doubling his stakes every time. He'd lost tens of thousands of pounds in just over three hours. Finally, the *coup de grâce* was when he'd disappeared into a private poker game. What happened in there, Bill didn't know. There was no way he could follow him, but he was still in there now, and if he ran to form, he'd lose thousands more.

CHAPTER 36

Sitting at the table in Sophie's kitchen, Willis and Jonathan were having trouble concentrating. Not only had their night's sleep been interrupted, but they had spent a further two hours discussing what Bill Chalmers had relayed before retiring. They were not only closing in on the heart of this illicit operation, but they had possibly also uncovered the reasons that drove a senior member of the government to become involved in so many nefarious activities. Somehow, the man's gambling addiction had to be financed, and at the rate Bill described he was losing money, it would require a lot more than they'd uncovered so far.

Slowly, Jonathan drew patterns with the tip of his fork in some tomato ketchup remaining on his breakfast plate. 'It is going to be near impossible to get permission to properly investigate this guy. We even needed permission for yesterday's interview. Because it provided nothing of value, it means it will be all but impossible to get anyone to take us seriously a second time.'

Willis hummed and shook his head. 'We might not yet be able to prove anything, but we have collected invaluable information. That Pendleton-Smyth has a gambling problem is clear. That he sent at least some of the threatening emails is clear. If only we could get access to his bank accounts.'

'That won't happen. Not unless we find much more malefactions to incriminate him.'

'What about his partner?'

He hadn't gambled but only followed him around the various tables he visited.

They decided to investigate the second man. After all, as Jonathan explained, it might be easier to get permission to look into his private records. As soon as Bill Chalmers surfaced, they would ask him for a full report. Their wish was to be fulfilled sooner than expected. Willis's mobile rang. Groggily, the voice of Bill Chalmers hoarsely explained that he had waited for his targets to leave the casino, and it was after 5 a.m. before their taxi stopped at an apartment block. It would appear they'd spent the night together there. Chalmers had gone home to bed, and although he'd only had a few hours' sleep, he thought it best to update them.

'Where was the apartment block?' Willis glanced at Jonathan, expecting he already knew the answer.

It was on the Albert Embankment, and it wasn't too shoddy either. It would cost more than Bill's police salary to live there.

'Before you go back to bed, one more thing. Can you describe what his partner looked like?'

Bill hadn't paid too much attention to him. He was tall. Well built. Dark hair and a moustache. Other than that, he didn't have any distinguishing features. Bill had wanted to sneak a photo of them together with his phone, but knowing how awkward they could be in casinos when they saw a camera, he'd decided against it. He had a shot of them entering the apartment building, but it was useless as it was a silhouette. The reception area behind them had been brightly lit.

'Thanks. You'd better go back to bed and get your voice back before it goes completely.' Willis said that his information was very useful and that he deserved to spend what was left of the day asleep, but not until he had texted him a copy of the picture.

As Willis expected, the picture was next to useless. It showed the outline of two figures entering a building. Other than they were holding hands, he could spot nothing of interest.

'What's that?' asked Jonathan. He pointed to where one of the overhead lights on reception reflected off something on one of the men's wrists.

It looked like a watch face. It was pretty washed out and overexposed, so Willis asked Jonathan if anyone in his team might be able to process it enough to recognise the make because Willis would put money on that it wasn't a Casio or a Citizen. What did he think?

'This is where digital photos excel. Unless it is completely saturated, we can usually get something from it with careful processing. I'll send it to the forensic people. If they can't get anything from it, no one can.'

Jonathan said they needed a plan for the rest of the day. 'So far, we've made good progress, but I fear the forces of law and order might be stymied for a while until we uncover more evidence.'

'The forces of law and order might very well be, my dear Sherlock, but Watson here will relax for what's left of the morning and, later this afternoon, when I can be confident Pendleton-Smyth is back in his office, I will visit him. As a private citizen.'

'You won't get near him. He's protected. He has staff all around him, and I'm told his secretary is a formidable lady.'

'We will see. I have a cunning plan – a cunning but not-so-subtle plan.' Willis grinned the way Baldrick did. He remembered the grin from watching his favourite character in the *Blackadder* series on television. 'And you don't want to know what it is. In case it goes belly up, you'd better disassociate yourself from it.' Willis winked and took the final slug of his morning coffee.

***

Whitehall was everything Willis expected. He assumed that this department was typical of others in the historic building. It was well appointed, but in some areas, it showed a lack of maintenance, though nothing serious enough to impair its structure. It is sometimes the simplest of plans that work best, Willis thought. The hallway was full of security cameras covering every angle. Willis positioned himself looking into a corner facing a waste container. He dropped his copy of *The Times* newspaper into the bin and then poured the contents from a small glass bottle over it, followed by a lit disposable cigarette lighter. It wasn't exactly spontaneous combustion, he thought, but the burning liquid would have a similar effect. In a few minutes, the smoke would become so intense that it would require attention. He moved away and walked towards the security barrier, acting as casually as he could. His face would be recorded on the security cameras, but by the time they'd identified him, it would be too late. To delay his identification, he looked at his feet as he walked.

When the commotion started, the guards ran towards the billowing smoke. Willis sat on the ID card reader and swung his legs over the steel barrier. He was in. Now he had to get out of sight as soon as possible.

He was carrying a manilla folder in his hand to make him look busy. He wore his university pass untidily around his neck, supported by its ribbon, making sure that the important side was facing inwards and hidden from view. The map of Whitehall he had studied on the internet wasn't particularly detailed, for obvious reasons, but it had enough information to get him within yards of his target. He stood in the corridor, opened his folder and pretended to read it. It took longer than he hoped, but eventually, a bright-faced young man swung open the door to one of the offices and let it close slowly behind him. The man introduced himself and entered. He was the Deputy CE's four o'clock.

Willis stepped forward and placed his foot so that the door didn't close fully.

The secretary stood and headed for a pair of sturdy oak doors. She pulled the left one open. 'Your four o'clock, sir.' She stood back and allowed the man to enter.

Within seconds, Willis had crossed the outer office and barged in behind the young man. 'Sir, you can't—'

'Yes, I can,' said Willis as he threw a sealed envelope on the CE's desk. 'Read that.'

Pendleton-Smyth leaned forward, hesitated, and lifted the envelope. From his left-hand side, he lifted a silver letter opener and slit it open.

At that point, two security officers rushed into the office. Each grabbed one of Willis's arms. 'Don't worry, sir. We'll take care of this intruder.'

By this time, its recipient had removed the letter from the envelope, and a picture of two men holding hands dropped out. Pendleton-Smyth held his hand up, and the security guards released Willis. 'That will be all, officers. I will take it from here.' Turning to his original four o'clock appointment, he gave a wave of his hand, and the young man headed for the door. 'Ask Silvia to make another appointment tomorrow, early.' He sat and indicated to Willis to do similar. 'Mr Willis, is it? You've signed the letter. I can press my panic button at any time to have you removed.' He stretched and pushed another button. A red light illuminated.

'I expect you won't want to record this conversation.' Willis nodded towards the glowing LED.

'I can always erase it if it isn't to my liking.'

'Very well. You have big problems, Mr Archibald Pendleton-Smyth. You are living way beyond your means. I have checked your salary on the dot-gov website, and your official income would last you about a month at the rate you are losing money. You have a gambling problem.'

The tall man stared angrily at Willis. 'So what? I gamble. I pay my debts. That's not illegal. Or is it your intention to blackmail me for being gay?'

'Not only have I no intention of blackmailing you, sir, but I might stop whoever is.' The CE's mouth dropped open so slightly. A clear giveaway 'tell', thought Willis. No wonder this man makes such a poor gambler. He is easy to read. 'Two officers came to visit you recently from the Met. They were very circumspect and wore kid gloves, but their next visit might not be so accommodating.'

'Who the hell are you? What do you think you can do?'

'Call me a troubleshooter, sir. I can help you. I solve things off the books.'

'For whom do you work?'

'If I told you that, it would hardly be off the books. Now, do you want my help or not?' Willis raised his voice a shade, feigning impatience.

'How can I trust you if I don't know who you are?'

'Look, sir, there are other pictures taken in the casino last night, right up until 4.30 p.m. when you and your partner left and drove to the Albert Embankment.' Willis was lying again. He was becoming good at lying. 'If I intended to harm you, sir, I would have plenty of ammunition. So, what's it to be?' Willis was getting impatient for real. Revealing yet another 'tell', the left corner of the man's lips twitched. Willis went for it. 'Do I help you? Or do I walk out of your office and promise that you'll never see me again?'

'Okay. What do you need from me?'

'You will need to tell me where the funds are coming from to pay off your debts and who is blackmailing you.'

He unlocked a desk drawer and tossed an envelope in Willis's direction. He slid out the contents to see a familiar blackmail demand constructed from letters cut out from a magazine. 'I have a well-off man..., a well-off friend. All the money is legitimate. He owns a large estate in Hertfordshire. Both my friend's parents are dead, and he inherited his wealth from them. He even tells me they managed the inheritance tax so skilfully that he received one hundred per cent of the monies. He has been kind enough to settle both of the blackmail demands I received.'

'I'll need his name. And his address.'

'I can do better than that. I can introduce you. He's my assistant and is in the office next door. Follow me.'

Willis felt that progress was about to be made, but when the door swung open, the office was empty. 'I thought Robert would be here.' The disappointment in Pendleton-Smyth's voice was palpable. 'We were out late this morning together, as you know, but I thought he'd be in by now.' Turning to another man sitting at a desk outside, he asked a question. Willis watched as the man shook his head. 'He hasn't been in at all today.'

'Will you take me to where he lives?'

Archibald Pendleton-Smyth nodded and returned to his office to pick up his coat. 'Silvia, cancel all my diary appointments for what's left of the day. I don't expect to be back this afternoon.' His secretary rose to her feet to lock the door to the CE's office.

As the driver of the official car opened the door to let Pendleton-Smyth enter, Willis heard him tell him to drive to the Albert Embankment. Willis's heart rate increased. He was on his own without backup. If Pendleton-Smyth's friend were hostile, he would be in danger. He played with his mobile phone and glanced at his host, who wasn't in the least concerned by this action, so Willis sent off a joint text to Bill and Jonathan.

Going to address at Albert Embankment with Pendleton-Smyth. Might need backup. Do nothing unless I contact you.

Since Jonathan was too far away to reach him in time, Willis hoped Bill had recovered from his late night and was up and close to his mobile.

As they entered the building, the receptionist gave a knowing nod and turned back to the bank of security screens filling his desk. While they stood waiting for the elevator to arrive, Willis admired the array of rooms filling the ground floor. These included a gym and a small cinema. Another room had tinted windows, so its purpose was unclear. How the other half lives, he thought.

Mirrors, engraved with scenes from ancient Greek history, covered the walls of the lift. Pendleton-Smyth touched his key card against the pad. In its reflection, Willis could read three numbers on its underside – 801. Possibly the number of the penthouse suite reckoned Willis. He took note. The ascent was both silent and fast. 'Does this apartment belong to you or your friend?' But he knew what the answer would be.

'It belongs to my friend. Better let me enter first to make sure that he's dressed and decent.' Willis wasn't keen on being with the two men on his own. Once Pendleton-Smyth had entered the penthouse, Willis jammed his foot on the door to keep it ajar and watched as his host crossed the lounge, opened three doors in quick succession and looked inside. 'Come on in, Mr Willis. My friend isn't here. I have no idea where he is.'

Willis spotted a coffee maker on the worktop in the kitchen. 'Do you know how to operate this machine? I could do with a cup of coffee.' A well-manicured hand stretched in front of him, eager to get the machine going. Willis backed off and returned to the lounge. After he'd turned to ensure that he couldn't be seen from the kitchen, he opened each of the drawers in a long cabinet. In the third drawer, he found two invoices, one from a shipping company and a second from a leasing company. Neither shed any light on the situation, but Willis slipped both into his trouser pocket. Alongside them lay a shiny Rolex Oyster wristwatch. Probably the same watch that caught the light in last night's picture. Willis flipped it over and noted its serial number. It might come in handy later. In the fourth drawer was an envelope addressed to Pendleton-Smyth. Inside was a badly folded piece of paper with letters glued onto it – identical to the other that the CE had already shown him. It joined the others in his pocket.

The coffee made, they sat on two long settees, facing each other. 'This is how this works.' Willis snapped his fingers to get his audience's attention. 'You contact no one. All mobile communication is banned. Not even to your friend. Got it? You had better stay at home this evening, and I will call to have an armed officer come to guard you.'

'But I have responsibilities.'

'I am sure you can manage your diary discreetly for a couple of days.' Willis removed the invoice from his pocket and read the addressee from the top of the sheet. 'Is that your friend's address in Hertfordshire?'

'Yes. It is. How did you know?'

CHAPTER 37

With Willis, Jonathan and Bill Chalmers conferring for most of the evening, time moved quickly, but they had made several major decisions. Bill would put a reconnaissance team around the Hertfordshire address with instructions to report if any activity took place. Because of its size, this was no straightforward task. He had strategically placed vehicles at road junctions and lay-bys surrounding the property, but most of the roads around the estate were rural; therefore, an unusually high number of parked vehicles would stand out. For this reason, Bill put together a collection of the oldest and most run-down vehicles he could get, some with damaged wings, some with multi-coloured paintwork; some were even immobile and only served as cover for the officer inside. All were in radio contact. There was nothing left to do now but wait. Pendleton-Smyth had instructions to attend his office and to contact his partner as normal during the day but not to reveal any detail of the plan. His secretary, Silvia, would be told about the robust security officer in the outer office, filling one of the office chairs well beyond its design capacity.

All they could do now was wait.

***

By mid-afternoon, the call came. High sided trucks were entering the grounds and amassing in front of the large granite building that once had been palatial and the hub of the estate. Now it looked sad and in need of repair.

Once the onlookers were satisfied that the last truck had arrived, Bill Chalmers gave the signal, and his team moved and blocked each of the three iron gates that accessed the grounds. In these positions, they sat well back from the main building, with the many trees sprinkled throughout the estate obscuring them from view.

Led by Bill Chalmers, a small team moved from tree to tree until the façade of the long narrow country house came into view. He set up a pair of binoculars on a tripod. Four lorries stood in the house's curved driveway while a dozen or so men busied themselves loading crates and boxes. One driver climbed down from a cab carrying a flip chart and pen – a sign that everything was on board and needed final signatures.

'Everything's loaded,' said Bill. Pressing the button on his mobile radio, he shouted commands to his men. Six personnel carriers burst into action and headed for the mansion. Some men surrounding the trucks heard the roar of the engines and rushed into the house. Several of the drivers stood around confused, unaware of what was taking place. Within seconds, they'd surrounded the building. Armed Metropolitan Police officers were prepared and positioned behind the safety of the vehicles with their weapons pointed at its front door. An officer led the truck drivers away from the house.

Glass shattered. Two single shots rang out from inside a left-hand window.

'Come out with your hands held high, and no one will get hurt.' Bill was shouting through a megaphone.

'We have hostages,' came the reply. 'If you don't do as we say, they will be shot.'

Willis briefly spotted the outline of a second megaphone protruding from behind a pillar. 'Hostages? Where did they find hostages?'

As if in answer to Willis's question, the answer came. 'We have three of the drivers here. They have nothing to do with this. They will die. You have ten minutes to comply.' As if to add gravitas to his words, a burst of automatic gunfire spewed from an upstairs' window. The gravel in the driveway scattered as the shells buried themselves harmlessly into the ground. 'Next time, we will aim. You have ten minutes to comply.'

A man wearing a boiler suit appeared from the front door with his hands held high above his head. He walked unsteadily and shook as he did. Willis recognised the logo on the pocket of the outfit. 'It's a trucker,' he whispered to Bill, who was busy on the radio organising a hostage negotiator. When he'd finished, Bill shook his head and told Willis he'll never get here in ten minutes.

'What equipment did you bring?' Willis stood and moved towards the rear of the nearest police vehicle. An array of weapons covered the floor. Willis inspected each in turn. He lifted an automatic rifle and stuffed his pockets with various other items he could reach quickly. 'I'm going around the back of the building. Keep them talking for as long as possible.' Bill was about to stop him but thought better of it.

Willis walked straight back from the house, keeping a vehicle between him and the window where most of the action had taken place. Once he was far enough away, he circled, maintaining his distance from the building. Meanwhile, he could hear Bill's voice arguing with the gang's leader.

Luckily, the gable end of the house lacked windows. This allowed Willis to hug the wall and reach the rear of the building, unseen. He ducked below each window as he headed for the rear door. An officer from one of the two vehicles guarding the rear signalled to Willis that there was a gang member immediately to the left of the door. As he did, he released a burst of gunfire towards the window, intending it as a distraction. Willis rushed through the door as the man levelled his rifle in response to the shots. Willis put his left hand over the shooter's eyes and drew a knife swiftly across his throat. The rifle lowered, and the man sank to the floor. Thank heavens for my Swiss Army knife, he thought. They should supply these as routine to the police. Despite the size of the house, it was narrow, only two rooms wide. Willis edged his way towards the front of the building and eased open the adjoining door. Before him stood four men with weapons, all with their backs to him. In the corner sat two men in black boiler suits, who were the truckers. Willis heard a man say, 'You can't shoot him, Robert. Once you've done that, it'll be too late to negotiate. You shouldn't have given them a deadline.' A low grunt followed as Robert dug the butt of his Russian AK 47 assault rifle into the man's stomach. Willis did a quick stocktake of their weapons. All four men had rifles, but only Robert carried an automatic, and he was making all the decisions. Daylight shone in the window from behind, hiding their faces.

Willis threw three objects into the middle of the room. Clattering sounds made the gang swing around as the smoke grenades landed between the four men and burst open. Noxious vapour filled the air. The men struggled to breathe. Willis made out the outline of their leader, raising his gun to aim at the trucker standing outside the front door, and reactively Willis lifted his rifle and fired a burst of shots into Robert's legs. They buckled beneath him, and his rifle rattled shells into the walls as he slumped to the floor. But Willis had been too slow. He saw the trucker fall to his knees and collapse. The remaining members of the gang dropped their rifles and stepped back with their hands held high.

Bill Chalmers and two armed officers rushed to the front door, followed by two medics to assist the injured trucker. They handcuffed the three gang members and led them out to waiting vehicles. Robert was lying face down on the worn carpet in a puddle of blood spewing from his wounds. Before the medics could attend to him, Willis kicked his shoulder with enough force to make his body flip over. As his shoulder hit the ground, his head cracked against the bare wooden floor that surrounded the carpet. At once, Willis saw a narrow moustache he recognised. 'Fuck! I know him. I know his man. He is Edward Young. He pretended to be the friend of Diana Bishop, my sister-in-law.'

Willis dropped to his knees and rifled through the pockets of the limp figure. He pulled out a driving licence and a wallet of bank cards. 'He isn't Edward Young,' he said. 'His name is Robert Devlin. This explains everything.'

'Get him to a hospital before he bleeds to death.' Jonathan shouted to the medics.

Willis sprayed his bank cards over his chest. 'You won't need these where you're going.'

Once the inert body was on a stretcher and carried off, Willis pulled a chair from under the long table that occupied most of the room and sat with his hands behind his head. Inside he was pleased – pleased that he had gone through the day's events without losing the plot – pleased that his PTSD hadn't affected or assisted his actions. He felt confident that he had experienced the last of his irrational outbursts. And what's more, he hadn't needed them to help him succeed. Sophie would be so pleased when he told her.

The room looked sad and unloved. Its carpet was worn, the paintwork needed attention, and the curtains were old and frayed. Below the loose threads hanging from a curtain hem, something was protruding. A small corner of white was visible beneath the second fold in the curtain. Willis stood and lifted a sheet of paper that was partly covered by the heavy drapes. He read it, swallowed hard, folded it and put it in his shirt pocket. Its contents wiped the look of satisfaction from his face.

***

It was over four hours later when they met in Bill Chalmers's office in the Curtis Green Building in New Scotland Yard. Most of the people around the table had been active all day, and the slow pace of conversation reflected the mood. 'Now there's bloody paperwork to complete.' Bill was supping on a large-sized beaker of black coffee. 'We emptied the trucks. That was the straightforward part, but now we have to trace all the owners of the stolen artwork. There must be millions of pounds of canvases with unknown owners, and some of them might even have been stolen years ago, long forgotten, with their original owners now dead. We can hardly publish a list and ask potential owners to apply. We'd be inundated with claims.'

'If the paintings have been missing this long, their owners can wait a little longer,' said Willis. 'We ought to investigate the paintings that were sold before we got involved because they were used to finance Pendleton-Smyth's gambling addiction.'

Bill nodded in agreement. 'Fortunately, the Metropolitan Police's Art and Antiques Unit, which was disbanded after the Grenfell Tower fire, has been re-formed after fears that London was at risk from a worsening situation with the theft and fraud of cultural items. Its stolen Art Database holds details of fifty-four thousand stolen works. In my opinion, they were probably more worried about the use of stolen art for money laundering than the need to protect its culture. Anyway, we'll hand over the items to them to investigate.'

'Never mind the art,' interrupted Willis. 'There are people incarcerated who need to be released. We have blown the whole sad story wide open now that we have discovered the existence of Robert Devlin, Alec Devlin's brother. If we had checked the serial number of the Rolex watch found in the Thames apartment block, we would have known of Robert Devlin's existence earlier. The gang members have been talking their heads off in an attempt at plea bargaining. Young Rob Moore needs to be released as soon as possible since Helen Devlin confessed to killing William McLellan. Robert Devlin ordered his lackey to kill his brother's wife, Helen, to stop her from talking, so Alec Devlin is no longer considered a murderer. Although he is guilty of smuggling and people trafficking.'

'Robert Devlin made attempts on your and Sophie's lives,' said Jonathan, 'and also the life of Diana Bishop, albeit via Messrs Yin and Yang. And while their names are in the frame, let's not forget about young Georgie Maclean. He didn't deserve to die either.'

'There remains a question about Pendleton-Smyth. He is innocent of murder and smuggling, but he provided information on Customs logistics to a blackmailer – a blackmailer he didn't realise was his partner and his close assistant in the office.' Willis stared at Chalmers, waiting for an answer.

'Pendleton-Smyth will have to resign. Even if he doesn't, everything will come out at the trial, and he will be for the high jump, but don't feel sorry for him, because he brought it all on himself.'

'It explains Edward Young's ambivalent relationship with Diana. He was gay. My profiling friend, Theresa in Cambridge, was spot on with her analysis. She predicted that one of the people who wrote the threatening letters would be gay. She was right. I need to offer her another lunch, but my priority is to visit Diana. I need to tell her the good news that she can relax at last, and they will release young Rob as soon as the process allows.'

***

On his way to East Bergholt, Willis picked up Sophie at Madingley village, and they arrived in time to prevent Diana from retiring for the night. 'I decided not to call ahead, because I wanted my news to be a surprise.' Willis told her how the day had unfolded and provided every detail except the identity of the main villain.

'That means I wasn't at HMRC, because someone wanted to spy on me. I got there through merit.' Diana was grinning from ear to ear.

'There's other news that isn't so pleasant. Edward Young was the gang leader who was dealing in stolen artwork.' Willis waited for the information to sink in before adding, 'He was the brother of one of the other suspects.' Willis was dreading telling Diana the bad news and delayed it as long as possible. 'And he was gay.'

Diana burst out laughing. 'That's typical. All the guys I fancy turn out to be gay. But it's a relief. It means it wasn't that he didn't fancy me – well, he didn't – but you know what I mean.' Sophie burst out laughing too, which reduced the awkward tension. Diana pulled herself up straighter in her chair, all signs of laughter gone. 'Who sent me those horrible threats?'

'It was two different people,' explained Willis. 'The first set you received was full of poor grammar and bad spelling. Helen Devlin sent you those, attempting to stop your investigation. Robert Devlin, aka Edward Young, wrote the second batch. He was trying to ensure Helen could continue coercing her husband into smuggling the paintings into the country. They both wanted to derail your investigation, but your boyfriend succeeded the most by using all his information to neutralise all of your efforts.'

'I will sleep a lot better this evening. Have you seen the news this evening?'

Willis shook his head.

'There's been a revolt in the House that's been running for several days. MPs submitted letters of no-confidence to the 1922 Committee. That's the group that decides on the future of our Prime Minister, and there is likely to be a vote to replace him – Mariam Hodges, the Home Secretary, is tipped as the favourite. She and I are very close, so if she succeeds, it will do my career a lot of good.'

***

After they had said their goodbyes to Diana, Willis and Sophie set off home. 'In your conversation, you never mentioned Jim Pryce, the driver who killed Carole.' Sophie laid her hand gently on Willis's thigh.

'It wasn't Jim Pryce that we should blame for killing Carole. Jim was overzealous, trying to frighten Diana, but it was Robert Devlin who paid him to frighten Diana, and Pryce mistook Carole for her. It was a simple mistake, but it cost him his life. He was eliminated in prison on Devlin's instructions. I'll need to get Bill Chalmers to add Jim Pryce's death to the list of charges facing Robert Devlin.' Willis waved his hand in the air. 'But that's not the best news of the day. The great news is that I had no PTSD symptoms. I knew they would disappear when I solved Carole's death.'

***

Once they were home, Willis poured Sophie and him a stiff brandy and sank into the chair in front of the flickering wood burner Mrs Burns had kindly prepared in time for their return. Sophie switched on the television and caught up on the latest news regarding the Prime Minister.

Willis surreptitiously removed the piece of paper he had lifted from the manor. He unfolded it and faced it towards the wood burner, letting the soft flames from the fire illuminate the writing. He took a deep breath and read it slowly:

~~Jim Pryce~~
~~Sam Cordell~~
~~Georgie Maclean~~
Brad Willis
Sophie Willis
Diana Bishop
~~Helen Devlin~~

The list of Robert Devlin's targets brought a lump to Willis's throat. His, Sophie and Diana's names stared back from the page at him. Devlin had crossed names out because he had received news that they had been successfully eliminated, and only accidents of fate had prevented the last three from dying. What if something hadn't spooked the assassins when they arrived at their cottage? What if Diana hadn't taken her dad's box of letters and his pistol to her bedroom? Was it telling him it was time to curb his curiosity and go back to being a full-time astronomer?

He folded the paper and replaced it in his shirt pocket. He would give the list to Bill Chalmers as evidence. Robert Devlin's handwriting was distinct and easy to recognise. This 'to-do' list would make sure Devlin remained in prison for many years to come.

CHAPTER 38

Several weeks had passed since the showdown in Hertfordshire. Today Sophie was jumping with joy. She had returned the previous evening from her parents, Ruth and Allan, with an agreed date and venue for her and Brad's wedding. Now all she wanted to do was to invite her friends to attend. Opposite her sat Diana. 'Will you come? Please say that you'll be there.'

Diana rose and put her arms around Sophie, 'Of course I will. A team of wild horses couldn't stop me from coming. But I might have to bring a few invitees of my own.'

Sophie twisted her head to the side and looked at Diana through the corners of her eyes. 'What do you mean?'

'Well, you know we have a new prime minister?'

'Yeeess?'

'Miriam Hodge is the new Prime Minister. She will lead the House.'

'And?'

'And she has invited me to be Home Secretary to replace her.'

Sophie's eyes widened until they looked as though they might pop out of their sockets. 'That's terrific. Congratulations. Brad, come and hear this.' Willis came out of the kitchen, where he had been setting up the coffee machine without being asked. 'Tell him. You must tell him. It's your great news.'

After Diana repeated her message to Willis, he enveloped her in the tightest of hugs and held her for several seconds. 'That's great news. You deserve it. That's why you were assigned to HMRC. You are a star. Doesn't that mean you will need security at our wedding?'

'Of course it does, Brad. Diana has explained that to me. She can bring anyone she likes as long as they don't get in the way of the merriment.'

'Hey, I have a contact in the Government. I have someone who will help me with any future assignments.' Willis meant what he said, though he said it with a big grin on his face.

'Don't even go there, Dr Willis. You will need to make an appointment to see me in future, so enjoy your short-lived access.'

Sophie asked if she would sell her house at East Bergholt and move to London. Definitely not, she told her, but it meant she would need to spend a lot more of her time in the capital.

'Anyway, that isn't the news you want to discuss. When is the big event happening?' Diana picked up her diary and hovered over it with a ballpen.

'Eight weeks on Saturday.'

Diana turned eight pages in her diary and scribbled. 'Now show me the ring.'

Sophie held out her hand for Diana to admire the solitaire diamond sparkling on her finger. 'We didn't have proper rings when we married in Antarctica. We had to compromise. But I've made up for it now. Brad, show Diana your ring.'

Willis held up his hand for Diana to see his ring. She looked at it and frowned. 'I know,' said Sophie. 'It's made from a metal meteorite found at the base of a glacier in Antarctica. He says it's the oldest thing he owns, other than me, that is.'

***

The eight weeks flashed by. The church glowed with flowers of all sizes and colours, provided by friends of Ruth and Alan, who were members of the local flower arranging group. Much to the chagrin of the vicar, the aisle was scattered with flower petals. Both sides of the church were full. Friends had come from far and wide. Uncle Jon came with a new lady he'd met. Johnny White, his cyber specialist, had also turned up. Representing the Met was Bill Chalmers, his wife and a few of the men with their partners who had helped in the arrests. Theresa Quigg, Willis's unofficial profiler, was being her usual shy self, standing in the background, waving. Sophie had sent an invitation to Linda Foreman and Gabi Costa, who married at the same time as Willis and her in Antarctica, not expecting them to be able to attend. Linda and Gabi gave tiny waves to attract Willis's attention. He waved back with a huge smile. Sophie would be so happy to see them.

All they had to do now was wait for Sophie – the bride was always late.

Exactly at 10 a.m., the church organ groaned and burst into life. Sophie was on time. Willis tried to force himself to face the front but gave up and sneaked a quick look at his lovely bride. Her veil, like a cloud of heavenly mist, hovered around her beautiful features. Willis loved her so much. They had been through so much together, and Willis considered himself fortunate to have found such a wonderful lady. He would look after her and protect her for as long as he lived.

When her father came alongside, he positioned Sophie beside Brad, smiled and nodded his approval, and then retired to his seat beside her mother. Sophie's hand found Brad's, and they squeezed each other's fingers as the ceremony began.

***

Once the speeches were over and everyone was enjoying the alcohol, the newly married couple took to the floor for their first dance for the second time. 'Do you remember our first dance at the Pole?' asked Sophie.

'How could I possibly forget it? You wore a chunky knitted sweater, as did Gabi.'

The rest of the evening went well. Dancing was set to continue into the small hours. Bill Chalmers came and sat on an empty chair next to Willis and handed him an envelope. 'You shouldn't have bothered,' said Willis. 'We asked for no presents.' He moved to hand the envelope back to Bill.

'I'm not sure that this counts as a wedding present. That's up to you. I've held this back for over two weeks to save it for tonight.'

Willis slowly opened the flap and removed the contents. He unfolded the sheet and read it in silence. 'Robert Devlin was killed trying to escape. An officer shot him. He died instantly.'

Bill turned and looked at Willis. 'I wasn't sure whether this would please you.'

A red candle stood burning in the centre of the table. Willis placed the paper in the flame and held it while it slowly burnt. 'It gives final closure,' he said. 'And it saves the British taxpayer a lot of money by avoiding a trial. Robert Devlin deserved all he got. Thank you for this.'

Willis stood and walked towards his housekeeper, Mrs Burns and her husband, John. 'I finished the model of *The Clipper*,' said John. 'It looks magnificent even without its hold in place.'

'Put it somewhere where I can see it,' said Willis, 'because it's a magnificent model, but the real thing was something else.' He put his hand out and asked Mrs Burns for a dance.

'Oh my. Oh my. I haven't done this for so long.'

'We'll take it slowly, Mrs Burns. From now on, everything will be much slower.' Mrs Burns paid no heed to his words. She was concentrating on what her feet were doing.

***

'It's that time of the evening, Brad. I need to change my clothes and prepare to make a stealthy exit from our party.' Sophie was hugging his arm and smiling. He bent over and gave her the longest kiss ever. Time froze for minutes as they embraced. Sophie took a large intake of air. 'Gosh. I'm off to change, and we won't need pizza tonight.'

Twenty minutes later, Sophie reappeared with Linda and Gabi in tow. Sophie and Gabi both had changed. Now they wore chunky Arran knitted sweaters. The same sweaters they'd worn at their first wedding. The same sweaters that Linda and Gabi had carried halfway around the world. 'We needed some continuity,' said Sophie. 'How do I look?'

'You look beautiful, my sweetheart, absolutely beautiful.'

If you enjoyed this story, please consider leaving a review on Amazon. Reviews help attract readers' attention to books and promote sales.

Thank You

Contact the author:
tom.boles@tomboles.org

Follow Tom Boles on Bookbub:

https://www.bookbub.com/authors/tom-boles

About The Author

Tom Boles has discovered more supernovae than any other person in history. Tom is a Fellow of the Royal Astronomical Society and a past President of The British Astronomical Association. He was awarded the Merlin Medal and the Walter Goodacre Award for his contribution to astronomy. The International Astronomical Union named main-belt asteroid 7648, Tomboles, in his honour. He has published many scientific papers on supernovae and written numerous articles for popular astronomy magazines. He has made many television appearances, ranging from BBC's Tomorrow's World to The Sky at Night. During recent years he has given Enrichment Lectures on astronomy aboard Cunard liners, mainly their flagship Queen Mary 2. During these trips, he has designed and presented shows using the ship's onboard planetarium, the only one at sea. His experience as an astronomer inspired this story. His first novel, DARK ENERGY, was published in June 2021. He lives in rural Suffolk, where he enjoys regular cloudless nights and dark skies, free from light pollution.

BOOKS BY THIS AUTHOR

DARK ENERGY

The first book in the Brad Willis series

When renowned scientists start dying, the scientific community is on full alert. The explosions appear to be unrelated. Their only connection is that they happened in scientific centres of excellence in Switzerland and the United States. Brad Willis knows that he must uncover the secret to save more lives from being lost. MI6 calls on Willis to use his background as a renowned astronomer to infiltrate the scientists to discover the truth behind the deaths. When Willis starts to uncover the facts, everyone is under suspicion until they start dying. The situation gets more dangerous as two hired assassins hunt him down.

SHADES of WHITE

The second book in the Brad Willis series

MI6 calls on Brad Willis to go to Antarctica to investigate powerful and dangerous radio surges. Their strength cannot be rationally explained. They are interfering with experiments and instrumentation. Laboratories have been damaged. People are dying. Electrical supplies are mysteriously failing. Planes are dropping from the sky. Who is doing this? How are they doing this? Murder and sabotage impede his investigations. Brad Willis must stop them before the Antarctic base is locked down for the winter. If he fails, everyone on the base will freeze to death.

Printed in Great Britain
by Amazon